QUEEN OF HEARTS

QUEEN OF HEARTS

A Composite Novel by

Laurie Lisa

Published in the United States by Homeless Media Co.

Cover design by Homeless Media and Elite Authors.

Interior design and layout by Homeless Media and Elite Authors.

For more information, visit: www.LaurieLisa.com

ISBN (paperback): 978-1-956420-04-3
ISBN (eBook): 978-1-956420-05-0

First Edition: 2025

All hearts lead to her. Not all make it back.

TABLE OF CONTENTS

Part One:
The Reckoning

HOMECOMING

The town looked the same but older, sadder. Robert wasn't surprised by this. He had the same thought every time he came back to his hometown of Liberty, Illinois, which was probably one reason why he returned so infrequently. But it wasn't the real reason. The real reason was waiting impatiently for him at the not-so-grand Colonial house on Waverly Road. Robert didn't like to think about how long it had been since his last visit to the place—three years, four, six? But the old woman would know. She could probably even tell him the number of hours and minutes that measured his neglect, although she wouldn't come right out and say that. He was supposed to already *know*.

Robert was in no hurry to confront the monumental task that lay before him or the judgment in the woman's eyes, so he decided to take a drive through town. It wouldn't take long. At one time, back in its heyday, when the coal mines were operating and hiring, Liberty's population topped 5,000. Small businesses thrived, too, and people could make a decent living. That wasn't the case now. Like most small midwestern towns, Liberty had been valiantly trying to stave off the steady, inevitable decline brought about by unemployment and a receding population. And an aging population, Robert thought ruefully. The heartland exemplified the "graying of America." The old woman had lost two more friends in the last year, and the Presbyterian Church, where she still played the piano, had a median age of seventy.

But as he slowly drove through town, the thing about Liberty that Robert had to grudgingly admire was that the people who stayed put and made lives for themselves tried hard; they were civically proud. Robert did drive past houses with unkempt yards, a rusted-out car on blocks, or a pit bull behind a battered chain link fence. Still, for the most part, yards were mowed, flags flew from holders attached to doorways in celebration of Flag Day the next day, petunias bloomed in window boxes, and lace curtains fluttered in windows. The places looked idyllic; they were supposed to be idyllic. Those places, the homes and yards that tried too hard, made Robert uneasy. He knew better.

Liberty still boasted a town square, and it was still green at this time of summer, with white wrought iron benches, a gazebo, and a bandstand. When he was a kid, Robert had thought it was the most magical place on earth. It was a place of twinkling lights at Christmas time. And on the Fourth of July, which was an especially big deal in this southern Illinois town, it was decked out in red, white, and blue bunting, local bands played on the bandstand, and antique cars sparkled in the hot sun, all spit and polished and waiting for the judgment of the mayor. Even later, as a teenager, he and his friends had hung out at the gazebo, waiting for one of the older kids with a fake ID to bring them a case of Old Style. Robert had kissed his first girlfriend in this square. Her name was Ginger, for the obvious reason, and she wore braces. What he remembered most about that first kiss was her braces cutting his bottom lip. His first kiss tasted of blood, but he told Ginger that he was pretty sure they'd done it right, just like they did in the movies. That had made her happy.

The businesses surrounding the square were all different now. Manny's VCR Repair had been replaced by a Verizon store, the one upscale boutique in town that the old woman had frequented—Maybelline's—was now a gun shop, and the Variety Store where he had bought penny candy now hosted a consignment shop. Hugo's, a diner his dad used to take him to for burgers, was now a Subway, and the pinball arcade where he had spent countless wasted hours had transformed itself into a pool hall with the same unoriginal name: Funtown. On the corner, Gaylord's Theatre stood abandoned and forlorn. The plywood planks on the windows had been there so long that they looked mildewed and damp. It was vaguely disappointing, yes, but not surprising. Even back in the day, the place had been a dump, its only saving grace the ten-cent bag of popcorn, which you ate at your own risk. Everyone knew the place was overrun with mice.

It was getting late in the afternoon, and the old woman was expecting him, but Robert continued his drive through the southern end of town. There, a Circle K had replaced Arlo's Garage, and a newish-looking, thriving RV sales center had swallowed up what used to be a field where he and his buddies would target practice on empty beer cans and Fanta soda bottles. As Robert continued on his journey, he saw the Goliath, the death and life force of so many small towns: the Walmart Supercenter. Robert knew it was there, of course—he hadn't been away *that* long—but it still shocked him every single time. It looked jarringly large and out of place in this town of carefully tended, modest homes, small taverns, and white clapboard churches. Yet cars crowded the parking lot, and he could see a man loading a blue plastic wading pool into the back of his pickup. Robert could count on one hand the number of cars he had passed in town on this lazy Saturday afternoon, but it made an odd sense now. Saturday, everyone flocked to Walmart. It's what people did.

Robert pulled into the cemetery nestled by the Mississippi River, another place he didn't particularly want to visit but had to. She would ask him if he'd gone, and if he said no, she would insist that they go together to "pay their respects." For the old woman, that meant sparing thirty minutes to stand silently and stare spitefully at the engraved tombstone, which eerily had her name and birthdate already engraved next to his. If Robert lied and said he had gone when he hadn't, the old woman would quiz him: "What colors are the flowers in the shepherd's basket this year?" she would ask. She'd nail him in nothing flat like she used to do when he was a kid. And God knew he was too old for that now. At forty-five years old, he was too goddamn old to be caught in any more lies.

The plastic flowers this year were white and blue. Robert could see that as he drew closer, as he tiptoed carefully between the graves to get to his father's, forming the joke in his head. "Hey, Pop, I tried not to step on any toes to get here. Haha," he said when he reached the grave under the tree, near the back of the cemetery. Robert imagined his pop laughing appreciatively at the lame joke. The man possessed a sense of humor, unlike his wife. Granted, his sense of humor had been on the silly, prankish side. He'd been a guy who preferred a whoopee cushion over a *New Yorker* quip. Still, it had been nice to know that dear old dad would rather smile at you than snarl. And everyone in town knew that Jacob Walker would give you the shirt off his back.

It drove his wife crazy. "Did you or did you not loan Joanie twenty dollars, Jacob Walker? And don't you lie to me. She told me herself."

"She didn't have enough money for groceries, Angela. She's got three little kids to feed."

"Is it my fault that her husband drinks away his paycheck at Meyer's tavern every single week? Joanie's husband is a coal miner, Jacob, and you are a school-teacher. They make twice as much money as we do!"

Pop, though, had this ability to tuck into his dinner and somehow block out the rest of his wife's harangue. It was as if he pulled down a mental shade while still managing to keep a pleasant look on his face. Neither Robert nor his sister inherited that ability. Robert remembered sitting across the supper table from Jillian, watching her stab savagely at her cubed steak while their mother went on and on. Her glare, when she looked up at him, could have frozen the warmest of intentions. Robert would kick her under the table or childishly stick out his tongue. Jillian would kick him back, harder. Somehow, they never seemed to get over those suppertime battles, which neither of them started. Over the years, Robert had often wondered if that was why they still avoided each other at every opportunity. The last time he had seen Jillian was at his second wedding, which she surprisingly attended, probably trying to figure out how much the whole shindig was going to set him back (it was a lot). She had whispered in his ear: "She's a bigger loser than your first one." Unfortunately, she had been right.

Looking at the engraved dates on the tombstone, Robert realized with a start that the twenty-fifth anniversary of Pop's death was coming up in November. Subconsciously, he must have known that, but he hadn't allowed himself to recognize it. Robert had lived longer without his father than he had with him. How could that be? And why did it still hurt so much?

"You know, Pop, if you hadn't been such a nice guy, you wouldn't be in this predicament. Haha." Robert's voice sounded croaky. Now that he worked from home, he didn't talk to many people. Some days, he didn't speak to another living soul. He half-heartedly thought he should get a parrot, just for the company.

"But you might have dodged a bullet there, buddy. Once you were out of the picture, she got crankier and meaner. I'm not kidding, Pop. Old age does not agree with her."

Robert heard the crunch of gravel and saw an older model Buick LeSabre creep into the cemetery's narrow lane. Over the steering wheel, he could barely make out the top of a white head, and next to that, an equally diminutive grey orb. More of the town's widows, Robert guessed, probably friends of the old woman waiting for him in her stuffed-to-the-gills house. They parked at the other end of the cemetery, and as Robert watched them slowly get out of the car, each one stooped over a basket of flowers that threatened to topple her over, he felt a lump forming in his throat.

His voice was now shaky as he said, "What's that you're saying, Pop? Am I being too hard on her? Old age doesn't agree with anybody?" Robert's hands clenched at his sides, and his breath, like an asthmatic's, came out in short puffs. "What in the hell do you know about old age? You dodged that bullet too, buddy."

Robert suddenly squatted, out of breath. The widows across the cemetery might think he was praying or picking up stray twigs or weeds from the grave. He wasn't doing either, and he wasn't crying. He was too goddamn old to cry. "I've made a mess of things, Pop. I want to help her, but she makes it too fucking hard."

Robert didn't know how long he remained squatting on the grave, but when he tried to straighten up, he had to grab onto the tombstone for support, his cramped legs audibly creaking. "What's that you said, Pop? Should I stop by the Legion for a beer before I go to the house? I've got to say, that sounds like a splendid idea. It always helped you, didn't it? Thanks for the advice." He patted the top of the stone, feeling foolish. What was he doing here, besides procrastinating? The man had been dead for a quarter of a century. And what the hell did he know anyway?

The Liberty American Legion Post 998 looked the same as Robert remembered. It was a white, ranch-style building, with a parking lot in front, a small, pretty park with playground equipment and picnic benches to the north, the baseball diamond and soccer fields to the south. Robert didn't know why, but it was a relief to see that it hadn't changed. Pop, a Korean War vet, had spent considerable time in this place, and consequently, so had Robert when he waited for his dad to drive them home for supper. When he was younger, Robert had played ball on that diamond, and later, the few times he came home from college, he would go to the wedding receptions of used-to-be friends or attend dances in the large hall behind the front bar. However, instead of the marquee sign over the door announcing an upcoming band or community event, it proclaimed: Queen of Hearts Drawing, Thursday at 8 o'clock, Jackpot: $1,000,142!!!

Robert immediately felt better as he thought: *Some things never change.* He knew what had happened; some idiot had used commas instead of decimal points. A kid who used to work in this place in the 1980s had some mental challenges. (Robert and his friends had called him *retard,* but he hadn't seemed to mind.) Could it be that he still worked here? What was his name, Dale? The kid—man—would be in his late 40s or early 50s now, but it was not outside the realm of possibility. It was a small town, and *some things never changed.*

The bar in front was about as no-nonsense as a bar could get: a long Formica-topped counter with fake wood trim, backless vinyl barstools, and a few wooden tables with low chairs scattered across the linoleum floor. One corner boasted a couple of dartboards and what looked like an old pinball machine. It was now a late afternoon Saturday, and the dedicated drinkers hadn't come in yet, so only a handful of patrons, all men, occupied the barstools and chairs. When Robert walked in, the bell above the bar tinkled, and everyone automatically looked up, questioning, assessing, ready to say, "Hey, Rufus, you old son of a gun," or to dismiss the newcomer, with a whispered: "He's not from around here."

Robert joined two other baseball-capped men at the bar, choosing the seat at the end, closest to the door. It wasn't like he thought he might need to make a quick escape. But he would do just that if he ran into any old friends. (Could he still consider those boyhood pals friends?) What if they wanted to catch up, or worse, wanted to rehash their so-called glory days, the high school years when they thought they were each the next Michael Jordan because they had a winning basketball team and were, therefore, hotter than shit? Robert had liked high school, thought of himself as popular, and he'd had plenty of dates and fun times. But thinking about it now made him uneasy. He'd been there, done that, and sad to say, hadn't ever topped it. Maybe it wasn't old age that sucked. Maybe it was growing up.

Robert caught himself before he ordered a Stella and ordered a Bud from the bartender, who looked like he was in his early 30s. That was a good thing. "Hey, what's with the sign? Did some idiot make a mistake? A million bucks for some drawing? Come on."

The bartender looked incredulous. "Where've you been, under a rock? This thing's been going on for weeks now, and the pot keeps growing. It's way past record territory now. Someone's going to win himself a million bucks any week now. It's all this town can talk about these days: Who's going to win the Queen of Hearts?"

"I don't live in Liberty. I mean, I used to, but I haven't lived here for a long time." Robert hated that he sounded apologetic. What did he have to apologize for? He wouldn't live in this town again if he won or someone *paid* him a million bucks.

"You can't be local then either. We've got people coming here every Thursday from towns all over southern Illinois. Personally, I hope a local guy wins, but what can you do? If you've got two bucks, you can buy a ticket. And hope you get lucky."

Robert took a long swig of his beer. "I'm from Chicago, so I plead ignorance." Robert meant it as a joke, but the bartender shrugged, acknowledging that it was so. Robert was suddenly parched. He drained the beer and ordered another. "I'm Robert."

"Brian." The other two guys at the end of the bar finished their beers and left, so Brian decided he had some time. He leaned his elbows on the bar. "So, who are you visiting in town?"

Robert hesitated a fraction of a second. "My mother."

"What's her name? Maybe I know her."

"You wouldn't know her."

"Holy shit, man, I've lived in this town my entire life. I know everybody."

Robert vehemently shook his head. "You wouldn't know her." It was true. His mother, Angela Walker, liked to pretend to the people in this town that she was the sweetest little old Christian lady who ever lived here. Most of them believed it. But Robert knew her to be someone else.

"Try me," Brian taunted.

"Tell me about the rules of this game," Robert threw back.

"It's a drawing, man, not a game. It's so simple. Everyone knows the rules."

"I'm from Chicago, remember?"

"Oh, yeah. Right." Brian grinned and then went on to explain. Each Queen of Hearts drawing started with the fifty-two cards in a playing deck, plus the two jokers for a total of fifty-four cards. Each card was put in a sealed envelope and given a number from 1-54. People bought raffle tickets for $2 a ticket. If you didn't think you would be able to attend the drawing, you could put a number on the back of your ticket, keeping in mind that you only got half the prize money if you weren't there in person. Every Thursday, all the tickets sold that week were put into a big drum. Then one ticket was drawn. The owner of the ticket then chose a numbered envelope.

"Obviously," Brian finished up, "you're hoping the envelope you choose has the Queen of Hearts. Each week that she isn't drawn, the game continues, and the pot gets bigger."

"How many envelopes are left in this game?"

"Six. I can't show you the board because Commander Atkins has it encased in glass and locked in the office safe."

Robert was on his third beer. "So this drawing is a really big deal, huh?"

"You bet it is, man. All the restaurants are doing good business on Thursday nights, and the high school track team has set up a business of parking cars. Queen of Hearts is the biggest thing that has happened in this town in a long time."

"God, the poor sucker who finally wins is going to have to hire a security guard to walk him to his car." Robert meant it as a joke.

But Brian nodded. "We pretty much have a fight in the parking lot every week. You know, a lot of beer, disappointed people. People around here really need that money. This isn't the richest town in the country."

"I can see that," Robert said.

"It's a really big deal," Brian repeated. "Queen of Hearts is giving people hope, you know. It's helping a lot of people around here. Seriously, man."

"Yeah." Robert knew it was finally time for him to go see the old woman. He couldn't put it off any longer. He reached into his pocket for his wallet.

"While you're at it, do you want to buy a couple of tickets?" Brian was very serious. "The excitement around here is what you could call *contagious*."

Robert threw a twenty on the bar. "Maybe another time, Brian." He'd never been a gambling man. To him, the Queen of Hearts-inspired mania did sound contagious. And he didn't want to catch whatever fever it was festering.

Maybe he was being too hard on the old woman. After he stopped by the convenience store to buy Certs to cover up his beer breath and walked up the sidewalk to the white house with its four columns across the small front porch, she opened the door and said simply, "You're here."

Robert stopped in his tracks. My God, had the woman always been that small? Even now, he expected to see her as she used to be, a tallish, thin woman with dark hair and eyes, an imposing woman who meted out judgment daily. But there she stood framed in the doorway, small and frail, white-haired and slightly stooped. She looked just like the two ladies he had seen earlier in the cemetery. All she needed was a basket of flowers weighing her down.

Immediately, out of habit, he started in with the apologies. "I'm sorry I'm late, Mother. Traffic was bad."

"You didn't give me your specific arrival time, Robert, so how can you be late?"

Robert searched for the accusation in her voice but didn't find it. "Very true." He hadn't given her a specific arrival time because he didn't want to make anything about this homecoming concrete. In the back of his mind, he had still considered doing the cowardly thing and not showing up.

"I made a ham." His mother opened the door wider.

"Sounds good." Robert didn't particularly like ham, but he would accept this as a peace offering of sorts. They would have to be civil to each other—like it or not—if they were ever going to get this house with its fifty-five years of memories, memorabilia, and useless relics cleaned out and ready to put on the market.

How long *had* it been since he'd been home? The enormity of what lay before them hit Robert as soon as he crossed the threshold into his childhood home. His mother's "collecting" had started immediately after Pop died. The woman, frugal in every other aspect of her life, was a sucker when it came to all the treasures one could find at craft fairs, flea markets, and yard sales. She had collections of Raggedy Ann and Andy dolls, Precious Moments figurines, old oil lamps, hymnals, teacups, vinyl records, and decorations for every holiday, real or imagined. She had probably started other collections in his absence, but Robert hadn't been worried. They could box it all up and let the estate agent that his mother had contacted come and take everything away. The idea was that she might get a little bit of money for all her crap. He had been coaching himself not to say *crap* in front of her.

But now, looking around, Robert could see how much smaller the rooms had become. The furniture in every room had been pushed forward to accommodate the boxes and mountains of *stuff* behind them. Robert could see the stairs to the left. Every step had more clutter piled on it, making the trek upstairs as narrow as a single footprint. It was a wonder his mother hadn't fallen down them and broken her neck.

Instead, it had been her hip that was the wake-up call. She had tripped on a chair leg, she'd said. She hadn't been paying attention to where she was going. She'd been lucky, with her osteoporosis, not to have broken that, the doctor had said when Robert spoke to him on the phone. It was only bruised.

"There's no need for you to make the long trip down here, Robert," his mother had said on the phone. "I know you lead a very busy life."

He did not lead a busy life. When his second wife left him three years ago, he had become something of a hermit. He'd let her have the condo in the West Loop, and he'd taken an apartment in an old row house in a Serbian neighborhood in Irving Park. He went to the local bar on occasion and would sometimes take the bartender to bed afterward. He worked from his apartment as a graphic designer for a few ad agencies in town. He was half-heartedly thinking about getting a parrot. But he'd said to his mother, "Well, if you're sure?"

"I'm sure, Robert."

"Promise me that you'll start wearing a Life Alert then."

"I will not."

He'd let it go and so had Jillian. Still, six months after the bruised hip, he got another call from his mother, saying that she had decided it was time to sell the house. Her handyman, the pastor at the Assembly of God Church, had told her that she needed a new roof. She didn't want to pay for a new roof, and now the boy who mowed her yard—he was in his thirties—wanted to charge her five dollars more a week. It was time to move.

The unspoken question, the elephant in the room, was this: Where was she going to move to? Answering that question was another one of his duties while he was home. He'd given himself a week to take care of things here, but he'd either been stupid or in denial. He could see that reflected in the clutter hemming him in with each step into the house. The small rooms were stifling. His mother refused to pay for central air and pretended to cool the house with a window air conditioner in the kitchen and her bedroom and three or four rotating floor fans scattered through the rooms. The heat made the place even more claustrophobic.

"We'll eat supper first."

It was only five o'clock, and Robert wasn't hungry, but it seemed like the right thing to do. They probably did need to get reacquainted again before starting this huge project, a project that seemed to lack a beginning and an ending right now. In the kitchen, Robert could see that she had prepared for him. A large spiral cut ham sat uncovered on the stove, and amid the stacks of yard sale mismatched plates and pitchers and salt and pepper shakers, piles of unopened mail peeked out from the counter. Had his mother stopped opening her mail? Was she in the early stages of dementia? He would know the answers to these questions if he talked to her more, or if she would learn to text. But talking to her had become even more stilted and painful as the years went by. If Pop hadn't died, maybe things would be different. But he did die, and Mother had made everything worse.

"Do you have any beer?" Robert meant it as a joke, something to break the ice.

"There has never been, and never will be, any alcohol in this house, Robert. We're having sun tea."

He should have known better; his mother had no sense of humor whatsoever. Plus, she literally thought alcohol was the devil's drink. It was one of Pop's many little secrets that he kept a six-pack of Pabst in the garage. His mother would have blown a gasket if she knew, and as Robert watched her pour the sun tea into glasses with a lemon decal, he almost told her. He'd been in this house for ten minutes and was already threatening to revert to the smart-mouthed kid he used to be. How would he make it through this week?

Who was he kidding? As Robert watched a row of ants crawl over a stack of mail and head for an apple pie that sat uncovered on the counter, with one piece missing, he knew that clearing out his mother's past would take much longer than that. He was going to have to call Jillian. She would say she was too busy—"I have three kids and a job, Robert"—but he would insist that she come. Fair was fair, and if he had to go through hell in this house, she had to go through hell, too. Robert quickly got up from the table and put the apple pie in the refrigerator.

The ham must have been sitting out for some time because it tasted dry, and the potato salad and baked beans were too salty, but Robert kept eating. If his mouth was full, he couldn't talk; she had taught him that. His mother also had her avoidance tactic. She cut her ham into tiny, precise bites and speared each chunk of potato and bean separately. The window air conditioner rattled. That, too, had seen better days.

It was 5:15, and Robert had finished. He had to say something. "I'm going to have a dumpster delivered tomorrow."

His mother's head snapped up. "You will do no such thing, Robert. I will not have my neighbors think I have a lot of trash in my house."

"You do have a lot of trash in your house, Mother." Robert tried to smile, but she had that tight, grim look on her mouth that he remembered too well. She was eighty years old, but that look was exactly the same.

"It is not trash, Robert. Every single item in this house has a purpose."

"Oh, yeah?" Robert went to the cabinet below the kitchen sink and opened it. It was still there, as he knew it would be. He held up the volleyball-sized globe of aluminum foil. "What is the purpose of this, Mother?"

"You never know when you're going to need that tiny little bit of tin foil to cover an odd-sized dish."

"And what about this?" He held up a glass pitcher that had a crack running its length. "This pitcher would leak if you put anything in it."

"That's why they make super glue, Robert."

"And this—" Robert was about to hold up something that might have been a warped spatula.

"Stop it, Robert." His mother carefully put down her knife and fork. She'd barely eaten anything. She took a few seconds to compose herself before she looked up at him. "You must understand that my parents lived through The Great Depression. When a person has so little, what that person does come to possess means a great deal. Plus, everything has a use—if not now, maybe at a later time. My parents instilled those values in me, and I am not going to sit here and let you tell me that my possessions belong in a dumpster."

Robert sat heavily back down in the kitchen chair opposite her. It was a small, round table, and for the first time, he could see that the lower rims of her eyes were red through her glasses. "Are you telling me that it's going to be difficult for you to part with anything in this house?"

She nodded slowly. "Everything in this house has meaning for me, Robert. Every single item is a memory. During the last two months, I have tried to organize, to sort through my belongings, to decide what I could give away." She cleared her throat. "It's very difficult."

His first instinct, which seemed totally foreign to him, was to reach out and put his hand over hers, and for once, he followed it. His mother was eighty years old, after all, and alone. "Then what are we going to do here, Mother?"

"I have no idea."

Robert let his mother convince him to wait until the morning to start clearing the house. She said that she wanted to sit and "visit" with him for a while; they needed to catch up. The visit went as well as Robert had expected. His mother talked about various people in town, the marriages and divorces, the addictions and illnesses. The illnesses especially intrigued her.

"You remember Debra Gallow, don't you? She married the brother of that boy you went to school with, the tall one who should have had braces but didn't."

"I have no idea who you're talking about, Mother."

"Of course you do! That boy with the crooked teeth was over here all the time."

Robert could hear the kitchen clock ticking off each painful second. He honestly tried to remember a tall boy with crooked teeth but could not bring forth a mental image. "Nope. Sorry."

She tried again. "The tall boy with the crooked teeth whose cousin was playing on the railroad tracks and got both legs amputated by a coal train?"

"Jesus, Mother."

"Do not take the Lord's name in vain in my house, Robert. I will not allow it."

"Sorry." Then to divert her away from his egregious sin, he said, "Go on."

She stared at him as if she could see beneath his skin.

"Go on. Debra Gallow," he prompted.

"Yes, well." She gathered her thoughts. "She has lung cancer. From what I hear, she never smoked a cigarette in her life, and she ends up with lung cancer. Now, a smoker getting lung cancer is one thing, but a nonsmoker? That is not fair. It's very sad, isn't it?"

"It's very sad."

He was not convincing, and she gave him that stare again. "Do you not understand, Robert? Her prognosis is dire. She is going to *die*, Robert."

"That is very sad," he said again. Mother crossed her arms over her sunken chest, offended, and the thought of this kind of back-and-forth volleying going on any longer exhausted him. "Why don't we watch a movie? You choose."

His mother chose *Scarface*—strangely, she loved violent gangster movies—from the teetering pile of VCR tapes stacked next to a bookcase that was also crammed full of old tapes. She had been highly offended when DVDs replaced VCRs. And she was not going to part with those movies. To watch the cassettes, she needed a genuine VCR player, so she started stockpiling them. Robert knew she had five or six of them in the laundry room that she had picked up at yard sales over the years. How would he ever convince her to get rid of those?

At 9:30, they dutifully pecked each other on the cheek and called it a night. Robert couldn't remember ever being so grateful to go to bed, but that didn't last long. After he had threaded his way up the narrow footpath of the stairs and settled into his boyhood twin bed, sleep would not come. For one thing, it was hotter than hell upstairs, and for another, his mother had not touched one thing in the room since he left. Above the desk, the bulletin board still displayed his various basketball pictures and track ribbons and movie ticket stubs. A wrought iron bookshelf had his tattered paperbacks, mostly westerns: Zane Grey and Louis L'Amour. On a lark, he decided to look in the closet to see if his Letterman jacket still hung there, wondering if it still fit. He hadn't been to the gym since his second wife left him. He couldn't see the point.

But when he opened the door, he faced a wall of *stuff.* He could see linens and trash bags filled with the unknown, and box after box of Barbie Dolls. When, and why, had his mother decided that she needed *Barbie Dolls?* This chore of cleaning out Mother's house, this duty that he had dreaded for as long as he could remember, would take months. He had always known that he would have to do it eventually, but he'd always thought it would be after she died. Then he could have just razed the house and all its contents. He wouldn't have to deal with the refuse of her life, his recollected childhood, the memories of Pop.

He needed help; he needed someone to share the burden. He called Jillian. "Our mother has become a first-class hoarder," he said before she even said hello. "This house is full of crap."

Jillian sighed. "Hold on." Robert could hear the glug of wine being poured into a tumbler. Jillian liked her tumblers of wine. "On a scale of 1 to 10, how bad is it?"

"Definitely a 10. My old closet is full of Barbie Dolls."

Jillian snickered. "So the old broad is finally full-blown crazy, huh?"

Robert felt slightly annoyed by the remark for his mother's sake. While his relationship with the woman had always been difficult, Jillian's bordered on hostile. "I don't think she's crazy. I think she started hoarding because she was lonely." As soon as he said it, Robert knew it was true.

"Am I supposed to feel guilty about that?"

Leave it to Jillian to immediately get defensive. She'd always been like that. Maybe it was because she was the older child in the family, or maybe it was because she was a girl, but their mother had always been tough on her, and Jillian had grown porcupine quills at an early age. Robert heard more gulping sounds and wondered if she was drunk. If so, he envied her. She wasn't yet stuck in this God-fearing, teetotaling house smack dab in the Bible Belt. Jillian lived in West Des Moines, Iowa, far enough away to be a tad too long to drive to southern Illinois. It was also far enough away to bitch and moan about having to buy an airline ticket to St. Louis, then pay for a rental car to get all the way down to Liberty.

"We should probably both feel a little guilty about leaving her alone for so long, but that's not why I'm calling."

"I don't want to come," Jillian said immediately.

"I don't want to be here either, but we have to help her. She can't do it alone."

"Can we hire someone to come and clean out the place?"

"Who's going to pay for that?" Robert knew his frugal mother wouldn't, and he couldn't afford it right now. He'd pretty much given his second wife everything out of guilt. And Jillian had two of her three kids in college, so she couldn't pitch in.

"Why don't we call that A&E show *Hoarders* and get Mother on as a guest? They'd bring in all those people to help, and it would be free."

Jillian was definitely on the road to getting drunk. "You need to get your ass down here and help me, Jillian."

"My ass is perfectly fine in West Des Moines."

"My ass was perfectly fine in Chicago, Jillian." It was a lie. He was thinking of buying a parrot, for fuck's sake. "But I'm here now, and the fact of the matter is that it's too big of a job for two people."

Jillian sipped on the other end. "You could ask someone from the church to help."

"A bunch of old ladies can't haul boxes, Jillian."

"What about that crazy Cliff Neeley who lives across the street? He doesn't have a job, and he's always lurking around. I bet he'd work for dirt cheap, Robert. Half of that town lives paycheck to paycheck."

"He's been carting around a wheelbarrow full of bricks through town, and everyone thinks he's going to end up back in the psych ward at Anna." His mother had told Robert that this evening. He was surprised he'd been paying enough attention to remember.

Jillian sighed heavily. "Shit." He could hear her take another drink. "Are Pop's clothes still in their bedroom closet?"

"I don't know." His mother had not let him enter her bedroom. "We'll have to save that job for later, Robert," she'd said before supper. It didn't bode well. "Probably," he said to Jillian.

"I don't want to see Pop's clothes hanging in the closet. They'll look sad, you know? She's probably still got that powder blue leisure suit from the 1970s stashed in there. He wore that leisure suit to church every Sunday for years, with those white shoes and white belt."

"I remember." A photographer had been at the church one Sunday to take pictures of the members for the church's annual directory. The photo had been taken outside, on the church steps, Pop wearing that powder blue outfit, Mother a yellow seersucker dress, Jillian a tie-dyed dress that she had worn to defy Mother, and he had been in his one gray suit. Robert had always liked that picture. They were all smiling, the happy family. Robert had thought they were before he knew better.

"I know I should come."

"Good. When can I expect you?"

"But I don't want to come."

Robert couldn't hide his exasperation. "Damn it, Jillian, do you want me to beg? Okay, I'm begging. I can't do this job by myself. Please come down here and help me clean out all the crap that has accumulated for fifty-five fucking years. Please!"

Jillian remained silent for so long that Robert wondered if she had passed out or walked away from her phone, but then she said, "I'll have to see when I can get time off." Jillian worked at a payroll company and had earned several promotions over the years. She was a big deal, even if she did say so herself.

"Thank you." Robert's hand cramped. He didn't realize how tightly he'd been clutching his phone, like a lifeline.

"I'm bringing a case of wine. I don't care what she says about alcohol in the house."

"You can smuggle in the bottles one at a time," Robert suggested.

"Just great. I'm not even there yet, and that woman already has me sneaking around and feeling guilty. It'll be like high school all over again. Shit."

"If it's like you in high school, bring some pot. It's legal in Illinois now—"

Jillian had hung up.

It was too hot to sleep. Robert considered going downstairs where it felt slightly cooler and watching some TV, but he didn't want to risk running into her and having to bear another non-conversation. His mother was a nocturnal being, and as he lay on the narrow bed, he thought he heard the occasional footstep, the occasional creaking floorboard. He'd left his computer bag and charger downstairs, and his phone was dead. Jillian had been right. Being here felt like he was in high school again, the pre-electronic age. Unlike her, though, Robert hadn't been a kid filled with angst and anger. He'd had a good time, good friends (why hadn't he kept in touch?), and he'd been happy, for the most part. It was only after he left for college, after his mother and Pop became empty-nesters, that the simmering became a boil, and no one could pretend any longer.

Robert gave up, turned on the bedside lamp, and got up. Maybe if he had something to read he could coax a few hours of sleep out of this night. His old westerns didn't hold any appeal anymore. Maybe they never had. Robert suspected he only bought those books because Pop was such a big fan of *Gunsmoke*. Pop had never traveled west of Missouri in his life, but he was enamored with the Old West mystique, the gunfighters and the sheriffs, the cowboys and the Indians, the horses and the stagecoaches. That must have been why he went to the gun show in Belleville that year and bought the Colt .45. When he got home from Belleville, he had gone into the house to get Robert. "I have something I have to show you," he'd whispered, looking around to make sure his wife wasn't within hearing distance.

Robert followed Pop into the garage. "Isn't she a beauty?" Pop said when he unwrapped the cloth it was carefully wrapped in. "Wyatt Earp used one like this during the shootout at the OK Corral."

Robert agreed that the gun was a beauty. "Can I use it to target practice with the guys?"

Pop considered. "Ask me again when you're a little older."

"Okay." Robert was only ten at the time, and that seemed fair.

Pop rewrapped the gun in its oilcloth. Then he put his hands on Robert's shoulders and bent down to look him in the eye. "This is our secret, Robert. Don't tell your mother."

"I won't," he promised, and he never did. As it turned out, he didn't have to.

In his cramped and airless childhood bedroom, Robert was about to give up and take his chances of navigating the dark and treacherous stairs and finding his mother puttering around downstairs when he saw the royal blue corner sticking out on the bottom shelf of the bookshelf. He pulled it out, not wanting to dislodge yet another treacherous pile, and saw that it was the 1992 *Falconer*, his yearbook from senior year. Robert wondered why he never took it with him when he left home for good. There must have been a reason, one that he no longer remembered. He took the yearbook and settled back in the damp sheets. It should be good for a couple of laughs if it didn't make him feel like a sad, tired old man.

The front and back covers were covered, along with many of the pages, with his classmates' messages. Robert remembered that had been the point. The more people who wanted to sign your yearbook, the more popular you were. Well, he had been very popular according to that criteria. But he only glanced at the barely legible declarations of *we'll always be friends* and *remember the championship game* and *see you in the NBA, Scorer.* That had been his nickname, Scorer, because he was the only one on the team who could consistently shoot a three-pointer. And because he was the guy in the senior class who'd had the most girlfriends. His friends thought he had slept with them all, but he had not. He didn't dispel the notion, though, only shrugged and grinned when someone asked him how a date had gone. That's all it took to seal his reputation. He was the Scorer of the Class of '92. His second wife—wherever she was—would think that was the funniest thing she had ever heard.

Robert flipped through the pages, and to his surprise, he remembered where to look for the pictures of him. There were a lot: he was poised midair, number 9, waiting to sink a shot; he was with a group of guys, lounging on the bleachers during lunch, trying to look cool; he could be found in pictures for the student council and drama club. Robert had to admit he had been a good-looking kid, with his dark hair flopping over his eyes and his slim, athletic build. There was no question about it. He'd thought he was hot shit in high school. That sarcastic little smile said it all.

"You stupid punk," Robert said aloud. "If you only knew, you'd wipe that obnoxious smirk off your face. You were only a big fish in a small pond."

Still, he kept thumbing through the pages until he found the picture that he realized he'd been looking for, the one of the Homecoming Court where he stood next to a stunning young girl holding long-stemmed roses and wearing a crown. As the homecoming king, he was supposed to wear a crown, too, but he'd refused. He was too cool for that, and the guys on the basketball team would never have let him live that one down. But he had been honored to have been voted king, even though he tried not to show it. And the best part was his queen, Mandy Malone, the prettiest and most popular girl in school.

Robert remembered very little about the actual dance, other than it was held in the gym, and the theme was Camelot. The decorating committee hadn't had much time to transform the gym into Camelot after the game, and the meager decorations did not live up to the dance's lofty theme. There had been some kind of archway where couples could take pictures and some posters of knights and a paper mâché rock that was supposed to be the stone that King Arthur pulled Excalibur from. It was hokey as all get-out, but he hadn't minded. As soon as he was crowned king, he set out on a mission to win his queen.

He'd had his eye on Mandy Malone since freshman year. She was probably out of his league, and she always seemed to have some older, mysterious boyfriend from another town. But Robert had grown cocky by his senior year, and with a couple of conquests under his belt, he decided he would make his move on that night. He was so cocky, in fact, so sure of his prowess, that he had not even brought a date to homecoming. When it was announced that he and Mandy had been voted king and queen, that further convinced Robert that the time was right.

He felt nervous during their first dance together as king and queen. All eyes in the gym were upon them as they led that inaugural dance. Robert was not a great dancer, but Mandy was. She subtly led him around the gym floor, elevating the dance from the common slow dance swaying, and he had a strange impulse to lick her hair. Mandy had the most amazing hair, blond and slightly wavy, draping to her waist, and it smelled like peaches.

"What kind of shampoo do you use?" he whispered into her ear. The student population of Liberty High was small, but Robert had never had the opportunity or the nerve to speak to her directly before. And those were his first words.

She giggled, a throaty, sexy sound if Robert ever heard one, and said, "I don't remember. It was on sale."

"You should keep buying it." He could have kicked himself. The beautiful Mandy Malone fit so perfectly into his arms—the top of her head came to his chin—and the bare skin on her back where his hand chastely rested felt silky. And he was talking about shampoo.

"Is this silly crown scratching you?" She lifted her head back to look at him, her blue eyes large in her small, heart-shaped face.

It was, but he barely noticed it. "I'd like to take you out." He smiled. His mother always said he had been blessed with perfect teeth, white and straight. His mother had a thing about nice teeth, among other things. She'd started playing the piano at church, and she was obsessed with that, too.

Mandy smiled back. "You move fast, buddy."

"So I've been told."

"So I've heard."

They were flirting! Plus, he was flattered that she had heard anything about him at all. "How about tonight? I know of a party at Boss' Lake."

"I don't usually go to those beer parties."

Robert almost tripped over her long tulle dress but caught himself just in time. He hoped he didn't know where this was going. "Do you have a boyfriend?" According to the Liberty lore, Mandy always had a boyfriend. However, a guy never showed up with her at school functions or events. How old were these mysterious boyfriends?

Mandy cocked her head to the side. At that moment, she looked far older and sexier than her seventeen years. "As it so happens, I've recently become single."

If he had the skill, Robert would have twirled her around right then. "Then my timing is perfect."

"I guess we'll see about that."

Robert and Mandy's relationship began on that homecoming night. They did go to the party at Boss' Lake, but Robert didn't have one beer. Instead, they sat in his lovingly restored Mustang—the one he and Pop had spent hours on—talking and making out. Mostly making out. He dropped her off at home that night, at an old farmhouse on the outskirts of town where Mandy lived with her daddy, grandmother, and four brothers. Robert was so smitten by that point that he wasn't concerned about the dark shadow lurking behind the living room curtain. "That's just Daddy," Mandy had said hurriedly before jumping out of the car and running to the house. At the door, she turned and blew him a kiss.

Within a week, they were sleeping together almost daily, and his Mustang saw a lot of action that fall and into the spring. Mandy never once invited him into her house to meet her family, and Robert did not find that to be strange. He wouldn't have minded bringing her home to see Pop, who already knew her because he had been her eighth-grade social studies teacher, but his mother was another story. Robert could just imagine her asking Mandy if she had taken the Lord Jesus as her savior. Or worse, she might sit Mandy down and grill her about her family. Or even worse, she might feel the need to lecture Mandy on the perils of premarital sex. Robert wouldn't put any of those things past his mother, who had been acting even more dissatisfied than usual lately.

Robert received his letter of acceptance from U of I in early April, and that's when things began to change between him and Mandy. She was not overjoyed with the news. "Why do you have to go so far away?" she asked. "What can't you go to SIU in Carbondale?" She was toying with the idea of going to Logan Community College but hadn't done anything about applying yet.

He was not as kind to her as he should have been. "God, Mandy, don't you want to get out of this small town? There aren't that many job opportunities here, and besides, don't you want to meet new people, go to different places? Come on, this town is downright claustrophobic sometimes."

"I like this town," she said in a small voice.

"This podunk town is fine for some people." He waved both hands in the air, trying to prove his point. "But some people want more out of life, you know?"

"What about me? Don't you love me?"

It was dark in the car, but Robert could hear her pout. He was getting tired of her recent mood swings and sudden neediness. "Sure." They'd said they loved each other, and he supposed he did love her some, but that wasn't the point here. His friends had been taunting him lately, telling him he was pussy whipped. Robert hotly denied it, but it did have a ring of truth. He didn't like it one bit.

"Take me home, Robert."

They limped along for another three weeks before she told him she was pregnant. He was blindsided, baffled. "How can that be? We use rubbers every time."

"Rubbers are not one hundred percent effective."

"Are you sure?"

"Yes, I'm sure. I took a home pregnancy test." One glance at his face and she said next: "If you ask me if it's yours, I will kill you, Robert."

"No, I wouldn't—" he stammered. "I mean, I know it's mine." He ran his hands through his hair and stared straight ahead, and it was like he could see all of his dreams go up in smoke. "What are we going to do?" He should have left it there, but he did not. "I can scrape together a couple of hundred dollars." He would have to ask his friends for the money; he hoped they would understand. He hadn't been around much since he started going with Mandy.

"For what?" she asked innocently.

He wanted to shake her. "Planned Parenthood in Carbondale, Mandy. Don't be dense."

"Take me home, Robert."

He and Mandy avoided each other for the next week, which was hard to do in their small high school. "Trouble in paradise," he told his buddies, which made them laugh. Robert wasn't laughing, and he couldn't sleep or eat. He didn't call Mandy, and she didn't call him, yet for some reason, they kept their date for the senior prom. He picked her up at 6:30.

She slammed the door when she got in. She didn't waste any time. "You're off the hook, Robert. I lost the baby."

Again, he was blindsided, baffled. His first thought was: *How could she lose a baby?* Her meaning finally sunk in. "Are you sure?"

"Yes, I'm sure, Robert. I was there."

"I'm sorry, I guess?"

Mandy looked at him like he was the dumbest person on earth. "And for your information, this is our last date. I'm going back to my old boyfriend. He's the one who truly cares about me."

He reluctantly started the car. "Then why are we going to the prom at all?"

"Because it's what people *do*, Robert. Don't you know anything?" She turned from him, her head held high, and added, "Maybe you'll learn something in college. You sure as hell need to learn a lesson or two."

Their relationship lasted from dance to dance, from homecoming to prom. Robert might have told her years later that he didn't learn much in college, that she had been right about almost everything, and that he probably did love her in the only way a selfish, arrogant young man could love a beautiful girl. He might have told her that it had been his one chance to have a child, and he had blown it spectacularly.

But he never did, and after the years turned into decades, it was too late.

Robert had been in Liberty for five days, and the only thing he could say with any certainty about what had been accomplished was that a dumpster squatted in the alley behind the garage. He had been sly in the way he had gone about getting his mother to concede. Instead of harping on the subject, he had started to put their "discards," as minimal as he thought they were, on the side patio. People driving by the front of the house or those taking an evening stroll on the adjacent sidewalk could see the black trash bags. It took his mother—a woman formerly so sharp that she noticed if you had moved one of her many knick-knacks an inch—two days before she figured out what he was doing.

Her eyes widened in alarm when she saw the meager pile. "This won't do at all, Robert. What will the neighbors think?"

"They'll think you're moving."

"But I haven't told anyone that I'm moving yet."

"Why not?"

She shrugged her narrow, shrinking shoulders. "There's plenty of time. I don't want to upset my friends, and Pastor Mulholland will be beside himself when I tell him that I won't be playing the piano anymore. The news will upset so many people, Robert."

"You're going to have to tell people eventually, Mother."

Her hands fluttered around her face, tucking in stray wisps of hair. "There's plenty of time, Robert. No need to rush things."

Robert suppressed a sigh, along with the many things he could have pointed out. She didn't have many friends left, and Pastor Mulholland could find another piano player. Plus, if his mother ended up at the nursing home in Liberty, both those points were moot. Or if she ended up at a newer assisted living place in a neighboring town, she could still drive to the church every Sunday, as scary as that prospect was. "I'll have a dumpster delivered."

She looked again at the trash bags. "I suppose that's for the best," she said quietly.

Robert had to turn away. As the days passed, he began to feel sorry for his mother. He wasn't used to feeling that way when it came to her, and he didn't quite know what to do with it. This was an excruciating process for her, and he could do nothing about that. He kept her busy sorting through various piles of books, pictures, magazines, and clothes. She didn't accomplish much. Those piles grew into multiple smaller heaps, which he suspected she surreptitiously moved to another corner of the house when he wasn't looking. Each day, she seemed to dwindle a little more. The piles did not.

Meanwhile, he alone went through closets with a trash bag at his side because Jillian had not called, and Robert suspected that she never had any intention to come home at all. He alone was the one who stank from sweat and frustration, and as he searched through the accumulation of his mother's lifetime, he alternated between anger and guilt. Why did she keep so much damn junk, and what was he doing to her by throwing it away? He was cruel to put her through this, but it was her fault for keeping so much worthless crap. Back and forth it went, the anger and the guilt. And the shame. Even if he couldn't afford to hire an estate company to come in and manage this chaos, he should have taken out a loan. Someone should have kept an eye on her all these years, but then again, she was an impossible woman to be around. Back and forth, back and forth.

And where in the hell would she live when they finished this heartbreaking, godawful job? To his and Jillian's great relief, his mother had told them a few years back that she didn't want to be a burden to them in her old age. She didn't want to live in Chicago or West Des Moines. Robert thought it was the nicest thing she had ever said to them, and Jillian had celebrated by turning her spare bedroom into a home gym. Neither he nor Jillian had brought up the subject again after that. They didn't want to know if she had reconsidered. They were terrible people, but their mother was a bitch.

As Robert dragged another full trash bag out to the dumpster, he noticed his mother had fallen asleep in the middle of her piles. Her head rested on a stack of clothes, and she had curled into a fetal position, her hands clenched. From a distance, she looked like a child who had fallen asleep in the middle of her cluttered playroom. Robert swallowed the lump in his throat. It was becoming familiar to him, and he hurried about his business.

The two middle-aged ladies from the house across the alley were there again, diving into the dumpster and tearing open bags. He had given them permission to do so. Many people in this town now lived below the poverty level, and as far as he was concerned, they were welcome to his mother's crap. Better they take it than her. The night before, just past midnight, his mother had dragged a ladder over to the dumpster to see what was inside, to find out what treasures her ungrateful son had thrown away. It was a good thing he had spotted her out his bedroom window. She was teetering precariously, reaching for a bag when he came out to rescue her. Neither of them said a word when he led her back into the house.

With his mother still asleep on the living room floor, Robert decided it was time to face his parents' closet. He hadn't been in their bedroom for many years and was surprised at how small and dark it seemed. The curtains were drawn, and the window air conditioner in here rattled as much as the one in the kitchen, but it was still the coolest room in the stifling house. He remembered the orange bedspread on the neatly made double bed. It had probably not occurred to his mother to get a new one in forty years. In fact, everything in the room seemed vaguely familiar. Pop's dresser stood on one wall, his mother's on another. An old cedar chest stood under the back window, and a metal rack next to the closet displayed the collection of Avon cars filled with men's cologne. On every birthday, anniversary, and Christmas for many years, his mother had given Pop a glass car filled with cologne. But he wasn't allowed to use the cologne. It was a *collection*, she had told him, one that might be worth money someday. Pop would wink at Robert and kiss his wife on the cheek. She always blushed. Robert remembered that now.

Robert took a deep breath and opened the closet. For some reason, it was almost as if he expected to find something sinister in there. That had been the case all week. Every time he reached behind a box or a bag, picked up something from the floor, or opened a drawer, he expected to see a dead rat carcass or a dead squirrel or a pile of some unidentifiable, mummified remains. None of that had happened, and Robert was almost positive he expected to come across something frightening because he hadn't slept at all since he returned to this house. The lack of sleep and stress played tricks on his mind. He had been imagining awful things in this place, his childhood home, and they were not there.

Sure enough, Pop's clothes were still hung up neatly, and the powder blue leisure suit peeked out from the very end of the row. Jillian had been right. The clothes did look sad, outdated, and strangely small. Pop had not been a tall man—at six feet, Robert had towered a good six inches over him—but Robert's memories always forgot that fact about the man. In his recollections, he always looked up at his father, not the other way around. Robert guessed a psychologist would have a field day with that one.

But it wasn't the sight of the clothes that made Robert feel a sudden and almost unbearable wave of sadness. It was the fact that she had kept them all these years. Did his mother want to be reminded of him every time she opened the closet? Did keeping her husband's outdated clothes mean that she actually missed him? Granted, the old woman had a hard time parting with anything, but she had been so angry with Pop after he died. She didn't shed a tear at the funeral, not even when the casket was lowered into the ground. Nor did a tear fall at the luncheon afterward in the church basement. Her friends offered condolences, but she remained dry-eyed and rigid. Robert might have understood if the woman didn't want to display her grief to the world—she was an inordinately proud person—but her anger seemed completely unjustified.

"That stupid, stupid man," she said the day after the funeral.

"How can you say that?" Robert looked up from the plate of food in front of him. He didn't remember pulling out all the casseroles from the refrigerator. Their friends and neighbors had been very generous with their gifts of food. That's what people did in small towns when someone's family member passed away. They brought over food before quickly leaving you alone. They'd stay longer when they came to collect their washed dishes that had their names written on masking tape on the bottom.

His mother shook her head. "So very, very stupid."

Robert threw down his fork. Was his mother truly that cold-hearted? She had always held herself apart from her own family, but this was going too far. Her husband had just died, goddammit. "Pop was a fucking hero, Mother. He was the first one on the scene, and if he hadn't gone into that burning house, those two little kids would have died!"

His mother looked him directly in the eye. "It was his choice to go over there."

"What do you mean? He was a volunteer firefighter. When a house catches fire, the firemen go and try to put it out. Don't you understand? It was his duty to go over there!" Robert pounded on the table with his fists. "Pop was a fucking hero, Mother!"

"He was a very stupid man." She turned away from him then and went to the sink. She ran water and started the dishes.

Robert couldn't stand to be around her one more second after that. Jillian had been the smart one, only coming with her family for the funeral and immediately leaving when it was over. Robert, unfortunately, had come into town for the homecoming weekend at Liberty High. He wasn't home because he missed the glory of high school or anything as pathetic as that. He had a good reason. His senior basketball squad was being inducted into the high school's Athletic Hall of Fame during the homecoming game's halftime. He thought it would be a lark to come back home, the college frat boy coming to receive his laurels. He'd thought it was a big deal, but it wasn't. Four of his former team members already sprouted beer bellies, and most people were too busy buying popcorn and soda to pay attention to the presentation on the gym floor. No one had acted like their outstanding high school basketball team—and he had been the top scorer; they had called him Scorer—had been that big of a deal.

He'd thought he might see Mandy, so he stayed until the very end of the dismal game, searching the crowd and watching the door. But either she had changed so much he didn't recognize her, which he doubted, or she hadn't bothered to come. He was still arrogant enough at that time to think she would want to see him; he was still cocky enough to hope that she still loved him. He was one of the last people to leave the gym, and it was only then that he heard about the fire as he walked to his car in the almost deserted parking lot.

The Rathbone house was on fire. Robert did what most of the people leaving the high school did. He headed over to the house. He could see the ash in the air a few blocks away and smell the acrid burning wood. It had been an old house, and the wiring was faulty, he heard as he got out of his car. He moved closer to the smoldering ruins. Most of the firefighters had taken off their helmets, their soot-smudged faces grim.

"Smoke inhalation," one of them said. "That's what got him when he went back in to get Tina."

Robert knew Tina. She had been one of the bartenders at the American Legion where Pop liked to hang out.

"He got the kids, though. That's something," another firefighter said.

"Jacob doted on that family," the first said.

"Everyone thought Tina was a great gal," the second said.

It took Robert a few more stunned seconds before it sank in. It took him seeing the two stretchers carried out of the house before he started to run, crying out, "Pop!" It took three of the firefighters to tackle him before he could reach the stretchers. And it took every ounce of courage he would ever possess to go home and tell his mother that Pop was dead.

But she already knew.

Robert found the Colt .45 in one of Pop's work boots, the same boots he wore as a volunteer firefighter. What was it doing in the closet? The last he knew, it had been hidden in the back of a shelf of wrenches. But that had been many years ago. Still, the thought of the gun in the house startled him. It had been his mother's house alone for almost twenty-five years, and it did not belong. He took it out of the boot, wondering if he should take it back out to the garage, or if he should take it to the gun shop downtown and sell it. He was holding it in his hand, gingerly, when his mother walked into the bedroom.

She seemed to be a little dazed from her nap. "I thought I heard you in here." She perched on the edge of the bed, lowering herself slowly. "I see you found the gun."

"You knew about the gun?" Robert still thought Pop had moved it there for protection, but that didn't make any sense. On the night he died, Pop had been wearing those boots. But now they were cleaned and polished a shiny black.

"I found that gun years ago when I went to the garage to get a wrench to tighten that pipe under the sink. As you may remember, your father wasn't very handy around the house." She waited for Robert to nod. "It was not a very good hiding place."

Robert continued to stare at the boots. His mother must have been the one who cleaned and polished them. "Aren't these the boots Pop wore the night of the fire?"

She nodded.

"If you wanted a gun for protection, you should keep it in your nightstand. I mean, what is it doing in Pop's boot?"

"I keep it there as a reminder."

"A reminder?" Robert looked at her. That uneasy feeling of finding something unexpected and unwelcome started to creep up his spine. He shivered.

"Sit down, Robert." She patted the space next to her.

Reluctantly, he did so, his unease growing.

"On the night of the fire, I gave your father a choice. I pointed that gun at him, and I said, 'You have to choose, Jacob. It's that woman or me.'"

"But there was a fire, and Pop was a volunteer firefighter. He went over to Tina's house when he heard the alarm."

She shook her head. "Your father was already over there when the fire broke out, Robert. He'd been seeing that woman for several years by then."

Robert's mind reeled, trying to make sense of what she was saying. "And you knew?"

"Everybody knew, Robert. It's a small town."

Another thought careened from the corner of his brain. "Those two little boys. Were they—" He couldn't bring himself to say, *Pop's.*

"I don't know, Robert." She shook her head again. "As long as your father came home to me each night, I could stand it. I could keep our family together. I could pray. I could hope that he would come to his senses. But then he told me that he loved her. Things got much harder after that."

Robert remembered how her anger escalated over the years. "Why did you put up with it for so long? Were you afraid of what people would say if you got a divorce?"

She still had it, that scathing look. "People get divorced, Robert."

He dropped his gaze. "Yes, I know." He was living proof of the fall-out from two failed marriages. Being left for someone else could carve away messy chunks of your self-esteem and happiness.

"I let it go on for so long, Robert," she enunciated every word, but her voice sounded shaky, old, "because I loved him. You can't help who you love, Robert."

Robert sighed heavily. On his bleakest days, he sometimes wondered if he had ever loved his first wife, his college sweetheart. They got married the week after graduation, and once they were out of school and in the "real world," things fizzled fast. Without a party to go to, they'd had nothing in common. He had loved his second wife very much, too much. She said he smothered her. Maybe, long ago, he had loved Mandy Malone, the homecoming queen who had taken his breath away every time he looked at her.

Finally, Robert said, "No, you can't. You can't help who you love."

"Damn shame, isn't it?" his mother trilled.

He stared at her, shocked. He couldn't believe that his mother had sworn under her very own roof. What was next? Then he started to laugh. "Yep, it's a damn shame."

She reached for Robert's hand so he could help pull her up. "That's enough work for one day. I'm going to start supper." She seemed fully awake now, her step lighter.

"I'll be right there to help you," Robert called after her. But first, he was going to take the Colt .45 out to his car for safekeeping. Tomorrow, he would take it to the gun shop and sell it. It finally needed to be out of this house; it was time.

And more importantly, even though it might be too late, Robert didn't want his mother to get hurt.

FEVER

Trudy would like to say that she didn't know when it started, but she did. She knew exactly when it began.

That second Thursday in June promised heat the moment she opened her eyes, and it did not disappoint. As the morning turned to afternoon, the temperature continued to rise until the thermometer outside of her hair salon, Trudy's Beauty Boutique, read 98 degrees. It was all that her clients would talk about, the unseasonable heatwave. Well, that and the Queen of Hearts drawing at the American Legion that night. It was too hot to breathe, they said. The jackpot was over $1,000,000, they said.

"What would you do with that kind of money, Trudy?" Gina Hardish asked.

Trudy was in the middle of cutting her hair into a long shag, the same style she had worn for decades, the style that made her look like Carol Brady. It was not flattering on the woman. Trudy cut another inch off the back, letting the dyed blond hair fall to the floor. "I think the first thing I would do is remodel my kitchen."

Gina snorted. "Are you kidding me? You just got rich, and you'd remodel your kitchen? Did you hear that, Joanne?"

"I heard." Joanne pretended to read a magazine as she waited her turn, but everyone knew she always eavesdropped on your conversation. Joanne was one of the biggest gossips in town.

"My dishwasher hasn't worked in two years, and my stove was in the house when we bought the place nineteen years ago. It's olive green. That's how old it is." Trudy tried to remember if Carol Brady had an olive green stove. Cutting Gina's hair always made her mind wander to *The Brady Bunch*.

"Why doesn't that hunk of a husband of yours fix your dishwasher?" Gina looked at Trudy in the mirror, arching her eyebrows. Joanne might be one of Liberty's biggest gossips, but Gina qualified as the town's biggest flirt over the age of fifty.

"Wayne works the third shift at American Aluminum and sleeps during the day. When he's not sleeping, he's fishing, or if it's deer season, he's hunting." Trudy worked hard to keep the tinge of annoyance out of her voice. After nineteen years of marriage, she was used to it. And she knew from experience that it did no good at all to complain. Wayne refused to bother with anything household-related. That was her job.

"Whatever." Gina shrugged. "I'd go on an around-the-world cruise if I had that kind of money."

"I'd buy a Mercedes," Joanne said.

"Or maybe I'd go to Italy and eat pasta all day and flirt with all the men. Those Italian men are so sexy."

"The men in France are sexier," Joanne said.

"Look at you and me, Joanne. We're out traveling the world, and our little Trudy is cooking up meatloaf in her new kitchen." Gina snorted again.

"You know that you'd only get about half of the money, ladies. The taxman gets a big chunk." Trudy raked a comb through Gina's dry hair. The woman was so cheap that she dyed her hair with Clairol Nice 'N Easy, then came to the salon to get it cut. And forget about her ever leaving a tip. Yet now she was spending her make-believe money on trips around the world.

"You need to lighten up a little bit, honey," Gina said.

Joanne tossed the magazine to the side. "Yeah, there shouldn't be any taxes in daydreams. They're a tax-free zone."

"Someone has to be the practical one." Trudy smiled stiffly. She couldn't afford daydreams. She knew from experience that they were very expensive—and costly in so many heartbreaking ways.

Gina brushed that remark aside with a wave of her hand. "I know you, Trudy. You'd buy that son of yours a nice new truck."

"A Dually, all decked out," Joanne added.

"With antlers on the front and a gun rack on top."

"And don't forget the mudflaps."

"Right. The ones that have that drawing of a pink naked lady with pointy tits." Gina smiled broadly in the mirror at Trudy.

"I'm glad you ladies have figured out how I'd spend my pretend money." The looks on their faces said this disappointed them. "But you're right. Travis would love a truck like that. I'm sure that's what I would buy if I won the Queen of Hearts drawing."

"I knew it." Gina slapped her knee.

"Travis is a good boy," Joanne said.

"He is." Trudy nodded.

"I heard he joined the Army right after graduation. When does he leave for basic training?"

Trudy glanced over at Joanne. She had no idea how the woman had come across that information, but if she knew, it was now all over town. "He leaves next month for Fort Leonard Wood."

"You must be so proud."

Trudy nodded, not trusting herself to speak. She was proud of her son. He was a lovely, sweet boy, but that was just it. He was a *boy*. The thought of him leaving soon and going into basic training cut through her like a knife, and the thought of losing him terrified her. He was her only son, her only child.

Joanne continued. "We have so many young ones around here joining the military shortly after graduating from high school. It only goes to prove how patriotic southern Illinois is. We should all be proud that we live here."

"Amen to that, sister." Gina nodded vigorously, and Trudy barely missed her ear with the scissors.

"I bet that Wayne is proud, too," Joanne persisted.

"Of course." Trudy kept her eyes down as she unsnapped the plastic gown covering Gina. Joining the Army had been Wayne's idea. To his way of thinking, it would toughen up their son, who in Wayne's opinion—and he was not quiet about it—was something of a wimp. Trudy knew he suspected Travis was gay. However, neither she nor Wayne had ever asked Travis, and Travis wasn't volunteering any information. He had learned that lesson the hard way.

Trudy took off Gina's gown with a flourish. "You are back to your beautiful self, Gina."

And that's when the shop's large front window exploded, shards of glass ricocheted in every direction, and Gina's high-pitched scream filled the air. Trudy's immediate reaction was to duck, and she did so, pulling Gina off the styling chair to the ground and shouting at Joanne to *get down, get down!*

It was a brick, an ordinary reddish brick that had exploded through her window. Trudy could see that when the terror eased and she could breathe again. Gina whimpered in her arms, and Joanne cowered in the far corner, her arms crossed over her head. "Is everyone okay?" Trudy's voice shook as she slowly got to her feet. Her first thought was that maybe the brick had fallen off the back of a passing truck, but she didn't remember seeing or hearing any automobile before the brick crashed through the window.

"I need a medic," Gina whimpered. "I'm bleeding."

Joanne unfurled herself in the corner, and bracing herself against the wall, inched into a standing position. "I'm okay."

"I've been shot!" Gina cried.

"Oh, for god's sake, woman! It was a damn brick through the window. Get a hold of yourself!"

"I am bleeding!"

"It's a goddamn scratch. Don't be such a baby, Gina." Joanne crunched her way over the broken glass to Trudy. "You better call the police. I'll get a Band-Aid for Gina's tiny little scratch. Talk about someone who's not good in a crisis. Sheesh."

"Right." Trudy was happy that someone told her what to do. A brick had just come flying through her window, and nothing made sense. Liberty was a small town, and while there were the occasional acts of vandalism, mostly committed by high school students, they usually occurred at night, not in broad daylight. Who would want to throw a brick through her window? She went out of her way to be nice to people, and as far as she knew, she didn't have any enemies. Yet this attack—could she call it an attack?—felt personal. It was unnerving. She dialed the local police.

"What the hell?" Roxy must have parked in the lot behind the salon and walked through the back door. Roxy, her young stylist, who was supposed to be here two hours ago, was higher than a kite. She stood weaving and could barely keep her eyes open. It was typical.

"Someone threw a brick through the front window. The police are on the way."

"Why?"

"I don't know *why*, Roxy. I can't think of any earthly reason for someone to do that, but there you have it." Trudy motioned to the brick.

Roxy plunked her outsized, heavy purse down at her station. "It was probably that weird Cliff Neeley guy. He's standing across the street, staring over here."

"That doesn't mean anything. Before long, the whole town will be here gawking. Cliff's only the first one here."

"Maybe. But he's got a wheelbarrow full of bricks."

"What?" Trudy's eyes flew to the cracked window. She couldn't see the guy from here, and she was not about to go to that window again. He might decide to blast another brick through it. And she was not about to open the door. What if he charged her? She was thinking crazy thoughts; she knew that.

"I said," Roxy spoke slowly as if Trudy had not understood her, "he has a wheelbarrow full of bricks. It's something a person notices, you know?"

"I heard you the first time, Roxy." It took a fair amount of self-control not to snap at the girl, even though Trudy was not the type of person who generally lashed out at people. That brick through the window had really rattled her.

Joanne, as she put a tiny Band-Aid on Gina's teensy cut on her knee, had not missed a thing. "He was always an odd one, even when he was a little kid. He was in my Roger's grade at school. I told my Roger to be nice to him, but once Cliff flushed the class pet hamster down the toilet, I told him to steer clear."

Gina, now that she had been tended to, jumped back into the conversation. "The poor man. I hear his sister lives in Springfield and won't have anything to do with him. And once his mother died—six or seven years ago, was it?—he quit taking his meds."

"I gave him a sandwich once." Roxy had no problem peering through the hole in the window. "He's such a skinny old man, and I felt sorry for him, you know? But it is creepy how he just walks up and down the street all day, every day. I bet he knows everything that goes on in this town."

Joanne cleared her throat. "Roxy, Cliff is forty-four, which does not make him old. Furthermore, I would imagine it's more likely that he's listening to the voices in his head. I don't think he can pay attention to what goes on around him."

"The poor man," Gina said again. "I bet he gets lonely in that big, old house by himself."

"Now wait a minute, ladies." Trudy crunched over the glass and pulled Roxy away from the window. "The fact of the matter is that Cliff Neeley threw a brick through my window. Another fact is that someone could have gotten hurt."

"I'm hurt," Gina piped up.

"Would you stop whining about a little cut, Gina? Sheesh."

Trudy continued, her voice louder. "Look, everyone in this town knows that Cliff Neeley is not quite right in the head. He's schizophrenic or bipolar or what-ever, but that doesn't excuse him from throwing a brick through my window."

"Did you do something to get on his bad side?" Joanne asked.

"Of course not! Why would I do something like that? I always wave at him and—" Trudy stopped, remembering. Oh, God, she had said something to him about a month or so ago. She had looked up from cutting Tory Gleeson's hair, and there he was. Cliff stood right in front of her, pressing his face against the glass, hands cupped around his eyes, peering. Trudy had been so startled that she jumped, the scissors clattering to the floor.

Tory had her back to the window, her head bent to her magazine. "I hope you're going to sterilize those scissors again, Trudy."

"I'll be right back." And she had marched outside and told Cliff that he was trespassing on private property, that he was scaring her customers, and that he ought to mind his own business. She'd told the man to *shoo!* Trudy shivered, remembering that she hadn't been kind to him at all. She'd had a bad morning at home with Wayne, and she had not been kind to Cliff.

"And what?" Joanne prompted.

Trudy shook her head. "Nothing."

"The cop is here, and he's talking to Cliff across the street." Roxy had made her way back to the broken window. "You should get a load of this new cop Liberty just hired. He's hot."

The large hole in the front window must have been letting in outside air because the salon sizzled with heat by the time the new cop questioned Trudy. It hadn't taken long for Officer Morrison to interview Gina, Joanne, and Roxy. But the seconds in those few minutes seemed to stretch like pulled taffy as Trudy watched the handsome, uniformed young man write the women's statements, nod sympathetically, and reassure them in his deep voice that he had everything under control. They didn't need to worry about a thing. Trudy couldn't take her eyes off of him, his sandy blond, curly hair, his lashes as long and thick as a Maybelline model.

"Are you sure you don't want to take a picture of my knee, Officer?" Gina hiked up her summer dress a couple more inches.

"I have all the information I need from you ladies right now." He smiled.

"I can remove the bandage," Gina said hopefully.

"God Almighty!" Joanne took Gina's arm. "I'm taking you out of here before you embarrass yourself any more."

Even Roxy, who had slipped into the bathroom to put Visine in her bloodshot eyes, had perked up during her short interview. She seemed to have forgotten that, a few feet away, her oversized purse held enough illegal substances to land her in jail. "Are you sure there isn't anything else I can help you with, Officer?" she asked in a throaty, sexy voice.

"Not right now." Again, that winning smile. "Good afternoon, ladies."

It was Trudy's turn to be questioned, and on their own accord, her legs started to quiver, and she couldn't catch her breath. She landed clumsily in the nearest chair, one of the two chairs against the wall for waiting customers.

"Are you all right, Mrs. Bickford?" His voice seemed warm with concern. "You look flushed. I'll get you a glass of water."

When he returned from the small kitchenette in the back of the salon and handed the water to her, Trudy could only hold on tightly to the glass. She didn't dare bring it to her lips because she would slosh the water all over her lap. She stared at his hands, his lovely hands, as he held his pad of paper. He didn't wear a wedding ring.

He clicked his pen. "Do you want to add anything else to what the other ladies said about the incident?"

Trudy tried to steady her breathing. She was acting like a fool. He was a handsome young man, yes, but she was a thirty-nine-year-old married woman. However, people still said she looked good for her age. She had always been small-boned, and at five feet, two inches, on the short side. She had not let herself go like so many of her former classmates had. She walked three miles on a treadmill every morning, watched what she ate, and tried to keep up with the latest styles she saw in magazines. Her hair, shoulder-length, light brown with honey highlights, was her best feature, of course. And she never walked out of her house without a full face of makeup. It was her job to look good, and she took it seriously.

"It was like they said. I had just finished cutting Gina's hair, and that brick blasted through the front picture window. It scared us all half to death."

Officer Morrison took the seat next to her and nodded sympathetically. "I bet. You were lucky no one was seriously injured."

He was so close that Trudy would swear she could feel the heat coming from his body. Involuntarily, she crossed her legs. "Aren't you hot in that uniform?"

"It is a little warm today," he acknowledged.

"How long have you been a cop? I mean," Trudy felt her face grow redder, "you're probably only twenty-five or so, right?"

"I'm twenty-nine, and I've been working in law enforcement for five years. Now, if we can get back to the incident, ma'am?"

"No ma'am. I'm Trudy. Please call me Trudy."

He nodded slightly. "Trudy."

"And what can I call you? Officer Morrison seems like a mouthful, doesn't it?" Trudy didn't know what she was doing, being so forward, rushing her words, leaning toward him too eagerly. It wasn't like her. It must be the heat—the heat and the unsettling events of the day.

"Okay," he said slowly. "My name is Alan."

"Alan." It was Travis' middle name. That was odd, wasn't it? Or maybe it was a sign. It could be a sign.

Then a completely different thought rushed at Trudy, and she took a sharp intake of breath. "Is Cliff Neeley still out there across the street? Is he going to throw more bricks through my window?"

"He claims he doesn't remember throwing the brick."

"He definitely threw the brick! Oh, my God! Is he still out there?" Trudy didn't remember setting the water glass down, but her hands were now free, and she reached for Alan's.

"Calm down, Mrs.—Trudy—Officer Pyle has taken him in for questioning. I understand he has some mental health issues that we're going to sort out." He gently extricated his hands from hers. "Now, can you think of anything that would have provoked Mr. Neeley into doing something like this?"

He had such warmth and sympathy in his green-gold eyes. Trudy could not remember the last time someone looked at her like that, looked at her as if she mattered, looked at her as if she were important. She would tell him the truth. "About a month ago, I was with a client, and Cliff peered into the front window." She nodded at the broken window. "He scared the bejesus out of me, with his face pressed against the glass. I told him in no uncertain terms to go away and stay away."

"Is that all?" Alan's pen was poised above his pad. "Could your client verify this information?"

"She had her back to the window and was reading a magazine."

Alan scribbled something on his pad.

Trudy looked into his eyes. What did he want from her? Was she not saying it right? "Cliff had a very strange look on his face, his lips all flattened out like that. I was *terrified*."

Alan waited, searching her face, wanting more.

"I," Trudy hesitated only a split second, "I thought he was going to expose himself to me, right there and then. His hands—"

"Where were his hands?"

Cupped around his face, on the glass. "It looked like he reached for the zipper of his jeans. He had a strange look on his face . . ."

"And that's when you went outside and told him to go away?"

"Yes. I was terrified," Trudy said again. "I mean, who knows what a man like that would do next, right? What if he had been stalking me, and some night when I've worked late, and I'm closing up the shop, he comes in and . . ."

Alan looked genuinely concerned. "Do you think Mr. Neeley has been stalking you?"

"I don't know, but it's possible. The man wanders the streets of this town at all hours of the day and night." Looking at Alan's beautiful, concerned face, Trudy wanted him to believe her. She wanted him to keep looking at her that way. She wanted to keep him near. The blood in her veins felt like it was boiling. If Alan touched her now, he could feel the heat, the fever coursing through her body.

He closed his notepad. "I guarantee that I will follow up on this, Trudy. And I'll make sure to drive by this salon a couple of times a night on my patrol. If you have any concerns at all, you can just call me, okay?"

"You're going to protect me?" Trudy didn't care if he saw the naked hope in her eyes, and she knew she would start coming to the salon in the evenings. She would wait in the front window with a cup of coffee. She would wave at him, point at the cup of coffee, and silently will him to stop and come inside.

"I'm going to do my best. Now, if you have a piece of cardboard, I can tape it over the hole until you can get someone in here to fix this window." His smile was boyishly shy.

"Do you always go above and beyond your call of duty like this?" Trudy almost expected to burst into flame at any moment.

"I give it my best shot," he said and went to look for something to mend the damage.

Wayne Bickford asked Trudy to marry him at the beginning of their senior year. They had been going together for two years, and Trudy thought she might love him, a little. He was a defensive tackle on their high school football team—never mind that Liberty's crummy team hadn't won a game in two years—and was considered something of a big deal. Trudy knew she was supposed to be flattered that someone that tall and broad-shouldered and good-looking would ask her to marry him. She was, a little. She said no.

Wayne asked her to marry him the next time at Christmas and even produced a diamond ring the size of a speck of sand. They were standing under the twinkling lights of her family's Christmas tree, and her parents were overjoyed at the prospect. Their little Trudy had landed a whopper of a fish. However, Trudy was not overjoyed. She said no.

Wayne asked Trudy to marry him again on the night of graduation. He was already working part-time at American Aluminum by then, his future set, and he had rented a tuxedo for the evening. That time, he produced a slightly bigger ring with a diamond the size of a small pebble when they went parking afterward at Boss' Lake, an old strip mine pit. He waved the ring under her nose like it was a vial of smelling salts, and she was supposed to wake up and smell the roses. "Will you marry me, Trudy?"

Trudy smoothed down the tulle of her scarlet dress. "I'm going to have to take a raincheck on that, Wayne."

"What in the hell is that supposed to mean?" He kept waving the ring in front of her. It had now become the grand prize of her life.

"I have things I want to do before I settle down. You know that, Wayne." She had told him repeatedly what she planned to do, but Wayne never seemed to hear anything he didn't want to hear.

"You're not going to do any better than me, Trudy, and this is the last time I'm going to ask you. Will you marry me?"

"No."

After Wayne threw the ring out the car window, slammed the car into reverse, peeled out of their parking spot, drove her home at breakneck speed, and dumped her on her parents' doorstep, Trudy packed her bag. Then she retrieved the business card from the miniature cedar chest where she kept all her valuables and tucked it safely in her purse. By the next morning, she was on the Amtrak to Chicago.

For as long as she could remember, Trudy had dreamed of becoming a singer. She'd started singing in church at the age of five when she debuted with "Silent Night" in the Baptist Church's Christmas pageant. Some of the older ladies had wept and told her mother that Trudy had the voice of an angel. She had continued to sing in the choir at school, and in the four years of high school, she had won the lead in the annual musical four years running. She had sung Laurey's part in *Oklahoma!*, Maria in *The Sound of Music*, Anna Loenowens in *The King and I*, and Magnolia Hawks in *Showboat*. After her show-stopping performance in *The Sound of Music*, Mitchell McHenry had cornered her in the hall and told Trudy that she sang "as good as Celine Dion." Everyone knew Mitchell McHenry was a perpetual drunk, but Trudy took his lofty compliment as a statement of fact.

Trudy hadn't known what she was waiting for until it happened. She'd been asked to sing a couple of songs at a wedding dance held at the American

Legion in March of her senior year. The bride's mother somehow knew Trudy's mother, and even though Trudy didn't know either the bride or groom—they were older, and Trudy heard they lived somewhere in the Chicago area—Trudy happily accepted. It was her first paying gig! She felt like a professional as she crooned "At Last" and "From This Moment On" into the microphone. Trudy, eyes closed, poured her heart and soul into those songs, and when she opened her eyes and saw how tearful her audience was, she knew she had nailed it. She knew she had what it took. Most of the people in the hall didn't know her, yet she had moved them.

After the performance, Trudy stood at the bar, sipping a ginger ale. A short, blond man wearing an expensive-looking suit walked up and ordered a dry martini with a twist. That immediately impressed Trudy. Most people around this town drank beer or basic mixed drinks, like 7&7s and rum and Cokes.

"Nice job." He lifted his drink in a toast.

"Thanks. I was a little nervous at first." She wasn't nervous at all. Singing in front of a crowd of strangers had seemed as natural as breathing.

"You didn't show it." He took a sip of his drink and made a face. "Where in this town can you go to get a decent martini?"

"I wouldn't know." Trudy almost told him she was in high school but changed her mind. "I don't drink martinis."

"What do you drink?" He peered at her glass, which was almost empty.

"7&7." Trudy knew the drink was clear, like her ginger ale.

The man ordered her one and then introduced himself as Tyler Colby. "You've got some real talent, Trudy. Who represents you?"

Trudy blinked. Again, she didn't mention that she was in high school. She was glad she'd worn her black dress, the one she thought was the most sophisticated in her closet. Maybe it made her look older. "Why do you want to know?" she stalled. She thought she knew what he meant by "representation" but wasn't entirely sure.

Tyler reached into the pocket of his suit and pulled out a business card. He handed it to her. "I'm always looking for new talent."

It was a professional business card, shiny black with metallic letters: TYLER COLBY TALENT AGENCY. Trudy glanced back up at him. She couldn't believe it; this was really happening. "I guess I can tell you. I'm looking for a new agent. The one I have now… Well, he's not meeting my needs." Trudy quickly looked back down at the card. She guessed her "agent" would be her mother. She knew she was blushing.

"If you're serious about new representation, please consider me. As I said, I'm always looking for new talent."

"I'll do that." Her heart was beating fast and hard, and Trudy's head spun with excitement. She prayed not to faint.

"It looks like you need another drink."

Trudy was surprised to see that her drink was almost empty. "Sure."

The bride floated over to the bar in a sea of crinkling taffeta. She was not a pretty bride, with her long nose and pronounced jaw, but she acted like she owned the place. Trudy could respect that. "Tyler, you old hound dog." She threw a glance at Trudy. "I see you're up to your old tricks."

Tyler kissed her on the cheek. "Now, Connie. I'm only trying to get this pretty little lady to let me represent her. No harm in mixing business with pleasure, is there?"

"Uh-huh. Is that what they call it these days?" The bride threw back a shot of Wild Turkey. "God, I don't know why I let my mother talk me into having the wedding here. 'You know your grandparents can't travel anymore, Connie,'" she mimicked in a high, scratchy voice. She threw back a second shot. "This place sucks." She flounced off, her long train dragging along the floor. Trudy could see that three or four crumpled paper napkins had become ensnared in the material as the train swept the floor.

"This place isn't so bad." Trudy felt a need to defend the Legion Hall, but looking around at the exposed brick walls and metal folding chairs and blinking fluorescent lights, she felt a flush of shame. She had always thought this place was special, but now she could see it with new eyes. If she married Wayne, this was where they would have their wedding reception, too. It wasn't good enough.

"This place has free booze, so it suits me just fine." Tyler motioned to the bartender. "And Connie's a bitch. The only guy she could get to marry her had to be deaf."

"The groom's deaf?" That was sad. And it meant that he hadn't heard her sing, which was even sadder.

Tyler grinned. "Nah. But after a year or two of marriage, I bet he can't hear a thing she says."

"Oh, you." Trudy playfully slapped at his arm. The alcohol was starting to dull her inhibitions. Plus, Connie had seemed to know Tyler was a talent agent, which meant that he was legitimate. Trudy had heard there were a lot of scumbags in the entertainment industry, but Tyler was a bonafide agent who wanted to represent *her*.

Tyler was easy to talk to, and Trudy relaxed even more after another couple of drinks. She didn't know anyone at this wedding dance, which was probably the first time that had happened in her entire life. On most days, she couldn't go to the post office without running into at least three people she knew. She'd always thought she liked that aspect of living in a small town, but now, talking with Tyler, she wasn't so sure. He made Chicago sound exciting, and Liberty grew paler and paler. Trudy lost track of how many drinks she had.

When Trudy's mother found her much later, Trudy was locked in a toilet stall, her head against the cool brick wall, willing herself not to throw up. Her lips were bruised from Tyler's kisses, her pantyhose torn at the waist, and she was flushed with excitement and desire. Tyler wanted to represent her; he wanted her. She said yes.

Trudy should have called, but she wanted to surprise Tyler. In the two months since they'd met, she'd almost called him many times but had resisted the urge. Even when the train deposited her in the bustling, confusing Union Station, Trudy did not try to find a payphone to call Tyler to let him know that she had arrived. She would surprise him at his office as an independent young woman ready to start her career. She'd changed into her good black dress in the bathroom on the train because it was still the most sophisticated thing she owned. He had said that he liked the dress, and she wanted to please him.

Trudy was afraid to ask any of the hurried-looking people for directions, so once she was out of the station on Canal Street, she let the crowd move her until she found a drugstore. She bought a map to locate the address on the business card: 69 E. Madison Street. Trudy was relieved. It was only a little over a mile walk, which was a good thing. Her high heels, the only pair she owned, were already killing her feet. She noticed that many of the women walking to and from the train wore tennis shoes and carried bags with their dress shoes. She shuffled that useful information away. She had so much to learn about living in a city.

When Trudy arrived at 69 E. Madison, she thought there must have been some mistake. It wasn't an office building like the many skyscrapers she had passed. It wasn't even an apartment building where Tyler perhaps had his office. It was a bar called Red's. Confident that there was an easy explanation for this, Trudy pushed through the revolving door. She would take a seat, rest her aching feet, order a Coke, and ask the bartender what nearby building housed Tyler Colby Talent Agency.

The room was dark and narrow, with a bar running along the length of one wall. A few gruff-looking men, some wearing Blackhawk t-shirts or hats, nursed their drafts and barely looked up when they heard the door. Behind the bar, Trudy could see a room with tables and a staircase twisting out of sight. She almost laughed with relief. Tyler's office must be upstairs. She was in the right place after all, and the niggling doubt that had started to pester her ever since she reached Union Station had only been her nerves. Tyler Colby was the real deal, and he was going to represent her.

Trudy set her old suitcase on the floor and climbed onto the barstool. She might as well order that Coke and maybe a hamburger, too. She was suddenly starving. She had been too nervous to eat on the train. Plus, the prices were exorbitant. Trudy had brought every penny she'd ever earned with her, which only amounted to a little over $800. She was going to have to conserve her money carefully until the jobs started pouring in. She might even have to get a job waitressing or something to keep her afloat until she started making real money. Trudy was not afraid of hard work.

The bartender turned from the cash register and stood in front of Trudy in two strides. "What'll you have?"

Trudy stared, speechless. This couldn't be true, but there it was. The man she had dreamed about for the last two months stood before her: same blond hair, light blue eyes, and lazy grin. But instead of an expensive suit, he wore jeans and a white t-shirt. He also had an apron around his waist and a towel draped over his shoulders. "I, uh—"

"I'll need to see an ID." He leaned on the bar. "You don't look old enough to vote either, sweetheart. Are you old enough?" And there came the lazy grin. Tyler was flirting with her. Again.

Trudy flushed. She knew she looked ridiculous, overdressed, and out of place. She had even put the pearl-encrusted comb she had inherited from her grandmother in her hair. She might as well have stamped "Liberty, Illinois" on her forehead.

"I don't have all day, sweetheart."

"Don't you remember me?" Her voice was a whisper.

Tyler squinted his eyes, considering. "Maybe."

"The wedding dance in Liberty at the American Legion. I sang, and you gave me your business card. You said you were a talent agent." She fished the business card out of her purse and pushed it across the bar. "Here."

The lazy grin never left Tyler's face as he studied the card. Then he spread his arms wide. "Welcome to Tyler Colby Talent Agency, sweetheart!"

This was the thing. Even though Tyler wasn't exactly a talent agent—he liked to dabble in many things, he said—Trudy, for some reason, decided to trust him. She could have hightailed it back to Liberty on the evening train after she realized that she had fallen for the oldest trick in the book before the ink on her diploma had even dried. She could have chalked up her mistake to her small-town naiveté or her young age or her foolish dreams, but she didn't. She stayed. After Tyler bought her a Coke and a hamburger and apologized for the confusion, he said, "You know, maybe I could be your agent. You have a great voice and a pretty face. What do you say we give it a go?"

Trudy could remember kissing those full lips; she could remember their heat. She'd had to look away. When she really thought about it, Tyler hadn't promised her anything, had he? And what Connie, the bride, had said—*Is that what they call it these days?*—could be taken in any number of ways. Tyler wasn't actually the bad guy in this situation. She had read too much into their one night together. Trudy had straightened up on her stool and squared her shoulders. But she was here now, and she liked the way he looked at her. He had said she was pretty. She reached across the bar and shook his hand. "I'd say we have a deal."

Trudy could never remember how it came to be that she moved in with Tyler that day. Whether he asked her, or she asked him, or it was mutually understood didn't matter. Tyler had a small, cramped studio apartment in an old building on Hubbard Street. His bed was a fold-out couch, so it was a given that she slept with him, too, and those first few weeks in the city were a heady blur of constant sex and thrilling discoveries. Trudy could not believe how much there was to see and do in such a big place. Every street held the promise of a new adventure, and every night, a free concert played in the park, or someone that Tyler knew had a party. Chicago, in the summer, was a wonderful place to live.

To his credit, Tyler tried to live up to his end of the bargain for the first week or two. He made some phone calls to friends who knew people in the entertainment industry. "It's all about connections," he said confidently to Trudy, or he would say: "This town is all about networking."

Since she didn't know anyone at all, this sounded like a good plan to Trudy. "It's really going to happen, isn't it, Tyler?" She kissed him then and held him tightly. It was so nice to hug a man that she could put her arms around, unlike Wayne, who was a big bear of a guy. She rarely thought about Wayne, or if she did, he always came up lacking in comparison with Tyler. Trudy could not believe that such a smart, worldly, older man—Tyler was thirty!—would want to be with her. She felt giddy and slightly drunk all the time.

She was slightly drunk all the time during that summer. Just as he had in Liberty at the wedding reception, Tyler liked it when the drinks kept coming. And when they were free. Tyler was a self-professed master at finding out about all the free events in town, the gallery and restaurant openings, the fundraisers where there was a nominal cover charge, and all the booze was included. Tyler needed free drinks because he never had any money. Tyler never had any money because he spent lavishly on his other favorite hobby: drugs.

Tyler was not partial to any drug in particular. Instead, Tyler's favorite drug was the one available at any given moment. Trudy, the first time she walked into the apartment and saw Tyler snorting cocaine off the coffee table, knew she should pack up her bag and go back to Liberty. Everything suddenly made sense: why they never had any money and why Tyler could be so manic before he would fall into a moody depression that might last for days. But she didn't pack up her bags. Likewise, the first time she came back to the apartment after working her shift at the McDonald's on Wabash and found Tyler in bed with a waitress from Red's, she should have packed her bag and left.

But Trudy didn't leave because she didn't have any place to go. Returning to Liberty was not an option. She'd been writing glowing letters to her mother for weeks now, telling her about the nightclub she sang in. Then she landed an impressive gig singing in the lounge at the Drake Hotel. Her mother also learned about the tantalizing prospect of a record deal with a big music producer in town, who had come to hear her sing and taken her out for a ritzy dinner at a very expensive restaurant called Alinea. She told her mother that the offers were pouring in. She also told her mother that she lived in a roomy two-bedroom apartment with a graduate student named Sari from India. According to her letters, Trudy lived such a glamorous, successful life in Chicago that her mother could be very proud of her. Her mother had nothing to worry about, not a thing. Trudy had been right to follow her dream, and she was living it.

And Trudy didn't leave because of Tyler. She loved the man, and it seemed to Trudy that Tyler had, whether she liked it or not, become her drug of choice as summer gave way to a brisk fall. She couldn't seem to get enough of him and thought of him incessantly. When Trudy got off work from McDonald's—the only place that would hire her because of her age and lack of experience—and smelled of grease and french fries, she would find herself automatically heading for Red's. She would walk quickly by the front window, furtively glancing to see if Tyler tended the bar, to see if he flirted with another woman, to see if he snuck drinks on the side, which he had started to do. Trudy would walk by once, then wait a few minutes before walking by again. Sometimes she spent over an hour making those trips back and forth in front of Red's. Sometimes Trudy waited long enough that she followed him home. From a safe distance, dodging from doorway to doorway, she would watch as Tyler stopped by one of his drug-dealing friends or ran into CVS for Trojans or Gatorade.

Then one day, Trudy walked quickly by Red's, and Tyler wasn't behind the bar. It was a Thursday afternoon, and Tyler always worked that shift. Trudy wasn't especially alarmed at first. Tyler might have gone into the back storeroom for a bottle of Maker's Mark or a keg of beer. He might have gone to the restroom because he hadn't been feeling well when he got up that morning. Somehow, Tyler had fallen out of bed and spent the night on the apartment's cold, wood floor. His eyes had been red-rimmed, and he had a nasty cough that called for a bottle of cough syrup. Then he'd vomited into the kitchen sink. He shouldn't have gone to work, but they needed the money. They always needed money.

Trudy hurried home, only stopping to get some Campbell's chicken noodle soup and Vicks Vapor Rub at the Walgreens on their corner. The relief she felt when she opened the door to their apartment brought tears to her eyes. Tyler had come home! But he looked terrible, sitting on the couch, wrapped in a blanket, shivering, and his cough sounded even worse. "You poor baby. You had to come home because you're sick. I knew you shouldn't have gone to work today. Your cold is worse now."

Tyler shook his head in misery. "It's not a cold, Trudy."

"Yes, it is. I'll rub the Vicks on your chest, and you'll feel better in no time. And I bought some chicken soup, too."

"It's not a damn cold, Trudy." He flinched away from her when she sat down next to him and uncapped the Vicks with its strong smell of eucalyptus and menthol. "I think that fucker D'Marco sold me some worthless shit."

"For heaven's sake, Tyler. I know a bad cold when I see one. Don't be such a baby, and let me put some of this on your chest."

"I'm the baby here?" Tyler glared at her with his red-rimmed eyes. "I know you come from a small town, Trudy, but sometimes you act like you've crawled out from under a rock."

Trudy stood up. He had never talked to her like that before, but he was sick. She would make excuses for him. "What a terrible thing to say, Tyler, but I'm going to make you some soup anyway." She tried to wedge a pillow behind his back.

"For the love of God, Trudy, stop *hovering*. Sometimes I feel like I can't breathe around you."

Tears stung the back of Trudy's eyes, but she blinked them back. "You might be sick, but there's no need to be mean."

"Shit!" Tyler groaned, throwing back his head. It hit the wall above their couch with a sharp crack. "Shit!"

She stood in front of him, waiting for his apology.

She didn't get one. "I got fired today, Trudy. We don't have any money, and everything is going to hell. Is your Vicks Vapor Rub going to make that any better?"

"You know how prickly Gavin is. He probably had a fight with his wife. If you ask him, I bet he'll give you your job back."

"Gavin fired me because I've been drinking on the job, Trudy. I didn't dispute it because it's true. I'm sick of that place anyway." All the fight seemed to have seeped out of Tyler. He closed his eyes.

Trudy swayed unsteadily on her feet. This was bad. Without Tyler's income, they couldn't make it. They wouldn't be able to afford to eat, let alone pay for the apartment. She made minimum wage at her part-time job and handed her paltry paycheck over to Tyler. She had even given him her savings when they moved in. She'd been a fool to let him handle the money. "What are we going to do?"

Tyler shrugged, and minutes ticked by before he said, "I guess you could always sing for your supper. You're the talented one, right, Trudy?" His laugh was not kind and ended up in a jagged coughing fit.

She resisted going to him and clenched her fists at her side. "I'll do what I have to do, Tyler. I'm stronger than you think."

Trudy started to sing on the streets of Chicago the very next day. It was October, and the weather was brisk but not too bad, so there were plenty of broke people out there, counting on the kindness of strangers. It did not take long for Trudy to learn that the competition was stiff on those city streets. Drummers drummed on overturned buckets; guitarists and saxophonists and flutists and even a xylophonist vied for change. Mimes, acrobats, struggling young painters, and evangelists also entered the competition, and Trudy discovered that the panhandlers were incredibly territorial about their spots. More than one of them shook his battered plastic cup of loose change at her and told her to get the hell away from his turf.

On that very first day, as Trudy learned the ropes of her new craft, she decided she needed a gimmick. Most of the panhandlers held cardboard signs designed to tug at the heartstrings of strangers: "homeless vet," "struggling artist," "my ticket home was stolen," and "my child needs medicine." Some signs targeted the passersby's funny bone: "will work for food but don't want to," and "I'm not going to lie. I'll buy a drink with the money." Trudy didn't want to think of herself as a beggar—even as all signs pointed in that direction—but she needed to make money. And she needed something to make her stand out from the rest of the crowd. After walking around for a couple of hours, Trudy went into Walgreens and bought a crisp, white poster board. On it, she neatly printed: "Name your tune. I will sing any song to brighten your day." Trudy felt pretty good about her sign. It demonstrated that she wanted to help people. She wasn't begging, not really.

During that fall, Trudy sang all over the Loop. She sang on the steps of the Art Institute, and she sang in front of Sears Tower. The various corners up and down State Street seemed more lucrative for her, but she had to get there early. The competition was keen on that street, even though the people passing by could be very rude. On way too many occasions, people told her she needed to get a real job, a few screamed at her that her voice sucked, and one young man not much older than her actually spat on her. But Trudy persisted. Tyler counted on her to bring home money every night. He still hadn't gotten another job and had to ask his parents for money. They sent a check from Florida but told their son that it was the end of the gravy train. Trudy suspected it wasn't the first time Tyler, too, had begged.

It was a cold winter, even by Chicago standards, but Trudy went outside and sang on various street corners throughout the city every day. But as the weather turned bitter and harsh, the pedestrians dwindled. Most tourists had disappeared, and the Chicagoans hurrying to their various office buildings kept their heads down and hands in their pockets. It was on a day at the end of January—a day so bitterly cold that Trudy was afraid she'd gotten frostbite on her fingers and toes—that Trudy finally felt like giving up. She only made three or four dollars a day during this freezing weather, and she'd had a bad cold for three weeks now. Her singing sounded nasal and weak. Why was she putting herself through this? She'd given Tyler every penny she'd earned, and she had nothing to show for it.

Well, they had the apartment, Tyler said. They still had a roof over their heads, and that had to count for something. As the snow started to fall, Trudy picked up her sign and trudged home to Hubbard Street. Her throat now began to hurt. She climbed the four flights of stairs to their apartment—the elevator in their building had never worked—and inserted her key into the lock. Nothing happened. *I have the wrong key*, she thought to herself, even as she knew she didn't. She tried the lock again. *The cold has frozen the lock*, she thought next, even though she knew it hadn't. Then she started to pound on the door. "Tyler! Let me in!"

Trudy was so surprised when Tyler opened the door that her knees buckled. He caught her before she fell and pulled her inside. "Shh," he said. "Don't let Gower hear you."

"Why?" Trudy pulled herself away from Tyler's arms and saw the empty apartment. "What's happening here?" She could only whisper because her throat burned.

"The piece of shit took all our stuff and changed the locks. Gower says I owe him back rent, the piece of shit. But I showed him. I refused to leave! He said he would call the cops, but that was over an hour ago. I think we're safe now."

Trudy looked at him, really looked at him for the first time in months. His face was gaunt, the hollows beneath his eyes a dark purple. His hair was no longer blond and barely covered his skull. When had Tyler started to lose his hair? But the important thing was this: He had waited for her. He could have left, but he had stayed. That had to count for something, didn't it? "What are we going to do?" Trudy looked around. Their landlord had taken everything, even the pearl-encrusted comb she inherited from her grandmother. It was the only thing of value she might have been able to sell.

"We're staying right here." Tyler plopped down on the dirty floor. "It's unconstitutional to throw people out of their homes. We're going to squat right here. Then I'm going to sue the bastard. I'm going to sue him for a million bucks, Trudy! That'll show him!"

Tyler continued to rant, but Trudy no longer heard him. She didn't know if he was drunk or on heroin or if he had just gone mad. She had a hard time focusing and felt hot and cold at the same time. She was probably burning up with a fever. She wanted to crawl into bed and cover her head with a blanket, but of course, that was impossible. Their landlord had taken everything.

"I have my dignity!" Tyler shouted.

Trudy sank to the floor beside him and put her heavy head on Tyler's shoulder. She was so tired that she could barely keep her eyes open.

She must have fallen asleep because the next thing she knew, two burly cops escorted Tyler and her from their apartment. Tyler had sobered up some by then and tried to reason with them. "It's too fucking cold for a human to be outside. Come on, man, have some pity."

The cops escorted them to the curb outside their building and left with a warning not to enter the premises again, or they would be arrested.

"Those fuckers!" Tyler muttered under his breath when they drove off. He pulled Trudy close to him. "We need to find someplace warm."

Trudy nodded into his shoulder. Tyler would take care of everything, and she let him lead her to Popeyes Louisiana Kitchen, then the Hampton Inn hotel lobby, then the food court in the mall on Michigan Avenue. They couldn't stay anywhere too long, Tyler said, or they would arouse suspicion. They ended up at the Chicago Public Library, where they sat until closing time.

"I have an idea. I know some people." Tyler half-led, half-dragged Trudy through the streets and then down, down to Lower Lower Wacker Drive. Small clusters of tents and cardboard boxes and piles of old clothes housed the homeless population down there. Tyler asked for a guy named Clyde, but no one seemed to have seen him. At one point, he propped Trudy against a concrete wall and told her to wait. She fell asleep again and only awakened when Tyler started to shake her.

"Trudy, this is Clyde. He's going to give us some money if you sing for him."

"She better sound like Diana Ross. She's my favorite," Clyde said.

"Come on, honey, sing for the man," Tyler urged.

Trudy obediently opened her mouth, but nothing came out.

"She's a little under the weather, man. Be patient. Come on, baby, sing something for Clyde."

Trudy shook her head. She was sick, yes, but that wasn't the reason she couldn't sing. She couldn't sing because the songs were gone. There was nothing left.

"Damn you, Colby." Clyde stalked off.

Tyler sat down heavily beside Trudy and put his arm around her, pulling her close. "It's not your fault, baby." He kissed her burning forehead.

When Trudy woke up the next morning, shaking with cold and fever, Tyler was gone, and Trudy, even in her delirium, knew with certainty that he wasn't ever coming back.

Trudy untaped the cardboard from her front window and peered through the hole. It had not been repaired yet because Henry Wydeck, who owned the only remodeling business in town, said he had to order a new window that large "special from St. Louis." It had been a week since Cliff Neeley threw the brick, and the heat hadn't abated at all. Trudy's clients started to complain about how hot it was in the shop, but Trudy didn't take it personally. Everyone was crabby lately with the heat, including Wayne and Travis, who were always at each other's throats. Two days before, while Travis banged on his drums and had his music blasting, Wayne had barged into his room and thrown his drum set out the window. Then, for no reason at all, Wayne had thrown out most of Travis' clothes. All of it was still on their front lawn, and neither Wayne nor Travis had budged.

But Trudy wasn't thinking about that now. Finally, after a week of longing to be with Alan again, he was coming to the shop tonight. Of course, she had seen him from time to time during the week. Trudy now knew that Alan had his morning coffee and a blueberry muffin at Lolly's Diner, and she knew that he rented an apartment on Maple Street and watched TV for a couple of hours when he got home from work at ten o'clock. Plus, Alan kept his word and drove by the shop nightly at 7:30. If he saw her peering at him through the hole in the window, he didn't acknowledge it, but Trudy reasoned that he probably had to keep to a schedule. It wasn't like Trudy was stalking him or anything like that. She just happened to be driving by places where she knew he would be. There was no harm in that.

Trudy heard the back door of the shop open and whipped around. It must be Alan, and he must have parked in the lot in the back, rather than on the street. Fewer people would know he was here that way; he was a smart man. She had a smile on her face, ready for him. He said he needed to talk to her, and she hoped she knew what he would say. He had felt the attraction, too, during their first meeting.

But it wasn't Alan. It was Roxy. "Unbelievable." She dropped her big bag on the floor by her station and plopped herself in the chair. She had dyed her hair pink this week and wore a matching pink halter top and tight cut-off jeans.

"What are you doing here, Roxy?" There was no earthly reason for the girl to be here at this hour, and Trudy needed to get her out of here before Alan showed up.

Roxy, looking at herself in the mirror, played with her hair. "This whole town is going crazy over this Queen of Hearts drawing, and no one won again tonight. Can you believe that? The jackpot is over a million dollars. I had a gut feeling they were going to draw my ticket tonight, but no such luck. Someone from Marion got his ticket drawn, and he picked the six of spades, so I guess that's some good news."

"Roxy, *what* are you doing here?"

"Oh, I'm going to dye my hair back to blonde. This color is not working for me." She swiveled around in her chair. "What are you doing here this late?"

"Inventory." Trudy wasn't about to tell her that she had gotten a phone call from Alan, saying he wanted to talk to her.

"Good. I need a new curling iron. Mine's sticky from hairspray, and it's starting to smell funny when I heat it up. What is it with old ladies and hairspray anyway? It's like helmet hair is a kind of code or something." Roxy started to get out squares of foil from her drawer.

"Roxy, can't this wait until morning?"

"Oh, and guess who else I saw tonight?" Roxy was good at pretending not to hear people.

"I don't care who you saw."

"But this is kind of important. I should have told you first thing, but I had a few beers, and then I started to think about my hair—"

They both heard the crunch of tires on gravel coming from the back parking lot.

"Who could that be at this time of night? Are you expecting someone, Trudy? Man, is this the place to be tonight, or what?"

But it wasn't Alan who walked into the salon from the back storage room. It was Wayne, and the look on his face made Trudy take a sharp intake of breath. And then she saw he had a towel clumsily wrapped around his hand, and it was seeping blood. Her eyes went back to his face. "What happened?" She stood rooted to the spot, even as every instinct told her to run home as fast as she could.

"It was my fault," Wayne said. "I told Travis that he needed to pick up his goddamn drum set and clothes from the front yard because it looked like rain. And he told me, and I quote, 'go fuck yourself.' I lost it, Trudy. I picked him up and slammed him against the kitchen wall. Then I punched him."

"I… I don't understand." In all the years of arguments and disagreements, Wayne had never physically hurt either her or Travis.

"Then he pulled a knife out of the kitchen drawer," Wayne continued, as if in a trance, "and when I reached for it, I sliced open my hand. We both said a lot of things that we shouldn't have. I told him that he was going to join the Army because it was the only thing that would make a man out of him. He told me that he would kill himself if he ever became a man like me. I didn't know my son hated me so much."

"He doesn't hate you," Trudy said automatically, but she didn't know if it was true. Her son and her husband were as different as two men could be. Trudy heard a clap of thunder that sounded very far away.

"It was my fault," Wayne repeated.

Roxy had fished a flask out of her purse and handed it to Wayne. "It looks like you need this more than I do."

"I'm going to go home and talk to him now. I will make this work." Isn't that what she'd said all those years ago to Wayne when he drove up to Chicago to get her? She hadn't known who else to call when she woke up that morning, feverish and ill and heartbroken. Tyler was gone, and so were all her childish dreams. So she called Wayne, and he drove nearly six hours to get her and took her home. He hadn't said a word on the entire drive home, as Trudy told him over and over again that she was sorry, that she would gladly become his wife, that she would figure out some way to make a living. *I will make this work,* she had said. *I will make this work if you marry me.* Two months later, after she had recovered from bronchial pneumonia, they married.

Wayne took a long gulp from the flask. "He's gone, Trudy."

"He'll listen to me," she said, reaching for her purse.

"He's not coming back," Wayne said. "We went too far. We said things that we can't take back."

"You should go to the emergency room." Roxy pointed at Wayne's hand. "It looks like you need stitches."

"Come with me, Trudy." Wayne had never begged for anything, but this was close.

Trudy was having a hard time making sense of things. She didn't believe Wayne when he said Travis would never come back. She couldn't let herself believe that. People who you loved were supposed to come back.

But then she remembered. Sometimes they didn't.

She looked at Wayne's sad, familiar face. She didn't want to go with him, not just yet, even though she knew that she would, once again. "I'm supposed to meet someone here, Wayne." She thought of Alan's young, handsome face. Travis' middle name was Alan.

"Right." Roxy snapped her fingers. "That's what I was trying to tell you. Officer Morrison said he wasn't going to make it over tonight—there was a lot of drunken fighting going on at the Legion—and to tell you that Cliff Neeley confessed to the crime, and he's going to be in Anna for a few months to sort out his meds. If you don't press charges, he won't go to jail. His sister is going to pay for the window. So, the investigation is closed."

"I won't press charges." The thunderclap sounded closer now, and soon, it would start to rain. The fevered heat spell would finally be broken.

So Trudy walked to Wayne and took his arm. It was the right thing to do. "Come on, Wayne, we need to get this taken care of." Her shop's front window would be replaced with new, clear glass; Wayne's hand would be stitched and mended.

But their hearts were another story.

THE CHURCH LADIES

"It's just scandalous," Marie said.

"Sinful." Nadine nodded.

"Disgraceful." Sophie had to add her two cents.

Yet the three women, all widows in their late 70s, continued to sit on Marie's porch across from the American Legion Post 998 and watch the bustling proceedings. The Queen of Hearts drawing started at 8:00 that night, and the jackpot now approached 1.1 million dollars. To Marie's way of thinking, there was no other way to put it: The whole town had gone crazy, crazy with greed, their heads filled with the prospect of more money than most people would make in their entire lives. Some of the businesses in town—the Subway shop and Lolly's Diner and the Tastee Freeze—had people lined up outside their doors until shortly before 8:00 when everyone made a beeline to the Legion, their faces flushed with booze and excitement, only to be disappointed once again. Even Liberty High's boys track team had decided to prosper off the craziness and had started parking cars at the drawing for five dollars a car. Those gangly boys were setting up their table now. Marie craned her neck and could see that every picnic table at the park next door to the Legion was also full of people eating picnic suppers before the madness started in earnest. After the drawing, the Legion's parking lot and the park would be chaotic, filled with loudly disappointed, quarreling people. It was utter nonsense.

Sophie took a sip of her sweet tea. "I don't understand how this drawing can be legal. I know that the Legion supposedly uses part of the money for town projects, but still."

"Illinois passed that video gaming law, but I don't think that has anything to do with this kind of drawing. It's sinful. That's what it is." Nadine looked at Marie. "Don't you agree, Marie?"

Marie fanned herself with a folded newspaper. They were old ladies, sitting out here in the wretched, humid heat when they could be inside her air-conditioned house reading the Bible or watching reruns of *Blue Bloods*. Watching the handsome Tom Selleck could brighten Marie's spirits almost more than anything, yet still, they sat, mesmerized and appalled at the unleashed greed of ordinary folk. "Isn't that your nephew, Jaxon, in that truck, Nadine?" Marie pointed at the battered blue Ford with her newspaper.

Nadine's eyes followed the line of the paper to the truck and watched as the bearded man parked and got out. "Sure enough, it is, and it doesn't surprise me a bit. That boy never had a lick of sense, dropped out of high school at sixteen and hasn't done a blessed thing since."

"Maybe he'll win and give you some of the money, Nadine," Sophie said.

Marie suppressed a sigh. She often thought that Sophie showed signs of dementia. Her watery blue eyes looked dazed at times, and Sophie sometimes did not grasp the thread of conversation. But then again, Marie had not known Sophie in her youth, so it was likely she'd always been a bit of an airhead. "Why would he do that, Sophie? If Nadine's nephew hasn't even paid her a visit in ten years, what makes you think he'll give her money if he suddenly, and surprisingly, becomes rich? Do you actually think that's a likely scenario?"

"Sometimes, people do surprising things." Sophie leaned forward in her chair. "Good lord, is that Mayor Aldean?"

"He comes every week, Sophie." Nadine looked at Marie and rolled her eyes.

"Does he? I don't remember seeing him last week." Sophie repositioned her sizable girth on the Adirondack chair. "Well, he does have all those kids to feed, and being mayor of this town doesn't pay much."

"I don't think he gets paid anything, which is why he also owns the lawnmower repair shop," Nadine said.

"Then he deserves to win, with all those kids to feed."

"We aren't rooting for anyone, Sophie. As good Christian women, we think the Queen of Hearts is just another form of gambling, so it's sinful. Isn't that right, Marie?"

"Uh-huh," Marie murmured. She did think that something was wrong about this drawing with its escalating jackpot and all the hoopla it was generating. However, the growing anticipation had been giving people in this town hope for weeks now. And that was sorely needed. She'd lived in Liberty for thirty years and had seen firsthand how the jobs had dried up after the strip mines started to close. She'd seen firsthand how many more people came to the food pantry in the Presbyterian Church's basement. Unfortunately, she'd also witnessed how many promising young people in her Sunday School class later turned to alcohol and drugs. While the drugs had changed over the years, from cocaine and Quaaludes to opioids and meth, the despair had not.

"Who wants more sweet tea?" Marie rose from her chair. Her thighs felt sticky under her linen dress. Even though it was too hot for linen, unlike her companions, Marie wouldn't be caught dead in an old lady-looking cotton shift (Sophie) or polyester stretch pants and a faded flowered shirt (Nadine). Marie rarely dwelled on the vanity inherent in her desire to always look her best, even though she supposed it didn't matter much now. When she looked in the mirror on some mornings, she felt startled at the white-haired, wrinkled face that stared back. On other mornings, she was frightened. Time was the ultimate thief. It took precious moments, days, and years from you when you weren't even looking.

Marie took her time refilling their glasses in the blessed coolness of her house. She had been a widow for a decade and had grown accustomed to solitude. It suited her. Her husband Leland had owned the home when Marie landed in this town thirty years ago, and the house, like him, had been tidy, compact, manageable. It hadn't taken long for Marie to decorate the two-bedroom bungalow to her own taste, replacing the orange shag carpet with a neutral beige, the somber wallpaper with pastel paint, the dark furniture with a light oak couch and love chairs. Just as it hadn't taken long for Marie to convince Leland that he loved her, that he needed her.

It was because of Leland that Marie became involved in the Presbyterian Church. Leland was active in the church, an elder, and the first person to arrive every Sunday morning, ready to hand out the church bulletins. Leland had once considered going into the ministry himself, but a lack of funds made the decision for him. Instead, he went to the community college and got his associate's degree in accounting, and with a partner, he opened his own business in downtown Liberty. While Leland's chosen career didn't set the world on fire, money-wise, they were comfortable enough—and happy enough. They went to church every Sunday, and Marie, who had never been much of a churchgoer before, found herself in a place that welcomed her with open arms. That, too, was a first.

The church was also the place she first met Sophie and Nadine, although they didn't really become friends until they all three were widowed within a single year: first Leland, then Sophie's husband, then Nadine's. They had all taught Sunday school and worked together on various projects throughout the years, such as numerous food and clothing drives. And once, when they wanted to raise money for the Head Start preschool program, a wrapping paper campaign turned out to be a disaster. The three of them sold scads of wrapping paper, but people reneged when it was time to collect the money. It was Christmas, they said. They didn't have extra cash for fancy gift wrap when any old paper from the drugstore would do just fine. Marie still had rolls of leftover wrapping paper in a box in her basement. It had likely disintegrated by now into a box of moldy crumbs. Marie never went down into her basement anymore. Too many relics reminded her of too many mistakes.

Those early years of forced togetherness with the churchwomen were pleasant enough, although Marie often felt left out when the discussions turned to children. God had not given her children; she had accepted that fact many, many years before. (Secretly, she had always thought it might be a blessing in disguise. Perhaps God knew, better than she, that she would not have been a good mother.) But when Sophie and Nadine's children were grown and gone, and when all three of them had buried their husbands in the cemetery on the south end of town, the three widows discovered they shared a fondness for gospel music. They took trips to listen to Legacy 5, the Gaither Family, the Collingsworth Family, and many others. In warm weather, they would travel as far as Nashville to hear a group—Marie was always the designated driver—and stay in motels for a night or two. They were Gospel Groupies, they laughed to each other, and Marie looked forward to those trips. They, like Tom Selleck in *Blue Bloods*, helped to brighten her spirits.

Marie took her time before going out onto the hot porch again. She arranged slices of strawberry shortcake and sliced strawberries on a serving platter. She gathered up her best china dessert plates and white lace napkins and set everything on a large tray. It was slow going, walking from the kitchen in the back of her house, through the small dining room and living room, to the porch. The tray was heavy, but rather than go back to the kitchen and take off the glasses of tea, it suddenly became very important to Marie that she make this presentation of refreshments in one trip. She hated that she had suddenly gotten old, hated that she feared tripping and falling, hated that she would bump an arm on a door frame and have a sordid purple-blue bruise marking her thin skin.

She was panting when she got to the front porch. "Would someone please open this door for me?"

"Oh, my." Sophie tried to get up, but her weight forced her back down.

Before she could try again, Nadine got to the door. "Let me help you with that, Marie. You shouldn't be lifting something so heavy," she scolded.

When the other two women navigated the tray onto the table in front of the three chairs, Sophie reached for a plate of cake. "Isn't this festive?"

"You have always made the best shortcake, Marie." Nadine reached for a plate. "Isn't that true, Sophie?"

Sophie's mouth was full, so she could only nod.

Marie murmured her thanks. Nadine had always been a bit of a suck-up. Usually, Marie didn't mind so much, but it wore on her nerves this evening. Maybe it was the heat. Maybe it was because of all the excitement going on across the street, while they, the three old ladies, sat on the outskirts, watching. Marie could not remember the last time she had felt excited about anything. She now anticipated the gospel concerts, but they were not what an average person would call exciting. It seemed very wrong, suddenly, the lack of excitement in her life. She was old, but she wasn't dead yet.

When she landed in this town thirty years ago, the last thing Marie wanted was excitement. After everything she'd been through, she only wanted a comfortable, quiet existence, an ordinary life with no drama. However, even then, Marie would not have chosen Liberty as her final perch. She had started driving aimlessly from Iowa with only the vaguest notion of getting to Florida. She had never seen the Atlantic Ocean, and she was tired of the cold Iowa winters. Miami had sounded nice. In a city that size, she could finally be anonymous.

But Gene's old Chevy truck, with its 200,000 plus miles, had another idea. When she reached the outskirts of town—a white wrought iron sign back then announced, WELCOME TO LIBERTY—that old truck had sputtered, clunked, coughed weakly, and died. Marie managed to maneuver the relic of an automobile to the ditch on the side of the road, and it wasn't two minutes before a dark, nondescript sedan stopped, parking behind her, and a man got out.

"Looks like you need some help." He was a small man, 5'6" or 5'7", Marie's height, with a neatly trimmed dark mustache, just beginning to gray. His trousers, too, were gray, with a crisply ironed shirt tucked in.

"People in this town must be very friendly. I just broke down a second ago." Marie became acutely aware of her wrinkled sundress. She'd slept in it the night before in a motel somewhere along the interstate. She couldn't remember the name of the town because she hadn't cared. She'd put her wiry black hair into a lazy bun at the nape of her neck. She'd been dying it since the incident; it had turned completely white overnight.

The man considered this, then nodded. "Yes, Liberty is a very friendly town."

"Does this friendly town have a tow truck? I was just passing through when—" Marie pointed at the Chevy, shrugged.

"Where are my manners?" The man stuck out his hand. "I'm Leland Sherman."

Marie hesitated before saying, "Marie." He didn't seem to recognize her, and this town was miles away from where she came from.

"I can give you a ride to Arlo's gas station. He ought to be able to take care of this for you. Arlo can fix almost anything."

Marie didn't have any other choice but to take Leland up on his offer. She had brought one suitcase with her—filled mostly with clothes—and she had very little money. It wasn't that she was being noble to her husband at this late stage of the game. No, it was because they had very little money left after all the doctor bills. Marie was a planner, but she hadn't seen that one coming.

"I don't want to keep you from anything," Marie said as she got into the cool comfort of Leland's car.

"I do believe I'm done working for the day." Leland smiled shyly. "I could show you around town while Arlo's fixing your truck."

True to his word, Leland showed Marie the various Liberty sights, which didn't take long. However, with a population of 5,000, Liberty was slightly larger than the town Marie had just left. She thought it was a nice enough town and even rather pretty. Many yards had their late spring flowers blooming, and by the time she and Leland stopped for an early supper, Marie was beginning to think that Gene's old truck had conked out here for a reason.

"So that's the story of my life," Leland said over pie at Lolly's Diner. He told her that he had been born and raised in Liberty, owned his own business, and cared for his mother until the day she died. He had been widowed for a little over a year. "Not too exciting, is it?" He gave his shy smile.

"It sounds to me like you've led a very nice life, Leland." Marie sincerely meant it. Leland already seemed like a dependable, hardworking, thoughtful man. In other words, he might be just the thing she needed after the tumult of the past year.

"Now it's your turn." Leland signaled to the waitress for more coffee. He'd said earlier that coffee was his only vice.

"I'm recently widowed, too," Marie lied. The tears came readily to her eyes. She'd had a lot of practice over the past year.

"Oh, you poor dear." Leland placed his hand over hers. "It gets lonely, doesn't it?"

"Yes," Marie choked out. "I've been very lonely." That, at least, was true.

"I wish you were staying in Liberty longer, but I'm sure you have people expecting you wherever it is that you're going."

Marie had not told Leland about the idea of traveling to Miami. It seemed rather silly now. She was forty-five years old and had never been out of the Midwest. She shook her head, and the tears fell steadily now. "No, I don't have anybody waiting for me." She reached into her purse for a tissue. "I've got no one."

"There, there." Leland patted her hand. "It looks like we're in the same boat."

Marie nodded and wrapped her fingers around his small hand. "Sad but true."

Always, Marie would think that's when she and Leland sealed the deal. When Arlo told them half an hour later that the Chevy could not be repaired, Marie was not surprised. When Leland shyly offered the use of his guest room, Marie wasn't surprised. The next day, when Leland came home from work, Marie had cleaned the dark house from top to bottom and prepared a roast and found the Chantilly lace tablecloth for the dining room table.

Tears came to Leland's eyes when he saw the beautifully appointed table. "This is what I've been missing."

Marie stayed. With a quiet, unassuming man like Leland, maybe she would be a good wife. Maybe she would finally be good.

At 9:30, the floodgates opened across the street, and people spilled out into the parking lot and adjacent park, just as they had in prior weeks. The three women on Marie's porch had been anticipating this moment. During the last hour or so, the conversation had trickled down to the occasional observation on the weather—"My, it's still hot"—and comment on the church music: "That Angela Walker always drags the beat on the Doxology." Now, they leaned forward eagerly in their chairs.

"Such a commotion!" Nadine said.

"I've never heard such hootin' and hollerin'." Sophie made this same observation every single week.

Marie fanned herself with the newspaper. "They're disturbing the peace." Yet she made no move to go inside, nor did the other two women make any move to leave. Someone from across the street laughed loudly, hysterically.

"Do you think someone drew the queen of hearts this week?" Sophie asked after a moment or two. "Can you imagine having that much money?"

"The eye of the needle, Sophie," Nadine said ominously.

Sophie bristled. "How do you know I wouldn't give that kind of money to the church, Nadine? If I won," she added.

"Would you?" Nadine challenged.

"Would *you*?" Sophie countered.

Marie slapped the newspaper on the table. "I wouldn't," she said, making the other two old women gasp. "I suppose I would feel some responsibility to tithe, but other than that, I'd spend the bulk of it."

"On what?" Nadine sputtered.

"Oh, I don't know, Nadine." All of a sudden, these two women, her best friends for the last decade, thoroughly irritated her. They were so predictable, so rutted in their ways that she could set her watch by their thoughts and actions. "Maybe I'd take a trip down to Miami to see the Atlantic Ocean. How about that?"

"That doesn't sound like you, Marie." Nadine bit her lip, worried. "You're not having a stroke, are you?"

"For the love of God, Nadine!" Marie spoke so loudly that a few people across the street heard and turned her way. "I'm not having a damn stroke! All I'm doing is using my imagination, which is something that seems to be in short supply for you."

"Oh, my." Sophie picked up the newspaper and started to fan herself.

"I don't know what in the world has gotten into you, Marie Sherman," Nadine huffed.

Marie didn't know what had gotten into her either. Maybe the commotion and boisterous voices from across the street had gotten under her skin. Maybe it was the heat. Maybe she was just cranky, but this urge had come unbidden.

For the first time in a very long time, she wanted to be in the midst of the excitement, not a passive observer. She wanted to feel something, *anything* other than old and bored. She had tried to do the right thing, the expected thing, for so long. Perhaps what it all boiled down to was this: Her true nature was trying to escape after decades of hibernation.

Nadine had tightly crossed her arms and now glared at Marie. "If you don't apologize, I have half a mind to stomp off this porch and go home."

Marie stopped herself from saying, *Suit yourself,* only because the thought of spending all her time with just Sophie was unbearable. "Fine, Nadine. I apologize." She didn't sound apologetic at all, however.

"Apology accepted."

"Good. Now everything can go back to normal." Sophie smiled happily.

Marie groaned inwardly. Going back to normal was the opposite of what she wanted. But what was it, exactly, that she wanted? She had been sixty-five when Leland died, and she could have packed up and left Liberty then. They had some money saved, not a lot, but enough to perhaps settle in a cheaper retirement community somewhere warm. But she hadn't gone, mostly because she thought she had a home in her church, that the church was a place where she could find solace. But now, tonight, Marie could see that it hadn't been enough.

"Oh, look, there's a fight." Sophie pointed across the street.

"There's always a fight," Marie said tiredly.

"Isn't one of the men Jaxon?" Nadine squinted into the darkness, as if it would help her poor eyesight.

"Oh, probably. That boy never did have a lick of sense. My poor sister almost died giving birth to him, and he's brought her nothing but heartbreak."

Nadine nodded sagely. "Some children are just bad seeds."

Oh, shut up! Marie silently screamed. *At least she had a child!*

"Well, that was a short fight." Nadine sounded disappointed. "That handsome new cop is already breaking it up."

Sophie shifted in her chair. "I hear he's really on top of things. Maybe I should have him meet my granddaughter, Rachel."

"Isn't Rachel the girl who's had every sexually transmitted disease known to mankind?" Marie could hear Nadine snigger.

"The unfortunate girl has a very poor immune system!"

"Right, Sophie, whatever you say." Marie saw something out of the corner of her eye and turned her attention back to the Legion. Brian Gyver, who had been a bartender at the Legion for years, propped a ladder next to the Queen of Hearts sign. And now climbed up, up, up. "Brian's changing the number on the sign."

"If it goes up, no one won this week."

"Brilliant deduction, Sophie." Nadine squinted. "I can't make it out."

Marie could. "He's increasing the amount of the jackpot. No one won."

"This is getting out of hand," Nadine sniffed.

"It's sinful," Sophie said obediently.

"Somebody should do something."

"Why don't we?" Both women turned to look at Marie. "Why don't we do something about all this craziness?"

"What can three old ladies do to stop this snowball rolling into hell?" Nadine looked skeptical.

The idea came to Marie like a jolt of electricity in her veins. "We could picket the Legion next Thursday night. You know, make signs that say something about the wrath of God and so on and so forth."

Nadine stood up slowly, waiting for the circulation to come back into her legs. "Now, you're having a stroke."

"No, now I have a brilliant idea. Are we going to spend one more Thursday evening sitting on this porch as passive observers?"

"Yes." Sophie nodded vigorously.

"No! Next Thursday, we're going to voice our opinion and be *heard* in this town." Marie was on her feet now, too, her enthusiasm building. "Ladies, next Thursday, we are going to create a little excitement of our own."

Because he was a forbidden love, Gene Ketchum became all the more desirable to Marie Tallo. She knew who he was, of course, long before she met him. Le Claire, Iowa, was a small town, and some families could trace their roots all the way back to LeClaire's inception in 1855, families like Gene Ketchum's. Their farm was one of the oldest and most profitable in the county, and if townspeople didn't personally know the Ketchums, they had undoubtedly heard of them. The same could not be said for Marie's family, which consisted only of Marie and her mother, Althea. Marie's father had deserted them shortly after Marie's birth, and Althea only leaked the sparsest of details of him over the years. He had been Sicilian; he liked to work on cars; he was a lying, cheating son of a bitch. "But you inherited his lovely hair, Marie," she would add. "The SOB had lovely, thick, dark hair."

So while one reason Marie had never crossed paths with Gene Ketchum was that they were not in the same social class, according to Le Claire standards, the other reason was that Gene was twelve years her senior. Marie was twenty years old, Gene thirty-two, a vast difference to her young mind. And he was a married man, which put him in an entirely different league than her, too.

Marie occasionally dated young men her age, but the pickings were slim in 1964 Le Claire. Too many of the young men had been drafted and were off fighting in Vietnam, a country most of the townspeople had never heard of before this mysterious war. Besides, she was too busy working at the drugstore to think about men, and she had a long-term plan. She planned on owning the store very soon. Old man Teton rapidly approached eighty, and in the two years she'd worked at Teton Drugs, Marie had proved to be invaluable in the day-to-day running of the business.

Marie was working at the soda fountain in the back of the long, narrow store on the day her life changed forever. She often worked there during her shifts because Mr. Teton's arthritis had gotten so bad that he could no longer dip the ice cream for the cones, or make the sundaes and milkshakes and cherry cokes. It was a hot July day, and the place had been busier than usual. The overhead fan did little to cool the still air in the shop, so when the final customer left the counter, Marie slumped against it tiredly, fanning herself with one of the folded silk fans the store sold. She unbuttoned the top two buttons of her blouse, and with the back of her hand, pushed the damp tendril of hair off her forehead. She closed her eyes for just a moment. She'd been working since 6:00 a.m. that morning, and it was now nearly 4:00.

When the bell over the front door tinkled an arrival, Marie didn't immediately open her eyes. "I'll be right there." Poor old man Teton had gone home to take a nap. The heat had been too much for him. Marie could understand why. Even she, usually a tornado of energy, felt dazed with the heated stillness.

At first, she thought a butterfly had slipped through the hole in the screen door and fluttered across her cheek. The touch was so soft, barely there, yet heated. Slowly, Marie opened her eyes and came face to face with Gene Ketchum. "Oh!" she said.

Gene straightened up, smiling. "Excuse me. I didn't mean to wake you. You looked so peaceful, and you had this curl of hair that escaped your ponytail. I don't know what got into me. I'm sorry."

Gene didn't look sorry at all, and the way he looked at her made Marie's already flushed skin burn hotter. "Do you make it a habit of touching strangers on their cheeks?"

"No, I don't. I do believe this is a first for me."

"For me, too." Marie couldn't stop staring at him. She'd only seen him from a distance before, and while she had always known he was a good-looking man—everyone in town said so—the effect he had on her now, in person, made her feel faint. He looked something like a sunburned Warren Beatty in *Splendor in the Grass,* a movie she had seen at the movie theater a couple of years before. But Gene's hair was lighter, his shoulders a little broader. And his very presence seemed to be sucking what little air there was out of the room.

"Again, my apologies." He lowered himself to a stool and placed his large hands on the counter. He wore a faded blue chambray shirt, the sleeves rolled up to his elbows. The fine hairs on his muscular forearms were almost white from the sun. "While I'm here, I think I'll have a strawberry milkshake. Could you do that for me, make me a milkshake?"

"Um, sure." It was a relief to turn away from him. The man made her feel dizzy, and her heart galloped a mile a minute. She was being ridiculous. Gene

Ketchum was only a man—granted, a handsome one—but only a man. And he was married.

With her back still turned, Marie took deep, steadying breaths. "So, what brings you into town today?" Her voice sounded too high, stilted.

"I needed a part for the tractor. I was kind of glad it broke, to tell you the truth. It's hotter than Hades out there."

Marie squirted the whipped cream on top of the shake and added a cherry. Reluctantly, she turned back around. She still didn't have her breathing under control. "Here you go." She placed it carefully before him.

Gene stirred the shake with the straw. "*Farmers' Almanac* says the heat's going to last all week."

"Do farmers always spend so much time talking about the weather?" Marie hadn't meant that to sound flirtatious, but for some reason, it did.

Gene looked up from the shake and smiled slowly, nodded. "Yep, I guess we pretty much do."

Marie could see that his right front tooth was slightly chipped, which made him seem younger. She couldn't help it; she smiled back. "I guess there are more boring topics of conversation."

"Like what?"

"Like how fast grass grows."

"Oh, us farmers talk about that, too." Gene had a full-blown grin on his face now.

"A group of brilliant conversationalists, aren't you?"

"Yep." Gene took a long drink of the shake. "This is a mighty fine milkshake, Marie Tallo."

This surprised Marie, yet she was flattered. "How do you know my name?"

Gene shrugged. "I've seen you around town, and a guy doesn't forget hair like yours. You have lovely hair, Marie."

Marie's hand went instinctively to her ponytail, which felt damp and sticky. If it was down, it would hang just past her waist, thick and wavy. "I look like a mess. Are you flirting with me, Gene Ketchum?"

"I thought that's what we were doing here, Marie Tallo. There's no harm in flirting." Gene slurped up the last of his shake. "Best milkshake I ever had." He was still grinning as he pulled out two quarters and placed them on the counter. "I'll see you around."

"Tell your wife I said hi," Marie called after him, pointedly.

"Will do." Gene saluted as he pushed open the screen door.

As soon as he left, Marie missed him. It was as if he had taken all the life out of the room, and it was once again an overly hot, dimly lit, dusty drugstore. She shook all over and leaned against the counter for support. She was being ridiculous, she told herself. They had only exchanged a harmless flirtation, and she would never have another conversation with the man. It meant nothing that he knew her name. And he was married. She would never get involved with another woman's husband. She wasn't that kind of person.

Marie would be proven wrong on all counts. The next day, Gene returned for another milkshake, and he returned the day after that. He didn't make any promises that he would come back, nor did she ask. But each day, she found herself anxiously waiting for him, hoping for his return. She dreamed of him at night, dreamed of him holding her, kissing her, touching her. The heatwave lasted for another five days, finally breaking with a thunderstorm that rained four inches on Le Claire. The rain came, and the next day, Gene did not appear at the drugstore.

But he called her on the store phone as she was about to lock up for the night. "I missed you," he said.

She wanted to be angry with him, but relief coursed through her body. She knew it was wrong for her to desire him so much. He wasn't hers to love, yet Marie had started to think that for the very first time, she was falling in love. She had no other name for the raging emotions she felt. "We can't do this," she said.

"I know." A long silence followed before he added, "But I don't think I can stop."

Again, the relief was overwhelming. "What are we going to do?"

"I don't know. I've never done this type of thing before, didn't think I ever would. Then I walked into the drugstore and saw you."

Marie could hear the sorrow in his voice, and her voice mirrored that sorrow when she said, "Maybe we could just be friends."

"That's not possible." There was another long pause. "Can I come to the store now? Will you wait for me?"

Tears silently streamed down Marie's cheeks when she whispered, "Please hurry."

Gene's wife's name was Tabitha, and during the first few months of their affair, Marie and Gene never mentioned her. That was fine with Marie, who preferred to pretend the woman didn't exist. When she was alone with Gene, Marie was so passionate about him that she could barely think of anything else at all. The way Gene made love to her, it was impossible for her to imagine that he had ever loved—let alone married—another woman. And even the secrecy enthralled her, the whispered phone conversations and the discreet planning involved to be together. Their "love nest," as Marie laughingly referred to it, was generally the hayloft in Gene's barn. That setting might not seem romantic to most people, but it was to Marie. She was with the man she loved, and nothing else mattered.

However, inevitably, Marie wanted more. Their affair had been going on for over a year, and Gene hadn't asked his wife for a divorce. Marie couldn't understand it. Gene obviously loved her, not Tabitha. And he and Tabitha didn't have any children, so what was the problem? Finally, one October night in the cold barn, Marie gathered up her courage and asked him, "Why don't you divorce Tabitha and marry me? Nothing is stopping you. You and Tabitha don't have children."

They were nestled together on a mound of blankets in the hay, but Gene propped himself on one elbow to stare down at her. "It would break her heart if I divorced her, Marie, and it breaks her heart that we don't have children. She feels like it's all her fault. She knows how much I want a son."

Marie saw her opportunity and grabbed it. "I could give you a son." She reached up and took his face in her hands. "I will give you a son."

He kissed her to silence her, and she let him, that time.

But as more months passed and their affair approached its second anniversary, Gene still hadn't asked Tabitha for a divorce. Marie decided to take matters into her own hands. Gene was a good man, a kind man, but enough was enough. She was supposed to be Gene's wife and the mother of his children. Tabitha had failed in both departments, and it would be better for all concerned if she bowed out gracefully. But she needed a little nudge. Without Gene knowing, Marie would tell Tabitha precisely what was going on.

She called Tabitha late on a Tuesday evening, right before the store customarily closed, and told her that her doctor had phoned in a prescription. Marie knew Tabitha had a prescription for something because she came into the drugstore every two months or so. On those short, infrequent visits, Marie would busy herself elsewhere in the store. It wasn't that she was ashamed or hiding. It was because the sight of Tabitha set her teeth on edge. Tiny little Tabitha, with her blond hair, blue eyes, and heart-shaped face, looked more like a doll than a person. She was the antithesis of Marie, who was relatively tall and angular and looked like her unknown Sicilian father with her thick black hair and olive complexion. Tabitha was apple pie, and Marie was cannoli. The sight of Tabitha made Marie wonder why Gene had ever thought she was attractive.

Tabitha arrived at the drugstore in a flattering floral dress with tiny straps. "I'm here to pick up my prescription." Even her voice was small, breathless.

Marie had decided she would come right to the point, but seeing Tabitha made her suddenly nervous. "Uh, there isn't any prescription, Tabitha."

Tabitha arched her perfect little brows. "Then, why did you call me?"

Marie took a deep breath. "Someone is having an affair with your husband." At Tabitha's skeptical look, Marie rushed on. "I'm having an affair with your husband."

Tabitha remained skeptical. "Is this some kind of joke? Because if it is, it's not funny."

"It's not a joke, Tabitha. Gene and I have been having an affair for two years now."

"This is not funny," Tabitha repeated, her lower lip trembling.

"Gene is not working late all those nights in the barn, Tabitha. He's with me."

Tabitha's eyes grew glassy with tears. "I don't believe you."

Marie had anticipated that. "Gene has a birthmark the size of a quarter on his inner left thigh."

Tabitha swayed on her feet. "There is no way Gene would have an affair with a girl like you. You're not his type!"

That remark stung, mostly because Marie sometimes feared it was true. But she pushed on. "You need to give Gene a divorce."

"Why would Gene want to divorce me? Even if this is true, which it is not, there is no reason he would ever divorce me."

"You can't have children."

Tabitha's face crumpled, and she covered it with her hands. "He said… he said that it didn't matter."

"It does matter. Gene wants a son."

Tabitha was moaning now, sobbing. "No, no, no!"

Marie did feel pity for the crying woman, but she was determined. The only way to get Tabitha to divorce Gene was to go to extremes. "Tabitha, I'm pregnant with Gene's child." She said it loudly, firmly.

"No!" Tabitha wailed and ran toward Marie.

Marie, taller and stronger, could easily ward off her flailing arms. "I am going to give Gene a son."

"You are an evil woman!" Tabitha screamed one more time and ran blindly from the store.

Marie watched her go, shaken. She should call Gene to tell him what she had done. She had driven his wife to hysteria and been unbelievably cruel. And she had lied; she'd gotten her period that morning. But still, she needed him to know that the only reason she had gone to such extremes was because she loved him so much. And the thought of living without him was unbearable. She should call Gene, yet she didn't move.

Gene called her later that night. His voice sounded worried when he told Marie that Tabitha had gone into town and hadn't returned. She hadn't, by any chance, seen Tabitha, had she? he asked. Marie told him no, she hadn't seen Tabitha, and no, she hadn't come into the drugstore. And Marie remained mum while the entire town searched for the missing woman. When they found Tabitha's body in her car in the pond behind the Dickersons' house two days later, even Marie was shocked at the extremes the woman had gone to.

"There weren't any skid marks," Mr. Dickerson told anyone who would listen. "She plowed straight into the pond."

Marie, like everyone else, agreed that it was the saddest story she had ever heard.

Twenty-odd years later, the local press, in its foolishness, dubbed her Milkshake Marie. But the press didn't know the whole story, never even bothered to ask. If they had, Marie could have set the record straight. She would have told them that theirs was a simple love story that grew more complicated through years of hardship and disappointment. She and Gene had good years mixed with the bad, just like everyone else. Despite what everyone said, and despite the burning anger, she continued to love the man. As it turned out, he loved her, too.

She and Gene waited a respectable amount of time—another two years—before they married. Marie quit her job at the drugstore (old man Teton still hadn't kicked the bucket yet) and settled happily into the role of farmer's wife. It was a good thing that Marie was no stranger to hard work because the work was hard, constant. She took care of the chickens, gathering eggs twice a day. She helped milk the four Jersey cows the farm still had. She planted a garden every spring, and every fall, she canned vegetables from the garden and fruit from the peach orchard in the back pasture. And she cooked. Good Lord, did she cook. Gene's parents had died tragically in a car accident some five years before, and his one sister lived in California, so Gene had to hire four men to help him with the plowing, planting, and harvesting. When the men arrived at dawn, Marie had bacon and eggs, potatoes and toast waiting for them. When they came in for the noon meal, Marie would serve a hearty lunch of meat and potatoes. (She once estimated that she had fried 3,000 chickens in her lifetime.)

In short, Marie did everything that Tabitha, before her, had not. In no time at all, she'd made herself invaluable to her husband. And she planned to keep it that way because the babies she had promised him did not come. It was not for lack of trying. She and Gene remained just as passionate for each other as they'd been in the beginning, but each month brought another disappointment. After they had been married for a while, the answer became obvious to Marie. It wasn't her—nor had it been Tabitha—who was at fault. It was Gene.

"I'm not going to go to a goddamn baby doctor!" Gene, who was usually patience personified, was belligerent on the subject. "There is nothing wrong with us! All we have to do is keep trying."

"They have doctors in Des Moines who—" But Gene wouldn't even let Marie finish the sentence before he stomped out the back door.

What surprised Marie most of all was how much she now wanted to have a baby. When she'd been a single working girl, she'd vaguely thought she might have babies one day, but she hadn't thought of it as crucial. Now, though, she did. When her period arrived each month like sadistic clockwork, Marie was devastated. Another month and another lost opportunity, and she wasn't getting any younger. Then she would give Gene the news at the supper table—the only meal they ate alone together—and wait for his resigned acceptance. As the months and then years passed, Marie wanted more and more to reach across the table and slap his sunburned, handsome face. If he would only go to a doctor, they could have a baby. She still loved him deeply, but it was all the stubborn man's fault that Marie would never become a mother. Her anger was a constant, niggling presence.

As she grew older, less fertile, and more resentful, Marie consoled herself by working even harder. She loved their farm—she now considered it hers as well as Gene's—and working on it and for it gave her purpose. Then came the 1980s Farm Crisis. The tight money policies by the Federal Reserve intended to bring down high-interest rates caused their farmland value to drop by 60%, and the record agricultural production of the 1970s resulted in a glut of farm commodities, forcing prices down. Gene had borrowed extensively from the bank for a new combine and grain silos, thinking the boon would go on forever. He was wrong. Although they tried everything they could think of to save their farm, they ultimately could not.

Losing their farm humiliated Marie and devastated Gene. They had no other choice but to move in with Althea, who had a small apartment in town over the hardware store. After having had the luxury of so much open space on the farm, Marie found Althea's apartment to be a claustrophobic emblem of the Ketchum disgrace. They were not the only ones in this predicament in Le Claire, but Marie and Gene had been considered by many to be the hardest working and most successful farming couple. All that was gone.

And at the age of forty, Marie found herself back where she started. Old man Teton's thirty-year-old grandson, Todd, now ran Teton's Drugs. He'd made improvements to the store, such as expanding the drug department and stocking the shelves with more useful items rather than sundries. But the soda fountain remained in the back, and Marie found herself, more often than not, mixing milkshakes and making sundaes. But she had no other choice. Althea, a seamstress, could not afford to feed all three of them, and Gene, once he left the farm, was not the same man. He spent a great deal of time staring mindlessly at the TV, too depressed and too proud to go out and look for another job. "I'm a farmer," he told Marie, as if that explained everything.

However, Gene did have one routine. He came in every afternoon around 4:00 for a strawberry milkshake. The man still loved his milkshakes, and it didn't seem to bother him in the least that his wife stood behind the counter serving him. Now Marie had served him meals for years, but this was completely different. Every sip he took out of every single milkshake was money out of her pocket. Gene never even offered to pay, nor did he seem to register that his drink wasn't free. Marie didn't dare to let Gene have the milkshakes for free; Todd's eagle eyes were always upon her as soon as Gene walked into the store. This routine went on for two more years. Marie felt that was plenty of time for Gene to pull himself up by his bootstraps, but he never did.

Her husband was too damn proud for his own good. First, the man couldn't give her a baby and refused to do anything about it. And now, he had lost their farm and refused to do anything about it. It was intolerable. Their life was going nowhere in slow motion, and once again, it was up to Marie to do something about it.

When she put arsenic in his strawberry milkshake that first time, Marie only meant it as a wake-up call for Gene. The man had languished for two years, and enough was enough. The arsenic was easy to get. Todd stored it in a locked cabinet in the pharmacy section. "I don't know why," he told Marie when he showed her around the store on her first day. "No one buys that stuff anymore. As far as I know, it's been there since Grandad first opened the store. I'll get around to throwing it out one of these days." But two years had gone by, and it still nestled there. Marie didn't think Todd would miss a little bit of arsenic, and she had a key to the cabinet.

Gene was still a robust man, and it took a full week of milkshakes before he got sick. Gene woke up one morning with abdominal pain, diarrhea, and muscle cramps. "I think I have the flu," he told Marie. "Do you think I should go to the doctor?"

Marie felt a sharp pang of guilt. Gene did not look at all well. What had she done? Marie took him to the doctor, and the doctor confirmed the diagnosis of the flu. Marie felt remorse and vowed that she wasn't going to do that again. Of course, after a few days with no milkshakes, Gene's health improved. Then he was back every day drinking the milkshakes, and things went back to normal. For Marie, it was intolerable.

The pattern continued for two more years. Every single time Gene got ill again, Marie thought she would stop poisoning her husband, but he would saunter into the drugstore, proud and jobless and sterile, and something in her would snap. Gene experienced many symptoms. His skin reddened, he had nausea and vomiting, his fingers and toes tingled, and he developed an abnormal heart rhythm. Marie took him to kindly old Dr. Bob, as everyone in town called the local GP, again and again. The poor doctor was perplexed as to the cause of this mysterious illness. As the arsenic slowly built up in Gene's system and his symptoms worsened to darkening skin, a constant sore throat, and persistent digestive issues, the doctor decided to put him in the county hospital for tests.

Marie wasn't worried. She doubted the testing done in the county hospital would be sophisticated enough to detect the arsenic. So she continued to bring Gene a strawberry milkshake every day. It was the highlight of his day, he told her, and she didn't want to disappoint him. One day, when Marie placed the milkshake on Gene's tray, he gently moved it to the side. "I'm going to save that for later."

When Marie arrived at the hospital the next day, two police officers were in Gene's room, waiting for her. "I didn't want them to test that milkshake," Gene said. "It offended me that the police think my wife would want to harm me. Tell them it isn't so," he urged her.

"While your husband has been in the hospital, his level of arsenic has increased," the older officer said.

Marie didn't know what to say. She honestly didn't remember putting the arsenic in the shakes she brought to the hospital. Had she done it subconsciously, or out of habit? "Excuse me?" she said.

"See? I told you my wife would never harm me." Gene's voice had a triumphant ring.

"You're under arrest, Mrs. Ketchum, for attempted murder," the younger officer said and produced handcuffs.

"Don't you dare arrest my wife!" Gene, still weakened, struggled to sit up in the bed.

"Mr. Ketchum, it's obvious that your wife has been poisoning you for some time." The older officer nodded, and the young officer cuffed Marie.

Marie spent the next week in the county jail, and the local press slurped up the Milkshake Marie story. She felt remorse for what she had done, but she couldn't say that she was truly sorry. She still loved her husband, but he had brought all this on himself. If he'd only listened to her, she would not have been forced to take such extreme measures. When the police finally conceded that Gene would never press charges against her, they released her.

After the officer walked her to the door of the jail, he said, "Your husband says to tell you that he still loves you. However, if you're going to visit him, you're going to need an escort."

"Thank you, but that won't be necessary." Marie could see Althea parked at the curb, waiting for her. She had already packed Marie's bag and would drive her to the rented garage where they stored Gene's old truck, one of the only things they had salvaged from the farm.

She turned one last time to the officer. "I know this is hard for you to believe, but I still love my husband." Then, with as much dignity as she could muster, Marie walked out of jail and on to a new life. She could never go back to Gene, not after what she had done. And the worst thing of all was that she couldn't trust herself not to do it again.

"I don't know if this is such a good idea, Marie." Nadine had repeated that mantra for the last week.

"We have the right to express our opinion." Marie would never let Nadine know she had second thoughts about picketing the Legion on this Thursday night. She'd been so excited about the project all week long. But now, as she looked across the street at the gathering throng, she, too, began to doubt the wiseness of this idea.

"I feel a little silly carrying this thing." Sophie hoisted the homemade sign—poster board taped to a yardstick—onto her shoulder. She had chosen to print Colossians 3:6 on hers: "On account of these, the wrath of God is coming." She'd written the verse in pen, and her shaky block letters were barely legible.

Marie thought Sophie did look a little silly with the sign, but she would not admit that either. "What's the worst thing that could happen to us?"

"Well, they could laugh at us." For her sign, Nadine had chosen Romans 1:18: "For the wrath of God is revealed from heaven against all ungodliness and unrighteousness of men, who by their unrighteousness suppress the truth." She hadn't planned well and had run out of room on her sign. The letters in TRUTH skittered off the edge of the poster board.

"They might think we're nuttier than a fruitcake," Sophie chimed in.

"What do we care what they think? We are three Christian ladies who happen to be in the right on this issue." Marie's sign looked slightly more professional than the others because she had kept at it until she got it right, even though she hated wasting all those sheets of poster board. On this sign, her fifth attempt, she'd used a black marker to carefully print James 4:17: "So whoever knows the right thing to do and fails to do it, for him it is a sin."

"Why don't we just sit here on your nice porch and hold up the signs, Marie? Wouldn't that work just as well? Do we really need to go traipsing over there?" Because of her weight, Sophie did not move all that well, and she was already perspiring.

Marie tried to rein in her impatience. "Ladies, didn't we all agree last week that we were going to picket the Legion tonight? Instead of sitting here and whining about how sinful this Queen of Hearts drawing is, we agreed to do something about it."

"I don't recall agreeing to anything. This was your idea, Marie, yours alone." Nadine stared at her defiantly. "Yours alone," she repeated for emphasis.

Marie knew she was not brave enough to go alone to that crowd and wave a sign. Once upon a time, she would have been, but not now. When she left Le Claire all those years ago, she had left her courage as well. However, she was undoubtedly braver than these old fuddy-duds, her best friends. She tried a different tack. "If we position ourselves just so by the door, we might be able to peek inside the Legion and see what's going on."

Sophie immediately perked up. "Now that would be something, wouldn't it?"

Even Nadine could not hide the temptation on her face. "Well, when you put it that way, it might be interesting to catch a glimpse of—"

Marie didn't wait for her to finish. "So, let's go." She picked up her sign to lead her ragtag crusaders across the street and through the parking lot to the door. It was a short walk, not even fifty yards, but Marie could hear Sophie huffing behind her.

With each step, the noise amplified around them. The crowd was loud enough when Marie sat on her porch, but it was deafening once they reached the door. Marie's ears rang, and her heart started to beat faster. She hadn't counted on the smell either, an acrid mix of sweat, stale beer, hope, and fear. And she shouldn't have worn the pearls Leland had given her for their tenth anniversary. The necklace stuck to her damp skin, the pearls heavy as a string of marbles, as Marie made her way through the crowd toward the door. "Excuse me," she kept repeating. "Excuse me."

But it did no good. No one paid the least bit of attention to Marie, and the crowd swallowed her whole, pushing and shoving and jostling. "The drawing's about to start!" Someone yelled excitedly, and then it was as if the crowd became a giant wave, surging forth. Marie could no more control the movement than she could an actual tide, and before she knew it, she was pushed through the door and into the Legion.

"Nadine! Sophie!" Marie called frantically, but they were nowhere in sight. Of course, her ragtag band of crusaders had abandoned her. And now, stuck amid this unruly mass of flesh, Marie felt more alone than she ever had before. She briefly wondered if she should be concerned about her friends' welfare. Marie was the hardiest of their group, and she didn't feel at all well. Her heart would not stop pounding, and she was light-headed from the heat and the noise. And her eyes would not focus correctly. Surely, she should recognize someone in this room, but all the faces blurred. Was this a panic attack? Oh, dear God, was she having a heart attack?

Marie did not want to die in this room.

Someone had her by the arm. "Ma'am? Ma'am? Can you hear me?"

As he hovered over her, Marie could feel that he was tall, as tall as Gene had been. "I... I . . ." Her mouth could not form the words.

"Someone should probably call an ambulance," the tall man announced.

Marie vehemently shook her head. She clutched at the man's arm and tried to peer into his face. It looked like he had a chipped front tooth, but she might be mistaken.

Another shorter man approached. "Come on, man, park the old lady somewhere. We drove a long way to get here, and the drawing is about to start. We bought $100 worth of tickets, and you know we don't have that kind of money to spend."

"Someone should probably help her," the tall man said. "She doesn't look so good."

The shorter man laughed meanly. "Since when did you become a Good Samaritan? Park the old lady, shithead. We've got everything riding on this."

"I just need some water." Marie's voice was fainter than a whisper.

"What'd you say, ma'am?" He leaned his head down. His hair smelled like the sun. Gene's hair had always smelled like the sun.

Marie leaned against him. She did not want to die in this hellish place. If he could just get her home, she would be all right. Her heartbeat would return to normal, and she would be able to breathe. After years of arsenic poisoning, Gene developed an abnormal heart rhythm. On many occasions, he had thought he might be having a heart attack. Had he felt like this? It was terrifying to have a faulty heart. Marie understood that now.

Marie pulled the man's face down to her lips. "Please, if you could just take me home. I live right across the street."

"What's the bitch whispering? Does she want you to be her boyfriend?" The shorter man's voice sounded harsh. He was getting angry.

"She wants me to take her home. She lives across the street."

"Goddamn it, man. We're here for a *reason*."

"She's wearing pearls." Marie's Good Samaritan lightly stroked her neck.

Marie could smell the mean man's beer breath as he leaned forward to take a look. "I'm starting to get the picture, man. How could I ever doubt you?" Again, that mean laugh.

"I'll be back in a few."

The man slowly navigated Marie through the crowd. The air thrummed with excitement and anticipation, but Marie felt slightly better once they were through the door. Her heart still didn't feel right. Maybe she would make an appointment at the clinic tomorrow, but Marie didn't need a doctor to tell her something was seriously wrong. As she and the man inched toward her home, Marie's jumbled thoughts turned to Gene. She wondered what he had ultimately died from. He would be eighty-seven now, so he could still be alive. Conceivably, Gene could end up outliving her.

Nadine and Sophie were not waiting at her house for her, and Marie was glad. She didn't want them to see her in this state. Always, she had been the strong one. Often, her strength had been fueled by anger, but someone had to be responsible. Someone had to take the bulls by the horn. Marie could not change that character trait, no matter how hard or how long she tried. She simply could not.

The front door, as always, was unlocked. The Good Samaritan led her in, and Marie settled herself gingerly on the sofa. "Thank you for being so kind. I don't know what came over me." Maybe she should offer to pay the man for escorting her across the street, or would he find that rude? Perhaps a glass of water would help her feel better. Should she ask the man to fetch it for her? She didn't feel able to do that just yet.

Marie reached over to turn on the table lamp, and as her eyes finally focused, she turned to the man. She would ask him for that glass of water, but the words stuck in her throat. Her Good Samaritan didn't look anything like Gene. He was tall, yes, but dangerously thin, with unkempt hair past his shoulders and a scraggly beard that looked stained with tobacco. His front tooth wasn't chipped but missing. He calmly reached behind him and locked the front door she never locked.

"What, what are you doing?" Marie could see a glinting object in his hand, and she gasped. After all was said and done, had it come down to this?

He raised the knife, pointing it directly at her. "We'll start with the pearls and see where this goes." His eyes bore into hers. "And if I were you, ma'am, I'd turn off that light."

RIVER PEOPLE

Calvin Phillips didn't mind the reporter's questions because he was a man who loved to talk. "Yes, sir, these river people along the Mississippi have been unbelievably kind to me. When I docked here in Liberty, I was out of food, wood, and propane, but people here have been very generous. A couple of these good folks even took me to the barbershop and got me a haircut and a shave." Calvin rubbed his freshly shaven face. "I needed that."

Calvin looked around the cluttered cabin of his houseboat, *Shameless*. He didn't particularly care for the name the previous owner had bestowed upon his craft, but everyone knew it was bad luck to change a boat's name. And Calvin didn't need any more bad luck. Two years before, he had been diagnosed with cancer. The cancerous cells came from his bone marrow and attached to his sinuses. He'd never heard of such a thing.

"I was in the hospital for forty-seven days, most of them on a ventilator. There were complications from chemotherapy, and I wasn't expected to live. They called my brother three times because they didn't think I'd live through the night." Calvin ruefully shook his head.

The young reporter from the *Liberty Gazette*, Brad, clucked his tongue. "That's terrible."

Calvin lit a Marlboro before continuing. "When I came to, I didn't know where I was or what had happened. A nurse told me that I was in hospice, and shortly after that, the doctor released me. I guess he figured they couldn't do any more for me."

Calvin did not think it was necessary to describe the fear and rage that he had felt to this young man. Why him? What had he done to deserve such a death sentence? He was forty-eight years old at the time and the owner of a dry cleaners business in Michigan. Married and divorced at a young age, Calvin had spent most of his adult life working in his shop. He didn't have any children, and his only hobby, if it could be called a hobby, was his fascination with the Mississippi River, its geography and its colorful history.

"That's when I decided that if I was going to die, I would do it on the Mississippi." Calvin stubbed out his cigarette in the overflowing ashtray. "Then my plans got all screwed up. I lived." Calvin laughed and slapped his thigh. "I bought the houseboat in Wisconsin and expected to be dead in a month. But a year later, I'm still here. It's the damnedest thing."

"So your cancer is in remission?" the reporter asked.

"When I was in Wisconsin, a doctor examined me and said the cancer is no longer in my sinuses. But I'm still weak from illness and chemotherapy." Calvin wanted to make sure the reporter knew he wasn't a freeloader. He would work if he could. He'd worked his entire life, after all—not that it had done him one bit of good. So far, he'd been living off his savings, but that fund was limited. It's why he depended upon the kindness of the river people he met along the way. They had not disappointed him.

Brad next asked, "Do you ever get lonely traveling in this houseboat by yourself?"

Calvin thought it was an odd question. Hadn't the young man been listening to him tell the stories of all the people he met? However, the fact of the matter was that Calvin did get lonesome sometimes. In bad weather, he had spent days at a time without speaking to another living soul, which had just given him more time to ponder the question: *Why am I still alive?* Calvin was not a religious man, but he had come to believe that there must be a Higher Power of some sort during his months on the Mississippi. The idea of a Higher Power made even more sense when Calvin fell into the river on his fiftieth birthday last December. He was attempting to tie *Shameless* to a work barge in St. Louis because there was nowhere else to dock. Calvin thought for sure he was a goner. The water was frigid, and he was not a strong swimmer, especially not now, after the chemo had weakened him. But miraculously, a worker on the barge appeared and pulled him out. Calvin called that tumble into the water his *baptism.*

However, Calvin wasn't going to share this information with the young man. Instead, he said, "Every day is an adventure. Every day, something happens. Whether it's the people I meet or the things I see, it's been amazing."

"I've taken up enough of your time." Brad started gathering his things, his notebook, iPad, and phone.

"Nonsense. I'm just getting warmed up." Calvin tried to remember if he'd told Brad about the military veteran in Arkansas who brought him a new American flag to replace the tattered one he'd been flying. That was a good story.

Brad glanced at his watch. "I've been here for three hours, Mr. Phillips."

"I do believe you know me well enough to call me Calvin. Goodness, we're practically best buddies by now." Calvin didn't want the young man to leave. He was good company, a rapt listener. "Did I tell you the story about the woman at the marina in Louisiana who brought me a pie every day during my stay? That woman really knew how to bake. I've never tasted a flakier crust. And the variety! I'm talking cherry, peach, apple, and rhubarb. I do believe that rhubarb was my favorite."

Brad smiled patiently. "Yes, you told that story. I have it in my notes."

"Make sure that one gets into the article, will you?"

"Sure thing."

Brad looked like he was on the verge of jumping up from the sagging armchair, so Calvin said conversationally, "What are the sights to see here in Liberty? I like to explore each town that I dock at."

A slight blush covered Brad's cheeks. "Well, Liberty is a regular type of small town. We've got a town square and a park next to the American Legion, and naturally, we have a Walmart. If you stick around for another week, you can go to the Fourth of July celebration. It's the biggest event of the summer around these parts. A carnival comes to town, and we have a parade and an antique auto show."

"I might have to take you up on that." Calvin smiled hopefully at Brad, but he got to his feet anyway.

"Thanks for your time, Calvin. My article will appear in this week's edition of the *Liberty Gazette*." Brad reached the door but then turned. "Oh, I just thought of something you could do. The Legion has a Queen of Hearts drawing every Thursday night. It's practically all anyone in this town talks about. The jackpot is over a million bucks now. Someone's going to be very rich one of these days."

Brad's hand might be on the doorknob, but he was still here, so Calvin kept talking. "A million bucks, huh? How do you win?"

Brad turned back around. "Each Queen of Hearts drawing starts with the 52 cards in a playing deck, plus the 2 jokers for a total of 54. Each card is put in a sealed envelope and given a number from 1-54. Then people buy raffle tickets for $2 a ticket. If you can't make it to the drawing, you can put a number on the back of your ticket, but you only get half the prize money if you don't attend. Then every Thursday, all the tickets sold for that week are put into a big drum. One ticket is drawn, and the owner of that ticket chooses a numbered envelope. The game continues until someone picks the queen of hearts."

Calvin took his time lighting another Marlboro and exhaled a long plume of smoke. "Do you attend this weekly drawing, Brad?"

This time, Brad's blush was deeper. "I do attend, but only in a journalistic capacity. I mean, when someone finally wins, it's going to be huge news around here."

Calvin nodded. He had become something of an expert on human behavior during his months on the Mississippi. "And do you, perhaps, buy a raffle ticket from time to time?"

Brad smiled sheepishly. "I plead the Fifth on that one."

"What would you do with a million dollars, Brad?"

Brad hesitated only a fraction of a second before saying, "The first thing I would do is buy a Lamborghini."

Calvin felt slightly disappointed at this. He'd thought this young man would be more imaginative than having his deepest desire be a car.

Brad warmed to the subject. "And I'd probably give my mom some money for a new roof. She's been talking about her leaky roof for ages. Wait a minute. I'd probably give her enough money so she could move to Arizona. Her sister lives in a retirement community in Mesa, and I know that would make her happy."

This was more like it, and Calvin's faith in the boy was restored. He wasn't a mercenary millennial after all. "That would be very noble of you, Brad."

"What would you do with a million dollars, buy a new boat?"

"Why would I do that? This one suits me just fine." Brad blushed again, and Calvin felt bad. If he looked at *Shameless* through Brad's eyes—the sagging shelf of canned goods, the ancient TV and radio, the peeling paint—he could see the logic of Brad's suggestion. "You know, on second thought, I probably would buy a new boat. The bed on this one is not very comfortable."

Brad smiled, relieved. "It's been really nice talking with you, Calvin, but I do have to go now. I want to get started on this story while my ideas are fresh."

"Of course. It was nice to meet you, too, Brad. If you have any more questions, you know where to find me."

After Brad left, Calvin lit another cigarette and continued to sit and rock and ponder in his old wooden rocking chair. He could have imparted so much wisdom to the young man on the subject of money. Namely, that it didn't do a body any good at all. He had worked his ass off for years in that stifling dry cleaners, the air laden with chemicals that had probably been the cause of his cancer. And he had scrimped and saved, living a miserly existence for the most part. He lived in a small rental house, rarely ate out at a decent restaurant, and never took vacations. And for what? He'd gotten deathly ill, and the medical bills wiped out most of that hard-earned money, leaving him with enough only for a used houseboat and a small monthly stipend.

But here on the Mississippi, he had learned how little he needed to get by and be happy. Whoever said that hearses didn't come with luggage racks had the right idea. You certainly couldn't take it with you. When your time came, you were gone. And Calvin should have told Brad that people matter in this life, not material possessions or money in the bank. He had met so many good, kind people at this late stage of the game. Maybe that was why he was still here. He had a lot of meeting and greeting yet to do.

Calvin suddenly stopped rocking. An idea had materialized out of nowhere and grabbed his full attention. He absolutely knew what he would do if he won that kind of money. He would retrace his route on this mightiest of rivers, and he would give money to all those people who had helped him. He would hand out rolls of hundred-dollar bills to people like the military veteran who had given him the flag and the lady who baked him all those pies in Louisiana. He would pay it forward.

Calvin decided to get a beer to celebrate. A nice man in town had stopped by earlier that day and given him a six-pack of Budweiser. Come to think of it, that nice man had said he was a bartender at the American Legion. Maybe it was some kind of sign? Calvin thought as he got stiffly out of his chair and hobbled to his miniature refrigerator. Maybe he was supposed to go to the Queen of Hearts drawing next Thursday night, and maybe he was supposed to purchase a raffle ticket for $2. Maybe his luck would finally change. It certainly seemed to Calvin that everything pointed in that direction.

Calvin opened the tab on the can of beer and stood sipping it as he stared out of the streaked window. Since he docked a week before, the girl had shown up on the banks of the river right about now. Calvin would guess she was in her early twenties. One day, her hair had been pink, but most of the time, it was blonde. From this distance, she seemed to be pretty, but she was much too thin. She usually wore cut-offs and a skimpy top, but Calvin figured it was because it was very hot for late June. She was not a tramp, of that he was sure. The girl would find a comfortable place to sit on the bank and produce something to drink from that big purse of hers. Then she would stare contemplatively at the river for an hour or so.

There, he could see her walking toward the river now, and she smiled in anticipation. One of these days, Calvin would meet her. Maybe she would even want to come on board and sit a spell. He would like that, and he would entertain her. After all, he had a lot of interesting stories to tell.

Roxy did not consider herself to be an addict; she just preferred to be happy all the time. And to Roxy's way of thinking, people should do whatever it was that made them happy. Take her mother, Rosemary, for example. She loved to go to bingo every Saturday night in the parish hall of St. Joe's. She looked forward to it all week, and every Saturday night before she walked out the door, Roxy would do her hair. That's what Roxy did for a living—she was a stylist at Trudy's Beauty Boutique—and she would style Rosemary's hair, teasing it until it poofed up in the back and covered the balding spot at the crown. And then Roxy would apply crimson nail color and the heavy blue eyeshadow that her mother still favored.

"I look like a million bucks," Rosemary would say when Roxy gave her the hand mirror. "Don't I look like a million bucks?" She would lift her eyes to Roxy's, imploring her to agree.

Roxy always did. "Yeah, Mom, you look like a million bucks." It was no hardship for Roxy to lie to her mom. It was easy, in fact, because the lie, like bingo, made her mom happy. "Don't you go picking up any strange men at that bingo parlor, you hear?"

Her mother would play along, laughing playfully before the phlegm caught in her throat, and she started to cough. "It's the parish hall at the Catholic Church! Believe me, honey, the kind of man who goes there on a Saturday night ain't my type."

That was true. Before, when Rosemary brought men home regularly, she'd favored the drunken redneck type. Roxy secretly thought it was that type of man who had prematurely aged her mom. She remembered many drunken fights and flying beer bottles in their trailer. And Roxy remembered other nights when Rosemary didn't come home until the next morning, her mascara dried on her cheeks in rivulets, her blouse torn, the heel of her shoe missing. Her mom would swear off men on those mornings, but by the next night, she'd go back to Meyers Tavern and do the same thing all over again.

Smoking almost three packs a day had not helped Rosemary in the age department either. One of Roxy's earliest memories was of Rosemary sitting in her recliner in front of the TV, a cigarette dangling from her left hand, and a bottle of Wild Turkey on the table beside her. It got worse after Rosemary fell at work and had to "retire" at the age of thirty-five. She'd worked at Gilster Mary Lee—all the locals referred to it as The Cake Mix Factory—since she dropped out of school at sixteen. She'd been happy working there, she said, working the assembly line in the cereal department. But then she slipped on some wet paper towels in the restroom and hurt her back. She had collected disability checks ever since.

"My career is over," Rosemary joked at the time. But then there were more men and more nights at Meyers Tavern, followed by depression and COPD.

Rosemary was only forty-four but looked twenty years older, and Roxy felt sorry for her. She'd had a hard life—some of which she'd brought on herself, true—and now she didn't do much of anything. The men were gone, along with the booze and cigarettes, and Rosemary had her *Housewives* shows to watch on Bravo and Saturday night bingo at St. Joe's parish hall to keep her happy.

And she had Roxy, who fiercely loved her mother. Roxy had never known her father. Rosemary had told her so many conflicting stories over the years that it could have been any number of men in town. When Roxy was a child, she had looked intently at all men of a certain age, scrutinizing their faces for green eyes or a high forehead or a long, straight nose like hers. She'd gotten so bad about the staring that her mom had finally said, exasperated, "He's dead, Roxy, so you can stop your goddamn gawking."

So it had always been just the two of them. "It's just you and me, *amigo*. We're all we've got," Rosemary had said all of Roxy's life. Roxy took this to heart; she knew it was her responsibility to take care of her mother. After all, she owed it to her. Rosemary, to the best of her capabilities, had been a good mother. No matter how many nights she used to get drunk, she always made sure that Roxy had enough to eat. Rosemary also protected her from the episodes of violence that erupted in the trailer, most of the time. (Roxy did have a small scar just below her right eye, pierced by a shard of a flying beer bottle when she took cover behind the kitchen counter.) And Rosemary had valiantly tried to protect Roxy from the more predatory men, most of the time.

Now Saturday evenings, when Roxy helped Rosemary get ready to go play bingo, were some of their best "together" times. Rosemary would be giddy with anticipation, and after Roxy finished her handiwork, everything seemed right with the world. "I'm gonna knock their socks off tonight." Rosemary would get slowly to her feet, using the kitchen table for support.

Roxy's heart would swell just looking at her. Her mom had gotten so frail over the last few years, and Roxy didn't think she weighed over a hundred pounds. She used to be a curvaceous, robust woman, something that Roxy didn't inherit. Instead, she must have taken after her unknown/maybe-dead dad in the looks department, with her long legs and skinny build. Rosemary used to tell her that she was "all skin and bones." Now that could apply to both of them.

"Your chariot awaits," Roxy would say. She wouldn't take her mom's arm for support unless she asked her to. Rosemary was proud that way.

Rosemary, smiling, would say, "I'm living the high life."

"You sure are." Roxy would then drive her to the parish hall and make sure she had a ride home. She would kiss her mom on the cheek before she went off to do her own thing. Her friends would be waiting for her.

So Roxy, at the age of twenty-two, still lived with her mom, and in many ways, they were better off than they had ever been. With her job at Trudy's Beauty Boutique, Roxy contributed to the household income, and they had what they needed. She also did the grocery shopping and what passed for cooking and cleaning in their home. (Roxy was the first to admit that she didn't care much for either.) She might have contributed more money if she worked harder, but there were days when she didn't feel like going to work. It might be beautiful out, or it might be a day that she felt the need to sit by the Mississippi and daydream. It was pretty much her favorite place in the whole world.

Roxy might also have contributed more money to the household income if the dang opioids weren't so dang expensive. But they were.

Most of Roxy's friends were tweakers. They preferred meth because it was cheaper and easier to get hold of in small, rural towns. Roxy could see the logic in this, but opioids—Percocet and Oxycontin—were still her drugs of choice. And she had ready access to them. When Rosemary fell and hurt her back, the drugs magically appeared in the trailer's medicine cabinet. Oddly enough, Rosemary, a woman who had spent a good portion of her adult life drunk on beer and Wild Turkey, did not take to the pills.

"They make my head feel funny," she'd said to thirteen-year-old Roxy.

To Roxy, that sounded like a fine idea. Who wouldn't want her head to feel funny? But when Roxy tried her first Percocet the very next day, she didn't feel funny at all. She felt gloriously happy. She had always had a sunny disposition— Rosemary called her "a ray of sunshine"—and the Percocet elevated that to a very satisfying sense of well-being. Liberty's oldest doctor, Doc Jenkins, did not have a problem writing out prescriptions for the drugs. And Roxy knew, in the way one addict recognizes another, that Doc Jenkins was a firm believer in the benefits of hillbilly heroin, too.

If Rosemary knew about Roxy's fondness for the drugs, and she must have known because Roxy did nothing to hide it from her and even took her to Doc Jenkins to get the refills, she insisted on turning a blind eye. Roxy sometimes wondered if it was because Rosemary understood addiction's power, but she didn't push the subject. Once, Rosemary said, "Just be sure you don't ruin your looks, Roxy." Another time, it was: "I guess I don't have to worry about you losing your teeth like all them tweakers." Roxy promised she would lose neither.

Roxy's best friend, Tommy, had already lost a few teeth. He'd been using meth for three or four years and had the sunken cheeks and skeletal frame to prove it. But he was generally a good guy. Roxy rarely slept with him anymore, not because she didn't want to but because every time they did it, Tommy thought he became the president of a mythological country called Fayland. She'd had to talk him out of phoning the White House more times than she cared to remember.

Roxy's other friends, Carl and Robbie, were sometimes hyperactive and irrational but generally decent, too. Neither of them looked so hot anymore, and they had been so hot in high school. All three of the guys had been a few years ahead of Roxy in school, and she knew who they were just like she knew almost everyone in Liberty. Then one day, they all happened to be at the shaded grove by the Mississippi at the same time. They struck up a conversation and discovered the mutual attraction to drugs over a shared bottle of tequila. They had been buddies for a couple of years now.

On this particular Saturday night, they were once again at the shaded grove. Roxy had already dropped off Rosemary at the parish hall, and they were sitting around on camp chairs that Tommy had found propped up against somebody's garbage can. The chairs were not in good shape, and neither was he. His eyes had that crazed, glazed look that spelled trouble, and he gulped down the cans of Miller High Life as if they were water.

He crumpled up the current can, his sixth, and tossed it over his shoulder. "Everybody in this miserable town has gone fucking insane."

Roxy immediately knew he was referring to the Queen of Hearts drawing held every Thursday night at the Legion. You couldn't walk past a street corner in town and not hear someone talking about it, and the frenzy grew as the jackpot mounted. It now hovered at the million-dollar mark. "I think it's exciting." She took a sip of her beer. "And it gives people something to look forward to."

"Yeah, if you're an idiot," Tommy sneered.

"Shut up, asshole." Roxy threw him a dirty look and then slapped at her arm. The dang mosquitoes were out in full force tonight and were eating her alive.

"Whoever wins is a dead man," Carl said somberly. "The poor slob will walk out the door of the Legion a millionaire and Bam!" Carl formed a gun with his hand. "He's dead."

"Not worth it in my book," Robbie said, shaking his head.

"What, you'd rather be a fucking tweaker than a millionaire?" Tommy reached for another beer.

"Yeah, man, I'd like to keep living, you know?"

"Then you're an idiot."

"Roxy was right. You are an asshole, Tommy."

Roxy didn't like it when her friends bickered like this. It didn't happen very often, but it seemed like everyone had arrived at the river in a foul mood. They had all gotten high on their preferred drugs first thing, but it didn't seem to be lifting anybody's spirits, including hers, which was very rare. The headlights from Tommy's old truck cut through the gloom, illuminating four disgruntled faces.

Roxy disliked being unhappy, so to brighten the mood, she said, "What would you all do with that kind of money? I'd open up my own salon, and I'd put in a tanning bed and hire a manicurist and someone to do facials. And I'd buy Rosemary a new trailer and one for myself right next door . . ." Her voice trailed off when she realized nobody was listening to her. They were too busy glaring at each other. She stood up. "If you all are going to act like sixth-graders, I'm going home. I don't need this shit."

Tommy grabbed her arm and pulled her back into the chair. "You're right. I'm sorry for being an asshole, guys." He crumpled another can and reached for a beer, sighing heavily. "It's just that everything sucks right now. I'm flat broke. My unemployment check don't stretch like a rubber band. Between my ex always having her hand out and the kid, I don't even have $2 to buy a damn raffle ticket."

And the meth, Roxy almost added but didn't. She patted his arm. They all knew Tommy had been laid off from Arlo's gas station months ago. It wasn't Arlo's fault—everyone knew he was a great guy—it was because Arlo couldn't compete with the new Circle K. It was also this group's general consensus that Donna, Tommy's ex-wife, was a bitch. If the truth were to be told, Roxy would also have to say that Tommy's three-year-old son, Devon, was something of a brat. She would never say that directly to Tommy because it would hurt his feelings, but Devon was the kind of kid who screamed for no reason at all. Once when Roxy had been in Walmart, she had heard Devon start to shriek a few aisles over. Before he was done, he'd pretty much cleared the store, and Roxy's ears rang for an hour after that.

Carl, who'd never held a job for more than two weeks, said, "I'd help you out, man, but I'm pretty much in the same boat."

"Same here." Robbie still worked at Dave's Market, but he had a respiratory infection last winter and spent two weeks in the hospital. He was still trying to pay that off.

"My money's at St. Joe's parish hall." Roxy had only gone to work for two days the past week because Trudy had been nagging her. "You're going to lose your clients, Roxy, if you keep canceling appointments." So Roxy decided she would show her and take the rest of the week off. What little tip money she still had, she'd given to Rosemary to play bingo.

Roxy reached into her purse for an Oxy, and the guys dug into their jeans pockets for their meth. All three had pills tonight, but Roxy had seen them do it all: smoking, snorting, and injecting. Ten minutes later, Roxy felt much better. Her mind roamed on different subjects before finally landing. "Where do you think the Legion keeps the million bucks?" she asked dreamily. "Do you think the money's in a safe in the Commander's office?"

"How do you know there's a safe there?" Carl's voice sounded two octaves higher than usual, and he wrung his hands. He'd reached the agitated state he always got to at this point.

Roxy shrugged. She was just throwing out random ideas. "They probably keep it at the bank until someone wins, and then they give him a check."

"Maybe they're making the whole thing up, and all the winner will get is a million dollars of Monopoly money." Robbie laughed uproariously.

Tommy jumped to his feet and began pacing excitedly back and forth in the circle their camp chairs made. "Why do some people have so much money, and others, like us, are flat broke?" Back and forth, back and forth. "It's not fair, goddamn it."

"So unfair," Roxy murmured. She had never really thought about it before, but it was surely unfair. She would love to buy Rosemary a decent wig and maybe a pair of pants that didn't droop and sag. That would be nice.

They had finished the case of beer, and Robbie juggled the empties. "Look at me, would you? I'm like that guy on TV, what's-his-name?"

"Awesome." Carl applauded.

We are so high, Roxy thought. *It is a very good thing.*

"We are so fucking going to do something about this." Tommy waved his arms in the air like he conducted an orchestra. "Who's with me on this?"

Roxy struggled to sit up straight in her wobbly, rusty chair. Half the nylon straps were busted, and her butt almost touched the ground. "On what?"

"We're going to rob the Partytime Liquor Store, and we're going to do it tonight."

The air against her skin felt humid and warm, yet Roxy couldn't stop shivering. She must have dozed off in Tommy's truck on the way here because she didn't remember the drive. She squinted at the clock on the tower in the town square: 3:15. Rosemary, after she returned from bingo, would have gone to bed hours ago. She would not be worried about Roxy, though. Roxy always came home eventually. Roxy was a loving, dutiful daughter.

And Roxy was about to rob a liquor store. "Guys, we can't do this," she whispered. They either didn't hear her, or they were ignoring her. Roxy suspected the latter. They were well into the crystal meth zone now, and in the dim light of the streetlamp, they looked like every bad picture of a crystal meth zombie she had ever seen: sunken cheeks, soulless eyes, missing teeth, scarred faces. Yet they were frenzied with agitation and misguided purpose.

"How are we going to get in?" Carl asked, hopping from one foot to another. "We don't have a key."

"You are such a shithead, Carl," Tommy hissed. "Robbers don't have keys."

"We could use a credit card like they do in the movies." Robbie had brought the empties with him and started juggling again.

No one had a credit card, and Roxy said again. "We can't do this. Let's go home and forget the whole thing."

"Nothing doing." Tommy eyed the front door as if he'd never seen one before. "We are on a mission."

"A mission from God," Carl intoned, which cracked up Robbie.

"Shut up, assholes!" Tommy hissed.

Roxy wondered how long they would stand there before they gave up and went home. She wished that the gorgeous new police officer would cruise by, but everyone in town knew Officer Morrison's shift ended at 10:00. She tried again, tugging on Tommy's arm. "They might have a security camera or an alarm system."

"Are you kidding me? Partytime Liquor is a dump. And Wilson's too cheap to spring for any of that crap. Besides, we're just going to run in and run out."

"If you can figure out a way to get into the store, Tommy."

"I wish I had a gun. I could shoot the lock off."

The three of them acted so high, so ridiculous, and so lost that Roxy felt sorry for them. There couldn't be that much money in the liquor store to steal, or maybe Wilson deposited it in the bank each night. Her tweaker friends had been dealt a bad hand in life. People in town avoided them like the plague now, as if the three of them were a constant reminder of how wrecked the human spirit could become. Right then, she wanted to take Tommy in her arms and tell him everything would be all right, but he was jumping up and down like a pogo stick and wildly waving his arms again.

"Cliff Neeley threw a brick through the front window of Trudy's a week ago." Roxy was still sorry she hadn't been there to see that. She had walked in right after it happened and missed all the excitement. But she was the one who told Trudy that Cliff Neeley was standing across the street with a wheelbarrow full of bricks. She'd done her part on that day, but Trudy did not bother to thank her.

Tommy had started to sweat profusely. "I heard about that, but… Oh, fuck me." Tommy began to laugh. "You think I should throw a brick through the window of this door and reach in and unlock it, right?"

"No, I don't think you should do that, but you're going to do it anyway."

"Damn right, I am."

Roxy looked long and hard into Tommy's wild, distant eyes. They had no soul right now, and to Roxy, that was the saddest thing about the tweakers. When the soul went out of their eyes, it seemed as if the heart followed. They were not the generally nice guys she knew anymore; they were irrational strangers. Without another word, she turned and left. She had walked half a block when she heard glass shattering behind her.

Roxy walked through the town square, passing the consignment shop, Zelda's, where she sometimes shopped for clothes. Mostly, though, like everybody else, she shopped at the Walmart Supercenter on the southern end of town. Roxy then passed the boarded-up movie theater where Rosemary occasionally took her for a Saturday matinee as a kid. When Rosemary used to do that, she usually felt guilty about something. Roxy walked faster. She crossed the railroad tracks that dissected the town. There used to be multiple daily trains carrying coal running on those tracks, but that hadn't been the case for a long time. When the strip mines closed years ago, the town grew poorer.

Almost all the Liberty houses were older, built in the 1940s and 50s, and some were better kept up than others. Roxy walked past a house with pretty petunias in the front window box and a concrete goose dressed up as Uncle Sam for the upcoming Fourth of July holiday on the porch. The house next to it had a scraggly lawn with an old car on blocks in the front yard and a sagging couch on a sagging porch. She passed a dog locked in a chain-link kennel behind one house, and it started to bark like crazy. *Poor thing*, Roxy thought, *it must be terrible to be cooped up like that.* And then she thought of Rosemary and walked faster.

The trailer park that she and Rosemary lived in was on the edge of town, next to the cemetery. Big, old oak trees shaded the thirty or so older model trailers in the park, and they could be considered the nicest feature of the place and responsible for its name, Oakwood. No one ever called it Oakwood, though. It was just the trailer park. Nanette Gilbert was the sole owner once her husband, Harold, died, and she was a lackadaisical landlady at best. If someone had a broken toilet or a leaking faucet, Nanette maybe would, maybe wouldn't call a plumber. But no one complained much; the rent was cheap.

Roxy had always known the trailer park wasn't an especially desirable place to live in Liberty, nor was it pretty. Because of the enormous trees' shade, very little grass grew, so the area surrounding each trailer was mostly hard-packed dirt. The trailers wedged in between the trees had been there since the 1970s, and many had rust spots or corrugated tin patched roofs. Roxy, using the flashlight on her phone, felt like she saw the place with new eyes on this night. The kitchen window's shades at the Dirksons were torn; the Duggans had placed a piece of cardboard over a broken window. The Langleys' satellite dish skewed dangerously to one side, and the Schroeders' kids had left their tiny plot of yard littered with toys.

Unlike most trailer parks, the residents in this one tended to stay put and were on reasonably good terms with one another, most of the time. Inevitably, because of the close proximity, shouting could be heard coming from the Suttons' place every so often. The expletives and slurs those two slung at each other would make a sailor blush, and the wife, Darlene, had packed her bag and left on countless occasions. She always came back. Like all the others in the trailer park, the Suttons' fights were rage-, drug-, and poverty-fueled.

But there had been celebrations and times of solidarity in this park, too. Roxy insisted on believing in that. The residents held celebratory birthday, wedding, graduation, and getting-out-of-jail parties, many of them. And when old Mrs. Pearson fell and broke her hip in trailer #21, everyone in the park had chipped in to buy her flowers. When the Trainers in trailer #18 fell on especially hard times—they both lost their jobs, and their kid got put in the hospital with pneumonia—every single neighbor had taken over a can of soup or corn or Chef Boyardee to tide them over until unemployment kicked in.

"Home, sweet home," Roxy whispered as she let herself into the unlocked door of trailer #9. She had lived in this trailer all her life, and she had never been ashamed of it. Two people could make a family, and two people together, in a trailer, could make a home. Granted, the couch and chair in the living room still bore witness to Rosemary's wild past with their beer smudges (and other stains Roxy didn't want to think about) and cigarette burns. The Goodwill wooden chairs in the kitchen had missing slats, and Roxy slept on a blow-up bed in the second bedroom that was the size of a large closet. But none of that mattered. Roxy insisted on believing in that.

Even though Roxy could hear Rosemary's loud snoring, she checked on her anyway before letting herself into the bathroom to get ready for bed. She stripped quickly before stepping into the small shower, where she scrubbed hard at her skin, hair, and face. Roxy had never felt so unclean before, and it wasn't only because of the humid night by the river with all those mosquitoes. She had participated in a robbery. No, that wasn't right. She had walked away *before* the robbery. But she was the one who had told Tommy how he could break into the liquor store. She should have kept her big mouth shut, and maybe she would have if the memory of Cliff Neeley throwing the brick through the window of Trudy's salon hadn't been so fresh in her mind.

She stepped out of the shower and toweled off. Her hands started to shake, then her whole body. She needed another Oxy, but it was more than that. She needed to tell someone what had happened tonight. Wilson wasn't a very nice man, but he had been the victim of a needless crime. On the other hand, Tommy, Carl, and Robbie were her friends, the only friends she had—other than Rosemary, if she could be counted as a friend. What would happen if Tommy and the others went to jail? Roxy didn't think any of them could withstand even the county jail. Their withdrawals alone would probably kill them.

Roxy felt faint from all the steam in the small, cramped bathroom. She had taken the hottest shower she could stand, and she still didn't feel clean. Furiously, she swiped at the cloudy mirror above the sink with her towel until the image of her face slowly came into focus. She gasped. She did not look at all well. Her cheeks, like the tweakers, were sunken, and her green eyes were bloodshot. With her wet hair matted to her skull, she looked like one of those poor unfortunates being released from the camps by the Allies. When was the last time she had taken a good, hard look at herself? Roxy couldn't remember.

She stumbled out of the bathroom and felt her way down the narrow hall to the living room where she had dropped her purse. With trembling hands, she uncapped the Oxy. After swallowing the pill, Roxy leaned back on the couch and waited for the release, the joy, the comfort. They didn't come, and she felt the hot tears of frustration and fear sting the back of her eyes before rolling down her cheeks. She was an addict; there was no denying it. She was an addict who lived with her ailing mother in a poor trailer park.

Maybe they should move out of this trailer, this town, this life. It was her last thought before the knocking started.

The knocking persisted, dragging Roxy reluctantly from whatever sleep or stupor she had fallen into. She blinked awake, and it took her a moment to remember where she was—the couch—but it was early morning. And the knocking came from the door.

She wrapped the towel tightly around her and peeked through the curtain on the door. It was Tommy. He hadn't gotten caught, and he was probably here to apologize. She opened the door. "Tommy."

"Here." He thrust a black garbage bag at her. In the light of early morning, he looked like a ghost, his sallow skin glowing a sickly whitish-gray.

"What is this?" Roxy was not fully conscious. Was he giving her garbage or a present? It made no sense.

"This is our haul, and you're going to keep it for us until this all blows over." He kept thrusting the bag at her, jabbing her with it. "Take it, Roxy."

Roxy shook her head to clear it. He said it was the *haul*. "I don't want it."

"Roxy, take the goddamn money, or if we get caught, I'll tell the cops it was all your idea."

The events of last night started to return. "You robbed the liquor store."

Tommy smiled his missing-teeth smile. "And nine other places, Roxy. We were in the zone, baby. We were invincible. We were on a mission."

"Then I for sure don't want it, Tommy." Roxy backed away from the door, her hands in the air as if she were surrendering.

"Like it or not, Roxy, you're already an accessory. This is just going to make it official." And with that, he threw the black garbage bag through the door and took off running, laughing like a madman.

There she was, the girl. She had not come to sit by the river for two days, and Calvin had first missed her, then worried that something was wrong. Had the girl moved away? Had she been in a car accident? Had she fallen ill? But no, there she was, and all his worries had been unfounded. He watched her as she moved through the tall grass and made her way to the riverbank. There was something different about her today, and it took Calvin a couple of minutes to figure out what it was. Oh, yes. She didn't have her big purse with her. Instead, she had a large black garbage bag that she dragged behind her through the weeds. Was this girl of his going to throw trash into the mightiest of rivers? Calvin fervently hoped not. If she did, it would mean he had misjudged her, and Calvin considered himself to be something of an expert when it came to human behavior.

The girl lifted the bag, cradling it in her arms like a baby, and stood staring at the river, still as a statue. Calvin held his breath as he heard the kitchen clock ticking away the minutes. After about fifteen minutes had passed, the girl dropped the bag and began dragging it back the way she had come. Calvin breathed a sigh of relief. He had not misjudged her. And since he had promised himself that the next time he saw the girl, he would speak to her, here was his chance. He stepped out onto the deck of *Shameless* and began to wave, shouting, "Hey, you!"

The girl stopped and turned toward him. Today she wore jeans and a blue t-shirt. Her blonde hair was in a ponytail, which made her look much younger than she usually looked.

Calvin had rehearsed what he would say to her. "You look like you could use a cold drink on such a hot day."

"Are you talking to me?"

"Yes." Who else would he be talking to? No one else was around. It was just the two of them, precisely like Calvin had been imagining it for days. "I made a pitcher of lemonade and wondered if you would like to join me."

The girl cocked her head to one side, assessing the situation. Perhaps she would think it was too dangerous to go onto a houseboat with a stranger. Perhaps she had somewhere else she needed to be, and if so, Calvin would be disappointed. He'd been thinking of her constantly during his time in Liberty, and when he walked into town for the few provisions he needed, he always looked for that blonde hair of hers.

"Do you have any beer?" she asked. "I've never much cared for lemonade."

Calvin nodded vigorously, relief flooding over him. "I have beer."

She shrugged. "Okay, then." She walked to the boat and up the slanted board that Calvin used to get onto dry land. She set the garbage bag down carefully and stuck out her hand. "I'm Roxy."

"Calvin." Up close, she wasn't as fresh-faced as Calvin had imagined. She could be called pretty, but there was something haggard about her appearance. The skin under her green eyes looked bruised.

"I know. I read about you in the *Liberty Gazette*." She followed him into the cabin. "Nice place," she said, looking around.

Calvin didn't know whether she was serious. His rooms were crowded with things he had picked up along the river: a rusted propeller blade, some empty propane tanks, various magazines and papers, and books on the Mississippi. He laughed self-consciously. "I guess you could say it's a typical bachelor pad, a little messy."

Then she asked something that surprised him. "How much does one of these things cost?"

Calvin told her what he had paid for *Shameless*. Then he launched into the story of why he had bought the boat, his near-death experience with cancer, and how he decided that if he was going to kick the bucket, he wanted to do it on the Mississippi River. It was only when he began to wind down his spiel that he realized she must have read the very same thing in the paper. However, she listened attentively and didn't interrupt him. He respected her for that.

"Is it hard to drive?" she asked when he was done.

"Piece of cake." Calvin showed her the steering wheel and the instrument panel. "If you can drive a car, you can drive one of these."

She took the can of Bud that Calvin offered. "Where are you going next?"

Calvin took a sip of his own beer and shrugged. "Wherever the wind takes me."

"I like the sound of that." Roxy clinked her beer against his. "I think a free and easy life would suit me just fine."

Calvin's heart skipped a beat. It almost sounded like the girl wanted him to invite her to go with him when he left Liberty. But he could be wrong. It had been so long since he'd had a meaningful relationship with a woman. Maybe she was flirting with him. Maybe she was teasing him, a man probably thirty years her senior. He smiled uncertainly. "What's not to like about a free and easy life?"

She smiled back. "Where's the most interesting place you've been?"

That's all it took for Calvin to get revved up. He told her that while he'd be hesitant to name a specific place as his favorite, he could tell her about all the wonderful river people he'd met during his journey. Just as Calvin had imagined, she was as avid a listener as the newspaper reporter had been. They finished their beers while he talked, and Roxy got them two more. As he talked, he stared intently at her face, which seemed to grow more hauntingly beautiful the longer she stayed. She asked occasional, intelligent questions, and Calvin couldn't believe that when he finally stopped to take a breath, the sun had dipped low in the sky.

"Goodness, it's late," she said. "I better be getting home and fixing Rosemary her supper."

Calvin knew Rosemary was her mother, she was a hairstylist, and she was twenty-two. Those were the meager facts that she'd revealed. Yet he still felt as if he knew and really understood this lovely young woman, and he liked being in her company. He did not want her to leave. "One more beer?" He tried, unsuccessfully, to keep the desperation out of his voice.

"You're out of beer." She picked up the empty cans and put them by the kitchen sink.

"I'll buy more beer tomorrow." He followed her out to the deck. "Will you be coming back tomorrow, Roxy?" Calvin didn't care if he sounded desperate now. He *was* desperate for her to return tomorrow and the next day and the next.

"Sure." Roxy's voice already sounded as if she were a million miles away, and Calvin didn't know if she meant it or not. She picked up the black garbage bag.

"What's in the bag?" Calvin pointed.

"Nothing," she said hurriedly. "It's not important."

"When I saw you earlier, I thought you were going to throw the trash into the river. I hoped you wouldn't do that—"

"I changed my mind," Roxy interrupted. She had the bag slung over her shoulder like a Santa about to deliver toys.

"I'm glad."

"Me, too."

"So, tomorrow?"

Roxy skipped down the wooden plank without looking back. "Sure."

Calvin watched her until she was out of sight. He didn't think he would ever see that lovely young woman again.

But Roxy did return the next day, and he had the beer ice-cold and ready. She had a few more questions to ask about the boat: How much did it cost to fill it up with gas? How long could it go on a tank? And what about propane? Was there a generator? She asked if he had a pen and paper so she could take notes. No one had ever asked Calvin such specific questions about his boat before, and he felt flattered. He answered all of her questions to the best of his ability.

Then it was Calvin's turn to talk again, and he told her how scared he'd been when he heard he had cancer. He had been afraid to die, he told her. He had been afraid of dying because he had never fully lived. He had never shared those thoughts and feelings with anyone before, but he shared them with Roxy.

He thought she had tears in her eyes as he told his story. Her eyes had a glassy sheen to them, and Calvin was moved by her genuine compassion. "You're a good person," he said to her when he was done with his heart-wrenching tale.

"You don't really know me."

"Oh, but I do. I'm an excellent judge of character, Roxy, and you are a good person." He dared to reach out a hand and pat her shockingly thin arm.

Roxy smiled wanly and then did a surprising thing. She leaned over and kissed Calvin lightly, sadly on the cheek. "I think you're a good person, too."

"'What comes around, goes around.' That's always been my motto." The spot her lips had touched burned hotly on his cheek.

"And I think you're an honest man."

Calvin believed this was true about him as it pertained to other people. He had never deliberately tried to cheat another person out of anything in all the years he owned the dry cleaners. He had never overcharged for services rendered or lost an item of clothing, and he had never tried to cheat the IRS either, always paying what he owed and not looking for any phony deductions. However, when it came to himself, Calvin had not been honest. He had cheated himself out of a full life for far too long. He had convinced himself that the wrong things were important. He had told himself that he didn't need marriage or children to make him happy, and he didn't need love. He had been devastatingly wrong. It was only the wake-up call from cancer that finally made him see the light.

"Because you're an honest man," Roxy continued, "I'm going to ask you a favor. Would you do me a favor, Calvin?"

"It would be my honor to do you a favor, Roxy." Even at this early stage in their relationship, he wanted to tell her that he would do anything she asked. But even he knew that it would be too much to say, too soon."

"I would like for you to keep that black bag for me for a while." Roxy nodded her head toward the deck of the boat, where she'd dropped it before coming into the cabin.

Calvin had thought it was a little strange that she would be carrying around a bag of trash again—was it the same one or another?—when she came to their river today. But then she'd walked through his door, and it was all that mattered. He had quickly forgotten about the mysterious bag filled with "nothing." He was only half-kidding when he said, "I'll guard it with my life."

Her pure smile of gratitude was reward enough. "Oh, thank you, Calvin! I knew I could count on you."

Calvin hoped she would throw her arms around his neck, but when she didn't, he quickly launched into another story about his travels, the one about the young couple in Memphis who took him grocery shopping at the Piggly Wiggly in Olive Branch. Roxy listened, and they drank their ice-cold beers. She stayed as late as she had the day before and rose to leave when the sun dipped low in the sky.

"Say, Calvin, I was wondering if you'd want to meet me at the Queen of Hearts drawing at the Legion tonight? It's the most exciting thing to do in this town on a Thursday night, or any night, really. What do you say?"

Could it be? Was this lovely young woman asking him on a date? It sure seemed like it to Calvin, and his words tripped off his tongue. "I, I, sure. I'd like, like that very much."

"Great. I'll see you there at 8:00." She shook her finger at him flirtatiously. "Now don't you be late, you hear?"

"I will be prompt." Calvin struggled to sit up if she wanted to hug him, but she moved to the door.

Once there, she turned. "And promise me you won't look in that bag. There's nothing good in that bag."

"You have my word." He'd managed to stand up and blew her a kiss, but she'd already skipped down the wooden plank, her blonde ponytail bobbing.

"I am in love," Calvin said to the emptiness of the cabin. He wondered if he had loved his wife, who he barely remembered. Deena had been the opposite of Roxy, short, with cropped dark hair. They'd been nineteen, and their marriage lasted nine months before she ran off with one of the dry cleaners' customers. Calvin supposed he had been devastated at the time, but now he couldn't conjure up any feelings about her, one way or the other. One thing he did know, though. He had not felt about Deena the way he did about Roxy. With Roxy, it was love.

It was already 7:00, so Calvin didn't have much time. The first thing he did was bring in the black bag. It wasn't as heavy as he expected, but he didn't look inside. It was not tied shut, but he still didn't look inside. He had promised Roxy, and he would not break that vow. He stuffed it in the narrow space under his bed. Then quickly, he washed his face and hands, put on his finest, a pair of tan Dickey's and a blue plaid shirt, and slicked down his hair with water. He hummed with happiness as he walked down the plank and toward the Legion. This was his first date with Roxy, and he would make it special. He would arrive early and secure good seats close to the action. That would make Roxy happy.

To his dismay, the Legion was already packed when Calvin arrived at 7:45. He didn't see Roxy anywhere in the throng milling about outside, so he pushed his way through the door and then through the thick, sweaty crowd to the bar. The bar was in the front room, along with a pool table and dartboard and tables already filled with people. Behind the bar was a fairly large room. The bulging drum sat on the west side in front of a table where women still sold raffle tickets. Other long tables and chairs facing the drum occupied the rest of the room. All these, too, were filled.

We shouldn't have come here, Calvin thought. For their first date, he should have insisted they do something romantic, like have a picnic on the banks of the mighty Mississippi, the river that had brought them together. Calvin didn't have a phone, nor had he thought to ask for Roxy's number. He had no way to communicate with her, so he would wait. She'd said she would meet him here, and Calvin knew in his heart that she would keep her word. Roxy was like that, honest to her very core.

He wedged himself between two barstools and stood his ground. When he finally got the attention of the bartender, the nice young man who had brought him the six-pack of Bud earlier in the week, he ordered two beers. But all the time, he craned his neck, looking over his shoulder, searching for that blonde hair of hers. The buzzing in the room grew with each passing minute, sounding more and more like a cloud of locusts. By the time he got the bartender's attention again and tried to ask him if he'd seen Roxy, the bartender could only point to his ears and shrug. It was then that Calvin realized he did not know his girlfriend's last name.

Calvin held onto his dying hope like a lifeline. The proceedings started. The initial drawings were for some smaller prizes: a gift certificate to Dave's Market, a toaster oven, $100, $500. Calvin wasn't paying any attention at all to those. He didn't care about money, not even a million dollars, not anymore. Calvin had, perhaps too late, discovered that love was the only important thing in life. He had not yet told Roxy that he loved her—it was much too soon—but he had thought she felt the same way about him. It was time for the main event, and Roxy was still not here.

Roxy wasn't coming. He had only been acquainted with the hauntingly beautiful young woman for a short time, and he didn't really know her at all. Calvin could see now that Roxy had revealed very little information about herself during their time together. He was the one who had done all the talking. Oh, he was a big talker, the fanciful storyteller with his tales of the river people on the Mississippi. Most of the stories he told were true, some merely embellishments of wishful thinking. The realization stabbed Calvin in the heart at the exact moment that a collective groan went up in the audience. No one was a winner tonight. No one had chosen the queen of hearts.

Calvin looked up when the new round of shouting started. The bar area had cleared quite a bit, and he could see that the commotion came from the corner with the dartboard. There, three uniformed policemen handcuffed three of the sorriest-looking people he had ever seen. They looked like they hadn't eaten in days; they looked like they were ill with some contagious, deadly plague. Calvin had seen this type of person, too, along the river.

"Serves those fucking tweakers right," the bartender said behind him.

Calvin turned. "What did they do?"

"They robbed ten businesses in town the other night. God knows that people in this town struggle enough without having losers like that steal from them."

The three men being arrested were no match against the stronger, healthier policemen, but they struggled as they were dragged across the room. One of them sobbed, and another laughed hysterically between repeating the phrase: "They got us, Tommy. They fucking got us, Tommy."

Tommy, the one being dragged in the lead, started shouting his own mantra. "It was all Roxy's idea. She told me to throw those bricks. Where in the hell is Roxy? She's the bitch you should be arresting. It was all Roxy's idea!"

Hers was not a common name. Haltingly, Calvin turned again to the bartender. "Do you know a young woman named Roxy?"

"Roxy Morton? Sure. Some people around here call her Hillbilly H-e-r-o-i-n-e." He spelled it out. "Get it? Hillbilly h-e-r-o-i-n."

Calvin didn't wait another second. He had to get to his houseboat.

Roxy knew she should call the police and tell them who had burglarized the ten businesses in Liberty. But it seemed as if every time she picked up her phone to do so, Tommy had left another menacing text. He would tell the police that the robberies had been all her idea, that she had enlisted the others to help her, and the topper: She was the one holding the loot (which, thanks to Tommy, was true). Roxy had seen enough detective shows on TV to know that just the fact they had a chain text going was probably enough to incriminate her. She didn't know what to do. She was scared.

Her first thought, irrational or not, was to get rid of the money. If the cops couldn't find the end result of the robberies in her trailer, then maybe it would be her word against Tommy's. So she took the garbage bag of money down to the river, planning to dump it. She'd looked inside the bag, and it didn't seem like an exorbitant amount of cash, mostly ones, but Roxy did not want to touch the tainted bills. Tainted money should be thrown away. However, when she got to the river, she couldn't do it. That ill-gotten windfall was still more than she had ever seen in one place at one time, and while tempted, she would not keep it. She thought about returning the money to its rightful owners, but she'd bet her bottom dollar that all of the business owners would say more was stolen than actually was. And there was no sense in pitting citizen against citizen in this town.

And then Calvin waved to her from the deck of his boat, and her thinking took a different track. Roxy did like listening to Calvin's stories. The man certainly loved the sound of his own voice, but the more she looked around the houseboat, the more the idea grew on her that she and Rosemary could be happy there. Plus, the only vacation she and Rosemary had ever taken, to Branson, MO, had been years ago. They could see new places and have new adventures on this boat, just as Calvin had done, while Rosemary could still get around. Rosemary would always be Roxy's number one priority, and that's what sealed the deal to Roxy's way of thinking.

She would ask Calvin if she and Rosemary could join him in his travels on the mighty Mississippi. To Roxy, it would be a perfect plan for all concerned. She could help Calvin take care of the place, and she had a half-baked notion that maybe Rosemary and Calvin would hit it off. She almost asked him that first day they met, but then Calvin ruined everything. He got all moony on her, and the look in his eye gave Roxy the creeps. Calvin used every opportunity he could to touch her, her hair, her arms, her legs, and he brought back memories of the one boyfriend of Rosemary's who she hadn't protected Roxy from. The guy was pretty old, and as soon as Rosemary fell asleep, he pawed at Roxy and tried to tug down her jeans. Roxy tried never to think of that man, but Calvin brought it all back. They couldn't travel with Calvin.

Yet it was truly mean to steal not only a man's boat but also his home. It was not in Roxy's nature to be that unkind, but the way she saw it, she had no choice. She needed to get out of town as quickly as possible. Things were going to boil over soon. Tweakers were not very good at keeping secrets, and one way or the other, she would be implicated. She and Rosemary needed the boat more than Calvin did. Besides, wasn't the moral of all his stories that people along the river were good, kind, and generous? If he had relied on them for the past year, and they had not disappointed, it wouldn't hurt him one little bit to stay in Liberty.

Rosemary was easy. "We're going on a little vacation, Mom. We're taking a cruise down the Mississippi on a houseboat." Roxy told her as they were eating their dinner of frank and beans.

"Ha!" Rosemary laughed. "We don't have the kind of money to do that. Nice one, baby."

"A friend is loaning it to me," Roxy tried.

"You don't have that kind of a friend," Rosemary pointed out.

"Right." Roxy couldn't argue with the truth. "What if I told you that I need to get out of town?"

Rosemary carefully put down her fork and looked Roxy directly in the eye. "That sounds more like the crowd that you run around with."

Even though it was hard, Roxy kept her gaze level. "Yes, that's why we're leaving on a houseboat tonight."

"The man in the paper? Are you going to steal his boat?"

"Yes."

"Now, Roxy." Rosemary shook her head. "That's not right."

"Rosemary," Roxy never called her mom by name unless she was dead serious, "do you remember that time after the old Harley rider spent the night? The next day, you took me to the Saturday matinee and let me have popcorn and a candy bar and a soda? It was like that."

"Oh." Rosemary looked stricken.

"We're taking a vacation on a houseboat," Roxy said firmly.

Rosemary nodded. "Damn right, we are."

Roxy didn't have much time to get everything onto the boat before the Queen of Hearts drawing was over, and she counted on Calvin to wait for her until the bitter end as she hauled their suitcases up the plank. They'd probably brought too much, but Rosemary refused to part with certain things, like the falling-apart quilt her grandmother had made and a shadow box of pictures from Roxy's short stint as a majorette. Roxy, of course, had to bring the tools of her trade, the scissors and brushes, and some boxes of hair dye. All of that went into the boat fairly quickly. It was getting Rosemary up the narrow plank that took some serious time. She was too wobbly to do it by herself, so Roxy ended up finding an old tire on the boat, plopping Rosemary's butt in the middle, and dragging her up the plank.

At 9:10, Roxy started the motor. She held her breath until it coughed weakly to life, and that was when she saw Calvin wading into the river. He was waving his arms and yelling. A sick feeling of disappointment washed over Roxy. He might be able to get on the boat using the side ladder. On the bank of the river, where the plank used to dig into the mud, she'd left an envelope with some money from the garbage bag. A note on top read: "With this and the help of river people, you'll be fine, Calvin. Love, Roxy." She had added that last part out of kindness. Had Calvin not seen that she'd been kind?

But Rosemary was on guard on deck. She threw the tire with enough force to knock Calvin off balance. He flailed in the water as a siren screamed closer.

Roxy continued to back out, straightened the boat, and pushed the accelerator to the floor, hoping this old houseboat would be as good to them as it had been to Calvin. And that she and Rosemary, too, could rely on the kindness of river people.

CONSIGNMENT

Mandy perched on a stool behind the counter of Zelda's Consignment Shop, staring moodily out the window. There was nothing more she could do. She had mended the latest box to come in, a collection of little boys' clothes with tears in the sleeves of the t-shirts and knees of the jeans. Then she washed and dried them in the machines she had in the back of her shop before carefully folding the items and putting them in the Boys' section, where they joined the company of equally overly-used clothing. This mother, Darlene Sutton, like all the mothers who had come before her, had wanted reassurances from Mandy that she would get top dollar for the box of worn clothes, and Mandy, as always, had told her that she would try her best. It was the same old, sad story over and over again. When the coal mines shut down, half the people of Liberty were jobless, and even though that had been years ago, it was a blow the town never recovered from. Jobs were still scarce, and pennies were precious.

Mandy shifted on the stool, sighing. She couldn't help poor Darlene even if she wanted to. She barely kept Zelda's head above water, and even she knew she couldn't ask Mr. Winters at the bank for one more loan. It was not that she would be embarrassed to do so; it was that Mr. Winters would be embarrassed for her. He would shake his head sorrowfully and say something along the lines of: "This town needs to keep small businesses like yours going, Mandy, but you've already taken out three loans, and then there's your mortgage to consider. It breaks my heart to tell you *no*, but . . ."

That damn Walmart. Mandy sometimes wished the megastore would burn to the ground. Then perhaps people would come to her store and discover that she had some real treasures here buried among all the worn-out jeans and dresses. She had a faux fox fur jacket and a couple of Jackie O-vintage dresses that Marie Sherman had brought in days before her terrible ordeal. Rumor had it that a man broke into her house. Some said he had been across the street at the American Legion for the Queen of Hearts drawing before he attacked her with a knife and stole the pearls her husband had given her. Some said she was sexually assaulted—the poor woman was in her late 70s—and some said she escaped out the back door. Some said Marie had a nervous breakdown, and some said she moved to assisted living at The Cedars. Any way you looked at it, it was a terrible story. But those vintage dresses Marie brought in were truly beautiful, classic.

It was July 3rd, so business dragged here at Zelda's (but Mandy would bet good money that damn Walmart still had a crowd). Mandy could see across the street to the town square and the gazebo covered in red, white, and blue bunting from her vantage point on her stool. Tomorrow, there would be a Dixieland band on the gazebo and antique cars lined up to be admired. And there would be a parade with marching high school bands and floats and people perched on antique fire trucks throwing out candy. But plenty of people were out and about today, too, riding the rides at the carnival in the nearby park. However, those people weren't making it a point to come into her store. Why had she even bothered to come in today?

Mandy knew the answer to that one. It was because she wanted to save her store. She'd been the sole proprietor of Zelda's for fifteen years now since buying it from its namesake, Zelda, who retired and moved to Florida. And it had been a dream come true for Mandy. When Zelda handed over the keys to the place, Mandy had been naive enough to think that she'd made it. Before, she had worked in a series of menial jobs: food worker in the grade school cafeteria, flower arranger at the local florist, assistant at Tots Daycare, and school bus driver. Owning her own business had seemed an elusive goal, but Mandy had made it happen through hard work and sheer determination. However, despite her best efforts, her store was on the verge of failing. Mandy wasn't glad that Zelda had died, but she was happy that Zelda wouldn't hear about her disgrace if she was forced to give up. So Mandy worked six days a week and kept mending, washing, and drying overly-used clothes, wishing that Walmart would magically disappear.

Her door pushed open, and there stood Trisha. Mandy's first reaction was, *Oh no, not again.* The thought was unkind because Trisha, after all, was Mandy's best friend and had been since high school. However, ever since the jackpot for the Queen of Hearts drawing at the Legion went over a million dollars, Trisha could talk of nothing else.

She did not disappoint. "Please tell me you're going to the drawing with me tomorrow night."

Mandy's stock answer was, *I'll think about it*, but Trisha evidently hadn't heard the news. "Because of the Fourth of July festivities at the park and Legion, they're not holding a drawing this week."

Trisha's face fell, which was saying a lot. Trisha had regular Botox treatments in Carbondale. "I don't know if I can wait for an entire week. This excitement is killing me. I can't sleep. I can't eat."

"You don't eat anyway." Unlike Mandy, who carried an extra twenty pounds since going through early menopause last year at forty-four, Trisha followed a strict high-protein, low-carb diet. She was also married to her elliptical trainer, unlike Mandy, who felt lucky if she could squeeze in a short daily walk.

Trisha eyed Mandy up and down. "All it takes is a little discipline."

"I have discipline—just not when it comes to the fresh donuts at Dave's Market."

"Whatever floats your boat." Trisha shrugged. She sauntered closer to the counter in her high-heeled wedgies, a sly look on her face.

Mandy knew that look all too well. "Don't keep me in suspense. Just tell me."

"I have some news, too. Guess who's back in town?"

Mandy folded her arms over her chest and waited.

"Robert Walker! He's been back in town for about a month now. He's helping his mother clear out her house."

Mandy felt like the wind had been knocked out of her, and she sat back on her stool, hard. She started dating Robert Walker senior year in high school when they were crowned homecoming queen and king. The relationship lasted until the prom. She had loved him fiercely, but he couldn't wait to shake the dust of Liberty off his Nikes and left town shortly after graduation. Mandy hadn't heard anything about him for years.

Trisha looked genuinely distressed. "I'm sorry. I shouldn't have sprung it on you like that. It was just such a shocker. The man disappears for twenty-seven years and then *poof!* He's back in town."

"At least he had the decency to come home and help out his mother."

Trisha looked at her closely. "That's all you're going to say about him?"

"There's nothing to say, Trisha. It's all water under the bridge now. I doubt that we would even recognize each other on the street."

"Right. In high school, Robert was too good-looking for his own good, and now he's probably fat and bald. And you—" Trisha stopped herself short.

She didn't have to say it; Mandy knew. During the last few years, she had let herself go. She didn't look awful—she knew that—but constant worrying had made the crow's feet around her eyes deeper and her hair, now dyed blonde and cut short, thinner. That's what constant worry could do to a person. It made you a shadow of your former self.

"I think you should go and see him."

"Absolutely not!" Mandy slapped her hands down hard on the counter.

"And tell him," Trisha finished.

There were times, like this one, that Trisha just went too far. "Don't you get it, Trisha? It doesn't matter anymore." Unlike her annoying, meddling best friend, Mandy had long ago accepted that there was nothing more she could do.

"Don't fool yourself, Mandy. It matters to you." Trisha turned and walked out with a flourish, slamming the door behind her.

These days, Mandy's primary source of worry was her younger daughter, Clara. Mandy could not remember the last time she had seen her daughter smile, and she sometimes felt that Clara simply refused to be happy. And she wanted everyone around her to be miserable, too. Tonight, apparently, would not be an exception.

"You keep telling me how fat I am, so what do you do? You bring home fried chicken for supper." Clara stared at her accusingly.

"I have never said you were fat." At least Mandy didn't think she had. She thought she'd been subtle about it, fixing more salads and steamed vegetables and refusing to buy Clara's beloved Doritos. When Mandy stopped by Dave's Market after closing the shop, she hadn't given any thought at all to picking up the chicken for dinner. She only wanted something already prepared, fresh, easy. And the chicken had been on sale.

"You say it all the time," Clara argued.

"I do not." Mandy pulled out a kitchen chair and sat tiredly.

"You do."

"For the love of God, can't a man eat his supper in peace?" Neal, Mandy's husband, reached for the bucket of chicken. "If you don't want to eat the chicken, Clara, fix yourself something else to eat."

"I have a couple of Lean Cuisines in the freezer."

"See?" The smug look of triumph on Clara's round face was not becoming. "Mom just proved my point."

"I did no such thing, Clara."

"That's it." Neal wadded up his paper napkin and threw it on the table. "I'm going to the Tastee Freeze to eat." He pushed back his chair and stomped out the back door.

"Now look what you've done." Clara stared out the door for only a second, as if considering whether or not she would follow her father, before reaching for the chicken and putting three pieces on her plate. Then she pushed back her chair. "I'm eating in the family room."

Mandy didn't try to stop her either. What was the point? All her family did anymore was bicker, and when that proved to be too tiring, they avoided each other. It was exhausting. Giving up on the idea of dinner altogether, Mandy decided to pour herself a glass of chardonnay and take it out to the front porch. Thankfully, old Mrs. Schneider, her nearest neighbor on the east, wasn't outside on account of the heat, and Mandy wasn't obligated to make small talk. She sat down in the swing and rocked slowly, thinking.

Clara had always been a little overweight. She took after Neal's side of the family in that regard. They were all tall and big-boned. (Back in the day, when she and Neal still joked around, they called his sisters the Amazon Aunts.) So from the very beginning, Mandy had accepted that Clara would never be a petite girl. It wasn't a big deal; it was just the way things were. Clara hadn't seemed to mind either. She had plenty of friends and was a standout catcher on the girls' softball team. Naturally, Clara sometimes lamented the fact that she didn't have a boyfriend, but Mandy had always told her, without going into any detail, "Trust me, honey, you're better off without a boyfriend in high school."

But six or seven months ago, something changed. Clara quit the softball team and became moody and withdrawn. At first, Mandy wasn't too worried. She just figured Clara had gotten into a fight with one of her friends or something like that. Girls in high school were all drama queens, and Mandy convinced herself that whatever bothered Clara would sooner or later blow over. That didn't happen, and Clara's behavior became even more sullen as she piled on the pounds. Then came the anger. The intensity of this mysteriously-sourced anger frightened and bewildered Mandy, mostly because Clara usually directed it at her.

Mandy begged Clara to tell her what was wrong, but Clara refused. "Nothing," she would say.

"Maybe I could help," Mandy, still begging, had said.

"You can't help, Mom. There's nothing here for you to fix."

That stung. In her family, Mandy was "the fixer," the one who always tried to remedy a bad situation. But Mandy pressed on. "I could make an appointment with a psychologist in Carbondale."

"I am not crazy, Mom!"

"I know that. All I'm saying is that people get depressed, and sometimes it helps to talk to someone who is objective."

"Maybe you're the one who should talk to a psychologist, Mom. Did you ever think of that?"

Mandy had let that go because she was trying so hard to get through to her daughter; she was trying to help her. And Mandy wasn't going to make the same mistakes she had made before. So in desperation, she said, "Why don't you call your sister? Maybe you could talk to her?"

Clara stared at her, incredulous. Her pale blue eyes were large in her round face, framed by uneven dark bangs that Clara had decided to cut herself. The bangs hung as limp and stringy as the rest of her unwashed hair. "Why would I do that, Mom?"

"Because she's a nurse?" Mandy knew she grasped at straws.

"So she says."

"What's that supposed to mean?" Three years ago, Stephanie had sent Mandy a text saying that she was graduating from Barnes School of Nursing in St. Louis. Mandy had been thrilled that her older daughter had found a purpose in life after several false starts. Things had never been easy with her now twenty-seven-year-old daughter, and Mandy had always thought it was because of the circumstances of her birth. Mandy had texted back, asking for details about the graduation. She wanted to attend. Stephanie had not replied.

"Stephanie is a big, fat liar. Every time she says she's going to come home for a visit, she never shows up." Clara had the bowl filled with leftover Halloween miniature candy bars on her lap. Methodically, she unwrapped the next one and popped it into her mouth. The pile of wrappers on the coffee table suggested she had been at it for a while.

"I know you're disappointed she didn't come home for Christmas—"

"Mom," Clara interrupted, "Stephanie hasn't been home for Christmas in *years*! Maybe you really should think about calling that psychologist in Carbondale. For yourself."

Mandy decided to get another glass of wine. On her way to the kitchen, she passed the doorway to the family room and paused. Clara had fallen asleep on the couch while the contestants on *Survivor* ran through a sandy obstacle course. Her body looked enormous, bloated, her ankles and feet swollen. None of her clothes fit, and she had taken to wearing Neal's old flannel shirts and boxer shorts. Laying there, with her arm flung over her eyes and her mouth ajar, she looked just like Neal did when sleeping.

At least that's how Mandy remembered him looking. She and Neal hadn't slept in the same bed for over two years now, ever since he came home one night and said, "I'm not sexually attracted to you anymore, Mandy."

She'd been caught completely off guard. They'd had sex the week before, an early morning, rushed coupling that was over almost as soon as it began. Mandy could think of only one reason for this startling announcement. "Are you cheating on me?"

Neal briefly closed his eyes before speaking, a sure sign that the next thing out of his mouth would be a lie. "No, there's not another woman."

"Who is she?" Mandy tried to concentrate on her anger and ignore the sickening sense of *déjà vu* that washed over her. Neal was her fourth husband. Was she never going to get it right, the complicated business of being married? It seemed that no matter how hard she tried, the fantasy of a happy marriage eluded her.

"There's not another woman."

The fixer in Mandy immediately went into overdrive. "You can see a doctor. They have all kinds of pills now, like Cialis. ED is nothing to be ashamed of. You've seen those commercials." In the various drug commercials for ED, the couples involved were always good-looking, the point being that even attractive people could have sexual problems. They were supposed to make you feel better. They did make Mandy feel better.

Neal's cheeks colored. "I don't have any problems. I mean, that's not it."

"Come on." Mandy grabbed his hand and started to pull him toward the stairs. "We'll prove right now that we don't have problems in the bedroom."

Neal gently extracted his hand. "Mandy, I don't want to sleep with you anymore. That's all there is to it."

Mandy could only stare at him helplessly. "But, but . . ." She couldn't bring herself to ask the question, *Do you still love me?*

Neal kissed her hand. "I'm sure it's just a phase, honey."

The phase had been going on for two years, and Neal had given no indication that he would be moving back into their bedroom soon. Mandy told herself that it was okay, that she was used to it. Who didn't sleep better alone? But on some nights when the loneliness overwhelmed her, she would creep into the den and watch him sleep, silently crying over how everything inevitably went wrong.

Mandy refilled her wine glass and went back to the porch. She sometimes wondered if she had been born unlucky. She was the only daughter in a family with four older sons. Her father, Darryl, eked out a living as a farmer, but his bitterness was too great to be only about the farm. Mandy never did find out what made him so bitter and so mean. He was the type of man who kicked a kitten for no good reason at all (and she had seen him do that). Unfortunately, he passed on that mean streak to her brothers, who were too ornery to ever amount to much of anything. Ina, her poor mother, died when Mandy was four, and Ina probably thought the day of her death was the happiest day of her life. She was no longer a punching bag. She no longer had to be a slave to a household of ungrateful, foul-mouthed, punch-drunk rednecks. Mandy still put flowers on her grave every Memorial Day, but not the others who rotted in hell beside her. Those, she left barren.

Another glass of wine later, Mandy waved when Neal pulled into their narrow driveway, heading to the garage at the back of the yard. He returned the wave, but Mandy knew he would not come out and sit on the porch with her. They didn't do that together anymore either, and Mandy missed those shared moments out here on the porch swing more than she missed the sex. Not that she would tell Neal how she really felt about the lack of either. Because of how she'd been brought up, it was not her style to freely volunteer how she felt. No, she was the type of person who pasted a smile on her face and got on with things. She knew full well that it did no good to bellyache, especially with Neal. Neal tended to tuck tail and run at the very idea of a woman complaining.

And Mandy wanted to hold onto Neal. Despite the lack of sex—and companionship, for that matter—he was good to her. Mandy knew she had set the bar extremely low with her first three husbands, but everyone in town knew Neal Tanner was a decent man. He worked at Damon's RV World by Walmart, and it was common knowledge that if you wanted to buy an RV, you went to Neal.

Some years Neal made good money, and some years he didn't. Mandy tried not to worry too much about the lean years, although it did seem as if there had been more lean years than fat. And this year, so far, had been downright skinny. June and July were usually good months for RV sales, but Neal didn't bring home fat paychecks. When Mandy asked him about it, Neal just shrugged and said he guessed it was because everyone wanted to buy timeshares now. It was yet another reason to worry, and another reason she needed to keep Zelda's afloat.

But no matter what, they had their house, and that greatly consoled Mandy. Thanks to his parents' frugality and hard work, they passed on a debt-free house to their only son. Neal's two sisters bitched and moaned a little about it, but there was nothing they could do. It was in black and white in the will. The house wasn't fancy by any means, but it was considered fairly large by Liberty standards, with its three bedrooms, two bathrooms, and a separate family room. By far, it was the grandest house that Mandy had ever lived in. The first time she set foot in the place and saw the mahogany staircase and floral wallpaper in the dining room, she knew she'd marry Neal. She'd always wanted to live in a decent house, and the fact that Neal was also decent sealed the deal for her.

It had grown dark, and the mosquitoes whined above her head. Mandy didn't want to go in, but the thought of tracking down some bug spray seemed too daunting a task at this time of evening. Besides, she planned on being at the shop early the next morning. The idea had come to her sometime during the second glass of wine. She should decorate her store. People loved that sort of thing on the holidays, and maybe, if her front window looked promising enough, she could entice some of the revelers inside after the parade. She could even offer free lemonade and sweet tea. That ought to do the trick. People always loved to get something for nothing; it was a fact of human nature. So Mandy's first stop tomorrow morning would be the Dollar Store to buy some crepe paper and glitter.

Mandy washed her wine glass out at the kitchen sink and put it in the drainer on the counter. On her way to the mahogany staircase that she still loved, she decided to take one last peek into the family room to check on Clara. The nightly news droned on the TV, and Clara hadn't changed positions. The girl had been napping for three hours now, and that spelled out one thing to Mandy. Clara was seriously depressed. It wasn't like she had done anything taxing enough during the day to wear herself out. She'd gotten a part-time summer job at the Cake Mix Factory sweeping up the powdery floor but had quit after two days. Mandy would have to do something about the situation. If Clara wouldn't see a psychologist, maybe Mandy could get online and find a self-help book about maintaining a positive attitude. That's what her daughter needed—a lesson in attitude adjustment.

Mandy tip-toed across the floor, side-stepping the candy wrappers and an empty Ruffles bag. She and Clara were going to have a serious discussion to-morrow about attitude adjustment and cleaning up after yourself. Enough was enough. She would be kind, yet firm. She would tell Clara, *This has got to stop.* She turned from the TV, a gasp catching in her throat. Clara had shifted slightly, and Neal's old flannel shirt had hiked up on her stomach. The tautness of the white skin on Clara's lower belly looked vaguely familiar, vaguely threatening. But no, Mandy told herself, it couldn't be. Clara didn't have a boyfriend; Clara had never even had a date. Not that teenagers dated anymore. They "hung out," or whatever. As far as Mandy knew, when Clara "hung out," she did so with a group of girlfriends.

Without pausing to think about it, Mandy walked swiftly to the couch and lifted Clara's shirt. She was a large girl and had always had a bit of a tummy, so could it be that Mandy had just not noticed the roundness or that the shape of her stomach had taken on a more pronounced form? The gasp escaped her throat this time.

Clara's eyes flew open at Mandy's touch, and she struggled to sit up. "What are you doing, Mom? Get your hands off me!"

Mandy had tried so hard not to let her daughters make the same mistakes she had made or get caught in the traps that loomed large for all women, especially in small, rural towns. She'd pushed too hard with Stephanie and driven her off, but she'd thought that with Clara, she was finally getting it right. And now this.

Clara ripped the shirt from Mandy's outstretched hands. "What in the hell are you doing, Mom?" Her face held a moment of fear before the impassive mask returned.

"You're pregnant." Mandy was breathing hard, trying to fight back the tears.

"And you're fucking crazy!" her fifteen-year-old daughter spat back. "Bat-shit crazy."

"You're off the hook, Robert. I lost the baby." That's what she'd said to Robert, her high school boyfriend, on the night of prom. Even at that late date, she still hoped he would act crestfallen, or that he would actually cry and say he'd wanted the baby all along, that they should get married, that he would never leave her. But Robert said, "Are you sure?"

The naked hope in his voice was the final nail in the coffin of their short-lived romance. She'd turned away from him then and said, "Yes, I'm sure, Robert. I was there." She'd been so disappointed, hurt, and terrified—a Molotov cocktail of emotion—that she'd lashed back. "And for your information, this is our last date. I'm going back to my old boyfriend. He's the one who truly cares about me."

Mandy didn't have an old boyfriend. All through high school, before she started to date Robert after they were crowned homecoming queen and king, she had made up a story of a mysterious, older boyfriend from out of town. The lie served a dual purpose. Not only was it a means of self-preservation, but it also served as protection for any guys who were thinking of asking her out, even though they didn't know it. If her daddy got wind that she was seeing someone, or God forbid, that a man had touched her, he might get drunk and go after him, her four brothers in tow. All five of them were just mean and crazy enough to do such a thing. So Mandy went out of her way to prevent that possibility from happening.

The strange thing, though, was that her imaginary boyfriend made Mandy very popular. The idea that she was "off-limits" seemed to appeal to all teenage boys with raging hormones, which included every single boy at Liberty High, so Mandy rode the crest of popularity, her secret intact. Then she was crowned queen to Robert's king, and all her defenses came tumbling down when they danced their first dance, and he couldn't stop smelling her hair. She'd had long, blonde, wavy hair to her waist back then, and his fascination with her hair changed everything for her. It was that simple.

She thought she loved him. It was a small high school, and she certainly knew all about his reputation. Everyone called him Scorer, for his exploits on and off the basketball court. And he was cocky because of that and because of his good looks. Mandy, in turn, was fascinated with Robert's dark mop of hair that he constantly shook out of his blue eyes. He had a slim, athletic build, and the way he carried himself made him seem taller than he actually was. It was Robert's confidence that most attracted Mandy to him. As popular as she supposedly was, she was not a confident person, but Robert was. And why not? He came from a good family—his father was a middle school social studies teacher—lived in one of the grandest houses in town, and got good enough grades to land himself a college scholarship. In short, he was everything that Mandy was not.

Robert had already grown tired of her even before she told him she was pregnant. She could tell. All he could talk about was graduating and leaving Liberty. Never once did he mention that he wanted her to go with him. So it was her pride, probably more than anything, that caused her to tell the lie that would change the course of her life. And Mandy, over so many years, had come to deeply regret telling that lie. Essentially, she had let Robert off the hook, scot-free. As far as he knew, he was no longer responsible for anything. Oh, she had thought of marching over to Robert's parents' house during that first miserable year of Stephanie's life, handing over Stephanie, and saying, "Here. She's your granddaughter. Tell Robert that it's his turn to take care of her." But she didn't, and then nice Mr. Walker died in a house fire—with a woman who wasn't his wife—and Mandy couldn't bring herself to do it. Time passed, and the opportunity wasn't there anymore.

Mandy didn't want to tell her father, and as it turned out, she didn't have to. She was small-boned, and inevitably, she woke up during her fourth month, and her belly had "popped." She tried to cover it with an old housedress of Ina's she'd found in a box in the musty attic before hustling down the stairs to start breakfast. That's what she'd been doing in the weeks since graduating. She'd been cooking and cleaning, trying to soften up Daddy for when the news finally broke. It didn't work.

"Morning." Mandy fried bacon at the stove, but she heard his heavy footsteps behind her.

"Get me some coffee." Daddy's voice sounded gruff. He'd been up late drinking whiskey the night before, railing at CNN and "the goddamn liberals ruining this country."

Without thinking, she reached for the coffee pot, poured a cup, and turned. She realized her mistake immediately, as his face went from hungover slack to purple rage. She would try to explain, even though she knew it was useless. "Daddy."

"Who. Is. Responsible. For. This." Each word punched the air like a jackhammer.

She'd known he would ask. Of course he would ask. Her words tumbled out, futile as they were. "You don't know him. He's from another town. It was a mistake, Daddy."

"I will kill the sonofabitch." Now his words were calm, deliberate, and infinitely more frightening.

Instinctively, Mandy backed away, knowing what would come. She had entertained a fleeting hope that Daddy would not hit her in this condition. She should have known better. Daddy lashed out at everyone, all the time. Once, when he caught Fred, her least favorite brother, trying to sneak into her room, he'd punched Fred so hard and repeatedly in the face that he never looked the same again. His nose now was off-center and crooked, and one smashed cheekbone never did heal properly. Fred, of course, never went to the ER; none of them ever did. So Daddy took that as a license to hit anyone who provoked him. Which happened to be everybody, eventually. Being around Daddy felt like walking on eggshells all the time.

Daddy did hit her, but it was only one hard slap. Then he picked her up from the corner she cowered in and shook her so hard that she thought her neck would break. Her mouth filled with blood when she bit her tongue, and then the blood began to seep out of the corners of her mouth. But Daddy didn't stop, and that's when Mandy understood. Daddy was trying to shake the baby out of her, wasn't he? Mandy didn't know if that was even possible, but Daddy panted and shook and grunted and shook; he was a man on a mission. His hot breath on her face still smelled like whiskey. Mandy tried to scream, but she couldn't get enough air in her lungs. However, the tears had no problem escaping and mixing with the blood on her face.

Mandy would never know what made him finally stop, but he did stop suddenly, and she fell to the linoleum floor like a limp dishrag. "Goddamn it." Daddy's face was red with exertion. "Why'd you have to go and get yourself in this condition?"

Mandy shook her head, too afraid to speak. She kept swallowing mouthfuls of blood.

"I expected better of you than this." He nudged her newly rounded stomach with the toe of his work boot. "Those brothers of yours ain't worth shit, but you? I expected more from you, Mandy Lee." He swiped at his eyes with his forearm.

Was Daddy crying? Mandy stared at him, transfixed. She had never seen the man cry before, not even when Ina died. On the day of Ina's funeral, Daddy got so drunk that he tripped on a mound of dirt and almost fell into the grave with the casket. Her brothers thought it was the funniest thing they ever saw until Daddy came up swinging. Then everyone scattered, leaving the bewildered minister holding his Bible and saying Ina's eulogy to no one at all.

"I'm going to ask you one last time, Mandy Lee. Who's the sonofabitch who did this to you?"

"He moved away," Mandy whispered, which was true. Robert had already left town, so he was safe. Daddy never traveled outside of Liberty if he could help it.

Daddy stared at her intently. "Are you telling me the truth?"

"Yes."

Daddy gave her one more hard look and then turned and walked as slowly as a man walking through a knee-deep creek to the back door. Mandy didn't know what he would do next, but she felt almost lucky that she'd escaped the incident with only a thorough shaking. She was still young enough, naive enough, to hope that the worst had passed. Mandy could bide her time here on the farm for the next few months until she had the baby. Then she would give it up for adoption and move somewhere far enough away that Daddy and her dreadful brothers would never find her. That was her plan.

It wasn't Daddy's. He came home later that day drunk again, or perhaps still drunk, with Sam Nelson, a distant cousin whom Mandy had only met a couple of times. He'd been "away" for a few years and liked to tell people that he'd been in the Navy. Mandy suspected Sam's Navy was a euphemism for jail, but it was something she would never ask in their short, doomed marriage. Sam was nearly thirty, tall and thin to the point that he looked malnourished. He also still sported a dirty blonde mullet. A neck couldn't get any redder than Sam Nelson's.

"Put on a dress," Daddy told her. "We're going to the courthouse."

Mandy could only stare at Daddy. Everybody knew Sam Nelson had never worked an honest day in his life, and it was like the next eighteen months unrolled in front of her like a dirty rug. Sam would become Daddy's best drinking buddy while the farm went to hell, and he would probably treat her as poorly as he did his hound dog. He would be one more mouth to feed, one more load of laundry per week, and another pair of fists to avoid.

Daddy, beaming, clapped Sam on his scrawny shoulder. "Sam here has agreed to take you on, Mandy Lee. Today is your wedding day."

The red, white, and blue crepe paper from the Dollar Store, now draped in Zelda's front window, did not have the desired effect. Neither did the cardboard sign promising free lemonade and sweet tea. The parade had ended two hours before, and although the sidewalk had been crowded with people, none had ventured into Mandy's store to sift through her immaculately cleaned and mended used clothing and chipped kitchenware. Instead, all of her potential customers were at the antique car show or the park drinking beer and eating the VFW's fish sandwiches. Mandy had always thought there was something strange about the attraction those sandwiches had for folks on the Fourth of July. They consisted of a frozen piece of cod deep-fried in a vat of sizzling grease and two slices of Wonder Bread. That was it, yet people looked forward to those plain sandwiches all year long.

However, mulling over her lack of customers in her lonely store suited Mandy. It was infinitely preferable to being at home with her possibly pregnant fifteen-year-old daughter and neglectful husband. The morning had not gone well. After she had pounded on Clara's locked bedroom door for a solid ten minutes, begging her to come out and talk to her, Mandy had admitted defeat. "Fine," she called through the door, "you win this round, young lady. However, we are going to have a serious discussion tonight when I get home from work. And I will not take *no* for an answer."

She'd already brewed her second cup of coffee by the time Neal appeared in the kitchen. He wasn't working today because Damon's RV World was closed, or so he said. "What was all that commotion about?"

"We need to talk to our daughter."

"We talk to her all the time." Neal plopped a pod of coffee in the Keurig.

When had her husband become so indifferent? Mandy wondered. Could he not see that their daughter was pregnant? But she stopped herself before she could voice those thoughts. She, too, had been oblivious until last night. "I think Clara is pregnant."

Neal, to Mandy's dismay, laughed. "Don't be ridiculous, Mandy. I know she's put on a few extra pounds, but come on. She doesn't even have a boyfriend."

"Clara doesn't need a *boyfriend* to get pregnant, Neal. Any male on any night could impregnate our daughter."

Neal blew on his coffee before taking a sip. "And how did you reach this outlandish conclusion, Mandy?"

Her husband could be so damn maddening. Usually, Mandy liked how deliberate he was about things, how steady, but not when it came to something this important. And damn him because he looked so good right now. Two years ago, right about the time Neal informed her that he wasn't sexually attracted to her anymore, he'd started going out to the garage and getting on the stationary bike that had sat idle for years. He dropped weight, and while he was still a large man, he certainly looked more muscular than paunchy these days. And his hair. He was in his mid-fifties, but he was no longer all gray. Instead, his hair was back to his original dark brown, with just a hint of gray at the temples. Her husband had started to dye his hair, and she had failed to notice.

Mandy shook her head. She needed to get her thoughts in order. "Last night, before I went to bed, I went in to check on Clara. Her shirt had inched up, and I could see her belly."

"How much of her belly?"

Mandy let out an exasperated sigh. "An inch, maybe two? I don't know, Neal, but all the signs point to her being pregnant: the weight gain, the moodiness, the withdrawal from her friends. Don't you see?"

"How much wine did you drink last night, Mandy?"

"Two glasses." Maybe she had three. Mandy couldn't remember, but he was missing the point. "And that has nothing to do with what I saw. I *know* what I saw, Neal."

"Do you remember the time after the Ratherts' Christmas party when you swore up and down that you saw a raccoon in our bedroom?"

"This is not even remotely the same situation." She'd had way too many glasses of rum punch that night, and while it was an embarrassing, perhaps even funny story, it didn't apply here.

"And it turned out to be one of your fuzzy slippers," Neal continued. "All I'm saying is that you sometimes hallucinate when you've been drinking."

"I do not!" Not only was Neal being far too nonchalant about this situation, but he was also being unfair. Mandy didn't drink very often, and once she thought her fuzzy slipper was a raccoon. So what? He wasn't comprehending the gravity of this situation, but then again, he was a man. He'd never had to face an unwanted pregnancy when he was scared, tired, and alone.

"How many lights were on in the family room when you saw the inch of Clara's stomach?" Neal removed the lid from a cup of Dannon's yogurt. Her husband had now become a man who ate yogurt for breakfast.

Mandy wasn't about to tell him that the only light in the room, other than that from the TV, was the small floor lamp in the corner. "Why are you grilling me? I know what I saw, Neal." However, his questions started to raise some doubts in her mind. Clara had freaked out when Mandy asked her if she was pregnant, and she had flat-out called Mandy *crazy*. Was it possible that the shadows in the room had caused her to see something that wasn't there?

"All I'm saying is that I think you sometimes try to find something to worry about."

Mandy could only stutter that she was leaving for work before grabbing her purse and rushing out the door. That was probably the most hurtful thing Neal had ever said to her, and it was completely unwarranted. She didn't want him to see her break down in tears, nor did she want to say something that she would later regret, so she had to leave immediately. Their marriage, Mandy could see now, was on even shakier ground than she had thought.

Not having anything else to do in the store, Mandy poured herself a glass of sweet tea, perched herself on the stool behind the counter, and stared moodily out the window once again. Maybe Neal was right. Maybe she did find things to worry about. It was an unsettling and unwelcome thought, one that Mandy quickly dismissed. Perhaps the problem was that she had been worrying about the wrong things. Instead of her overweight daughter, Mandy should focus more on her marriage to a man who now ate yogurt for breakfast and dyed his hair. The only reason Mandy didn't think he was having an affair was that she would have heard about it. Nobody in this town could keep a secret when it came to something like that, especially Trisha. Trisha would be the person who would come running to Mandy if she heard anything about Neal fooling around. Mandy knew that with certainty. Neal wasn't cheating on her. He just didn't want her anymore. And that, unfortunately, was infinitely worse.

Mandy had been wrong. She recognized him immediately. Robert Walker crossed the street, his hand cupped around his mother's elbow as he guided her over the uneven pavement. He still carried himself like an athlete, and although he had filled out some, he was still relatively thin, especially compared to a lot of the men in this town, who sported beer bellies hanging over their belt buckles. His dark hair was shorter with sprinkles of white, and he didn't have that endearing forelock flopping into his eyes anymore, but it was definitely Robert. And he was headed toward the store.

Mandy wasn't prepared for this meeting. She had long ago concluded that she would never see him again, and she had long ago accepted that she had missed her opportunity to let him know he had a daughter. But she did not think of that now. Dressed in pressed jeans and an expensive-looking polo shirt, he looked handsome, accomplished, successful. She suddenly felt dowdy and unattractive and middle-aged. She needed to lose twenty pounds and kept putting off any pretense of dieting. Plus, she'd put on a pair of unflattering jean shorts this morning, and her flip-flops announced to the world that she hadn't had a pedicure in quite some time. Robert looked up as he stepped up the curb directly in front of her window, and his eyes met hers.

Instinctively, Mandy ducked behind the counter. It was such a juvenile thing to do that Mandy immediately regretted it. She could feel the hot flush spread across her cheeks, which made the situation even worse. Yet she still clung to the hope that he hadn't seen her through the window. Perhaps the glare from the sun made it impossible to see inside. Perhaps her homemade sign offering free lemonade and sweet tea didn't look as amateurish as it probably did, and her crepe-paper decorations weren't as gaudy as she knew they were. Mandy, crouched behind the counter and breathing heavily, clung to the last shred of hope that Robert hadn't been heading to her store but to the laundromat next door.

But she'd never been a lucky person. The bell above the door tinkled, and Mandy felt the whoosh of hot, humid air. And then the still familiar voice calling, "Hello? Are you open for business?"

"Just a second." Her voice sounded wobbly. "I'm… doing inventory." Mandy frantically combed at her hair with her fingers and wiped her damp face with her t-shirt. Naturally, it was one of the few days she hadn't bothered with makeup. She'd been too preoccupied with Clara and then too mad at Neal to bother.

"Now, Mother," Mandy could hear Robert say, "we're not here to buy anything today. Please put those cow salt and pepper shakers down. You already have a collection of those things that we need to get rid of."

Mandy took a deep breath to steady her nerves and hoisted herself up by holding onto the edge of the counter. It was not a graceful movement that brought her face to face with Robert Walker, her first love and the father of her firstborn, after twenty-seven years. "Hello, Robert," she said. "It's been a long time."

Robert kept his eyes on his mother as if he were afraid that, unwatched, she would manage to smuggle every item out of the store. "Are you Zelda? My mother is in the process of moving to a smaller place, and rather than give some of her possessions to Goodwill, we thought it would be nice if she could make a little profit." He lowered his voice. "A lot of her stuff isn't worth anything, but it would make her happier to get something for her so-called treasures."

So Robert either hadn't seen her through the glare on the window, or he had and didn't recognize her. Mandy cleared her throat. "It's me, Robert."

Robert's eyes swiveled to Mandy, and a slow recognition dawned over his face. "I'll be damned. Mandy Malone. I didn't, I mean, I wasn't expecting… Well, I'll be damned. Mandy Malone." And then he stuck out his hand. "It's good to see you."

Mandy stared at his outstretched hand. That was all he would offer after twenty-seven years of abandonment? "I think we can do better than that after all this time, don't you?" And she reached across the counter to hug him. But it was awkward, more like a long-distance grappling, and it was Robert's turn to look embarrassed.

Robert shifted on his feet, took a step back. "Uh, how have you been, Mandy Malone?"

"It's Tanner now." At Robert's blank expression, Mandy babbled on. "Before that, it was Gray, and before that, it was Beckman, and before that, it was Nelson."

A smile crept across his face. "Wow. You've got me beat. I've only got two divorces under my belt."

His smile wasn't the same. This one was slower, somehow sad, and lacked Robert's former swagger. Over time, she might like this new version better. "I think this one's a keeper. I've been married to Neal for seventeen years."

"Lucky him."

Mandy took a sharp intake of breath. She didn't know what he meant by that remark. He might be kidding her, or he might be implying more. Maybe he was flirting with her? If so, she was woefully out of practice, but she smiled back. "You'd have to ask him."

"How much would you take for this scarf?" Robert's mother Angela asked, holding up a multi-colored, handknit wool scarf.

"Please put that back, Mother," Robert said tiredly.

"You can have it for free, Mrs. Walker," Mandy said.

"Put it down, Mother." Then Robert turned back to Mandy and lowered his voice. "She's something of a hoarder. I've been here for three weeks now and can barely get her to part with a broken shoelace. I knew it would be tough, but not like this." Robert shrugged.

Mandy nodded. "Families can be tough." She liked this new Robert, who didn't act like he had all the answers.

Politely, Robert asked, "How's your family? I remember you lived with your dad and brothers."

"They're all gone," Mandy said quickly. Robert arched his brows, and Mandy added, "It was a house fire."

"It's always a fire around here, isn't it? These old houses, with their faulty wiring and rotting timber . . ." He trailed off, thinking about his own daddy, Mandy supposed.

Mandy's phone rang, and of all people, it was Clara. She should take the call because she needed to talk to her daughter. However, Robert was here; he had finally returned. Mandy didn't pick up the phone. "It's my daughter," she explained to Robert, who hadn't asked who it was. "My younger daughter. My older daughter lives in St. Louis. She's a nurse."

"That's nice," Robert said politely, but he seemed more interested in checking out the display of troll dolls by the cash register. Mandy had been collecting them for years, and they weren't for sale.

"She said I could keep the scarf." Angela still held the scarf to her cheek like it was precious and not moth-eaten and stained.

Robert's jaw was set, and through gritted teeth, he said, "Fine, Mother. You can keep the damn scarf."

Mandy was losing his interest—again. "Do you have any kids?" She tried to keep the desperation out of her voice.

Robert looked up from the troll collection. "Uh, no. I guess it wasn't in the cards for me."

Now was her opportunity. She could tell him, *Oh, but it was in the cards for you, Robert. You have a daughter.*

But Robert beat her to the punch. "Speaking of cards, do you go to that Queen of Hearts drawing every week?"

Mandy shook her head. She couldn't speak.

"Yeah, me neither. It's like the whole town has caught a highly contagious virus, but I have a feeling it's going to get worse when someone finally wins. Most of the people in Liberty have already mentally spent the money, and when they inevitably lose, the disappointment will make them even crazier. Disappointment makes people crazy," he repeated.

"I don't know about that." Mandy's disappointment had already sprouted, but she didn't feel crazy. She felt slightly ill.

Robert glanced over at his mother, who now had the two Jackie O-vintage dresses over her arm. "I better get her out of here before she talks me into letting her take home any more crap."

"Those dresses aren't crap," Mandy said quietly.

"Oh, sorry. I didn't mean it like that. I'm just tired of losing this war with her. My sister is supposed to be here any day now to help, but who knows?" Robert smiled his sad, slow smile. "I'll bring over some of Mother's stuff in a couple of days. It was good to see you, Mandy Malone Nelson Beckman Gray Tanner."

Not only had Robert remembered all her married names, but he had also put them in their proper order. A long-dormant spark ignited in Mandy's chest. Without thinking about it, she reached across the counter and repeated the long-distance, grappling hug. This time, Robert seemed to hug her back.

It was the story of her life. An opportunity had presented itself to Mandy, and she hadn't taken it. She should have answered the phone when Clara called earlier, but she had been so hypnotized by the reappearance of Robert Walker that she had not bothered to take the call. Clara was making her pay for that mistake, big time. She was once again locked in her room and refused to come downstairs. She hadn't even bothered to come down for supper, which was a first for her. And it only made Mandy worry more. Was Clara so upset because she was pregnant, or was she furious with her mother for mistakenly thinking that she was because she had gained so much weight?

"I'm sorry I didn't take your call this afternoon," Mandy apologized for the twentieth time as she stood outside Clara's bedroom door. "I was busy with a customer." Clara might or might not have grunted something on the other side of the door, so Mandy pressed on. "But I'm here now, honey. We can talk about whatever's on your mind."

Mandy gave up after another ten minutes and went to finish loading the dishwasher. Neal, still sitting at the kitchen table, had not lifted a finger to help while she was upstairs. But at least he was here and hadn't left to see the fireworks without her. They always took a blanket and joined the many other townspeople who spread blankets and towels over the tombstones in the cemetery to watch the show. The cemetery was the best seat in town on this one night of the year.

"So Clara gains a little weight, and you assume she's pregnant," Neal said, continuing their same conversation as if Mandy hadn't just spent twenty minutes upstairs begging Clara to come out of her room.

"I am not going to repeat this conversation yet again." Mandy scraped the last of the Caesar salad into a container. When she stopped at Dave's Market on the way home from work, she'd decided that it was time for her to start dieting.

She wouldn't let herself closely examine the reason for this, but she couldn't get Robert's sweet, sad smile out of her head.

"It's no wonder she's so mad at you," Neal goaded. He might be sitting, but he seemed antsy. He tapped his feet and drummed his fingers on the table.

"If you're so convinced that I'm wrong, why don't you go up and talk to her?" Mandy rinsed the plates and silverware. She might buy a lot of take-out food, but they always used real plates and silverware, never plastic. It made her feel not quite so guilty.

"That's not my area of expertise."

Mandy turned from the sink. No, it wasn't Neal's expertise. He'd been the indulgent, doting father, and Mandy had always thought it was because he became a father so much later in life than the other men in this town. It was she who had been the disciplinarian, the one who set rules and curfews. After Stephanie, she had learned her lesson the hard way. She'd always backed down with Stephanie, letting her stay out late and hang around with the wrong people. Stephanie said she acted out because Mandy wouldn't tell her who her real father was—and because Mandy had substituted her mythical, perfect, real Daddy with a string of very poor substitutes. Unfortunately, Mandy couldn't argue with that.

She kept her voice calm. "I guess we'll find out sooner or later if she's pregnant."

"What do you mean?" Neal glanced at the clock on the wall.

"If she's as pregnant as I think she is, she will give birth one day soon." The stunned look on Neal's face satisfied her, even if the reason for that look did not.

Neal stared at her accusingly as he rose from his chair. "I've had enough of this. I'm going out."

Mandy watched him leave. It amazed her how quickly he could move when it came to getting away from her. And he was running to someone else. Maybe she was a very slow learner, but it was obvious to her now. She turned back to the sink to finish the dishes and then stopped. Screw the dishes. She grabbed a tall glass from the cabinet and filled it with wine from the Franzia box in the refrigerator. She carried it out and took her place on the swing. Even old Mrs. Schneider next door was probably downtown watching the fireworks. Everyone loved the fireworks. Everyone, that was, but her. It was the sound she couldn't stand, the rumbling, ominous sound that filled the sky, promising to gloriously explode.

It was, as she had told Robert that afternoon, a house fire that killed all the male Malones, but it wasn't an accident. It was arson. Sort of. All Mandy had done was plant the seed in an already deviously fertile mind. And her despicable brother Fred proved to be the perfect candidate.

"You owe me, Fred," she had said to him one night when they were sitting in the backyard. Well, she had been sitting, looking at the stars when Fred, drunk as usual, had plopped down beside her.

"Goddamn it, Mandy. Not that same old shit again."

"I never told Daddy what you did to me for years before he caught you sneaking into my room. Just think what he would have done to you, Fred. I mean, it's bad enough that he ruined your face."

Not only had Fred taken after Daddy in the kicking-the-kitten department, but he also carried serious, seething grudges. According to Fred, everyone in the world had it in for him, and in turn, he despised them right back. Fred gently touched his face. "He made me into a freak, the bastard."

"He did." Mandy nodded into the darkness. "And that has to be the reason you don't have a girlfriend." Mandy thought the real reason Fred didn't have a girlfriend was that he was an inherently unlikeable person, but she had thought long and hard about this plan. Once again, she was living at home after her third divorce, and she needed to get Stephanie away from these people, her family. They were a bad influence on her, and at eight, Stephanie was already a handful, running wild with the boys on the next farm over and telling needless lies. Mandy had caught her red-handed eating a candy bar right before supper, and when she called Stephanie on it, Stephanie crammed the Snickers into her mouth and said she hadn't eaten a candy bar through a mouthful of chocolate. Mandy blamed her daddy and brothers for this behavior. They, too, the bunch of them, were all liars.

"It's his fault," Fred agreed.

"He made you a freak, and if I had told Daddy what you did, he would have killed you."

"The bastard." Fred had gotten up and started pacing around the yard. "He ruined my life."

"Maybe you should get even with him?" Mandy held her breath. She had to convince Fred of this for her plan to work. "Maybe you could threaten him with something."

"I should show that old SOB what's what," Fred yelled. And then he stopped pacing. "But how would I do that?"

"Remember when you used to build pipe bombs?"

"I still know how to do it," Fred boasted.

That's what Mandy counted on, and she also counted on the fact that Fred was careless around incendiary devices. In his younger years, he had blown off three fingers on his right hand and set the pasture barn on fire. Mandy also knew premature detonation was a hazard when attempting to construct any homemade bomb. It didn't take much more coaxing to convince Fred that he should go back to his hobby and that the barely used basement in the house would be the perfect place to build his crude bombs.

Mandy left with Stephanie the next day, temporarily moving in with Trisha until she could get her own place. She didn't know if her plan would work, and she knew she certainly couldn't trust Fred. But Mandy had planted the seed, and for the first time in her life, Mandy felt free. She would never go back to that house of horrors filled with drunk, crude, abusive men. She was twenty-six years old, and finally, free. Weeks went by, and Mandy almost forgot about the discussion with Fred. When the house inevitably went up in flames, Mandy acted as surprised as everyone else. And then, like everyone else, she quickly forgot about it.

Mandy hadn't thought about her daddy and brothers in years, not until Robert asked about them today. She was not sorry for whatever role she had played in that house fire. Instead, she thought of it as one of the few times in her life that she had made a decision and then acted upon it. She'd stood up for herself and her daughter when she planted the seed in Fred's twisted mind. And what she had really felt when she heard about the explosion that killed her entire family was satisfaction. Sometimes people did get what they deserved in life, and even if she hadn't planted the seed, the chances were great that the old farmhouse would have eventually gone up in flames from a dropped lit cigarette from one of the five drunk men. The chances were great.

Mandy was about to refill her tall glass of wine when she saw the picture of nine-year-old Stephanie on the refrigerator. She had looked at that picture for years but had not really seen it. And now, as Mandy studied it closely, she saw how much Stephanie resembled Robert. She had his dark hair and aquamarine eyes, and her tiny smile had that secretive, know-it-all look that Robert had in high school. Mandy had denied Stephanie the opportunity to ever know her real father, and both she and Stephanie had suffered for it. And perhaps Robert had suffered, too. Hadn't she detected an aura of loneliness around him today? Wouldn't he be happy to know that he wasn't alone in the world anymore, that he had a daughter who would love him more than she had ever loved anybody else?

Mandy snatched the picture from underneath its magnet. It had faded, sure, but Stephanie's resemblance to Robert was undeniable. When Robert saw the picture, he would finally know the truth, and Mandy felt certain that everything would change for the better when that truth finally came to light. She could hear the distant rumblings of the fireworks when she stepped off her front porch, the picture clutched in one hand, and for some reason, the empty wine glass in the other. Robert's family home was on Waverly, not too far, but it seemed to take Mandy forever to get there. She walked as fast as she could, but everything—the waving tree branches, the flight of a robin, a leaf falling to the ground—seemed to be moving in slow motion as she passed through the familiar streets.

She stepped onto Robert's small front porch with its four white columns. It was strange that she had never been here before. Even when she dated Robert in high school, he had never invited her over for a Sunday dinner or a family barbecue, and she wondered for the first time if he had been ashamed of her. She had not been brought up in a respectable family as he had, nor did her family participate in ordinary things like going to church or chatting with people on the way to the post office. She had her hand up to rap on the front door, but she paused. Maybe, after all this time, she was making a mistake by bringing Robert this gift.

"Hey, Mandy." It was Robert, coming around the side of the house. "What a surprise."

Mandy found her voice. "You have no idea." The picture shook in her hand. "I have something to show you."

"Um, sure," he said uncertainly. The puzzled expression on his face did not look welcoming.

"Here," and she thrust the picture at him.

"Who's this?" He frowned as he looked at the faded photo.

"My daughter, Stephanie." Too late, she realized she should have said, *our daughter.*

He glanced at the picture without a shred of recognition passing over his face. "Cute kid." He handed it back to Mandy.

"Don't you see?" she begged. She willed Robert to recognize his own flesh and blood. She had come so far to get here.

"See what?"

Angela was at the front door. "I thought I heard someone out here. I thought it was that boy across the street who keeps ringing my bell and running away."

"It's just me, Mother." Robert turned back to Mandy. "See what?"

As they stood under the porch light, Mandy could see that he looked much older than he had this morning. She hadn't noticed the wrinkles around his eyes, and dressed in baggy shorts and a t-shirt, he looked like every other average guy in this town. He was nothing like she remembered and reimagined over the years. Robert, she could see now, was nothing special.

"Never mind." Mandy turned and stepped off the lighted porch, back into the darkness of night. It was too late. She could not offer up Stephanie to Robert like a piece of used and patched clothing and ask him to give her a second chance. He did not deserve even that.

THE DRUNKEN POET

The small town of Liberty, Illinois, boasted about its five churches on signs leading into and out of town on Route 7. It did not boast of its taverns, of which there were seven. Nor did it boast about the drunken poet, as the town referred to Mitchell McHenry, although many people frequenting the busy taverns found him to be amusing enough. After a proper number of beers, and if someone bought him a shot of Jack, the old man could be coaxed to climb precariously upon a barstool and recite: "O Captain! My Captain! Our fearful trip is done, / The ship has weather'd every rack, the prize we sought is won." If the bar patrons caught Mitchell early enough in his nightly drinking process, his voice rang out deep and resonant and sure. If they asked him too late, the timbre of his voice was not quite as grand, his stature not as rigid, and they might have to catch him before he swayed himself right off the barstool. They would laugh, clap him on the back, and buy him another drink.

Other than his resonant recitations of Walt Whitman's "O Captain! My Captain!" or "When Lilacs Last in the Dooryard Bloom'd" or "Out of the Cradle Endlessly Rocking" or "Song of Myself," Mitchell was a quiet man. His performance finished, Mitchell would nurse as many beers as he could afford or that the kinder patrons would buy. Naturally, all the bartenders in town were well acquainted with Mitchell, but even they knew little about the man. He lived in one of the four duplex apartments on Pine Street, but when he wasn't out drinking, he kept to himself. He could sometimes be seen puttering around in his small front yard, but that was rare. And another strange thing about the man was that he didn't even have a car, which was unheard of in these parts where you had to drive miles and miles to get to any city of note. But Mitchell always walked home from the taverns after drinking his fill. People used to ask the man if he needed a lift, but after years of refusals, they stopped asking.

As far as anyone in Liberty knew, poor Mitchell McHenry didn't have a family, which was a very sad state of affairs indeed. Mitchell didn't offer up any stories about a wife who ran away or succumbed to cancer, nor did he recount any stories of now-grown children who were too busy or self-absorbed or selfish to come and visit. What's more, people didn't even know the man's exact age, and estimates ran anywhere from fifty to eighty. With his long, gray shaggy hair and beard, a baggy tweed jacket and brown corduroy trousers covering his rail-thin frame winter and summer, the man's age was indeterminate. The man had a pronounced limp, and some speculated that it was an old war injury, others that the man must have had polio as a child. The townspeople didn't dwell on the man's mysteries, however. As long as the drunk bum kept to himself, there wasn't a problem. The man wasn't a mean or belligerent drunk, so they let him be.

Brad Taylor knew a man named Mitchell McHenry was Liberty's drunken poet, of course. But tonight was the first night he'd ever sat at a bar at the same time as the man. There was a very good reason for that. Brad, as a rule, didn't frequent the town's taverns. Number one, his mother, with whom he still lived at the embarrassing age of twenty-eight, did not approve. And number two, Brad, at least in his own mind, had a reputation to uphold in this town. He was one of the three reporters working for the *Liberty Gazette,* and he took that job very seriously. The other two guys, Moody and Chuck, were in their fifties and cheerfully admitted they were too damn old to go chasing down stories. They waited until they got a call from the volunteer fire department about a house or barn fire. Or they waited until someone physically walked through the doors of the newspaper office, offering news about what was happening that week at the senior citizen center or the weekly arrests—mostly DUIs, domestic battery, trespassing, and drug-related charges.

But Brad, as the youngest, still took the job very seriously. When he enrolled at SIU-Carbondale, he'd known from the get-go that he would major in journalism. And Brad had always wanted to be a reporter, not a newscaster. He had set his sights on papers in larger towns, like Murphysboro or Vandalia or even St. Louis, but when that didn't pan out—not one of those papers offered him a job—he came back to Liberty where he was born and raised and took a job at his hometown newspaper. Never mind that it was a small-town operation. And never mind that the publishing industry seemed to be in rapid decline. Brad took his job very seriously, even going so far as to think of himself as a real investigative reporter. He knew Moody and Chuck thought he was "an overly ambitious little prick." He'd overheard them use that term more than once, but Brad ignored them. His goal was to excel at this job.

The only problem, though, was that in a town this small, the meaty, juicy stories were few and far between. The highlight of Brad's career so far was when he got the chance to interview Calvin Phillips, a man who had been told he was dying of cancer but then miraculously lived. So he bought a houseboat named *Shameless* to travel up and down the Mississippi River. He told Brad a lot of interesting stories about the people he'd met along the river. Calvin called them river people, and even though Brad suspected that the man fabricated most of it, he had dutifully written a glowing article about Calvin's belief in the goodness of people.

Brad thought it was a good story, if tame, but he hadn't seen anything yet. About a week later, a young local woman named Roxy Morton, a hairstylist at Trudy's Beauty Boutique and well-known opioid addict, commandeered *Shameless*. That was newsworthy enough, but she had somehow managed to get her disabled mother up a plank and onto the boat. The mother, Rosemary, had her own entertaining story. As Brad soon discovered, Rosemary was at one time considered to be something of Liberty's town slut. It was even rumored that she had one time had sex with five men at the same time. As titillating as that tidbit might be, Brad was too polite to include it in the article.

So Brad thought he might be on the verge of something big as the search for Calvin's boat began. Some people were stupid enough and drunk enough from the Queen of Hearts drawing that had just ended at the Legion to go home and got their fishing and motorboats, intoxicatingly determined to chase down Roxy. Liberty's new police officer, Alan Morrison, put a stop to that immediately and declared they would notify the Coast Guard. Everyone was astounded—and a little disappointed—when Calvin tried to put a stop to that. "Roxy will come back to me," he said. Brad noted in his finished story that Calvin had tears in his eyes.

No one believed Roxy and her mother would return. Some people thought she would get high and crash the houseboat before she'd made it to the next town, and others believed she'd sell the boat as quickly as she could to get more money for her hillbilly heroin. But lo and behold, Roxy arrived back the next morning and clumsily maneuvered the boat back to its original position by the bank of the river. Quite a few people had decided to make a night of it and camp on the bank. Most of the people who had gone home to get their boats were too drunk to drive back again in front of Officer Morrison, who would have immediately arrested them for DUIs. Roxy came out onto the deck of the boat and made a public apology to Calvin.

Roxy's exact words were, "I'm sorry, Calvin. I brought your boat back. It was wrong of me to take it, and I'm sorry." Brad, in his article, noted that Roxy sounded very sincere.

"I knew you'd come back." Tears and dirt smeared across Calvin's face. He'd spent the night with his face pressed against the very edge of the bank. In his article, Brad noted that Calvin seemed to be listening for the sound of his boat, or perhaps he was willing Roxy to come back.

By then, Brad had realized Calvin was in love with Roxy, who must have been close to thirty years his junior. And he wasn't surprised by what came next. Embarrassed for the man, yes. Surprised? No.

Calvin got down on one knee, beseeching. "Roxy, will you marry me?"

It had taken a while for Rosemary to hobble onto the deck of the houseboat, but she stood there now. She glanced at Roxy, who wrung her hands. "Now, Calvin, my Roxy here is young enough to be your daughter." Brad thought she might be flirting with the man, but her voice was so raspy from years of heavy smoking that he wasn't positive.

"You are a very nice man, Calvin . . ." Roxy looked at Rosemary to finish.

"But I'm closer to your age, honey. Why don't you come onto the boat, and we can talk about this?"

"I want to marry Roxy," Calvin said.

"Just give me a chance," Rosemary teased.

"Come on, Calvin." Roxy reached out her arms.

And that was all the invitation Calvin needed. He sloshed through the knee-deep water and over to the ladder on the side of *Shameless*. Calvin was still weak from his cancer treatments, so it took both women to pull him aboard. He fell onto the deck in a heap, but both women helped him up. All three of them walked into the cabin. Brad, tempted to slosh through the water to get the story, wanted to hear what was happening inside that small, cluttered, sad cabin. He would have, too, for the sake of good journalism, but he kept hearing his mother's voice in the back of his head, the one that told him to *respect people's privacy*. Since that admonition went against everything good journalism entailed, Brad usually ignored it. But unfortunately, he listened to it while on the brink of the best story of his career. Twenty minutes later, the boat left its makeshift dock, Calvin at the helm, the two women on either side of him waving at the sizable crowd.

Brad could only imagine what the content of their three-way conversation had been. As a journalist, though, he could not speculate. However, if he were to speculate, he would like to imagine that somewhere in their short journey up the Mississippi, Roxy and Rosemary had realized they would not get far before someone apprehended them. They might have realized they were better off having Calvin with them than without them. And Brad would like to think that right before they turned back to Liberty, Rosemary, the former town wild woman, had said: "I'll take this one for the team, baby." But Brad would never know for sure, and as a journalist, he'd missed the most crucial part of the story.

He wouldn't let it happen again. Since that lost opportunity, Brad had been concentrating most of his investigative energy on the Queen of Hearts drawing at the American Legion. The town was in a frenetic uproar about the drawing for an obvious reason. The Queen of Hearts had been going on for weeks without a winner. No one had yet chosen the queen of hearts from the board that contained the sealed envelopes, numbered 1-54. And the jackpot now stood at

$1,100,000. It was an obscene amount of money, and the town, in turn, acted like a pack of wild mustangs galloping out of control.

Every Thursday, Brad dutifully attended the drawing, only to watch the excitement crescendo unbearably before the person whose ticket was drawn selected a card that didn't turn out to be the queen of hearts. The anticlimactic end to the evening contained a mixture of disappointment and relief, the relief stemming from the remaining hope that everyone still had a chance to become a millionaire. The game remained open to possibilities and dreams. It was the same old story, followed by the same old misunderstandings and drunken brawls. The only exciting piece Brad had gotten out of the weekly event so far was when the mayor sprained his wrist trying to break up a fight between the Ehlers brothers.

But tonight, Brad saw another opportunity sitting at the end of the bar in the Hideaway Tavern in the form of Mitchell McHenry, the drunken poet who spouted Whitman when he reached the zenith of his drunken arc before settling into a quiet solitude that no one disturbed. Who was the man? Brad wondered. Something seemed lost about him, yet Brad detected a remaining streak of quiet dignity. It was a very strange thing that no one in this town knew who Mitchell McHenry was, where he came from, or who he was related to. Small towns had a long memory when it came to that type of information. Take his mother, for example. She could recite who was related to whom, going back generations. Her verve for the relations of generations made Brad uneasy. If she were to be believed, everyone in this town would be related. Brad didn't want to believe the possible truth of that, but his mother wasn't a liar. She exaggerated, sure, but she was not a liar.

Brad decided to test his theory. He nudged the bearded man next to him. "Do you know the guy at the end of the bar?" He nodded toward Mitchell.

The guy glanced over. "Sure. That's the drunken poet. Everyone knows that."

"That's not what I mean." Brad tried again. "I mean, do you know anything about him, like where he used to work, if he went to Liberty High, or if he's on disability? Things like that."

"Nope." The guy took a swig of beer, holding the longneck with two thick, calloused fingers. "And I don't give a shit. He stands up and says these funny verses from time to time, but other than that, he's got his nose in a beer. That's A-OK in my book."

"Right." It was just as Brad thought. No one had even tried to uncover the mystery of the man, and there had to be a story there. There had to be, and the first thing to do was go to the primary source. "He looks like he's had enough. I'm going to see if he needs a ride home."

The guy next to him snorted. "Good luck, buddy. He don't let nobody give him a lift. He walks."

"It's worth a try." Brad slid off his barstool and dug in his pants pockets for some change, and by the time he'd found a few crumpled bills, Mitchell McHenry had vanished from his stool at the other end of the bar, as if he'd sensed Brad coming, as if any threat to his mysterious life served as a reason to disappear.

Mitchell McHenry was an idealistic young man. Growing up in Brookline, Massachusetts, his preference had always been to stay inside and read rather than participate in the outdoor activities of boys his age. Ice skating and hockey held no appeal for him, and that suited his mother just fine. His younger sister, Adeline, had been born frail and weak, and it often fell to Mitchell to care for her while his mother went to her various charity meetings and church activities. Mitchell's father, a prominent corporate lawyer, was always too busy to pay much attention to his children, so Mitchell felt free to immerse himself in books. His favorite subject was transcendentalism, with its optimistic tenet that divinity pervaded all nature and humanity. That lovely idea appealed to the young Mitchell very much, and he reread his favorite authors over and over: Ralph Waldo Emerson, Henry David Thoreau, and Walt Whitman.

It was only when Mitchell got accepted at Harvard that his father sat up and took notice. "You'll study law, of course," his father pronounced one rare night when all four of them sat around the dinner table.

"I would rather study nineteenth-century American literature," Mitchell said in a small voice. Mitchell had always been slightly afraid of his father, a large, balding man in steel-framed glasses. That night his father still had on his suit and vest from work and looked especially imposing.

"Nonsense. You'll study law." His father pushed himself away from the table, crossed his legs, and lit a fat cigar. "It is the noblest profession, and the McHenry men have studied law for generations."

"Mother?" Mitchell turned toward the small-boned, porcelain-skinned woman at the other end of the table. He resembled his mother, a fact that had always seemed to disturb his father, and it was his mother who was by far the most approachable, more so when her husband wasn't home. If anyone in this family could help him plead his case, it would be her.

She wiped her mouth daintily with the linen napkin. "Perhaps Mitchell could study both? He could major in literature and then go to law school?" Her voice sounded so soft that Mitchell wondered if Father could hear her.

It didn't matter. His father's mind was made up. "He will major in pre-law and then go to Harvard Law, just as I did, and my father before me, and his father before him. The matter is settled." He blew out a big plume of smoke, causing Adeline to have one of her frequent, wrenching coughing spells.

That's when Mitchell realized that not only was he afraid of the man, but he also intensely disliked him. He was a bully and a tyrant, and just because they lived in a very nice house and had a cook and a housecleaner did not give him the authority to rule everyone's life. But Mitchell kept those thoughts to himself, and instead said, "All right, then. Pre-law."

When his parents dropped off Mitchell in front of his dormitory that fall, they didn't know it would be the last time they ever saw him. But he did. He also knew that once his father discovered that he did not attend any of the pre-law classes he was enrolled in but sat in on English lectures instead, the bully would cut off his money supply. With that certainty hanging over his head—and with the naive notion that he didn't need his father's money—Mitchell knew he had one semester to figure out what he wanted to do with his life. Again, naively, Mitchell thought that was plenty of time to map out his future.

However, that all changed as soon as Mitchell got his first taste of freedom. Boston was only about five miles from Brookline, but it might as well have been on the moon. Up until then, he had lived a sheltered, privileged existence with only a few friends and never a girlfriend. But in the dormitory and on campus, Mitchell discovered he could be the life of the party as soon as he had a few beers in him. It was his roommate, Sheffield, who introduced him to the pleasures of alcohol. Sheffield liked to brag that he was a "professional" when it came to chugging beer, and Mitchell knew that he earned the title. The first thing Sheffield did when he woke up was crack open a can of Budweiser and announce once he had gulped it down, "The breakfast of champions." Mitchell, not wanting to be left out, would do the same and say, "It's a pork chop in a can." They thought they were hilarious.

It was the late 1970s, and Mitchell grew his hair long. He grew a beard, too, because he thought it made him look more sophisticated. It was the first and only time in his life that Mitchell truly understood what the Transcendentalists meant. He could feel it in himself, the transcendence, as he metamorphosed from a shy, awkward boy into a new and better being. And after Sheffield found out that Mitchell was a virgin and took him to a local whorehouse called the Kitty Kat Klub, Mitchell knew he had become a man. Never mind that his first experience with an older, jaded, and slightly overweight hooker had been more embarrassing than profound. Mitchell felt as if he had shed the last stigma of childhood when he walked out of the whore's bedroom.

Sheffield waited for him in the hallway. "Did you do the deed?" Sheffield, as always, carried a can of Budweiser.

"I am a man," Mitchell said proudly, blushing.

"Way to go, dude!" And Sheffield high-fived him down the stairs.

When he wasn't hanging out and drinking with his roommate, Mitchell, unlike Sheffield, attended classes. He didn't attend his pre-law classes but would pore over the class schedules and attend any lecture that caught his fancy. He never took notes or a test, never wrote a paper, but would sit entranced as he heard lectures on the Beat poets, Emily Dickinson, Hemingway and Fitzgerald, and Faulkner and Steinbeck. He even dabbled in some courses on Marxism and Freud; his taste was eclectic. However, he never missed the lecture on the poetry of Walt Whitman. It was while leaving that vast lecture hall late one afternoon that Mitchell collided with his future.

He was looking over his shoulder when he walked straight into Kay Ballant. A heavy book bag hit his toes as he came face to face with the most astounding creature he had ever seen. Perhaps most people would not consider Kay to be beautiful, and she wasn't in the traditional sense. Her light green eyes were slightly too far apart, her small nose upturned at the end, her tiny rosebud mouth drooped at the corners, and her long, blonde hair feathered around her face like Farah Fawcett. She was petite, small-boned, and the bottom of her bell bottoms dragged along the ground. To Mitchell, everything fit together just as it should. To Mitchell, she was beautiful.

"Why don't you watch where you're going?" Kay said, although she didn't seem angry.

"I was captivated by your beauty," Mitchell tried. It sounded hokey, and he hoped she couldn't see the blush under his beard.

"Bullshit. You were checking out the boobs on that redhead behind you."

The redheaded girl walked by at that moment, and if possible, Mitchell's blush deepened, for that was indeed what he'd been doing. Since his flirting was so lame, he decided to be honest. "Guilty as charged."

Kay's eyes followed the redhead. "I don't blame you. She has nice boobs."

Mitchell stopped himself just in time. He'd been about to say, *So do you.* He would have to ask Sheffield for some flirting tips. He reached down and picked up her heavy bag. "What do you have in here, rocks?"

"Calculus books are heavy." She snatched the bag from his hand. Now she seemed angry.

He was blowing this, and he didn't want to. He wanted the girl to like him. He fell into step next to her. "Please let me carry that for you. It's the least I can do. What's your name?"

She let him buy her a cup of coffee, and the more they talked, the more captivated Mitchell became. He'd never had a girlfriend, but the way his heart flip-flopped in his chest told him that Kay Ballant was someone very, very special. They lingered so long over coffee that Mitchell bought her dinner. He now knew she was majoring in calculus, grew up in St. Louis, and liked Peter Frampton. He thought she was perfect.

He walked her home, and when their lips met, she tasted like bubblegum lip gloss. It was his first kiss—he hadn't dared kiss the whore—and he must have done it okay because she took a step back and said, "Wow."

He'd been thinking that, too. He smiled at her, then said, "Kay Ballant, I'm going to marry you one day."

When the admissions office contacted his father shortly before Christmas, his reaction was swift and decisive. His style was to go for the juggler, just as Mitchell had suspected, and without a phone call or terse, angry note, the weekly allowance stopped appearing in Mitchell's mailbox. What Mitchell hadn't expected, hadn't prepared for, was how devastatingly effective that action would be. He didn't have a place to sleep or a convenient meal plan in the cafeteria anymore. And because of all the drinking and hanging out with Sheffield and Kay during that first semester at Harvard, Mitchell hadn't even begun to prepare for the inevitable.

At first, Sheffield was kind enough to let Mitchell sneak into his dorm room at night and sleep on the floor, but Sheffield grew tired of that quickly when Mitchell kept sponging beers off him. He finally told him, "Look, man, you're going to have to get a job."

Kay's patience lasted a little longer. She said she didn't mind when Mitchell couldn't afford to take her out to a movie or for a beer. She said she had too much studying to do anyway. He believed her; he had to believe her. She even lent him money, initially, not a lot, but enough to "tide him over," she said. He was so blinded by love that everything seemed brighter and more hopeful when he was in her luminous presence, but when he wasn't with her, the bleakness of his situation became terrifying. So he was with Kay at every possible moment. He'd walk her to class during that bitterly cold winter, and then he would go sit in on another literature lecture until he could walk her to the next. He still pretended to be a student, still pretended he belonged at the elite, venerable institution.

Inevitably, Kay grew tired of his constant presence and attention. "You need to swallow your pride and go ask your father to help you out," she said.

"You know I can't do that." He sat on the floor of her room—she had been lucky enough to get a single—and watched her study. She said it gave her the creeps when he did that, but he did it anyway.

Kay sighed deeply, put down her highlighter, and turned all the way around in the chair. "Look, Mitchell, you've got to do something. I can't lend you any more money, and I can't keep letting you sneak into my room. I don't want to be expelled."

Kay was a good girl when it came to following school rules and codes. When they were in bed together, she was not such a good girl. Mitchell loved that dichotomy about her. He loved everything about her. "There's a fire escape right outside your window exactly for that purpose." He moved to her bed and patted the place beside him suggestively.

Kay ignored the gesture and said firmly, "I mean it, Mitchell. You have to do something for yourself, get a job, go to community college, or move back home. *Something.*"

"Are you trying to get rid of me?" He meant to tease her, but he sounded desperate instead. He swallowed hard. Kay was the only bright spot in his life. "Don't you love me?"

Kay sighed again. "I love you, Mitchell, but this can't go on. You need to get a *life.*"

Mitchell knew that, and it was precisely what he'd been avoiding for the last few months. Unfortunately, hearing Kay saying the words aloud made them real. He quickly glanced out the window so she couldn't see his tears.

"I've decided I'm going to med school after this, Mitchell. I have a *plan*. It's what we're supposed to be doing at this stage in our life."

Mitchell stared miserably out the window. He didn't have a clue what to do anymore. He had failed miserably as a student at this greatest of universities, and he kept pretending that he hadn't made such a terrible mistake. He should just swallow the bitter pill of failure and move on, but he couldn't. He was paralyzed with fear. He had no skills or talents. Other than drinking, his only hobby was reading the Transcendentalists. He was pathetic.

"I'm sorry to be so harsh, Mitchell, but you need to hear this." Kay did not sound sorry.

How could he make Kay proud of him? How could he rectify his mistake? It came to him so suddenly that Mitchell gasped. "I have a plan, too. I'm going to be a writer. I've been thinking about it for a while now," he lied. "And I'm going to do exactly what Thoreau did. I'll write my own *Walden*."

"I'm trying to be serious here, Mitchell."

Mitchell couldn't blame her for not believing him. Oddly enough, she hadn't even seen him read a book the entire time they'd been on campus. Her skepticism goaded him on. "It's been my plan all along. I don't need Harvard or a degree to write the best book of my generation." He stood up, excited now, and began to pace. "The next time I come back here, I'll be the one giving the lecture."

"Have you been drinking again, Mitchell?"

Mitchell didn't know when he grabbed her by the shoulders and shook her, not hard, not too hard. "Don't you believe in me, Kay?"

"I believe in you," she whispered shakily. "Let me go, Mitchell."

He released her as quickly as he must have grabbed her. He flung his winter coat over his shoulder and opened the window, letting in a cold, sharp blast of air. He gave a jaunty wave from his perch on the windowsill and wished he had a Fedora to tip. "I will come back for you."

That farewell to Kay, that ridiculously young, naively brave grand gesture would be Mitchell's first and last.

Brad wasn't pushy by nature, which could be considered an unfortunate liability in his profession. He'd gone to Mitchell McHenry's apartment on Pine Street twice and politely knocked on the door. Brad knew the old man was in there both times; he thought he heard the low hum of a television or radio through the closed and locked door. Both times, he'd left a folded note taped to the door, identifying himself and asking the drunken poet for an interview. On his third trip back to the shabby apartment, a note taped to the door waited for him.

It read: "Mind your own business and let me mind mine." The old-fashioned cursive handwriting looked a lot like Brad's aunt's, who sent him a card every Christmas with a five-dollar bill tucked inside. She was a woman who prided herself on her penmanship.

Brad still wanted to go to his primary source first, which meant that he should search the Liberty taverns every night. The old man managed to stay away from the Hideaway and Meyers and Zeke's, his favorite haunts, for three nights after Brad began his pursuit, and the man's self-control surprised and excited Brad. If a man who typically spent every night out drinking could manage to keep away from his beloved taverns to avoid an investigative reporter, he must have something to hide. Brad wanted very much to think that was the case. He had gotten it into his head that this story would be his big scoop of the summer. Other than the Queen of Hearts drawing and the stolen houseboat story, the only other big news of the summer was when ten businesses in town were robbed on the same night. Everyone thought the group of meth heads that loitered down by the river did it, but they hadn't been arrested yet. And unfortunately, Moody snagged that story first.

On the fourth night, Brad got lucky. He walked into Mr. Lucky's just as Mitchell righted himself on top of his barstool. Brad figured Mitchell took into account the short attention span of his audience when he launched into part two of "Song of Myself": "Houses and rooms are full of perfumes, the shelves are crowded with perfumes, / I breathe the fragrance myself and know it and like it, / The distillation would intoxicate me also, but I shall not let it." Not surprisingly, the crowd, mostly men, roared at the *distillation would intoxicate me,* but the drunken poet, eyes closed, seemed unaware of the noise. He was on a roll tonight, and he continued through parts three and four before helping hands steered him down from the stool. Then he sat heavily upon it as if exhausted, pulled his beer toward him, and bent his head like a bird taking a sip from a pond.

Brad made his way through the crowd. As always, the poet sat at the far end of the bar, the stool next to him empty. Brad wondered where that unspoken rule had come from, but it was always so. No one sat next to the drunken poet. Brad approached the empty stool, but he, too, hesitated a moment. He didn't want to offend anyone, especially the man he wanted to interview. But he was just doing his job, he reminded himself, as he tapped the drunken man on the shoulder. "Excuse me? Is this seat taken?"

"Hey, what're you doing?" It was the bartender, Lenny. Brad had gone to school with him. He hadn't liked him then, and he didn't like him now. He'd always been something of a bully.

"I'm going to sit at the bar and order a drink. And I'm going to buy this gentleman one, too." Brad nodded at the old man, who hadn't raised his eyes from the glass. Brad slapped a twenty-dollar bill on the bar. "Keep the change."

Lenny, unused to tips more than a quarter, eyed the bill. "Just don't bother him."

Brad felt absurdly proud of himself as he settled on the stool. He'd jumped over the first hurdle and felt ready for the next. "Here." He pushed the mug of beer in front of Mitchell when Lenny slopped it on the bar. "That's for the poem." He took a sip of his beer. "Walt Whitman's always been a favorite poet of mine."

The old man drained his first beer and reached for the full one, cupping it with two hands. He had small hands for a man, Brad thought, dainty hands, not the hands of a man who had spent a lifetime working in the fields, the mines, or with machinery. Uncalloused and smooth, they were the hands of a man who had worked in an office of some sort. The man bent his head to take a sip of beer. Foam stuck to his mustache, but he didn't bother to brush it off.

"I'll buy you another beer when you're finished with that one." Brad knew it sounded like a bribe, and it was. As an investigative journalist, he would use any means at his disposal to get his subject to talk. If the man had to get drunk before he would speak, so be it. Brad waited for some acknowledgment of his offer, but the man continued to stare into his beer.

He tried again. "You know, you look something like pictures I've seen of Whitman, with the beard and mustache. Do you do that on purpose?" Brad thought he heard something from the old man, a mumble, or a grunt. He leaned closer. "Excuse me, Mr. McHenry?"

Lenny appeared in front of them. "I told you not to bother the drunken poet, Taylor."

"I'm not bothering him." Brad knew what Lenny wanted. He was still the bully who would steal your lunch money. Brad pushed another twenty across the bar. "That's for the next round." He glanced at the old man, who seemed to have witnessed the exchange without lifting his eyes from his beer mug.

"Cocksucker." His voice was low but distinct.

Excited to have an opening, even one so small and crude, Brad hurriedly agreed. "Lenny's always been a bully. I remember when he slashed the tires of all the bikes parked in the bike rack in sixth grade. He got detention for that one." Brad's blue Schwinn had also had the seat torn off as if Lenny had singled him out. He didn't bother to tell the old man that part.

"How do you know I'm referring to Lenny?"

Brad ignored that and concentrated instead on the slight accent the man had in his low, quiet voice, an accent that didn't appear in his recitations. Brad thought he recognized it. "Are you originally from the East Coast, New York, or Massachusetts?" The drunken poet sounded vaguely like some politicians Brad had seen on TV from those states.

"What do you want from me?" The old man still stared into his beer as if it held all the answers.

Brad jumped in with both feet. "I want to interview you, Mr. McHenry. In the notes I left at your apartment, I explained that I'm an investigative reporter for the *Liberty Gazette,* and I think you would be a great subject for a human-interest story. Why do you only recite Walt Whitman? People would be interested to know," Brad reassured him. Guiltily, he looked down into his beer. He didn't want his story on Mitchell McHenry to be only a human-interest story. While Brad didn't hope the old man had led a tragic life—Brad didn't wish tragedy on anyone—he sure hoped for an angle that would evoke pathos in his readers. And he did feel guilty about that, but a man had to do what he could to get ahead in his career.

"There's no story." The old man reached for the new beer that Lenny had sloshed onto the counter, again cupping it with both small hands.

Brad couldn't take his eyes off those hands. "How about a little background information? For example, what did you do before you retired? Did you work in an office? Maybe you were a banker, or you sold insurance, or you were a CPA?" Brad could sense he was losing the guy, who was running out of both interest and patience, but he threw out one more thing just as it came to him. Suddenly, the poetry, the voice, and the clothes came together in a mental picture. "Were you a teacher?"

The drunken poet hadn't looked at him once all night, but now his head shot up, and his bloodshot, rheumy eyes locked with Brad's. "Mind your own business. Sometimes a man drinks just because he likes to drink. And I like to drink in peace." He slid off the stool, weaving, and grabbed the bar for support.

Lenny, the self-appointed bodyguard, appeared in an instant. "You can use the back door, old man. Do you need some help?"

The old man steadied himself, and in reply, raised his hand in a combination of salute and surrender. He shook his head, and moving slowly, inch by inch, made it to the back door and then out.

Lenny turned an accusing glare on Brad. "Now you've done it. In all the years I've been working here, the drunken poet's never left a drop of beer in a glass, and now he's left a full mug. You bothered him."

"Sorry," Brad said as he slipped off his stool. However, Brad didn't feel sorry at all. He'd hit a nerve with his last question. Brad's gut told him that the drunken poet used to be a professor or teacher. He wasn't sure of that yet, but it was a place to start.

After the night he broke into his parents' house and stole a sizable stack of cash from his father's not-so-secret safe, Mitchell did try to fulfill his promise to Kay. She might not have considered it to be a promise, but Mitchell did. By writing his own *Walden,* he would prove not only his love for Kay but also his worthiness. First, Mitchell bought a used Pontiac and rented a cabin on a lake in the Poconos. He had all the best intentions. He took long walks in the woods and built clumsy fires in the stone hearth. Then he would sit down in front of his typewriter and neatly stack the blank, white pages of paper at his side. He would insert a clean page and stare at it. After staring at it for a while, he would take another walk. Then it would be time to crack open another beer. It didn't take him long to realize that he was no Thoreau; he lasted one miserable week.

What Mitchell did write were long letters to Kay, declaring his devotion and describing in great detail his imaginary progress on his nonexistent opus. It was easy to lie in the letters, and by creating a fictional, more exciting life, he could almost believe he was the person who lived it. Imagining a more noble, ambitious Mitchell McHenry seemed infinitely preferable to the truth. Mitchell moved back to the Boston area, rented a small apartment, and began a series of menial jobs. He flipped burgers at McDonald's, bussed tables at one of the fancier restaurants in Boston, worked a short stint on a fishing boat, and held several telemarketing jobs. Meanwhile, in the letters that Mitchell continued to write to Kay, he traveled in Europe, talked to California agents about making a movie out of his book, and joined Greenpeace. But he never sent a single letter to the girl he loved, and it didn't matter. Writing those letters became Mitchell's lifeline.

Four years—the lost years, as Mitchell referred to them—passed numbly by. Without ever articulating it to himself, Mitchell knew he was waiting for the time when Kay would graduate from Harvard. In his romantic daydream, he would show up at graduation, Kay would spot him in the crowd of hundreds, their eyes would lock, and she would once again realize he was the true love of her life. Mitchell didn't dwell on the fact that he still had nothing to offer her, or that the life he led did not remotely resemble the one he had created for her in lavish, vivid, fictional detail. He might have secretly hoped that Kay would find him worthy enough just as he was, but he didn't dwell on that.

Then Mitchell's father died. The way Mitchell discovered his father's passing was either a stroke of luck or a sign of ominous things to come. Mitchell never read the obituaries in the *Boston Globe*, but he had been waiting at the DMV for hours, and someone had left an abandoned paper on the seat next to him. Mitchell was so shocked to see the jowly picture of his father next to the lengthy obituary filled with accolades and accomplishments that he ran out of the DMV without getting his license renewed. The most shocking thing contained in the obituary, perhaps, was that it listed him as a surviving family member. He called the family attorney, and miracle of miracles, he had been included in the will and not disowned. A trust fund had been set up for him, and while it was not large, Mitchell could survive on it if he was frugal enough. He did not contact his mother. According to the family attorney, she was already engaged to his father's law partner, also recently widowed.

Mitchell never made it to graduation and the romantic reunion with Kay. For the next five years, he focused on his new life. He found a new circle of friends that liked to drink as much as he did, and as it turned out, he could still be the life of the party. At twenty-seven, he was still attractive and charming. Many women told him that over the years, and Mitchell had no problem getting women. But they weren't Kay. Mitchell still believed that destiny would bring him and Kay together. Hadn't he told her the first night they met that he was going to marry her? He'd meant it then, and he meant it now, even though doubts had started to creep into his idealized illusions. What if Kay looked at him and saw him as he truly was—a deeply flawed human being? Mitchell could not stand the thought of that. He kept partying.

At one of those loud and raucous parties in the West End, Mitchell ran into his old friend Sheffield. Mitchell's girl of the moment had gone to fetch him another bourbon and water, and he heard someone laugh louder than anyone else. Mitchell knew that laugh and made his way over to the circle in the corner. Sure enough, the guy telling the joke was Sheffield, although Mitchell didn't think he'd recognize him on the street. Once an athlete, Sheffield had grown quite fleshy. His jowls hung over his collar, and his gut hung over his pants. As he got closer, Mitchell could see the broken blood vessels racing across his old friend's cheeks and nose.

But once he spotted Mitchell, he seemed like the same old Sheffield. "Mitch!" he cried, enveloping Mitchell in a sweaty, stinky bear hug. "What've you been up to all these years?"

"Drinking, mostly," Mitchell said when he escaped. Everyone laughed loudly, drunkenly.

"Same old Mitch," Sheffield said affectionately.

Mitchell had never allowed Sheffield or anyone else to call him Mitch, a fact that Sheffield must have forgotten, but Mitchell didn't correct him now. He was happy to see his friend again and didn't want to embarrass him in front of this crowd, but that wasn't the reason. Sheffield might know what had become of Kay. Through Mitchell, they had all three been friends. But he couldn't ask him just yet. People laughed and joked above the loud music. The smell of pot hung heavily over the room, and as usual, someone had the cocaine out on the coffee table. Mitchell didn't do pot or coke. He told people that alcohol, any alcohol, remained his drug of choice. It didn't take long to find out that Sheffield was game for everything.

It grew very late, and most of the partiers were gone before Mitchell got the chance to talk to Sheffield alone. He had wedged himself into a corner as if trying to prop up the structure, but clearly, it was the other way around. When Mitchell said his name, it took the very drunk and stoned man time to focus. "I am shitfaced, man," Sheffield said.

"So's everyone else." Mitchell handed him another vodka and soda, not that Sheffield needed it.

"No, man," Sheffield moaned. "I mean that I am shitfaced *all the time.*"

"Take it easy, pal." Mitchell patted him gingerly on the shoulder. The man was drenched with sweat, and it might not be long before he passed out. "Do you remember that girl I used to date freshman year, Kay Ballant?"

Sheffield's eyes again looked unfocused. "I lost my job last week, man, at a third-rate bank, and I fucking lost my job. Remember when I said I would set Wall Street on fire?" He barked a laugh. "Yeah, like I could make that happen. I worked in a bank in a strip mall." He tried to take a drink, but most of the liquid dribbled down the sides of his mouth. His shirt had come undone, exposing his white, hairy belly.

Repulsed, Mitchell pressed on. "Kay Ballant," he prompted. "She was tiny, with blonde hair. You called her Brainiac, remember?" Sheffield made him uneasy. The guy looked like a wreck, a drunken fool, and Mitchell hoped he never got that bad on heavy nights. But then he remembered just last week when he woke up in an alley next to a pile of trash. The last thing he remembered was getting in a cab, yet he somehow ended up in that creepy, dank alley. It mystified him; it frightened him.

"Oh, yeah." Sheffield seemed to have come back to reality for a moment. "She was a nice girl. Little Katie."

"Kay," Mitchell corrected. "Do you know what happened to her after graduation?"

Sheffield slowly slipped down the wall but didn't seem to notice. "Um, I don't . . ."

"Please, Sheffield, don't lose it yet. I want to know what happened to her. I'm still in love with her."

"Ah, Mitch." Tears came to Sheffield's eyes. "That's cool, man. My bitch of a wife left me last week. Right after I lost my job, she took off. Doesn't that suck, Mitch?"

"Yeah, it sucks," Mitchell quickly agreed. "What happened to Kay?"

"Uh, I don't think she graduated. I think she left school, went back to St. Louis. Something about her mother. I think her mother was sick."

Mitchell remembered Kay talking about her mother, who had battled breast cancer a few years before. It was the main reason Kay wanted to become a doctor. "Thanks, pal." He turned to go.

"Mitch!" Sheffield sobbed, lunging at him. "Don't leave me. I really need a friend tonight. Have one more drink with me."

It seemed like the right thing to do. Mitchell had already had plenty to drink, but one more wouldn't hurt. His old friend had become a drunken slob, and for the next few drinks, Mitchell could convince himself that he wasn't as bad, that he wasn't a sloppy, boo-hoo-ing kind of drunk. Sure, he couldn't remember some nights, a black eye he couldn't explain, a small heart tattoo on his ass that appeared out of nowhere, and former girlfriends who refused to take his calls. But Mitchell was a dignified drunk compared to Sheffield. He could hold his liquor.

But when Mitchell woke up on the floor of a jail cell the next morning, he knew the truth. Still-drunk people who stank of stale beer and despair crowded the holding cell. Sheffield, his old friend, was curled into a fetal position in the corner of the cell covered with his own vomit. Disregarding the bare, exposed toilet in the middle of the room, some of the men took turns pissing on Sheffield. And that was when Mitchell knew he was in as bad of shape as Sheffield; he was a hopeless drunk.

And he would quit. He didn't want to travel to St. Louis to reunite with Kay until he got sober. And he needed a decent job before he could come to her as an accomplished man. He would give himself five years. Those five years turned into ten, which turned into twenty. That was the funny thing about time, Mitchell thought over the years, it just seemed to trickle away, one drop at a time.

"What have you got?" The editor of the *Liberty Gazette* asked at the weekly editorial meeting. The meetings were mostly for appearance's sake. Moody and Chuck didn't give a damn about writing interesting stories. They had long since passed their prime. Best buddies, they spent more time fishing than they did in the office.

So, in Brad's opinion, Gilbert addressed the question solely to him. "I want to write an article on the drunken poet, Mitchell McHenry. I have a gut feeling there's a story there."

Moody guffawed. "Yeah, and here it is. Man goes to a bar, gets drunk, goes home. Man goes to a bar, gets drunk, goes home. Repeat."

Chuck chimed in. "It'd be a more interesting story to write about the guy's liver. Isn't he close to eighty? His liver, my ambitious cub reporter, just might be a marvel of modern medicine. There's your story." His laughter didn't sound especially kind.

"But why does McHenry only recite poems by Walt Whitman? Don't you think there's some significance there?" Brad knew looked young for his age, and his responding blush to the kidding didn't help matters.

"Maybe that's the only thing he memorized before he killed most of his brain cells," Moody offered, snickering.

Gilbert, usually kinder than the other two, didn't help Brad this time. "I think you're barking up a hollow tree, son. Right now, you should be focusing all your attention on The Queen of Hearts drawing. Who cares about a drunk old man? God knows that we have plenty of over-imbibers in this town." He looked pointedly at Moody and Chuck, who, grinning, raised their liberally spiked with brandy cups of coffee.

"But if I can get him to give me an interview, can I write the story?"

"Yeah, right," Chuck said. "The guy hasn't talked to anyone for years, so he's going to spill his guts to you?"

"Go to the American Legion tonight, son. If there's finally a winner in this damn drawing, it's going to be major news." Gilbert shuffled the papers on his desk. "Everyone, get back to work."

Brad ignored Moody and Chuck on his way out of Gilbert's small office and went straight to his desk. At least Gilbert hadn't asked him what he had discovered so far in his research. Brad hadn't uncovered anything yet. He had no idea where the man originally came from, so it was like trying to find a needle in a haystack. He'd even looked at old tax records, and unless Mitchell McHenry had changed his name, he'd never filed a tax return. Trying to follow up on his theory that McHenry had been a teacher, he'd gone through the online yearbooks of nearly every town, community college, and university in Illinois with no results. In desperation, he asked his mother if she remembered when McHenry came to town, and to Brad's disappointment, his mother, the woman who remembered everything about everyone in Liberty, had no idea. All that led Brad to one conclusion: He would have to get the man to talk to him if he had any shot at a story. And he could still hear Chuck's voice in his head, *Yeah, right.*

After a full day of futile research, Brad arrived at the packed Legion shortly before eight. The Liberty High boys' track team was making a killing by parking yet more cars. As the jackpot had grown over the weeks, so had the size of the crowd. Being Press, Brad had a reserved seat by the front table that held the big drum of tickets. If he'd been in a better mood, he might have noticed her before her ticket was picked for the Queen of Hearts drawing that night. She sat a few rows back from the front table and had blonde hair curling around her face. When she came to the front table to pick her card from the large board that only held five remaining envelopes, Brad could see she was petite, and her blue eyes danced with excitement. She looked to be about Brad's age, and Brad couldn't take his eyes off her.

When she picked the jack of diamonds, a moan whooshed out of the crowd, and Brad knew the moan would be followed by laughter and relieved tittering. The drawing would last for another week. The young woman, though, looked unperturbed. "I thought this was my lucky night." She shrugged, pointing to the board. "What are the odds?" That brought an appreciative chuckle from the crowd, and she joined in.

Brad didn't even have to think about it. He got up from his seat and reached for her elbow. "I'm Brad Taylor, a reporter for the *Liberty Gazette*, and I'd like to interview you."

"Me? I'm flattered, but I didn't win." She had the sweetest smile on her tiny rosebud lips.

Brad didn't care about that. He wanted to know who she was; he wanted to know her. He led her to his seat and pulled up another chair. He felt breathless with excitement and didn't waste any time. "Are you from around here? What's your name?"

She laughed. "I'm Ellie Ballant. I'm the new chemistry teacher at Liberty High. I moved into a place on Wilshire yesterday, and of course, the first thing everyone told me to do was to come to the Queen of Hearts drawing at the Legion, so here I am."

"I'm glad you came." And Brad, for once, didn't care if he was being unprofessional. He raked a shaking hand through his short, brown hair. He wished he'd stopped at home and put on a better shirt. He wished he'd brushed his teeth.

"What is the most interesting thing about you, Ellie Ballant?"

She didn't hesitate. "My 'father'—she used air quotes around the word—"is an anonymous sperm donor."

"Oh, I wasn't expecting that."

"Most people don't."

He grinned at her. His mother always told him he had a lovely smile that he should use more often. He would listen to that advice tonight. "I bet there are more interesting things about you than that."

Ellie cocked her head. "Are you flirting with me?"

"I'm trying to." He smiled again. Ellie seemed so natural and relaxed that Brad felt very comfortable with her.

"Oh, here comes my mom. She came down from St. Louis to help me move in."

Brad looked up to see an older version of Ellie, her blond hair laced with gray and tiny but distinct lines etched around her eyes. However, in Brad's opinion, she wasn't as attractive as her daughter. It was something about the eyes. "Hello, Ellie's mom," he said.

She reached out her hand. "Kay. Has Ellie already told you that she's a product of an anonymous sperm donor because her busy mother didn't want to take the time to get married?"

Brad could see instantly where Ellie's charm came from. He took her hand. "Only the sperm donor part."

"Mom's a doctor," Ellie explained.

"And this doctor is very thirsty. I'm going to check out the bar." She peered into the next room. "It looks like the crowd has thinned out." She leaned toward Ellie and said in a loud whisper, "Maybe you got lucky tonight after all."

Mitchell discovered that having friends in low places made it incredibly easy to get forged teaching credentials. And while the forger was at it, Mitchell had him generate a diploma from Roger Williams University, a small private college in Bristol, Rhode Island, that wouldn't raise as many red flags as a phony degree from Harvard. During one of his many relapses, Mitchell decided to become an English teacher. After an excessively maudlin night out with Sheffield, Mitchell found himself walking through the hallowed campus of Harvard. It filled him with such remorse and self-loathing that he immediately quit drinking once again and decided on a career. Aside from the short time with Kay, the classroom remained the only place he had ever been truly happy.

The next major decision Mitchell made was to leave Boston. Except for that one miserable week in the Poconos when he failed to write his *Walden,*

Mitchell had never been out of the Boston area. It was not only time to leave, but it was long overdue. Boston represented old habits and recurring patterns, and he wouldn't miss much about the area. But he would miss Sheffield. They tried to support each other in sobriety, but when one fell down the black hole, the other jumped in like a rabbit. They were always one phone call away, one bad day away, one drink away from the black, black hole. Mitchell didn't even dare tell Sheffield that he was leaving, fearing that Sheffield would beg him to stay. And that he would.

Rather than actively searching for teaching positions in newspapers and such—Mitchell had never bothered to learn how to use a computer—he used a different approach. He found it more to his liking to move to a new town and submit his phony credentials and resume to the local high school, telling the school principal that he was available to substitute. Finally, Mitchell felt he had found his true calling in substitute teaching. It was impermanent, not overly demanding work, and it didn't require much preparation or planning. For the most part, Mitchell could show up in a classroom and recite his beloved Whitman to the bored students, who didn't care what he said if they didn't have to do anything. Mitchell, drawing on his own experience, didn't make them take tests.

Mitchell preferred small towns, no more than pinpricks on a map, so during the years of substitute teaching, he traveled to and taught at many small high schools throughout Pennsylvania, Ohio, and Indiana. Always, he worked his way toward St. Louis, but it was slow progress indeed. Forty-four years old when he arrived in Worthington, Indiana, he'd been mostly sober for ten years. He rented a small basement apartment from a widow lady, who quickly realized Mitchell did not like to be cornered and bombarded with town gossip. "He's a bit of a loner," she told all her friends. "But I sometimes hear him reading aloud to himself. I don't know what he's reading, but he has a very nice voice." The old widow lady would then glance surreptitiously over her shoulder and whisper, "Don't go spreading this around, but I think he's queer." Her audience, of course, spread that juicy tidbit all around town.

As luck would have it, the local high school principal was desperate for a substitute English teacher because the current teacher had decided to take an extended maternity leave. So the grateful principal hired Mitchell on the spot for a two-month stint that would last until the end of the school year. "You're just what I've been looking for," he told Mitchell. He, too, had heard the rumors about the gay man who lived in Widow Carlson's basement, and he didn't feel the need to check Mitchell's references or do a background check. "You'll be teaching the freshman and sophomore English classes."

On his first day as a teacher at Worthington, Mitchell recited Whitman's "Among the Multitudes": "Ah lover and perfect equal, / I meant that you should discover me so by my faint indirections, / And I when I meet you mean to discover / you by the like in you." When he finished, a girl in glasses raised her hand.

"You." He pointed at her. Mitchell rarely bothered to learn his students' names. "What do you think of Walt Whitman?"

"We're supposed to be reading *The Great Gatsby*," she said. "It's on the syllabus." She waved a mimeographed sheet in the air.

"Shut up, Nancy," came a surprisingly mature-sounding voice from the back of the room.

Mitchell's eyes followed the sound, and he almost gasped at the sight of the stunning-looking girl with long, wavy auburn hair and deep green eyes. Her breasts strained against her lightweight sweater, and if Mitchell didn't know she was fifteen, he would have guessed she was in her twenties. She stared back at him with such raw sex appeal that he took an involuntary step backward. "Everyone read *Gatsby*, then." And Mitchell sat down heavily, surprised and chagrined by the rising in his trousers. He hadn't been with a woman in a couple of years, but his reaction to the girl's beauty was entirely inappropriate. Mitchell, too, picked up a copy of the novel left on the desk and pretended to read, pretending that he didn't look up from time to time to stare at the girl. He found the seating chart the teacher left. The beautiful young girl's name was Victoria Eldridge.

He knew she would come up to his desk after class, and she did. She waited until all the other students filed out before she said, "Your poem moved me. I felt like you were speaking directly to me."

"Whitman's poetry is quite powerful," he said carefully.

"You could teach me so much."

Mitchell felt confused. Was it possible that this beautiful, wonderful creature suggested what he thought she did? But she was so young! "I… hope you enjoy the class."

To his mortification, his face turned red. Did this girl know what power she possessed?

"Would you be willing to tutor me? English is not my strongest subject, and I really want to get into Purdue."

There, that seemed innocent enough. "I… I don't think that will be necessary. I'm only going to be here for a short time." Dear God, he stuttered under her watchful, frankly sensual gaze.

"We'll see." She turned and sauntered out of the room, and even the way she moved seemed sexual to Mitchell.

The next day, the principal informed Mitchell that he would be tutoring Ms. Eldridge. Her father was president of the school board, and he insisted on a private tutor for his eager daughter. "I'm only a substitute. It's not part of my job description," Mitchell pled.

But the principal remained resolute. "What Eldridge wants, Eldridge gets. Buck up, McHenry."

Mitchell tried vainly to resist Victoria's charms. He repeatedly reminded himself that he was almost thirty years older than the girl, old enough to be her father. At first, to protect himself, Mitchell insisted they meet in the classroom.

But when she would say to him, "I need some help with this," he would find himself bending over her, way too close, so close that he could smell her rose-scented shampoo and the animal heat from her body. The third time that occurred, she lifted her head and kissed him on the lips. To his everlasting shame, he kissed her back hungrily. And then there was no going back.

The first time they had sex, he took her to a cheap motel in nearby Spencer. "This place is not good enough for you," he told her. And he even told her: "We should not be doing this." But his passion for her consumed both his guilt and remorse.

"I want to do this." She gave him The Look, as he'd come to call it. "I love you."

She was not a virgin, which surprised and unnerved Mitchell. When he asked her about it, Victoria was vague. "Oh, some clumsy guy I met at church camp. He wasn't a man, not like you are."

Mitchell half-heartedly tried to stop the locomotive they found themselves on once or twice, but Victoria would silence him with a kiss and place his hand on her round, full breast or between her legs. He had no resistance when it came to her, none. Mitchell thought about her every moment, night and day, and when she sat in his class, it felt like sheer agony to look at her and not be able to touch her. It was so wrong, and yet he couldn't help himself. When he tried to explain this to Victoria, she gave him The Look and said, "It's our dirty little secret, my love."

Our dirty little secret.

Inevitably, blinded by passion, he became careless. Victoria would crawl into his car after school when the parking lot was almost deserted, and once, she followed him into the men's room at school. She was brazen, his Victoria, and she started coming to his basement apartment, which had its own exterior entrance. He cautioned her that first time, saying, "You shouldn't come here, Victoria. Widow Carlson watches this place like a hawk. And she gossips."

"Oh, yeah?" Victoria stood just outside the door and wore a tan trench coat in the light rain. "What would she have to say about this?" She opened the coat, revealing her naked splendor to Mitchell.

"Oh, God!" And he pulled her into his tiny living room. They didn't even make it to the bed before he pulled her down to the dubiously clean carpet and made love to her for hours.

It might have been Widow Carlson who eventually exposed his and Victoria's dirty little secret and spread the gossip to the ears of Victoria's father, but Mitchell would never know for sure. He had never asked Victoria how she managed to sneak out of her house almost every night under the strict, watchful eye of Vernon Eldridge. It could have been that she wasn't as careful as she claimed to be and that her father somehow caught onto her midnight jaunts and followed her. But it didn't matter how Vernon found out; he did.

Afterward, Mitchell felt grateful that Vernon, a tall, husky man, waited until his daughter left Mitchell's apartment before he banged on the door. He didn't identify himself as he pounded on the door, but Mitchell instinctively knew. He stood, shaking, with the smell of Victoria still on his skin. He couldn't have run even if he wanted to. The apartment only had one door and no windows. But Mitchell didn't want to run away. He'd always known he would eventually have to pay the consequences for his unconscionable behavior. And in some way, Mitchell had been expecting this moment ever since he crossed the forbidden line with Victoria. He was terrified, yes, but he also knew he deserved whatever punishment Vernon would mete out. He opened the door.

"You son of a bitch!" The large man barged into the apartment carrying a baseball bat. "You fucking pervert!"

Mitchell didn't try to defend himself as Victoria's father took his first swing. Mitchell heard more than felt the cracking of bone in his upper right leg. He went down hard, while Vernon Eldridge kept swinging and swearing. "Fucking pervert!" Pound, pound, pound. "Child molester!" Pound, pound, pound. Strangely enough, the pain of each blow made Mitchell feel more and more numb. When he couldn't feel anything at all, he passed out.

When Mitchell awoke sometime later, he was in the hospital. Someone finally told him that Widow Carlson had called an ambulance, but she hadn't accompanied him here. *She knows the dirty little secret*, Mitchell thought, which meant everyone in town knew by now. It would explain why the doctors and nurses only tended to him when they absolutely had to and would avert their eyes when changing his bandages. It would explain why no one sent flowers or came to visit, not that he expected either. Victoria did not call or send him a note, and he understood completely. What he'd done to her and with her was deplorable, illegal, and cowardly. Why didn't Vernon Eldridge call the police? Mitchell, the pariah, deserved to be jailed for his crimes.

But the police never came, leaving Mitchell utterly alone. When he recovered enough to hobble out of there, he would leave this town and drive to another town in another state, perhaps Illinois. Mitchell finally acknowledged he would never make it to St. Louis and see Kay. If he'd been unworthy before, he was now completely worthless. And he knew he would start drinking again; in fact, he would devote his life to drinking in solitude. It would be his punishment.

This night seemed different. Mitchell sat at the bar in Mr. Lucky's in his usual seat, but the beer tasted strange tonight, flat and bitter. Yet he kept drinking it; he was a man on a mission. However, if the next beer didn't start to numb his loneliness and erase all his failures, he would go home.

"Hey, McHenry, everyone wants to know when you're going to do your thing." Lenny placed another beer in front of Mitchell.

"I didn't order that."

"It's on the house," Lenny said.

Mitchell mumbled thanks, but he didn't particularly want the drink. Something definitely felt off about this night. Perhaps he was coming down with a summer cold. However, Lenny looked at him expectantly, so Mitchell dutifully climbed to the top of his barstool and began. Tonight, he decided, he would recite "When Lilacs Last in the Dooryard Bloom'd." He hadn't done that one in a while. He cleared his throat and began, relieved that his voice sounded resonant and sure, even though he did not feel that way: "When lilacs last in the dooryard bloom'd, / And the great star early droop'd in the western / sky in the night, / I mourn'd, and yet shall mourn with ever- / returning spring."

Mitchell saw her just as he heard Brad say, "There he is."

He stopped mid-breath. It wasn't ever supposed to happen like this. In all his fantasies over all the years, he would reunite with Kay under ideal circumstances. He would be sober and gainfully employed. He would have accomplished something worthwhile. But now, after forty-one years, Kay came into this bar on this night and saw him for what he truly was: a drunken, beaten man, a poet who recited the words of someone much more worthy than himself.

"I'm trying to write a story about the guy, but he won't cooperate."

Brad spoke in an overly loud voice, and then Mitchell, perched high on his barstool, saw the young woman standing next to him. She looked like the spitting image of her mother and could have been Kay forty-one years ago. The nosy young reporter was trying to impress the young woman, just as Mitchell had tried to impress Kay. And now Kay stared at him. Did she not recognize him? Mitchell hoped she had not. He scrambled down from his barstool. He should settle up with Lenny and get out of here. He should leave his impossible fantasies, the ones that had kept him going for all these years, intact.

But it was too late. Kay stood beside him. "I used to know a young man who loved the poetry of Walt Whitman. He recited it all the time." Without asking, she took the empty seat, the one supposed to always remain empty, next to him. "Hello, Mitchell. It's been a long time."

He couldn't stop staring at her. She had aged, of course, but he couldn't see that. To him, she looked like the young girl he had fallen in love with outside the lecture hall on the campus of Harvard. "You haven't changed."

Laughing, she reached up and touched the gray streaks in her hair. "Bullshit."

"Do you two know each other?" Brad stood annoyingly close.

"Mitchell McHenry and I go way back." Kay signaled Lenny for a beer.

"Wait a minute." Brad looked at Mitchell and then back at Kay. "How do you know each other?"

"Mitchell McHenry?" The younger version of Kay took Brad's arm. "We should leave them alone to reminisce. Mom and this guy were madly in love freshman year at Harvard. It's a love story for the ages, right, Mom?"

"You do tend to exaggerate, Ellie."

"Come on." Ellie started to lead Brad away. "I'll fill you in."

"It's a love story?" Brad said, incredulous. "I thought the guy probably had a deep, dark secret."

"*Come on,* Brad." Ellie tugged his arm more forcefully.

"My daughter's something else, isn't she?" Kay said, watching them leave.

Mitchell couldn't help but ask, "Are you married?"

Kay shook her head. "Never. You?"

"Never." Mitchell felt absurdly happy at her answer. Over the years, he had come to wonder if their romance had been more one-sided than he liked to remember. Perhaps she hadn't felt as strongly for him as he had for her. For the first time in years, Mitchell smiled. It felt awkward on his face.

"This is a strange coincidence, isn't it?"

"Maybe." Mitchell decided to take a chance. "But I'm glad you're here."

They could have talked about the past or what they'd been doing during the decades apart, but they didn't. Kay mentioned she had been at the Queen of Hearts drawing earlier. He said he never attended; he didn't like crowds. She said she thought it was even hotter in Liberty than in St. Louis. "It's the humidity," he said.

They sat in companionable silence as they nursed their beers. Then Mitchell decided to take one more chance. Gathering up whatever courage he had left, he said, "Please don't leave me again, Kay."

"I remember it being the other way around," she said.

That surprised him. He had never thought of it that way, but hadn't he been the one who climbed out her window, his coat thrown over his shoulder, with a promise he would write the book of his generation, the next *Walden*? He had never returned. He'd only written thousands of letters to her that she never received.

"If it was me who did the leaving, it was the stupidest decision I ever made."

"We all have regrets, Mitchell."

The look she gave him seemed so familiar that Mitchell felt that same transcendence he had felt all those years ago when in her presence. "Please don't leave me," he repeated.

Kay put her hand over his, pulling it away from the beer mug. "I promise that I won't leave you tonight, Mitchell. Tonight, I won't leave you."

DARK HORSE

"So, you got me to come back to this godforsaken town under false pretenses?" Stephanie picked up one of the troll dolls on display next to the cash register. She had never understood her mother's fascination with the ugly little dolls. The one in her hand had long, red Rapunzel hair tied with a tiny white ribbon and wore a bright pink tutu. Despite the adornment, it was still as ugly as sin.

"No, it is an emergency." Mandy, her mother, who owned and operated Zelda's Consignment Shop, snatched the doll out of Stephanie's hands. "You're messing up her hair."

"I've never understood why you collect these dolls. Not only are they ugly, but they're really kind of creepy, Mom."

"For your information, Stephanie, these little people are known as good luck trolls, or gonk trolls, in the United Kingdom."

"We're not in the United Kingdom. We're in Liberty, Illinois, or butt-fuck Egypt, as I like to call the old hometown. And they're not *little people*, Mom, they're *plastic dolls*." Stephanie picked up another with bright pink hair dressed in a purple Merlin the Magician outfit. She held it in front of her mom's face. "If this isn't creepy, I don't know what is."

Mandy snatched that one out of her hand, too. "I see that your attitude hasn't gotten any better."

This was precisely why Stephanie only came back to Liberty when absolutely necessary. Just being in this place brought out her surliness. She honestly couldn't help it. All she had to do was step foot into this town, and she immediately regressed into her teenage self. And her teenage self had been a royal pain in the ass, all mouth and sass and making it a point to do anything that she wasn't supposed to do. She was twenty-seven now and should be able to control herself better, and she had vowed to do so on the drive down from Champaign. Then she walked into her mom's immaculate consignment store stuffed with used clothing and mismatched china and immediately went back to ground zero.

The funny thing, though, was that Stephanie did love her mom. She just wasn't very nice to her. For years, her mom thought Stephanie's anger and resentment toward her were because Mandy had such terrible taste in men. And Stephanie let her think that. Mom had been married three times before landing on number four, a guy named Neal who seemed almost normal, wonder of wonders. Before that, it seemed as if she had subconsciously tried to marry big, fat losers. Stephanie's father was supposedly wretched husband number one, Sam Nelson, the biggest loser of them all. However, Stephanie knew Sam Nelson wasn't her biological father. Stephanie had begged her mom to tell her his identity, but Mandy refused to budge. That was the real reason Stephanie was so pissed off.

She needed to get over her Daddy Issues one of these days. And Mom was getting up there. At forty-five, her best years were probably behind her. Stephanie resisted reaching for another ugly troll doll just to irritate her. "Mom, what is this emergency? You called and texted me thirty times last week, yet you couldn't just come out and say what was wrong."

Mandy looked around the store to make sure no one could hear, which seemed slightly paranoid to Stephanie. She'd been in the store for ten minutes, and no one had come in. Stephanie suddenly had a sick feeling. What if something was wrong with Mom? What if she had been diagnosed with cancer? Stephanie hadn't really thought of that before. To her, Mandy had always seemed strong and capable. Whatever life handed her—and she had been handed a lot of crap—she invariably came up swinging. "Now, you're starting to scare me, Mom." Stephanie tried to swallow around the lump in her throat. "Are you sick?"

"Oh, goodness, no!" Mandy waved her hand in front of her face to dismiss the very notion. "I'm perfectly fine, healthy as a horse. And Neal is, too, although Neal has lost a lot of weight. But I'm pretty sure that he's doing it on purpose, and there's nothing to worry—"

"Mom!" Stephanie interrupted impatiently. "Would you stay on point?"

Still, Mom hesitated before she said, "It's Clara. She's pregnant."

"How the hell did *that* happen?" It was probably the last thing Stephanie had expected her to say. As far as she knew, her chubby, bubbly fifteen-year-old sister had never even gone on a date. Not that she had ever paid a lot of attention to her younger sister. Stephanie had been twelve when Clara was born, and she thought of her more as a nuisance than anything else. And when it became apparent that Clara was the good daughter, and Stephanie was the bad daughter, Stephanie ignored her completely. The line had been drawn, and neither would cross it.

"I would expect it happened the normal way," Mandy said drily. She picked up a stack of neatly folded t-shirts and started to refold them. "I should probably rephrase that. I *think* she's pregnant."

"Has she been to a doctor?"

"Clara flatly refuses to go to the doctor." Mandy stopped folding. "And that's where you come in, Stephanie." She leaned over the counter eagerly. "I thought that with you being a nurse and all, you could talk some sense into her."

"A nurse?" Stephanie said, confused.

"I was a little hurt that you didn't give me the details of the ceremony when you graduated from Barnes School of Nursing three years ago, but I got over it. When I started to think about it, I thought it was actually considerate of you. You know how nervous driving in St. Louis traffic makes me. I'm a Nervous Nelly once I cross over that bridge."

Stephanie had forgotten all about that lie. She had even forgotten why she felt the need to tell it. Had she simply been bored? And St. Louis? She'd forgotten about that one as well, or it could be that Mom just assumed she lived in St. Louis because that's what she'd told her when she left home all those years ago. Yes, she'd told her she was going to St. Louis, but when her friend dropped her off at the Amtrak station in Carbondale, she decided to take The Illini to Chicago. But she only had enough money to buy a ticket to Champaign. It was a college town and easy for an eighteen-year-old to get into the bars on campus, a definite plus in its favor. And when she saw a job offer for a nude model in the drawing classes at U of I, her career was born. Stephanie discovered that she not only didn't mind, but she liked taking her clothes off in front of people when she got paid for doing so.

Mandy looked at her expectantly, so Stephanie said, "What is it that you want me to say to her?"

"You know," Mandy kept her eyes on the folding project, "talk to her."

"No, I don't know," Stephanie said, exasperated. "Do you want me to talk her into an abortion?"

Mandy gasped. "Heavens, no! I think she's much too far along for that. Unless—"

Stephanie waited. Even after all these years, she knew when her mom was getting to the crux of the issue. Sometimes it took a while.

"I mean, you don't know how to do that sort of thing, do you?" She folded a faded Superman t-shirt into sharp creases, pressing and kneading. "I know that women sometimes have abortions in their third trimester if it's a medical necessity, isn't that right?" Then she looked up, her eyes imploring.

Stephanie picked up another troll with bright orange hair, a colorful lei around its neck, a green plastic grass skirt at its hips. It seemed to be staring at her accusingly. Wouldn't now be a good time to tell Mom the truth about so many things? She could simply shake the Etch-A-Sketch of lies and erase them forever.

"You know I'm proud of you," Mandy said, almost shyly.

"Abortions are not my area of expertise." Stephanie stared into the troll's accusing eyes.

"Well, you know what? That's a relief, honey. And really, I just want you to talk to your sister, to get her to open up. If we can find out when the baby is due and who's the father, we can make a plan. If we have a plan, we can all move forward, right?"

"Right." It seemed to be the answer her mom expected. "I'll try to talk to her tonight."

"I am so relieved to hear you say that."

She'd try to talk to Clara, but she wasn't making any promises. Clara had no reason to listen to anything she would say. She was the bad daughter—and a nurse. So she was the bad-daughter-fake-nurse, who had way too many lies and secrets to keep track of. She'd barely been in this town for fifteen minutes, and her head pounded.

Very carefully, Stephanie put the Hawaiian troll back where it belonged. "Do you ever sell any of these creepy little dolls?"

"They're not for sale, Stephanie. They're my personal collection."

"Why trolls? Why not thimbles or spoons or snow globes or even Barbie dolls? Barbie dolls might be perpetuating an unrealistic stereotype, but at least they're pretty."

Mandy laughed. "Like the British, I think they bring good luck."

Yeah, right, Stephanie thought. *Look at all the luck they've brought you.*

Stephanie, on the drive from the consignment shop to the house, refused to check her phone. She knew he had probably texted ten or eleven times since she left Champaign, and this time, she vowed, she would not respond. This time, she would break up with Jere Casper once and for all. Their relationship was toxic and destructive. At least that's what her closest friend Gigi, who wasn't all that close of a friend, had told her.

"You put up with all his shit, and then when he snaps his fingers, you go running back to him." Gigi was another dancer at the club, and when she decided to get implants to increase her tips, she went big. She was short with spiky, dyed straw-blond hair, and she went the DD route. She looked like a hairless, younger Dolly Parton.

"I don't do that." They were standing in front of the mirror in the shabby, crowded dressing room of the Fox Den, waiting for their turns to go on. Compared to the comical Gigi, Stephanie thought she looked pretty damn hot. With her short, dark hair cut in a bob, and with the long line of her neck and limbs sprinkled with body glitter, she looked as if she glowed. She'd been told once that she looked like Audrey Hepburn but with bigger boobs. Sure, the compliment came from Jere, but Stephanie decided to believe him. Audrey Hepburn, even now, remained a classic beauty.

"Yes, you do." Gigi generously applied more kohl eyeliner. She looked at Stephanie out of the corner of her eye and said softly, "He hurts you, yet you keep going back."

"I don't know where you got that idea, Gigi." Stephanie stared straight ahead into the mirror. Denial, she had learned the hard way, served as an excellent defense mechanism.

"I've seen bruises on your arms and shoulder and even your neck, for god's sake." Gigi went to work on her lips with candy pink lip gloss.

"That's just rough sex. We both like it that way."

Gigi tossed her makeup in the bag. "I don't care. If a man hits a woman, he's got to go."

"I hit him back." Stephanie, too, had given up the pretense of freshening her makeup and turned to Gigi. Her relationship with Jere was none of Gigi's or anyone else's business, but she felt the need to make Gigi understand. "If he hits me, I hit him back, and then we have incredible, passionate sex."

"I'm not judging you."

"It sure sounds like you are." Stephanie crossed her arms over her chest. "And you have no right to do so."

"But he's so much older than you." Gigi wasn't backing down, but her voice did sound pleading.

"So what?" Jere was in his mid-forties, and Stephanie had never considered that to be an issue. If anything, she thought it made Jere more sophisticated, sexier. "Believe me, he doesn't need Cialis, if that's what you're getting at."

"And he's married, with a family," Gigi finished. "And that, my friend, always spells trouble."

"He's planning on leaving his wife."

"Oh, they all say that," Gigi said dismissively. "Trust me. It's the cheating man's favorite line. Well, that and 'my wife doesn't understand me,' and 'we never have sex anymore.'"

"Jere doesn't say anything like that," Stephanie lied.

"And how long have you been 'dating' him?" Gigi used air quotes, and that further infuriated Stephanie.

"It hasn't been that long," but when Gigi's kohl-rimmed eyes continued to bore into hers, Stephanie added, "two years."

"Look, I'm only saying all this because you're my friend, and I'm worried about you."

"Don't be." Stephanie tried to put a jocular tone in her voice, but this conversation made her mad. She was a grown woman and could handle herself. "This ain't my first rodeo, darlin'."

"Nor mine." Gigi gave one final glance in the mirror. "There, I've said my piece, and now I've got to go. It's showtime." Stephanie could still hear her as she walked out the door and down the short hallway to the stage. "My god, I hope we have some decent tippers in the place tonight. I swear, the clientele in this place gets cheaper with every passing week."

"But I love him." Stephanie wanted the words to echo down the hall after Gigi, but they came out in a whisper. At least she thought she loved Jere, but maybe that, too, was another lie.

"My god, you're enormous," Stephanie said as soon as she walked into the house and got a load of Clara sitting on a kitchen chair. The chair seemed to wobble under her girth, threatening to splinter. She knew that she shouldn't have said that as soon as the words came out of her mouth. They were mean, and she had vowed on the way over here that she would be nice to her maybe-pregnant baby sister. After all she had put Mom through in her younger years, Stephanie supposed she owed it to her to be nice to Clara. But no. The first words out of her mouth were ugly and vicious.

Clara's round face wobbled, and tears sprang immediately to her eyes. But she rallied. "Why are you here? Don't you have some sick people to nurse, or do you poison them instead?"

Neal, rummaging through the refrigerator, turned at the sound of Stephanie's voice. He started right in with the placating, as he had always done when Stephanie and Clara were younger. "Now, Stephanie, Clara is rather sensitive about her recent weight gain. And it's not like it's all that much. It's nothing a good diet can't cure, right, Clara? And Clara, that was not a nice thing to say to your sister either."

Neal always acted like he was trying to be fair when he heard both sides of their fights and arguments, but Stephanie knew he usually sided with Clara. And why not? She was his real daughter. Stephanie didn't let it bother her too much. Neal was an okay guy if a little on the dull side. He sold RVs for a living, which spelled Boring with a capital B to Stephanie's way of thinking. But something seemed different about him now. Stephanie looked at him closely, and it took her a couple of seconds to realize what it was. He, unlike Clara, had trimmed down. And his hair. Had he started to dye his hair? When a middle-aged man began to do those things, a middle-aged wife should heed the red flags. Like Jere's wife should have. Stephanie quickly shook that thought off before it had time to settle.

Before Stephanie had time to apologize—and it wouldn't have been sincere because her younger sister looked like a beached whale—Mom breezed through the door with a sack from Dave's Market. "Oh, good, everyone's here. We can have a real family dinner tonight. I picked up some of Dave's homemade meatloaf, which is always a treat."

"I hate meatloaf," Clara said sullenly. Her lank, stringy hair looked like it hadn't been washed or combed in days.

"So do yourself a favor, kid. Don't eat."

"You're a bitch," Clara said.

"I've been called worse." Stephanie pulled out a kitchen chair. "So tell me, Clara, who knocked you up?"

"Stephanie!" Mom stopped midway to the table, the tray of soggy-looking meatloaf in her hands.

"You wanted me to ask her, Mom, and that's what I'm doing."

"But I didn't mean you should do it right after you walked in the door!"

"Mandy, did you call Stephanie home to grill our daughter?" Neal, normally so mild-mannered, looked like he was about to explode. "How many times does Clara have to tell you that she's not pregnant? For the love of God, woman, I sometimes think you're losing it. You make things up and then convince yourself they're true."

Stephanie turned to him in surprise. She had never heard him use that tone with her mom before. "Neal, calm down. If Clara's isn't pregnant then—"

"Don't you dare talk to me like that, Neal!" Mom, who had looked like she had just witnessed a horrific car wreck a few seconds before, snapped back to reality with a vengeance. "I'm only concerned about our daughter, who obviously has something going on."

"There you go again, talking like a crazy person," Neal said meanly.

"Maybe Clara's just doing some emotional eating?" Stephanie suggested.

"What are you going to do? Run out of here again? Isn't that what you always do at the first sign of trouble?" Mom and Neal glared at each other with equal ferocity.

"Why don't you leave things well enough alone?" Neal shouted.

"Maybe she has something wrong with her thyroid?" Stephanie made a feeble effort to break the tension. "I know a woman who once ballooned up to the size of a house because she had an underactive thyroid."

"I'm not making this up. Look at her." Mom gestured toward Clara with the tray of meatloaf. "This problem is real."

"All teenage girls gain weight," Neal said angrily.

"That's ridiculous," Mom sputtered. She finally made it to the table and plopped down the tray with a loud bang. "And when did you become an expert on teenage girls?"

"Maybe it's cancer," Stephanie said. "Maybe Clara has a gigantic tumor growing in her belly. That would make sense, wouldn't it?"

Clara finally piped up. "Why are you talking about me in the third person? I'm sitting right here."

Stephanie turned back to Clara. "Sure are. Can't miss you."

But before Clara could again call her a bitch—and Stephanie could see the word on her lips—Neal walked toward the back door, and Mom rushed at him, blocking his way. "Oh, no, you don't! You are not walking out on this argument or this family again, Neal Tanner."

"Just watch me," he said, his mouth a grim, set line.

Mom reached across him and grabbed her purse that still sat on the kitchen counter. "This time, I'm going to be the one to leave, and you can be the one who stays behind and cleans up the mess."

"Out of my way." Neal shoved her, not hard, toward the counter.

"Over my dead body!" Mom shouted and swung her purse at his head. It knocked Neal temporarily off balance, and she raced out the door. A second later, Neal followed, and the girls still sitting at the table heard two car motors start simultaneously.

Clara was staring at the door when Stephanie turned back to her. "Do they always fight like this?"

"No, this was a big one." Clara picked up a fork and speared a chunk of meatloaf and started to flatten it on the table with the tines. "I think it's worse because you're here."

That surprised Stephanie. "Me? What did I do?"

"It's what you always do," Clara said calmly. "You walk into a room, and things get messy fast."

Stephanie opened her mouth to deny this but then stopped. Maybe Clara did have a point. When she was younger and still lived at home, Mom and Neal fought more bitterly than they had in recent years. So Stephanie let that one go. Plus, she had something more pressing on her mind. "What's going on with your dad? He's lost weight, and now he dyes his hair. Do you think he's having an affair?" The Neal she had just witnessed fighting with Mom seemed like a changed man, perhaps a guilty one.

"Dad?" Clara shook her head. "I don't think so. Mom says that if Dad was having an affair, she'd have heard about it from Trisha. Trisha knows all the gossip, which is part of the reason why I can't stand her."

Stephanie had to smile at that one. She remembered Trisha, Mom's best friend since high school, as being something of a bossy snob. She, too, had tried to avoid her. "Maybe Neal is having an affair with Trisha?"

That coaxed a small smile from Clara. "I don't think she's his type and vice versa."

Stephanie saw her opening. "Who's your type, Clara? Do you have a boyfriend?"

"Do you?" she countered. Her pale blue eyes looked small in her round, bloated face.

"Right now, I honestly don't know." Stephanie thought about the unread texts from Jere. Maybe, after everything they'd been through, he'd decided to break up with her. They'd left things an uncertain mess. Gingerly, she touched her rib. She was almost sure that it was cracked.

"Me either."

"Fair enough." For the first time, Stephanie felt some pity for her sister. Mom was right. Something was definitely going on with her, and she wasn't happy.

"Why did you lie about nursing school?"

"Excuse me?" The question caught Stephanie off guard.

"I know you didn't graduate from Barnes School of Nursing. I looked it up online. And I'm pretty sure you don't live in St. Louis. I can't find any record of you there."

The challenge in Clara's small eyes stopped Stephanie from denying this truth. "You didn't tell Mom?"

Clara shook her head. "You're just lucky that she's not good with computers." Again, the small smile. "So tell me, where do you really live, and what do you actually do?"

"I'll tell you if you tell me whether or not you're pregnant, and if so, who's the baby daddy." Stephanie realized she wouldn't really mind if Clara found out what she did for a living. She wasn't ashamed of it, most of the time, although there had been times when she wished she had a profession that didn't raise eyebrows. When he got really mad at her, Jere would throw it in her face: "You're nothing more than a stripper cunt!" When he said it the first time, she'd thrown a heavy glass ashtray at his head, giving him a black eye. She never asked him how he explained that black eye to his wife.

"Fair enough." Clara sat there for another few minutes, staring somewhere over Stephanie's shoulder. Then she got up heavily and lumbered from the room.

"So tell me, Ms. Nelson." The man looked down at the paperwork on his desk. "Why do you need a loan for $68,998?"

Stephanie tried not to openly stare at the handsome bank manager. He was tall and broad-shouldered, with dark hair graying at the temples. He stood up to shake her hand when she walked into his office, and she immediately felt an electric charge at his touch. He'd been very professional so far, but Stephanie knew that he, too, felt the crackle of sexual tension in the room. She dropped her eyes to the gold nameplate on his desk, Jere Casper.

"I want to buy a car. Specifically, Jere—you don't mind if I call you Jere, do you?—I want to buy a 2012 911 Carrera 4 GTS Porsche that I found on Craigslist. It only has 21,000 miles on it, and the owner assures me that it's in excellent shape."

The skin crinkled around his dark eyes. "And I'm guessing the car costs exactly $68,998?"

Stephanie nodded. "That's the guy's asking price, and he's not budging."

Jere openly smiled now. "But I wouldn't have known that, would I? You could have come in here and applied for a $70,000 loan to cover the title and registration costs, and I wouldn't have known the difference."

That thought had never occurred to her, and Stephanie really wished it had. Damn, she could have asked for $75,000 to give herself a little bit of a safety net, but she hadn't thought of that either. "I don't want to be any more in debt than I have to be," she said, hoping that impressed him and proved she was a responsible money-seeker.

"I see." Jere leaned back in his chair and put his hands behind his head, perfectly at ease. "And why a Porsche, Ms. Nelson? Why not a more affordable Honda or Toyota?"

"Because this Porsche is my dream car." Actually, it wasn't. She'd never thought about cars before, other than the necessity of getting from Point A to Point B. But she'd been bored and decided to scroll through Craigslist on a lark. When she came to the ad for the Porsche, she suddenly knew what she'd been looking for, a classy convertible to drive around town in style. She had just started working at the Fox Den, and being the new girl, she received a lot of attention. The tips were rolling in, and Stephanie thought she deserved a reward.

"You must be a girl with expensive tastes."

He was flirting with her. Stephanie knew he was, even as his voice remained neutral, and the gold ring on his left hand shouted, *Taken!* "You bet. I have an entire closet filled with Jimmy Choo and Louboutin shoes. And I summer every year in the Hamptons."

Jere didn't bother looking at her file again. "What do you do at the Fox Den?"

"Well, I'm not a bouncer, bartender, or server, so what do you guess?"

"I'm not prying, Ms. Nelson. I'm just trying to ascertain if you could pay back the loan on your salary." He stared at her frankly now.

"My salary is paltry, but I'm making a killing in tips. I didn't put that on the application. You know, taxes and everything." Stephanie wondered if she should have left that part out.

But Jere seemed unperturbed. "So, you're a dancer."

"You should come and see me one of these nights. I'm fantastic."

Jere laughed out loud at that. "I bet you are, Ms. Nelson."

"Please call me Stephanie."

"Okay, Stephanie, so why haven't you asked your parents for a loan like most twenty-five-year-old women would do?"

"My parents are dead."

Jere unclasped his hands and leaned forward on his desk. "I'm sorry to hear that."

Stephanie was disappointed that he didn't reach for her hand, but he would eventually. She had a finely developed sixth sense when it came to the actions of men who were interested in her. "You don't have to be sorry. The car accident happened a long time ago. My grandmother raised me, but she died a few years ago, too. Lung cancer. I don't have any siblings, so I'm all alone in the world." She didn't know what prompted her to lie to him so early in the game. Perhaps she wanted his sympathy. Perhaps she just wanted money to buy her so-called dream car, although the Porsche grew less important by the minute.

To drive her point home, she said again, "I'm all alone in the world."

Then I would have you for myself. At the time, Stephanie wasn't sure if she heard Jere say those words, or if she just imagined it. Later, of course, she would know that he had inadvertently whispered them out loud, behind the hand cupping his mouth, as if he were trying to stop the thought from escaping.

"Do I get the money or not, Jere?" She smiled at him shyly. "I really want that Porsche."

The phone on Jere's desk rang, startling them both. Jere glanced at his watch. "I have to take this call." But he didn't pick up immediately.

"Why don't you stop by the Fox Den tonight, and we can discuss this further?"

He reluctantly reached for the phone. "Mixing business with pleasure, huh?"

"I'm insisting on it. My first show starts at nine."

When she walked out on the stage for her first number, Stephanie was not at all surprised to see Jere Casper sitting in the front row. He watched attentively as other men stuffed bills into her G-string, but he did not contribute. When her number finished, Stephanie knelt right in front of him as she scraped the random bills off the stage. "The dressing room has a bathroom," she said to him, and he nodded.

Stephanie met him at the dressing room door and then escorted him through the sea of half-naked women to the small bathroom in the back. She locked the door, and he was on her, pressing her hard against the wood, one hand pinning both of her arms above her head. After he fumbled with his zipper and thrust into her hard and deep, his other hand went around her neck, squeezing until the world turned black with streaks of silver. Stephanie had never had such an intense physical reaction to a man before, the pleasure and pain blending into an unbearably exquisite sensation. When it was over, she felt weak, satisfied, used. She wanted more.

"Did you like that?" Jere's hot breath whispered into her ear. His hand was still around her neck, but now he caressed it slowly, gently.

"Yes," she whispered when she found her voice.

"From the moment you came into my office, I knew you'd be the type of woman who liked what I like."

Stephanie had never had sex that rough before, and if someone had asked her five minutes ago if she liked to be strangled and restrained during sex, she would have said something like: "Do you mean do I like to be raped? Hell, no." But what had just happened wasn't rape. In its brutality, it was also completely honest, and she had never felt more turned on and alive. "I think you and I are a lot alike," she said.

"We'll see." Jere kissed her hungrily before opening the bathroom door and walking back through the sea of half-naked women. He didn't even glance at a bare breast, which further convinced Stephanie that she'd found the man she'd been looking for.

So she wasn't surprised when she got a call from the bank the next day; her loan for $68,998 had been approved. She immediately called the guy on Craigslist and bought the Porsche. When Jere got off work at five and walked out to the bank's parking lot, Stephanie, in her Porsche, was waiting for him.

Stephanie planned on leaving today. She'd done what Mom had asked her to do. She had asked Clara if she was pregnant, and Clara hadn't told her. Besides, she hated being stuck in this town. Even at the age of twenty-seven, when she came back to Liberty, she felt like she had traveled back in time to her frustrated, bored fifteen-year-old self, who was too young to drive and couldn't escape the claustrophobia of this old, dark house. She knew Mom loved this house; it was the nicest one she had ever lived in. She loved it and the safety it represented to her so much that she couldn't see how dreary and outdated the floral wallpaper in the dining room and the mahogany staircase and the furniture were. She couldn't see how unhappy everyone who lived here truly was.

Talk about denial. Mandy was a professional when it came to denial. Her mom blithely tottered to her little store every day, pretending nothing was wrong as her world fell apart all around her. Her husband was probably having an affair, and her daughter was probably about eight months pregnant, yet Mandy went to her store, brought home dinner, plastered a smile on her face, and willed it not to be true. When it came to denial, both Neal and Clara were also heading up to the professional level. Neither one would admit anything, so a river of denial ran through these rooms.

And then there was her. Last night, Stephanie finally read the seventeen texts from Jere, and they were as threatening as she'd suspected. Even the nice ones, the ones professing his undying love for her and the ones saying he couldn't live without her, sounded ominous. In one text, he said he would "hunt her down like a dog and bring her back." She didn't think he would do it, though. But on one rare, calm night, they had talked about installing that app on their phones that helps you track people. Stephanie wasn't going to check her phone to see if Jere had actually installed it. See? Denial ran in the family.

Stephanie walked into the kitchen, where Mandy was busy scrambling eggs. She'd heard her come in last night after ten, but she hadn't heard Neal. "Where's Neal? I didn't hear him come in last night."

Mandy shrugged. "Oh, he came in late, and he went out early this morning, too. How'd you sleep?"

Stephanie didn't buy it for a second. "My old room is now a combination office/storage room, and I slept on an air mattress on the floor. How do you think I slept?"

Mom turned from the stove then, a look of chagrin on her face. "Oh, no. I knew I should have made up the couch, but then I thought you'd want more privacy."

"I'm kidding, Mom," Stephanie said quickly. She'd done it again, hurt Mom. She needed to break that bad habit, but it was hard. "I slept fine."

"How did your talk with Clara go?"

Stephanie pulled out a kitchen chair like she had done hundreds of times before. "She wouldn't tell me anything."

Mom sighed and sunk into the chair across from Stephanie. The dark circles under her eyes made her look ten years older. "I suppose that's to be expected. You girls haven't seen each other in a few years, and it's going to take time for her to open up to you."

"What do you mean, *take time?*" Stephanie asked cautiously.

Mom took a paper napkin from the plastic holder on the table and started to fold it like she was an expert at origami. "I hoped you'd stay a week or so, Stephanie. It's been a long time since you've been home, and I'd like to talk to you about your work and what's going on in your life. Surely, you have some time off saved from the hospital? I mean, you've worked every major holiday for the last few years, so I think the hospital would understand if you took some personal time."

It was the perfect opportunity for Stephanie to tell the truth: *About that nursing thing, Mom? It's not true. I'm a stripper at a sleazy club in Champaign.* But Stephanie didn't utter those words. Instead, she said, "If I took some time off, don't you think I'd rather go to Cabo or the Bahamas or San Diego? Anywhere, really, except Liberty?"

Mom's head snapped back as if she'd been slapped. When she spoke, her voice trembled. "I would like to think you still have some feelings for your family."

She'd done it yet again, hurt Mom. It was as if she had a sickness that no amount of antibiotics could cure. And after the words popped carelessly out of her mouth, Stephanie always felt terrible, so why did she keep doing it? She must apologize once again. "I'm sorry, Mom. I swear, sometimes I think someone should cut out my tongue... Oh, God!" And suddenly, Stephanie had trouble breathing, and the room tilted around her. She grabbed onto the edge of the table.

Mom was immediately at her side. "Stephanie! What's wrong? Can you hear me, honey? Just hold on. My phone's on the counter. I'm going to call 911."

It had been their final argument two nights ago, the one that forced her hand, the one that brought her back to Liberty. She had a night off work and told Jere that she planned to stay home to dye her hair, which he would accept. He liked that she kept it jet black to distinguish herself from the other girls at the club, and back in the beginning, he sometimes called her the dark horse dancer. When she first took her position on the stage by the pole, many patrons didn't initially think she was as sexy as the girls with fake boobs and blond hair extensions, but as soon as she started dancing, they knew differently. By the time she finished her provocative set, she had collected more tips than any other dancer. Night after night, she was the winner.

And Stephanie did dye her hair that night, but at eight o'clock, she was bored. She wanted to go out. It had been such a long time since she'd had a night on the town. In the two years they'd been dating, Jere had slowly peeled off her friends like they were discarded gum wrappers. "I want you all to myself," he always told her. "We only need each other." So she didn't tell him about the nights she did make plans with the friends she had left. In many ways, it was like being back in high school and sneaking out her bedroom window, and Stephanie had to admit that it gave her a bit of a thrill. Jere didn't control her, no matter what he thought.

She met Peter and Dex at The Rose, a country bar in downtown Urbana, one of her regular haunts, pre-Jere. It had an old-time vibe with Sonny and The Playboys, clad in cowboy hats and big silver belt buckles, singing country classics like "Wasted Days and Wasted Nights" and "Rose Colored Glasses" and "He Stopped Loving Her Today." Peter and Dex were some of the first people Stephanie met when she landed in Champaign. She had even slept on their couch a few times when she had a hard time making ends meet, but there had never been anything sexual between the three of them. She hadn't seen them in ages, but when she called them, they were up for a night on the town.

They were into their fourth rounds of beer and shots, joking and laughing at the music—while secretly loving it—when Jere appeared at their table, his face a mottled red. "Come on," Jere said as he roughly grabbed Stephanie's arm. "We're going home."

"Hey, Grandpa, take your hands off her," Dex said.

"Who is this guy?" Peter asked. "Your long-lost Daddy?"

Right then, Stephanie felt more annoyed than frightened. She'd forgotten how much she liked hanging out with these two guys; she'd forgotten what it felt like to be young and free. "Cut it out, Jere. Enough with the theatrics. You can pull up a chair and join us, or you can leave. Take your pick, but I'm staying and having a drink with my friends."

Jere's hold on her arm tightened. "It's time to go home now, Stephanie," he hissed.

"Who does Grandpa think he is?" Dex laughed. "Is this a joke?"

"I am not her fucking Grandpa." Jere took a threatening step towards Dex.

Dex, unperturbed, shrugged. "I don't care who the hell you are. Just get the hell out of this bar."

Stephanie still wasn't frightened, and she'd had enough to drink to ignore all of Jere's warning signs: the mottled skin, the hard glint in his eye, the twitching tick around the corners of his mouth—all the signs threatening that he would erupt. "This Grandpa here is my married boyfriend. He says he's going to leave his wife for me, but it's been two years now. I don't think that's going to happen, do you? Oh, and when he gets mad, he likes to slap me around some. What kind of a man beats up on a girl? Seriously, I want to know."

Jere's hot breath hissed in her ear. "I'm going to cut out your goddamn tongue, you little bitch."

"Do you want me and Dex to take him on?" Peter asked. "I'm pretty sure we can take on this old geezer."

"Shut the fuck up!" And Jere lunged across the table at Peter, swinging.

It all happened so fast that Stephanie still couldn't believe she did it. She picked up the almost empty pitcher of beer and brought it down on Jere's head. The Rose was such an old-fashioned place that it still used glass pitchers, and the pitcher made a satisfying thunk on the back of Jere's skull. He howled, but Stephanie didn't stick around to see the damage she'd inflicted. She was out the door and into the hot night, running as fast as she could. She'd planned on taking an Uber home to neighboring Champaign, but she didn't call until she'd run for a good fifteen minutes. When she got home, she locked her door.

She should have barricaded it with a chair or her couch. Jere had a key, of course, and when he flung himself into the room, fresh blood still seeped from the back of his head. Usually impeccably dressed and groomed, his shirt was torn, and wet stains dotted his khakis. His hair was matted in clumps. During their many heated arguments, they both knew to keep their voices down so that Stephanie's neighbors in the apartment building didn't call the cops. So when Jere spoke, it was deadly quiet.

"I am going to cut out your tongue for saying what you did."

Now Stephanie was afraid, but she couldn't let him see that. Her fear seemed to elevate his violence. "What I said was true."

"But first, I'm going to use this knife elsewhere. Do you remember the movie, *Boxing Helena*? The last thing the guy cut off that loud-mouthed bitch was her tongue. Then all he had was her head in a box."

Stephanie remembered watching that creepy movie when she was way too young to be allowed. She'd had nightmares for weeks after about the doctor who was so obsessively infatuated with a beautiful woman that to keep her with him, he slowly dismembered her. She also remembered how the disturbing movie ended. "And in the end, he woke up, and it was all just a dream."

"But this will be oh-so-real, baby." Jere shook his hand at her. "This is real."

Jere did not hold a knife in his hand; he didn't even carry a pocketknife. That's when Stephanie knew the man's insatiable jealousy and possessiveness had made him crazy. She had three or four knives in her kitchen, and even though she didn't think he would cut her, she couldn't risk running into the kitchen and grabbing them. He was faster, taller, stronger, and he would be on her in a flash—with a real weapon in his hand. She had to keep playing this tired, dangerous game. She had to provoke him just far enough.

She braced herself against the back of the couch for the attack. "I don't think you're man enough to do it."

"What did you say?" he said between gritted teeth. He took a step closer. Stephanie's apartment was small, and the distance from the front door to where she stood at the couch was only six or seven feet.

Louder, she said, "You're not man enough to do it."

In three quick strides, he loomed over her. She slapped his face hard, and then, as she knew he would, he pushed her over the couch. Then they were on the floor, slapping and punching. He pummeled her ribs, grabbed her hair, and banged her head against the floor until his angry face swam before her eyes. He didn't touch her face—he never wanted to mar her beautiful face, he said—but his fists flew indiscriminately everywhere else. She fought back, slapping and biting until they were both exhausted. And then he kissed her, and she kissed him back passionately as they both tore off their clothes. In the morning, in addition to her other injuries, Stephanie had rug burns all over her back. In the morning, after Jere left, Stephanie packed her bag and drove to Liberty, finally admitting that they could not go on like this. Eventually, they would kill each other.

The water was ice cold when Clara threw it into her face. Stephanie sputtered. "What the hell?"

Clara stood in front of her, an empty glass in her hand. "She's all right now, Mom. But maybe I need to douse her again to make sure." Her smile looked wicked.

Mom, phone in hand, leaned down, getting directly in front of Stephanie's face. "Do you know where you are? I could still call 911."

"I'm fine." Stephanie mopped at her face with her t-shirt. The glass of water from Clara had been unnecessarily large. "I think I might have just been dehydrated."

Clara hurried to the sink. "I'll get you another glass of water."

"Hand this one to me, would you?"

Mom straightened up, her hand over her heart. "You scared me to death, Stephanie. Are you sure you feel better?"

"I'm sure." Stephanie looked warily at Clara as she took the newly full glass.

"Well, good." Mom nodded, satisfied. "I guess we can all sit down to breakfast and get on with our day." She scooped out scrambled eggs on three plates and added strips of greasy bacon. "I just had a great idea. Why don't you two girls go shopping today? You could drive to the mall in Carbondale and make a day out of it?"

Stephanie knew this had not been a random thought from the Queen of Denial. She'd had this preposterous plan all along. What were they supposed to shop for—maternity muumuus, baby clothes, a length of rope to hang themselves with? She looked at Clara, who rolled her eyes at her, a slight smile on her lips. Stephanie rolled her eyes back, smiling. She picked up her fork. "Great idea, Mom. Clara and I will go shopping today."

"How can you afford a Porsche?" Clara rubbed her hand over the leather seat. "A car like this must cost a fortune."

"It's used."

"Still, this is a ritzy car. What do you do, Stephanie? Cook meth, sell drugs, what?"

"I don't do drugs, and neither should you." It was more a stretching of the truth than an out-and-out lie. She'd probably tried them all at one time or another, but she considered herself to be more of a dabbler than a user. Come to think of it, she could really use an Oxy right now. Her right rib throbbed. It was definitely cracked or something.

"Yeah, right. You are so full of shit."

"Yep. I have shit running through my veins." Stephanie turned onto the blacktop toward Murphysboro. She remembered these well-traveled roads. Forty miles away, Carbondale was the closest thing to a big city for the residents of Liberty. "And by the way, I'm a stripper."

"Yeah, right," Clara said sarcastically. "Weren't you the one who flunked PE because you refused to get naked and shower with a bunch of girls?"

Oh, right. That's what Stephanie had told her Mom when the reason why was that she skipped class to make out with Raul, the sexy foreign exchange student that year. Stephanie peered ahead attentively. These two-lane country highways could be dangerous. It was daylight, but a deer could still appear out of nowhere. Even though the county now had two deer hunting seasons a year, the deer still multiplied like rabbits. "Hey, isn't that Neal's truck up ahead?" Neal drove a distinctive red Toyota truck with gold thunderbolt decals, a midlife crisis vehicle if Stephanie had ever seen one.

Clara looked ahead. "It's got to be. Where do you think he's going? He's supposed to be at work."

"Maybe he's going to meet his *lover*. Let's follow him and see what happens."

Clara gave her a sideways glance. She'd given up on buckling the seat belt. There was no way it would fit across her bulk now. "You say that like you think it would be funny if Dad was cheating on Mom. She would be devastated."

"I don't know about that," Stephanie said. She kept far enough behind Neal's truck to escape his notice. She sometimes forgot how young Clara was, but she was young and still naive enough to see matters of the heart in black and white. One of these days, too soon perhaps, she would see that relationships were mostly shaded gray.

"And I don't think it's funny that he might be cheating on Mom. However, she would have to be blind not to notice how Neal has changed." Stephanie stopped talking when she realized Clara's attention was focused out the window on a small farmhouse with chipped white paint. "Who lives there?"

"Nobody." Clara seemed to be searching for something.

"Is that where the Baby Daddy lives?"

Clara's head snapped back around, her sallow skin flushed a rosy pink. "For your information, I'm a virgin."

Stephanie couldn't help herself. She started to laugh. "Oh, come on, Clara, drop the act. Do you honestly want me to believe your pregnancy is the result of another Immaculate Conception?"

"Bitch," Clara mumbled under her breath. Then added, "A person can just get fat, you know. When I quit the softball team and stopped exercising, I gained weight. End of story."

"I don't believe a word you're saying, Clara."

"Now you know how I feel about you. A nurse? Ha! I knew that wouldn't be true in a million years."

Stephanie tried to keep the impatience out of her voice. Why wouldn't the silly girl give up the pretense? "All I'm saying is that you don't have to do this alone. You know Mom would help. And Neal, too," she added. It was so easy for her to forget that Clara's dad, unlike her own, had been an attentive and loving parent. And he was still here.

"And you?" Clara asked pointedly.

"You don't need my help. In fact, you probably wouldn't want it. My life is in something of a mess right now, and I'm in no position to be giving anybody advice."

"That, I believe," Clara said triumphantly. "You finally said something that sounds true."

Stephanie sighed. "I don't care what you believe, Clara, but if you are pregnant, there will eventually be a baby."

Clara folded her arms over the mound of her belly. "I call a truce."

"Fine. It's your life." Stephanie could see why Mom felt so frustrated with Clara. Talking to her was like talking to a large, immovable brick wall. She didn't need to come home after all; she wasn't helping here. If she'd been thinking clearly yesterday morning, if she hadn't been so bruised and frightened, she would have withdrawn all her savings from the bank, ditched her cell phone and bought a burner, and moved out of state. She could have moved to Colorado, a place she had always wanted to visit. Jere would never think of tracking her down there. Instead, she'd made the wrong decision and was now stuck. Jere had texted repeatedly throughout the night, badgering her, goading her. It was only a matter of time now before things came to a head.

"You know Dad is going to notice your Porsche following him. It's as conspicuous as his truck. This is a bad idea."

They were in Carbondale now, and Stephanie was trying her best to keep two or three cars behind Neal. She, too, had thought about her flashy Porsche. "Do you have a better idea of how we should spend the day? Do you want to go shopping?"

"No," Clara said sullenly. She sat up straighter and pointed. "There. He's pulling into that Wells Fargo bank. I thought we did all our banking at Liberty Savings and Loan. That's odd."

"Maybe he has a secret bank account for his mistress? If he set up another account in Liberty, everyone would know."

"You think you're so smart."

"I know something about cheaters," Stephanie said, but she didn't elaborate. She turned into the drive-thru at the McDonald's across the street while they waited for Neal to come out. She could hear Clara's stomach growling, so she bought her a Big Mac meal with large fries. Clara did not bother to thank her but ate every single bite.

Neal's next stop was at a hair salon, and when he came out, his hair looked just a shade darker than before. Clara offered an explanation for that one. "Dad can't go to Trudy's Beauty Boutique to get his hair dyed. That place is the hub for town gossip."

It was a long afternoon, and Neal only seemed to be running a series of random errands. He made stops at a dry cleaner's, Men's Wearhouse, Long John Silver's for lunch, LA Fitness, and a UPS store that advertised PO Boxes for rent. Stephanie found that to be especially interesting, but Clara seemed to have lost interest by then. Or perhaps she didn't want to acknowledge the growing evidence that her father led some kind of secret existence that her mother did not know about. Stephanie placated her by buying a dozen Krispy Kremes, Taco Bell, and Dairy Queen ice cream sandwiches. Every time Clara had to pee, they stopped and got something for her to eat. The amount of food Clara consumed made Stephanie feel slightly ill, but she kept her mouth shut for once.

At five that afternoon, Neal left Carbondale, but he didn't turn east back toward Liberty. Instead, he took a western route out of town. "I think he knows we're following him, and now he's leading us on a wild goose chase," Clara said.

Stephanie nodded. She felt stiff from sitting in the car all day, and the pain in her ribs had not relented. "Do you want to call it, or do you want to see this through to the bitter end?"

"What do you mean by *the bitter end*? Do you always think the worst of people?"

"It's just an expression, Clara," Stephanie said, but when Clara questioned her, she felt a shudder of apprehension. She was probably just grouchy from spending the day cooped up in the car with her exasperating sister, following her secretive stepfather, who must be cheating on his wife. Stephanie was 99.9 percent sure of it.

"We might as well see where he goes. I've got nothing to do when I get home."

Looking over at her, Stephanie would swear her sister had grown during the day—not only her belly but also her face, arms, and legs. She looked decidedly uncomfortable wedged into the bucket seat of the Porsche. "Your call," she said and continued following Neal's truck.

Neal drove ten miles west of town before turning into Coral Stables, a beautiful property with a large Colonial house and pastures on either side where horses quietly roamed. Stephanie didn't follow Neal down the lane to the house but parked on the side of the road in front, no longer caring if Neal saw them or not. "Why would your dad visit a horse property?"

"I used to want a pony when I was a kid," Clara offered as she stared at the horses.

"Oh, and you're a grownup now?" Stephanie meant it to be a joke, but Clara, naturally, took offense.

"You just can't help yourself, can you?" she said snidely. They let some minutes pass before she said, "There's an RV parked at the side of the barn. Dad is probably here because of that. Maybe he sold the unit to them, or maybe the guy wants to trade it in for a new model, something like that."

"Could be." But then Stephanie and Clara saw Neal and another man walking toward the pasture. The man called, and a beautiful black stallion came up to the railing. Neal rubbed the majestic creature's nose as if he were familiar with the animal. "I'll be damned," Stephanie said. "I never figured Neal for a horse lover."

"Me neither." Clara now stared straight ahead. "Even though Mom grew up on a farm, she's afraid of horses," she said, needlessly. They both knew that.

"I think we should head home." Stephanie started the car. They should not have followed Neal today. What had she been trying to prove? The only thing this surveillance had accomplished was to make Clara feel even worse than she already did. She must say it. "I'm sorry, Clara."

"What for?" Clara's sullen, angry eyes bored into Stephanie's. "What are you sorry for, Stephanie?"

"Just forget it." Stephanie stomped on the gas pedal, and they roared down the highway, full speed ahead.

They passed by the American Legion on their way back into town, and Stephanie noticed the sign and the cars already swarming the parking lot. "Are you kidding me? The jackpot for the Queen of Hearts drawing is 1.3 million dollars. How can that be?"

"That drawing has been going on for weeks now. It's all this town can talk about." Clara stared out the window at the gathering crowd. "Mom, of course, never goes. She doesn't believe in gambling. Dad doesn't go either… Well, maybe he does. Who knows?"

Stephanie changed the subject. She truly was sorry she'd upset Clara by suggesting they follow Neal. "How do you play?"

"The drawing is held every Thursday at eight o'clock. You buy a ticket for two dollars, and it goes into a big drum. Every week, they draw a ticket, and that person gets to pick a card in an envelope on a big board. The game starts with fifty-four cards—they include the two jokers—and it continues until someone picks the queen of hearts. Are you going to the drawing tonight?"

"Oh, I doubt it," Stephanie said, but she thought about what she could do with that kind of money. She could quit stripping and start a new life in Colorado. With that kind of money, she wouldn't even bother to go back to Champaign and pack up her belongings. Who needed decrepit old furniture when she could buy new stuff?

"You could go, and if you win, you could split the money with me. How about it?" Clara looked at her with something akin to happiness, a first for the day.

"It's a deal—if I go." Stephanie smiled back.

She didn't have any plans to go to the Queen of Hearts drawing. But after dinner was over—deli sandwiches bought from Dave's Market—Clara settled herself in front of the TV to watch some inane reality show, and Mom bustled around the kitchen, trying to look busy but accomplishing nothing. Stephanie needed to get out of the house. She was bored, as she always was when she came back home, but it was more than that. Neal had still not made an appearance, and every time Stephanie looked at Clara, it felt like they kept some deep, dark secret from Mom. Mom had not said a word about Neal's absence, but Stephanie could feel the tension emanating from her every movement. She kept cocking her head to the side as if listening for the sound of Neal's truck.

Mom finally finished refolding the dish towels, and as if struck suddenly with the memory, she said, "Did you and Clara have a good time shopping today?"

"We did more eating than shopping." Then at Mom's quizzical, probing look, Stephanie said, "I think I'll take a drive." She didn't want to talk about Clara, and she didn't want to tell Mom that Clara claimed she was still a virgin. All the pretenses of these people, her family, were getting on her last nerve.

Because of the crowd at the Legion, Stephanie had to park three blocks away, and as soon as she got out of her car and started walking, she could feel that something was different about this night. It must be because of the drawing, she thought. The very air seemed charged and static, almost as if a thunderstorm had started to brew. It wasn't a comfortable feeling, and her instinct told her to turn around and drive back home. But she really didn't want to be in that house with the sullen Clara and the beleaguered, sadly hopeful Mandy. She continued. She would drink one beer and then go back home. Maybe she would have two beers to take the edge off and silence her screaming rib. Maybe she would have old Doc Jenkins take a look at it tomorrow—if he was still alive. She would tell him that she fell down a flight of stairs or injured it in a skydiving accident. She would make him believe it.

Stephanie started walking faster; the sense of urgency propelling her was sudden and intense. She needed to be inside the packed Legion, enveloped in a crowd. Stephanie dodged between cars parked haphazardly in the lot and was comforted when she saw the police cruiser among them. She remembered Mom talking about the new police officer in town, how handsome he was, how kind.

"Maybe I should introduce you?" Mom had said with a wink. "Maybe it's time you settled down with a nice, reliable man, Stephanie. And it certainly helps that he's easy on the eyes." Wink, wink.

Stephanie hadn't bothered to tell her that she already had a boyfriend, or whatever it was that Jere could be called. Mom would ask a lot of questions that Stephanie couldn't answer even if she wanted to. Why was it that, after two years, she still stayed with a man whose rage and jealousy were out of control, a man who hit her more often than not? Her friend Gigi hadn't seen the worst bruises and scratches. She hadn't seen the place on Stephanie's inner thigh where Jere had held a cigarette lighter, burning her flesh. It was the last wound he inflicted two nights ago. "Now you're branded," Jere had said. "Now, you will belong to me forever."

She had to end it with Jere. She had been fooling herself for a long time, convincing herself that the abuse was worth it because of the sex, convincing herself that she wasn't abused if she hit him back. She had been lying to herself all this time. Ha! What a crock of shit! A liar, lying to herself. And that had to stop too. A roar went up from the crowd inside the Legion, and the building seemed to vibrate with the noise. *They all agree with me*, Stephanie thought. *They know it has to stop.*

Stephanie got her phone from the back pocket of her jeans. She would call Jere right now and tell him they were through. She was dialing when she heard a *crack*, and the phone flew from her hands and landed in pieces at her feet. At first, she didn't know what it all meant. Had someone thrown a rock? Had she tripped on something and accidentally dropped the phone? And then she heard the sound again, and the bullet hurtled through the passenger window of the car she stood next to, shattering it.

Then Stephanie saw a car door open a few feet ahead of her, a white Mercedes; Jere drove a white Mercedes. He walked toward her, slowly and deliberately, a strange smile on his face. "I've been waiting hours for you," he said. "And I don't like to be kept waiting."

"How… when… why . . ." But Stephanie was too stunned to formulate the questions. Somewhere, though, subconsciously, she wasn't all that surprised to see him. Hadn't she known that he would follow her, that he would make her pay for not answering his texts or telling him she was coming home to Liberty? She wanted to run, but she couldn't will her legs to move. Besides, what good would it do? Jere would follow her. Jere would track her down. Jere liked the hunt, and she was his prey.

He stood directly in front of her now, and he pointed the gun at her forehead. "It's time to go home now, Stephanie." His voice was eerily quiet.

"No," she whispered, even as she knew it wouldn't do any good. Another roar came from inside the Legion, and Stephanie knew that if she screamed for help, no one would hear her.

Jere grabbed her roughly by the arm and dragged her toward his car. She wanted to fight back, but he had the gun to her head, and Stephanie knew with certainty he would use it if she didn't obey. He opened the Mercedes passenger door, shoved her in, and then followed without loosening his grip. He pressed the automatic lock to lock the doors.

She was in the driver's seat. "Drive," he said.

She shook violently, and she tried to calm herself. She needed to stall Jere; she needed time to think. "What are you planning to do, take me to an old strip mine pit and shoot me?" She tried to sound flippant and not terrified, but it didn't work.

"Would you rather I do it here?" His voice was still eerily quiet. "Drive."

Stephanie instinctively knew she would be dead if she drove this car out of the parking lot. She shook her head. "No," she said, loudly this time. "We're not going anywhere. We need to talk about this, Jere. You don't want to shoot me."

"You left me," he said.

"I came home to visit my mother, Jere. That's all."

"You told me your mother was dead."

Had she told him that? She had told him so many lies in their time together. She could no longer keep them straight. "My younger sister might be pregnant," she tried again, uselessly.

"You told me you were all alone in the world. You told me that I would have you all to myself. You promised."

"No, I didn't—"

"Drive," he interrupted.

When she made no move to do so, he grabbed her by the back of the neck and rammed her face into the steering wheel again and again. He'd never struck her in the face before, but now he was breaking her nose and her cheeks, splitting her lips. Stephanie could taste blood, but she didn't know where it came from. He was breathing hard, and when he let up just for a second, Stephanie's fighting instinct came roaring back. She lunged at him, slapping and scratching like a madwoman. Vaguely, she thought she heard pounding and yelling, but nothing would come into focus except the outrage on Jere's face. They clawed at each other, writhing together on the plush seat, grappling in a bizarre and dangerous dance. Stephanie grabbed for the gun, but she couldn't quite get it out of his grip.

Seconds later, when the next and final shot rang out, Stephanie was finally free from Jere Casper.

Part Two:
The Aftermath

STRANGE INHERITANCE

It was the strangest thing. The call had come out of the blue on a day so non-descript that the only highlight had been when she walked to the mailbox station in her apartment complex to retrieve her weekly *People* magazine. Shelby almost didn't answer the phone. She didn't recognize the number, and she had been getting a lot of spam calls recently. But for some reason, she did answer, and the disembodied voice on the other end told her that she had inherited a movie theater in a small southern Illinois town called Liberty.

"That's impossible," she said. "I don't have any relatives in that town. And I've never even heard of it. There must be some mistake."

"You are Shelby Williams, aren't you?" He waited for her to acknowledge the fact. "I've spent a great deal of time tracking you down, Ms. Williams." The voice had grown slightly accusatory. "And according to the wishes of Mr. Errol Gaylord, you are hereby bequeathed Gaylord Movie Theatre in Liberty, Illinois."

"Why didn't he leave it to a member of his family?" She now walked quickly across the hot asphalt. Living in Scottsdale, Arizona, in July was like living in an oven. Or in hell. Today, it felt more like hell.

"Mr. Gaylord did not have any heirs." Papers rustled in the background.

"But why me?"

The voice said, "Apparently, Mr. Errol Gaylord was a great admirer of yours."

Shelby, now cocooned in the coolness of her air-conditioned apartment, laughed. "I haven't made a movie in years. Was the old guy crazy or something?"

"The will is notarized," the voice said, as if that explained everything.

"What if I don't want a movie theater?"

"It is legally yours," the voice insisted. "And Mr. Gaylord was a great admirer of yours," he reminded.

"I'm flattered." Shelby sunk into her couch. In a way, she was flattered that some random stranger would find her work admirable after so many years. She'd only made a handful of pictures before Hollywood moved on to another younger, prettier girl. She'd only ridden a small crest of popularity before the power players in Hollywood turned against her, saying she was no longer marketable after what happened.

The voice continued. "The property taxes are up to date, but I am informed that the theater has not been in use for quite some time."

"In other words, I've inherited a dump?"

"You can sell the property," he pointed out.

Shelby could use the money. She wasn't teaching her regular acting classes this summer at Scottsdale Community College. However, she wasn't keen on jumping in her car and driving thousands of miles to see this farce of an inheritance. "Why don't you sell it for me?"

"That is not my area of expertise," the voice said coldly. "I'm an attorney, not a real estate agent."

"Selling movie theaters is not my area of expertise either," she shot back. It was too late in the conversation to ask the voice to repeat his name, but Shelby pictured him as an older man in his early seventies, with sparse white hair and glasses perched on the end of a long, straight nose. And he had something snobby about him.

Then, surprisingly, the voice softened. "I do believe Mr. Gaylord meant this gift to be an homage to your talent."

"It's too bad Mr. Gaylord wasn't my agent. I could have used a cheerleader back then." The words sounded more bitter than Shelby had intended, so she added, "I am flattered—but surprised. It hasn't sunk in yet."

"That's understandable." More papers rustled. "Should I send the papers to your current address?" He rattled off the street name and zip code.

Shelby sighed dramatically. "Sure. Why not?"

After Shelby hung up the phone, she sat on her couch for a long time, thinking. She didn't delve immediately into the recent edition of *People* as she usually did. Even after all this time and bitterness, Shelby still wanted to be informed when it came to who was who in Hollywood, not that it mattered. At forty-two, she was a lost and forgotten relic. If she got lucky, she might be a footnote in Hollywood history, but it would not be a flattering mention.

The possibility remained, of course, that the phone call had been a joke. Perhaps a former student was reacting badly to a grade she'd given him, but other than that, Shelby could not think of anyone else who would want to pull this kind of prank on her, or who had this kind of twisted sense of humor. It puzzled and unsettled her, this strange inheritance from an old fan. What kind of a person would leave such a thing to a stranger he had seen on a movie screen?

From the ages of twenty to twenty-five, she made four movies. Some considered the horror film, *Don't Close Your Eyes*, to be something of a cult classic, although when Shelby occasionally came across it on TV, it came off as campy and outdated to her. She rarely saw reruns of her cop picture, *The Badge*, or the rom-com, *Fairy Dust*. Her last film, the one that sealed her fate, the one in which she played a murder suspect, *Deceit*, she refused to watch at all. What was it that had captivated Mr. Errol Gaylord in those films? What was it about her that had made him a great admirer?

Shelby got up from the couch. Tired of dwelling on the strange call, she needed to get ready for her Match.com date. He was a new guy, a fifty-year-old painter, who said he went to the gym five times a week, didn't smoke or drink, and loved long walks in the moonlight. None of it would turn out to be true. Shelby knew that from experience, yet she kept trying. This guy would probably be a house painter with a beer belly, who smoked like a chimney and hadn't walked longer than the ten feet it took to get to his refrigerator.

"What do you think?" Shelby said to her orchid plant beginning to slowly drop its petals onto her kitchen counter. "That phone call was a hoax, right?"

But two days later, a FedEx package arrived with a deed to Gaylord's Movie Theatre and a set of keys on an ornate brass theater mask keychain. Shelby recognized it as Melpomene, the Muse of Tragedy. *Errol Gaylord must have been quite a character,* Shelby thought. And then: *I now own a run-down movie theater in a small town that I inherited from a stranger.*

Shelby had never lived in a small town. She grew up in San Diego, then moved to LA before fleeing that traffic-clogged metropolis for the more sedate and suburban Scottsdale. So driving through Liberty was an eye-opening experience for her. Some homes were immaculate, with neatly tended yards and ornaments—she saw quite a few concrete geese on front porches dressed in red, white, and blue for the recent Fourth of July holiday—and others had run-down stoops and broken toys scattered on their brown grass. But Shelby found it to be quaint, even lovely. A few people waved from their yards or front porches, and after hesitating the first time it happened, Shelby began to happily wave back. After her last disastrous Match.com date, she was glad she had decided to come here. Shelby needed a break from the rut her life had fallen into. She needed a change of scenery.

She had gone online and rented a lovely bungalow on Elm Street for a month, and she decided to go there first and settle in a bit before seeing this strange inheritance. Her phone, which she had forgotten to charge in the hotel in Joplin the night before, was dying. So Shelby decided to stop at Circle K and ask for directions. The young-looking man behind the counter looked up when she walked in. "Howdy," he said.

"Hello." She smiled. She never worried about people recognizing her; they never did. She didn't look a thing like she had in her movie heyday: all svelte and auburn-haired and fresh-faced. She'd gained some weight, which happened so often with middle-aged women, and she wore her hair, now dyed Golden Brown, short with bangs. Shelby still thought of herself as an attractive woman, but she was no stunner. She'd made one attempt at plastic surgery on an ill-fated trip to Mexico. The only lasting result of that decision was that her left eye looked slightly higher than her right.

"What can I do you for?" the young man asked.

"Excuse me?" His thick Southern accent slurred the words while pushing them together. She had to ask him to repeat his question three times before she understood. She covered her lack of understanding and embarrassment by picking up three candy bars in the box on the counter and pushing them toward him. "I'll take these." She reached into the pocket of her jeans, now rumpled and wrinkled from the long trip, and showed him the slip of paper. "And could you please tell me how to get here? I've rented this house that belongs to Marie Sherman."

The young man's eyes widened, and he took a step back. "Miz Sherman's renting out her place?"

"Well, I went through a real estate agent here in town, but yes, I've rented it for a month."

He shook his head, whistling through his teeth. "Whadda ya know?" Still shaking his head, he gave her the directions. Then: "You be careful, hear? The place is right across from the Legion, and it gets mighty rowdy on Thursday nights at the Queen of Hearts drawing."

Shelby had no idea what he was talking about, so she thanked him hurriedly and left.

"Hey, you forgot your candy," he called after her.

Shelby found the house and pulled into the short driveway. The ad on the internet had not done the place justice. It was picture-perfect, a small white bungalow with green shutters and three Adirondack chairs on the porch. It was indeed across from the red-bricked American Legion, and Shelby could see a sign that said: Jackpot $1,500,000. It was a staggering amount of money. Shelby didn't have any idea what a Queen of Hearts drawing entailed, but the winner would become a millionaire. It seemed incongruous in a town this small, in a town that didn't seem very prosperous to begin with. But it didn't concern her. She was here to sell a movie theater. However, during the drive out, she started to flirt with the possibility that maybe she could make it operational again. It would be a lark to run an old-fashioned movie theater in a small town. Or if that didn't work, maybe she could open up an actor's workshop. Didn't a lot of small towns have community theater groups? It was an idea in progress.

The real estate agent, who couldn't meet her, had told Shelby that she would put the keys to the house under the porch mat, and even this delighted

Shelby. How friendly these people of Liberty were, how trusting! It reassured her that people in this country's heartland still had that kind of faith in each other. With a smile on her face, Shelby opened the front door to the fully furnished house—and then stopped. The place was immaculate, if somewhat old-fashioned in décor—the real estate agent had said it belonged to an older woman—but what immediately caught Shelby's attention was the dark stain by the couch. She walked closer. Someone had scrubbed at the stain, but the outline remained. *Someone must have spilled a glass of red wine,* Shelby thought. But she shivered involuntarily anyway.

It didn't take long for Shelby to tour the small house. From the living room, she passed into the dining room which had a short hallway to the left that housed two bedrooms and a bathroom. In the back was the kitchen that looked out over an overgrown garden of flowers and what looked like tomato plants. Maybe she would take up gardening during her time in Liberty. Shelby had never done anything like that before, but this small town might open up a world of possibilities. She could just feel it. On the way back to the car to retrieve her suitcase, Shelby paused again at the stained carpet. An older lady had lived here, and she grew tomatoes. Perhaps the woman used those tomatoes for her homemade spaghetti sauce. *She must have spilled tomato sauce,* Shelby thought.

Shelby had just finished unpacking her two suitcases when she heard a call from the front door, "Yoo-hoo!" Then she heard the door opening. Wondering who could be dropping by and wondering who would be so brazen to barge in uninvited, Shelby hurried to the door.

The woman who stood in the living room looked about her age but was impossibly thin with a sleek silvery-blond bob. She smiled, and not a crease appeared on her face. Shelby knew Botox when she saw it. The woman stuck out her hand. "I'm Trisha Yardley, the real estate agent. My appointment ended early, so I hurried right over to make sure you have everything you need."

Shelby shook her hand. "The house is perfect. Thank you. I should be very comfortable here." Shelby didn't know why, but her eyes drifted one more time to the stain. "But I do want you to know I didn't cause this stain."

Trisha's eyes followed Shelby's pointing finger, and she frowned. "Oh, goodness, no. I was told that problem had been taken care of. I'll call the cleaners and have them come back. Don't you worry about a thing."

"Someone must have spilled a glass of red wine." Shelby had gone back to her first theory.

"Isn't that always the case?" Trisha said with a rush. "Every time I spill wine, it just happens to be red, never white." She had a high-pitched, nervous laugh. "But enough about wine. What brings you to town, Shelby Williams? Liberty isn't what you would call a vacation destination."

Shelby had no way of knowing she was talking to one of the town's biggest gossips when she told her about the call from the lawyer and how shocked she'd been to inherit Gaylord's Movie Theatre from a stranger. Trisha raptly listened as Shelby recounted the steps that led her to Liberty.

"I always knew Errol Gaylord was a little bit off, not crazy, more like an eccentric. His wife, Nancy, died years ago from some rare disease. She was always sickly. They didn't have any children." Shelby could practically see the wheels turning in Trisha's head. "But why you?"

Shelby hesitated. She didn't like to bring up her past, but Trisha's very presence seemed to demand an answer. "Oh, I was a minor Hollywood actress years ago, and it seems that Mr. Gaylord was a fan of mine." She shrugged. "As you said, the man was eccentric."

"How interesting." Trisha's eyebrows would have shot up if they weren't pinioned in place. "Were you in any movies I might have seen?"

"I don't think so."

The answer clearly disappointed Trisha, but she let it pass. "Well, if you're thinking about selling the place, you know who to call. I'd be glad to handle it for you, even though it won't be an easy sale," she said magnanimously.

"Probably not. The lawyer told me it hasn't been used in a while, so it's probably fallen into disrepair."

"Errol closed the place about ten years ago before he moved to The Cedars, the nursing home here in Liberty. I haven't been inside it, but from the outside, it looks pretty run down. But that's not the reason why it won't sell." Trisha lowered her voice. "It won't sell because some people around here think it's haunted."

Shelby couldn't help it. She laughed. "That's ridiculous. Who in their right mind would think an old movie theater is haunted?"

"Some people," Trisha said ominously.

Gaylord's Movie Theatre stuck out like an eyesore on Liberty's town square, and it was a shame. The businesses circled a quaint common green with a bandstand and wrought iron benches. All were relatively well-maintained: Funtown Billiards, Zelda's Consignment Shop, Verizon, Vinny's Guns, and Subway. But Gaylord's, with its boarded-up windows and graffiti-marred surfaces, screamed of its neglect. Only the ornate marquee over the front door, its glass broken and bulb sockets empty, hinted at its former glory days. So now it stood there like a forgotten relic of a bygone era. And despite its sad state, Shelby felt an immediate kinship with the place. She, too, had been put out to pasture when she was still useful; forces beyond her control had decided for her.

Shelby parked her car and walked around the building. It wasn't large. She estimated that it could only hold about a hundred and fifty people at one time, so it must have offered only one movie at a time unless it showed double features. By the time she finished her tour around the perimeter, Shelby dripped sweat. The heat in southern Illinois, unlike the searing heat of the desert, was humid and heavy. Her t-shirt clung to her back and sweat ran in rivulets down the sides of her face. Still, she felt excited when she inserted the largest key on the Melpomene keychain into the front door lock next to the ticket booth. It took some jiggling and twisting, but the door finally swung open. Shelby peered over her shoulder before she stepped inside. For some reason, she felt that someone was watching her. But she didn't see anybody looking out of the other shops or walking along the street.

Because of the boarded-up windows, she couldn't see much in the musty, gloomy darkness. Even with the door open, not much light reached the interior of what would have been the lobby. She could see the outlines of a glass counter, a popcorn machine, and a soda fountain to her left. The projection room would be above her, but she couldn't make out any stairs off the lobby. Likewise, an office was probably here, but she didn't see the door. Directly in front of her, she could see dark, heavy drapes that led into the theater. She felt through cobwebs along the wall for a light switch, but no surge of electricity flipped on the lights. She should have brought a flashlight.

Shelby did not believe in ghosts. It was all superstitious nonsense, yet she tread softly and cautiously toward the curtains, hands outstretched, feeling her way through the darkness. Her hands touched the heavy, velvet fabric, and Shelby felt for the two halves. She pushed them apart, then hesitated before taking a small step over the threshold. If it was dark in the lobby, it was pitch black in this room. Were there rows of chairs parading down to the big screen in front? There must be a screen straight ahead, and Shelby strained her eyes to see. She heard a *snap* and thought she must have stepped on a creaky board, but then the sound became a distinct *click*, followed by a low whirring sound. It couldn't be, but it sounded like someone had turned on an old-fashioned projector. And was that a pinpoint of light on what would have been the screen? Did it grow larger as she stared at it?

"Is someone in here?" she called out in a shaky voice.

And the clicking, whirring sound of the projector stopped as suddenly as it began.

Shelby didn't believe in ghosts, but she couldn't deny that her first trip to Gaylord's Movie Theatre had rattled her. Despite her exhaustion, she slept fitfully that night, and the next day, instead of returning immediately to the old movie theater, she decided her time would be better spent by hiring someone to take the plywood boards off the windows and clean up the outside of the place. She called Trisha, who said the best handyman in town was a man named Greg Turner. "He also happens to be the minister at the Assembly of God Church, but don't let that put you off," Trisha said. Shelby, having no idea what Trisha meant by that remark, assured her that it wouldn't.

Greg Turner waited on the sidewalk when Shelby met him an hour later at the theater. Tall and lanky, he looked more like a cowboy than a minister. A surly cowboy. He did not return her smile. "You said you never met Errol Gaylord, yet he left this movie theater for you in his will?"

"That's right." They had gone over this information on the phone.

"That Errol was a peculiar man." Greg removed his baseball hat to scratch the back of his head.

"How so?" Shelby was curious. She knew nothing about the man who had left her this strange inheritance.

"I don't like to speak ill of the dead." Greg replaced his cap. "But he kept to himself a lot. And there are always stories swirling around this town, you know, especially when people keep to themselves."

"What kind of stories?"

Greg shrugged. "You know, the usual. Probably nothing to them."

For the second time that morning, Shelby felt bewildered. She was beginning to get the weird feeling that the entire town of Liberty had its own secret code, one that excluded her. "Could you be more specific?" Shelby had the foresight to wear a sundress today, but the sun on her bare shoulders burned.

"I'm not one to gossip, Ms. Williams."

"Of course not," she said hurriedly. It just figured that the town's best handyman would be a minister who looked like a surly cowboy who didn't gossip.

Greg stared up at the broken marquee, lost in thought. "I stole my first kiss in this movie house."

"That's lovely. It's the kind of story I like to hear about the place I inherited." Shelby didn't bring up Trisha's theory that the place was haunted.

"Not so lovely. I ended up marrying her. Not so lovely."

"Oh." Shelby could think of nothing else to say to that, so she changed the subject. "How long will it take to pry off the boards and get rid of the graffiti?"

"A couple of hours." Greg again removed his hat and scratched the back of his head. "And you don't want me to clean up inside?"

"No, I'm going to take care of that."

"That's good," he said.

"What do you mean?" she asked, not bothering to mask her growing exasperation.

"Not a thing. I'll get the crowbar from my truck."

"Do you take credit cards?"

"Nope." He walked over to his truck and pulled out a toolbox.

"Of course you don't." That was the way this odd day was going. "I'll go find an ATM."

Shelby started walking. Just yesterday, she'd been excited and optimistic about Liberty and the new opportunities it offered. But that had been replaced by a vague, restless unease, which stemmed from a suspicion that the entire town had a secret it didn't want her to know about. It was silly, really; she knew that. Except for Greg Turner, the people she had encountered were friendly. When she stopped at Dave's Market for groceries the night before, Shelby ended up talking with the older lady at the checkout counter for ten minutes. The woman could not stop talking about the upcoming Queen of Hearts drawing and the 1.5 million dollar jackpot. She had assumed that was why Shelby was in town, and Shelby hadn't felt the need to set her straight.

Shelby walked along Drury Street, one of the roads jutting out from the downtown area like spokes on a wheel, and she saw the small, red-bricked building, Trudy's Beauty Boutique. And directly below that, painted in a lurid pink, Walk-ins Welcome. She picked up her pace. Weren't small-town beauty shops centers for gossip? Granted, she relied on *Steel Magnolias* for that idea, but still. It was worth a shot. Someone in the place might know something about the strange Errol Gaylord. Plus, Shelby couldn't remember the last time she colored her hair, and this morning she noticed that the roots at the crown of her head had turned white. She pushed open the door.

With its two styling stations, two sinks, and mismatched chairs pushed against one wall, the room seemed to be disappointingly empty. "Hello," Shelby called. "Are you open?"

A few, long seconds passed before a petite, light brown-haired woman with golden highlights pushed through the saloon doors that led to a back room. "I sure am," she said brightly. "I'm Trudy. What can I do for you today?"

As she drew closer, Shelby could see she had been heavy-handed with the makeup, and it looked like her red-rimmed eyes had recently shed tears. "I want you to dazzle me," she said.

That coaxed a small smile from Trudy. "Your wish is my command."

Trudy, standing behind Shelby, studied her in the mirror of her station. "I think a warm, rich auburn would be a good color on you." She reached into a drawer and pulled out a book and pointed. "This one here."

It was precisely the shade Shelby's hair used to be all those years ago in Hollywood. She nodded. Somehow, it seemed appropriate. "Slow day today?" she asked Trudy, more to be sociable than anything else. This Trudy, who efficiently lined up the needed supplies, did not seem to be the talkative sort.

Trudy went to work. "I was busier earlier. The United Methodist Women had a meeting this morning, and a lot of ladies wanted their hair set. It'll get busy again this afternoon when people get off work. A lot of people want their hair done before the Queen of Hearts drawing tonight. You know, in case they win and get their picture in the paper." She began to paint on the dye and wrap locks of hair in foil squares. "I suppose that's why you're in town? Are you a reporter or something?"

"No." But before Shelby could utter another word, the door of the shop burst open, and a woman who looked like an aged Carol Brady and a woman about ten years older rushed in, breathless.

"Did you hear the news?" the Carol Brady look-alike asked, and without waiting for an answer, she blurted, "Errol Gaylord left his movie theater to a complete stranger! Can you imagine that? I always thought he was an odd little man, but really! He could have left it to the town or something."

"She's a woman," the older matron with steel-gray hair said. "Junior Busby talked to her in Circle K. He said she bought ten candy bars and a pack of Virginia Slims. He said she had a funny accent, but he didn't know what kind."

"Hello to you too, Gina and Joanne." Trudy nodded at each woman in turn. "Why don't you come back later, and we can talk then. I'm with a new customer right now."

Both Gina and Joanne seemed to register that Shelby was a stranger at the same time. "Oh," Gina said.

Again, Shelby had the feeling that she wasn't privy to town information, that she was an outsider not allowed into the inner circle. "I don't mind," she said quickly. "Just pretend I'm not here." In the mirror, she could see the questioning look that passed between the two women, but their need to spill their newfound gossip proved too great.

"Well," Gina said. "I heard Errol Gaylord completely lost his marbles during those last years in The Cedars. That would explain why he would leave valuable town property to a complete stranger."

"The place is an abandoned eyesore," Trudy, next to Shelby, said quietly.

If the gossips heard Trudy, they didn't let on. "No, Gina, you got it wrong. He would have moments of complete lucidity." Joanne lowered her voice. "One of the caretakers there told my neighbor who told me that Errol finally admitted to killing his wife!"

"No!" Gina's hand flew to her heart. "You know, I always had my suspicions about that, but he was never arrested or anything."

"Yet he didn't have a funeral service for poor Nancy because he didn't want to give a murdered, mangled body to the funeral home!" Joanne finished triumphantly.

Gina nodded thoughtfully. "That makes perfect sense, Joanne." Then she opened her eyes wide. "Oh, Trudy, your new front window finally came. We were so excited about the big news that we didn't notice. Shame on us."

"It came in yesterday, and Cliff Neeley's sister paid for it, as she said she would." She applied the last square of foil to Shelby's hair. "We had a little accident a few weeks ago. Someone threw a brick through my window."

"The town's crazy person," Gina said. "They carted him to the loony bin down in Anna."

"Why don't you two ladies go in the back and grab yourselves some coffee?" Trudy said firmly. The two women agreed that a cup of coffee would hit the spot, and when they disappeared through the saloon doors, Trudy said to Shelby, "Don't pay any attention to those two. They're just bored widows who have nothing better to do but talk about all the goings-on in this town."

"They don't bother me at all. But," Shelby felt she had to choose her words carefully, "is what they're saying true? Did Errol Gaylord murder his wife?"

Trudy led Shelby to the dryer and sat her in a chair before answering. "Oh, probably not, but who knows? I was only ten or eleven at the time, and all I remember is that Nancy Gaylord worked behind the concession stand every Saturday matinee, and then one day she wasn't there anymore."

"But she was a sickly lady, frail?" Shelby persisted, remembering that Trisha had told her Nancy Gaylord had some rare disease.

Trudy frowned as she lowered the dryer over Shelby's head. "Was she?"

Shelby spent the next twenty minutes under the loud, hot dryer, so when Gina and Joanne came back into the room and started talking again, she couldn't make out what they were saying. While listening to and watching them earlier, their exchanges had been as fast and furious as a volley in a professional Chinese ping-pong match. But now, their mouths moved as if they were ventriloquist dolls, and the sounds they made were distant, distorted. Shelby felt like a voyeur watching them, and she buried her nose in a six-month-old, tattered *Cosmopolitan*, which seemed to be as out of place in this room as she was. It didn't matter what they talked about now. They were probably bending another truth like melted taffy. Perfect example: She had bought ten candy bars and a pack of Virginia Slims at Circle K? Come on. People ought to have enough courtesy to get their stories straight, but they never did.

After her dryer time ended, and after Trudy rinsed out her hair and led her back to the styling chair, Shelby returned to her passive observer role in the conversation. The women were now talking about a former stylist at the salon named Roxy, and they dissected and speculated on the poor, unfortunate girl mercilessly. And what they said about the girl became so outlandish that Shelby had to suppress the urge to either shout in outrage or burst into hysterical laughter.

According to these two vicious women, Roxy was a meth head, a tweaker, who skipped town after the gang she ran with broke into ten of Liberty's businesses in a single night. Then Roxy stole a houseboat from a dying man spending his last months traveling up and down the Mississippi River. Oh, but before stealing the houseboat worth "over $100,000," she kidnapped her handicapped mother and forced her onto the boat. Then, believe it or not, she returned the next day and apologized to the owner, who was in love with her, and took him on board. The last anyone had heard, Roxy, her mother, and the houseboat owner were involved in a sinful three-way marriage.

When they stopped to take a breath after that story, Shelby couldn't help herself. Her voice low, she asked Trudy, "Is any of that true?"

Trudy glanced at the women. "More or less." Then she added, "You know what they say about gossip? It always contains a germ of truth."

"*Germ* is a good word for it," Shelby said wryly.

Trudy's smile seemed tired. "Say, you never answered my question. Are you a reporter here in town to cover the Queen of Hearts drawing?"

"No." After everything she'd heard—and not heard—in this salon, Shelby decided it was best to keep the information of her purpose in this town to a minimum. Gina and Joanne might be in the minority about the injustice of Errol Gaylord bequeathing his movie theater to a stranger, but she didn't want to take any chances just yet. And if Shelby decided to stay longer than a month and open the theater again or teach acting workshops, she didn't want to alienate people in this town right off the bat. She understood now that if she had any hope of fitting into Liberty or making a new life here, she would have to work at it like a moth on a wool sweater, slow and steady.

But Trudy seemed like a nice woman, and she still waited for her answer, her scissors poised above Shelby's right ear. "I have some business to attend to." Trudy still waited, so Shelby changed the subject. "I've rented a house owned by Marie Sherman for a month." Her statement exploded like a bomb into the sudden and unexpected silence.

Gina's hand flew to her heart again. "Marie Sherman?"

Shelby could see them in the mirror. "Yes, do you know her? The house is lovely—"

"That house should be razed!" Joanne interrupted rudely.

"The whole thing was shameful!" Gina put in.

"Don't tell me. Someone was murdered in the house." Shelby meant it as a joke, but it didn't go over well. And then she remembered the dark stain on the living room carpet. Her heart started to beat faster. "Was someone murdered there?"

"Almost," Joanne said ominously. "They say a man from the Queen of Hearts drawing at the Legion, a stranger," she said pointedly, "broke in and stole her jewelry and all the money she had in the place. Then he—"

"*Sexually assaulted* her," Gina said breathlessly. "And *slashed her throat.*"

"No, Gina, that isn't right," Joanne scolded. "I think he stabbed her in the abdomen."

"No, the throat," Gina argued. "And then the poor woman had a stroke, and now she's at The Cedars."

"No, she moved to Florida as soon as she was able. She didn't take a thing with her." Before Gina could argue, Joanne said, "Remember that I have a neighbor who has a friend who works at The Cedars. Don't you think she would have mentioned if Marie is there?"

"Ladies," Trudy said firmly, "don't you have a Beautification Committee meeting today?"

Joanne glanced at her watch. "Oh, my goodness. Come on, Gina. We're going to be late." Right as she reached the door, she turned back. "It was a pleasure to meet you," she said stiffly, as an afterthought. "Welcome to Liberty."

Trudy snipped the final hair and bent down, her face close to Shelby's. "Are you dazzled?"

Her hair looked better than it had in decades, so she nodded. She was dazzled, all right, but it had nothing to do with her new auburn hair with its Halle Berry short cut from *Monster's Ball*. "Tell me, Trudy. Why does it seem that people just disappear from this town, and why does it seem that people don't go to jail if they commit crimes?"

"I don't know," Trudy said thoughtfully. "That would be a good question for Officer Morrison." She straightened up, but not before Shelby noticed the sudden flush on her cheeks and the secret smile. "I'll have to call Officer Morrison and ask him."

Shelby stood outside of the old movie theater. She had to admit the surly minister did a decent job. The boards over the front windows and most of the graffiti had been removed. The minister had also picked up the trash that had accumulated against the outside walls. But the place still looked forlorn. The few windows were cracked and filthy, their sills warped, and for the first time, she saw that the old marquee tilted dangerously to one side as if unhinged. She hoped Greg didn't notice her involuntary shudder. The thought of walking back into that dark, gloomy space wasn't inviting. She asked Greg if he thought the wiring would hold up if she turned on the electricity.

For the first time, he cracked a wry smile. "Well, if you want to get rid of the place, that would be one way to do it." When Shelby gave him a questioning look, he added, "I think the place would go up like a box of matches. Mice have pretty much chewed up all the wires. If you want electricity, you're going to have to rewire the whole place."

Shelby doubted she had enough money for a project that large. Down the road, if she decided to stay, she could take out a loan, but for now, she would have to put new wiring on the back burner. Greg left, yet Shelby still stood staring at the building, willing herself to unlock the front door and start looking around. But she couldn't do it. She knew she had imagined the sound of a whirring projector and a light on a dark screen. She had been exhausted from the long drive from Arizona. That was the explanation, pure and simple. But she still couldn't dig the keys out of her purse and unlock the front door.

She made a bet with herself. If someone walked past her, she would ask them if they would go with her into the building. "Don't you want to see inside this old place?" she'd ask. "They don't make movie theaters like this anymore. It'll be a lark, won't it?" She waited, but oddly enough, no one walked past. Shelby had been told that things moved slowly in small towns, but shouldn't there be some commerce, some activity? It was a weekday afternoon, for crying out loud. Sure, it was blazing hot, but come on. Where were all the people? It was like she was standing in the middle of a ghost town.

Shelby didn't know how long she stood, lost in thought, in front of the movie theater before she came to a decision. What was the worst thing she could find in the old building: nests of mice, boxes of mildewed popcorn, old movie posters? *Come on*, she told herself sternly, *you are not a coward.* Even during the worst time of her life, Shelby held her ground and proclaimed her innocence. It had not, in the end, helped her situation at all, but she had not been a coward then. She'd left town, yes, but there was nothing left for her in LA, no love and no career, and no more choices. But she had a choice now. She would uncover the secrets of this old movie theater—if there were any to be found—and then she would decide whether she would sell it. But first, she needed to make a trip to Walmart.

With a new resolve, Shelby turned around to head to her car parked on the street. She happened to look up, and that's when she saw her. A woman watched her from the window of Zelda's Consignment Shop, an attractive woman who looked to be about her age. Feeling absurdly relieved to see another living soul close by, Shelby lifted her hand to wave, but the woman abruptly turned and vanished from sight.

One hour later, Shelby unlocked the movie theater door carrying a heavy bag from Walmart. She had purchased the largest flashlight the store had to offer, along with an assortment of candles. She quickly walked into the lobby, and leaving the door propped open with a rock, she wasted no time placing and lighting the candles on every available surface. With more light coming in from the newly liberated windows and the candles and flashlight, the room came into view. Shelby laughed out loud with relief. Just as she had suspected, it was nothing more than a small, quaint theater lobby. To her left was the concession stand Shelby had seen the day before, and now Shelby could see three doors, one leading to the restrooms, one to an office with a frosted glass panel, and one in the corner that must lead to the projection room. Panning the flashlight along the walls, she could see the still hanging posters: *The Curious Case of Benjamin Button, Twilight, The Dark Knight.*

Shelby decided she would start with the office. Another key from the Melpomene keychain unlocked the door, and she quickly scanned the room. She gasped. It, too, was adorned with movie posters, but the movies were all hers: *Don't Close Your Eyes, The Badge, Fairy Dust,* and *Deceit.* She supposed she shouldn't be surprised. The lawyer on the phone had said Errol Gaylord was an *ardent admirer* of hers, but her young face staring back at her was disconcerting. Shelby hadn't seen these posters in years. She hadn't even thought about them because it was too painful. She certainly wasn't the prettiest girl in Hollywood at the time, nor the most glamorous, but these posters reminded her of who she used to be, a girl with hope. Shelby again wondered why Errol Gaylord had been such a great fan of hers. Her B-movies never made big money, and compared with popular actresses of the day like Demi Moore or Meg Ryan, she'd been on the D-list, a bit player. *So why her?*

The room had a desk, chair, and two filing cabinets. Another key unlocked the drawers to the desk. The contents inside were not out of the ordinary: an old ledger, some receipts, stray scraps of paper with quickly jotted notes, such as "call plumber," "order Milk Duds," and "fix chair D-17," all perfectly ordinary stuff. But then Shelby got lucky. Stuck in the back of the bottom drawer was a black and white photo of a man and woman standing in front of the new-looking Gaylord's Movie Theatre with a banner proclaiming: Grand Opening. Shelby flipped the picture over and read, "Errol and Nancy, 1970," then studied the faces more closely. Errol had been a small man, bald, with elfin ears, while Nancy was even smaller, a wisp of a woman. Neither of them smiled, nor were they holding hands, which Shelby found odd. It was the theater's grand opening, and neither one of them looked particularly happy. Perhaps they fought right before the picture, or maybe they had a loveless marriage. Shelby would never know.

On a whim, and probably because she watched too many detective shows in her ample spare time, Shelby felt the underside of the top drawer. When she felt glossy paper, she pulled out the drawer all the way and turned it over to find an 8" by 10" black and white glossy, one of her first headshots, taken when she was nineteen. Shelby's heart started to beat a little faster. How could the man have gotten a hold of this? It made no sense at all, not unless he somehow knew that long-ago photographer in LA. She quickly pulled out all the other drawers. Each one contained another photo from that same session.

"This is getting a little creepy, Errol," Shelby said to the room. "I mean, a crush is one thing, but how did you get your hands on these pictures? Were you stalking me? Haha." But the joke wasn't funny, and it did nothing to staunch the slowly rising sense of dread. She took deep breaths of the musty air. There had to be a perfectly reasonable explanation for these pictures. Perhaps he got them on eBay or Craigslist, something like that. After the scandal, she heard that her memorabilia, what little there was of it, sold like hotcakes. Then people lost interest, and everything disappeared.

Shelby started to feel a little better when she went through the filing cabinets. For the most part, the drawers contained more old receipts and folders of yearly grosses and expenses. She flipped quickly through them, but one caught her eye. It was almost like she knew what was in the folder labeled Costumes before she looked inside to find receipts for costumes he had bought from her films: the bloody prom dress in *Don't Close Your Eyes*, the sexy lingerie in *Fairy Tale*, the red dress she wore as an undercover prostitute in *The Badge*, and the orange prison jumpsuit from *Deceit*. But these were written in what must have been Errol Tucker's handwriting. He did not note the source of the purchases.

He's dead, Shelby kept reminding herself. *He was an old man with a fetish*. Yet the sense of dread kept rising, rising, and when she found the manilla envelope in the bottom drawer of the second filing cabinet, she cried out in disbelief when she dumped the contents on the desk. All pictures of her. All pictures he should not have had access to. These were personal, pictures of her in a bikini in Malibu, sitting in a coffee shop off Sunset Strip, and shopping with Vanessa on Rodeo Drive. Had the crazed, obsessed man hired someone to stalk her? For a short time, a handful of paparazzi thought she was worth following, but she had never seen these pictures published anywhere before.

Shelby kept going. She would get to the bottom of this, one way or another. It didn't matter if a dead man had been obsessed with her. He'd never hurt her, had he? He'd never tried to contact her, as far as she knew, although a distant memory came back as she climbed the narrow stairs to the projection room on shaky legs. Her mother, who had nothing better to do at the time, had decided to "handle" Shelby's meager fan mail. Barbara Williams had been thrilled with her daughter's newfound success, as she called it, a success that had eluded Barbara in her own short-term career. "You've been getting some disturbing fan mail, darling," she'd said.

The horror flick had just come out, so Shelby didn't think it was too surprising. "Just toss it, Mother. There are a lot of weirdos out there."

"But a fan is a fan," Barbara persisted. "Maybe I can persuade him that you're not as mean and wily as the character you portrayed. I bet I could convince him that you're a good person."

"Why bother, Mother? There'll be plenty more supportive fans later." Oh, she had been so cocky and sure of herself back then. After one campy movie that received less than stellar reviews, she thought her success would continue to grow. On that night, she was primping to go out on a rare date with an up-and-coming actor, and she had her second movie in the can. She had the world by the balls.

"I'll handle this," Barbara said decisively. "Don't you worry about a thing, darling."

The low, narrow door to the projection room groaned as Shelby pushed it open, and with the flashlight leading her, Shelby stepped into the darkroom. Of course, there were no windows here, but the room seemed much larger than Shelby had anticipated. When her flashlight landed on the film projector, she was so startled that she scurried backward until her back hit the cobwebbed wall. She had almost convinced herself that what she heard the day before, the clicking and the whirring noise, had been nothing more than her exhausted imagination in overdrive. She had almost convinced herself that it wasn't likely a film projector because most movie theaters started to replace film with digital projectors in 2009. But here it stood, one more part of this strange inheritance to puzzle and confuse her.

"Someone must have snuck in here when I wasn't looking and turned this on just to scare me," she said out loud, not caring if talking to herself might make her as crazy as the man who had left this movie theater to her. The sound of her voice comforted her.

She went quickly through the bins of film in the room. Not surprisingly, they contained multiple copies of each of her four films, but apparently, Errol

Gaylord had hoarded romantic classics, too. Shelby found reels for *Casablanca, An Affair to Remember, It Happened One Night,* and *Roman Holiday.* Shelby wondered if these old films were the reason why Errol Gaylord kept the old film projector, and she wondered if he had crept into this theater at night to watch these classics on real film. That thought made her like the crazy old geezer a little bit. He had a romantic side, a romantic side that might have slipped over the edge into an obsession in her case. Unbidden, the memory of the man who had been obsessed with Jodie Foster, John Hinckley, Jr., came to her mind. He had been so obsessed with her that he tried to impress her with an assassination attempt on President Ronald Regan. At least Shelby's obsessed fan had never done anything that horrific. He had only been an eccentric, reclusive little man.

Shelby was about to leave the room, relieved that she hadn't found anything overtly creepy, but she decided to scan the walls with her flashlight just to make sure. She caught a glimpse of something metal on the far wall and moved closer. It seemed to be some kind of large metal box built into the wall, and once again, the dread returned. Shelby fumbled with two different keys before she found the right one. Taking a deep breath, she slowly opened the door and shined the beam of the flashlight inside.

The tunnel looked deep, probably six feet or so, and it was filled with packs of letters tied with string. Shelby picked up the first packet and flipped through it. They were all addressed to her, written but never sent in the year 2002. Shelby felt the bile rise in the back of her throat. That had been the worst year of her life. She felt even more nauseous when she saw the pile of tabloids underneath. It felt as if someone else's hand reached for the National Enquirer on the top. It felt as if someone else read the screaming headline: ACTRESS SEXUALLY MOLESTS CHILD!!

It was always assumed that Shelby would become an actress, mostly by her mother, Barbara. Barbara's career as a bit player in the occasional movie—she was always the best friend, secretary, or waitress, never the leading lady—had not amounted to much. Plus, they lived in West Hollywood—enough said. An only child, Shelby was an abnormally pretty girl, so Barbara started shuffling her around to commercial auditions at an early age. Shelby's father, Hal, a cameraman, wasn't around much, traveling as he did to location shoots in other states. He divorced Barbara when Shelby was four, so Barbara focused all her energy on Shelby. And she wanted Shelby to be an actress.

Shelby didn't mind. Sometimes she got a part, and sometimes she didn't. "Your big break will come," Barbara assured her, and surprisingly, it did. At twenty, Shelby went to an open casting call for a low-budget horror flick called *Don't Close Your Eyes.* And her career, according to Barbara, "was made in the shade." It appeared to be so. Immediately after that, she got another leading role in *Fairy Dust,* followed by *The Badge.* She regularly worked for three years and attracted some attention but not a lot. She wasn't a partier, one of those young starlets who sought attention by going to bars and clubs and having high-profile romances. Shelby suspected this disappointed Barbara to some degree, but Barbara took it in stride. "As long as there's money coming in," she said, "it's all good." Barbara could finally quit her job as a tour guide at Universal Studios and do a little more shopping.

After making three films in quick succession, Shelby decided to take some time off. She knew, even if Barbara didn't, that the movies she'd made were mediocre, at best. She needed a juicy role, a strong part in a film with good writing and a well-known director. However, directors and producers were not exactly knocking down her door with offers. So Shelby decided to take matters into her own hands. When she got invited to a party in Malibu hosted by the currently hot director Leo Spinelli, she decided to accept. He was Hollywood's golden boy at the moment. His last film had been nominated for an Academy Award, and even though he didn't win, he was making waves in Tinsel Town.

Shelby often thought the night she met Leo was like something that would happen in a movie. Everything seemed magical about that night. All the right people crowded his magnificent house, and waiters in bow ties passed champagne and canapes. She had been briefly introduced to her host shortly after she arrived, and she knew, and he knew that something immediately clicked. She'd never had that feeling before with other men she dated, but with Leo, she just *knew*. He was older, fifty-two, and distinguished looking with his thick, white hair that he wore long. Tall and tan and fit, he looked something like an Italian version of Peter Lawford in his prime, and Shelby was hooked not only by his good looks but also by his power. His power, his ability to accomplish things in that tricky town, was very sexy indeed. He was exactly what she needed.

When he could break away from his other guests, he found her on his balcony, sipping champagne and watching the waves crash on the rocks below. She knew he would be looking for her, and before they said another word to each other, he kissed her. "I've been looking for you," he said, his dark eyes glinting in the warm light.

"I've been waiting," she said, and then she kissed him.

On that night, Shelby believed in love at first sight and every other hokey, sappy thing she had heard about love. At twenty-three, she might be naive but thought she was invincible, which always turned into a combustible situation. In the very early morning hours, after all the other guests had gone, and after they made love on the tiger-striped rug in front of the fireplace, he told her that he wanted to cast her in his new movie. "It's called *Deceit*, with an ensemble cast. I've already lined up some of the top talent in this town."

"If you think I'm right for the part," she said demurely, cuddling into his chest. She'd only had one glass of champagne, but she felt drunk by his very presence.

Two weeks later, still drunk on what she thought was love, she moved in with a man she didn't know at all. Leo hadn't revealed much about himself during their two dates, which she assumed would happen over time. But most importantly, he didn't tell Shelby that he had a thirteen-year-old daughter who lived with him.

Or that she was a manipulative little bitch.

On the day Shelby moved in, it took Vanessa precisely five minutes to let her feelings be known. "Don't try to be my mother. It would not be in your best interests." She glared defiantly at Shelby with her dark eyes. Her eyes dominated the delicate features on her pale face. She was slight for her age, looking more like a child of ten than a teenager, and Shelby would learn soon enough that Vanessa used that misleading vision of childhood innocence to her advantage.

Caught entirely off guard by what she said and the surprising discovery that Leo had a daughter, Shelby stammered, "I would never do that, Vanessa." Leo had just left the kitchen a second before to put Shelby's suitcase in the master bedroom, and as soon as he stepped out, the smiling, charming Vanessa had been replaced with this angry, defiant version. "But I hope we can become friends."

"Don't hold your breath." Vanessa hoisted herself up onto the counter when they arrived to kiss her father on the cheek. Shelby thought it had been a charming thing for the girl to do, but the charming-little-girl act was gone.

"So what did dear old Dad promise you?" Vanessa held up her hand dramatically. "Don't tell me, a part in a movie. That's his M.O., you know. He offers all these pretty young starlets a part in his next movie and pretends like he falls in love with them. Then when he realizes they can't act, he dumps them." She eyed Shelby up and down. "You won't last long."

Five minutes into her acquaintance with the girl, Shelby still thought that, as an adult, she had the upper hand. She crossed her arms and leaned against the counter. It was normal for the girl to feel threatened by her. It was normal for her to want to keep her father to herself. So Shelby let the remark about Leo pretending to fall in love slide. "What makes you think I can't act?" she asked instead.

"I've seen your movies. Ewww." Vanessa pinched her fingers around her nose. "I did my research."

Unfortunately, Shelby had not. She had assumed Leo had been married before and probably had many lovers over the years. But that didn't matter now. They had found each other, and that was all that counted. Still, Shelby felt at a slight disadvantage. If she had known that Leo had a daughter, she would have done her own research. Shelby shifted uncomfortably on her stilettos. She'd worn a slinky, braless dress and sexy shoes, thinking that she and Leo would have sex as soon as they walked in the door. Instead, she met his child.

"Do you always do your research?" Shelby said it lightly, teasingly, smiling. "I bet you get good grades in school."

"Oh, please. I thought you'd be more interesting than that." Vanessa slid from the counter and placed her hands on her slim hips. "But you're just like all the others."

Shelby stopped smiling. She didn't want to get off on the wrong foot here, but this little girl was insufferably rude. "I think you'll find out differently," she said stiffly. "I'm in it for the long run."

Vanessa's smile was more sardonic than sincere. "We'll see about that."

The small girl barely reached her shoulder, so Shelby had to bend down to get face to face. "Yes, we will." And the battle lines were drawn.

She watched the little girl flounce out of the room and immediately reached for her phone. It took no time to do the research, and Shelby wanted to kick herself for being so besotted with Leo that she didn't try to find out about his past. It wasn't like it was a big secret that he had been married to a young Italian actress. The marriage had been turbulent, the divorce acrimonious when she left him for a Brazilian soccer player. Leo fought for sole custody of the then-eight-year-old Vanessa, and the actress, twenty years younger than Leo, finally relented when she received a large, undisclosed settlement.

Shelby felt rather sorry for Vanessa for that one brief moment. It didn't last long.

The girl should have been an actress. She was a master at switching from charming-little-girl in Leo's presence to vengeful, hateful teenager when she was in Shelby's. Shelby tried to avoid the girl as much as possible, but she always seemed to appear at the worst possible moments, such as when Leo loudly told Shelby everything she had done wrong in a scene that day. Shelby knew she had not performed her best—she'd had a raging headache—but Leo seemed to take it personally. Mortified, Shelby started to cry, which she rarely did, and looked up from blowing her nose to see Vanessa smirking in the doorframe.

Oh, yes, Vanessa had her sneaky, conniving act honed to perfection. On nights when Shelby and Leo cuddled on the couch or on days they went to the beach, if they became too intimate, or too happy with each other, the girl would show up. "Poppa," she would say with a sweet, wistful look on her face, "would you watch a movie with me," or "Poppa, would you hold my hand?" Leo melted every time the girl said, *Poppa*. So the girl said it often, and it always worked. "I swear, Leo," Shelby said to him one time they were finally alone. "If Vanessa wanted to keep an elephant in her room, you'd let her." Leo had laughed indulgently at the mention of his daughter's name. "You're right, Shelby. I'd probably let her have the elephant."

The girl was beyond spoiled, but when Shelby had lived in the Malibu house for two months, she noticed her sapphire ring was missing. She looked everywhere for it, but it didn't turn up. Then it was a pair of leopard print leggings, followed by her favorite bikini. After that, her Prada evening bag disappeared. Shelby knew it wasn't a coincidence. She also knew it was not something she could talk about to Leo. He would defend Vanessa to the death, no doubt about it, so Shelby knocked on the door to Vanessa's room one evening when Leo worked late on the dailies yet again. It was the perfect time to confront the thieving, spoiled child.

She didn't wait for an invitation after knocking, and when she walked into the room, Vanessa was already in bed reading *Anne of Green Gables*, cozy in a flannel nightgown that looked like it belonged on a doll. Shelby didn't let the picture-perfect scene stop her. "Vanessa, have you been stealing my stuff?"

Vanessa's large eyes grew even larger and rounder. "Me? Why would I take your stuff? If I want anything, all I have to do is ask Poppa."

Shelby was sick and tired of the girl's games. "Don't you think you're too old to call your father *Poppa*?" she snapped.

"Don't you think you're too young to be his girlfriend of the moment?" Vanessa volleyed right back.

"Where's my stuff, Vanessa?" Shelby said through gritted teeth.

Vanessa nodded toward the closet. "Feel free to take a look," she said coldly.

Naturally, the devious child wouldn't point her in the right direction, but Shelby walked into her vast closet and rifled through racks and racks of clothing, then the dresser that stood in the middle. Not surprisingly, the ring, leggings, bikini, and Prada bag weren't there.

When she came out of the closet, Shelby charged toward the bed, where Vanessa had serenely gone back to her book. Shelby leaned down close. "Why are you taking my things, Vanessa? Do you hate me that much?"

They both heard it simultaneously, or perhaps Vanessa heard Leo's car when Shelby was in the closet: footsteps coming down the hall, drawing nearer. Immediately, Vanessa clutched the book to her chest and worked up some righteous tears. "I think you should leave now," she said in a tremulous voice.

"What's going on here?" Leo stood in the doorway.

"Nothing," Shelby said. Even though her distrust and unease around the girl grew daily, she didn't want to accuse her of theft without proof. It did seem like a silly thing for the girl to do, and perhaps a maid had taken the items, but Shelby was almost positive it was the girl.

"Oh, Poppa," Vanessa wailed.

Leo was in the room in an instant, scooping his daughter into his arms.

Shelby was never sure if that night in Vanessa's bedroom became the actual turning point, or if things had been going downhill for some time, and she just refused to see it. But things changed after that. More and more, Shelby felt like the outsider in the house, like it was two against one, and nothing she did was good enough. It didn't help that work wasn't going any better either. Leo yelled at her onset now, along with everyone else, and the tension onset was as bad as the tension in the Malibu house. It was as if everyone involved in the movie could smell that they had a bomb on their hands. Despite Leo's best intentions and the talented cast, things weren't clicking.

Leo, overworked and stressed to the breaking point, suggested that Shelby take Vanessa shopping one Saturday afternoon. "I just need a break," he said.

"I don't feel like shopping," Shelby said. "I planned on taking a long walk on the beach." She, too, felt stressed, in case he hadn't realized it. He was very self-absorbed most of the time.

"Oh, Poppa! I'd love to go shopping!" Vanessa clapped her hands together like a little girl while giving Shelby a sly smile when Leo turned his back.

Shelby sighed. "Rodeo Drive, it is." Vanessa favored the expensive shops lining that road. Naturally, they would go there.

It wasn't that bad. Shelby, in retrospect, would have to admit that. Vanessa, once on the famed shopping avenue, acted like a kid in a candy shop. She gushed over the handbags in Tory Burch and the dresses in MaxMara, and even Shelby started to relax after they lunched on fettuccine at Il Fornaio. Vanessa was not only civil, but she was quite charming and entertaining. Shelby had never seen her smile so much—at least not directed at her. She should have known better.

They both agreed Versace would be their last stop of the afternoon, and even Shelby got into the swing of things by trying on a few dresses. She paid for their purchases with Leo's Amex Black Card, and as they pushed through the doors, she looked down at Vanessa and said, "You know, Vanessa, I had a really nice day with—" The beeping of the store alarm on the door stopped her. "They must have forgotten to take the tag off something."

"We'll see," and Vanessa reverted to her vengeful self.

Security found an expensive Hermès silk scarf in Shelby's purse that she hadn't paid for. And all the while that Shelby tried to explain that she didn't know how it got in there—but of course, she would be happy to pay for the item—Vanessa played her part. She would shake her head from time to time, saying, "Oh, Shelby, how could you?" After an hour of Shelby repeatedly proclaiming her innocence, and after the store called Leo to vouch for her, they allowed her to pay for the scarf she didn't want and let her go.

Shelby did not say a word to Vanessa on the drive home. She didn't trust herself to speak. What kind of devious mind would set her up like that? Vanessa must have slipped the scarf into Shelby's purse. Hadn't she conveniently said she would watch the bags when Shelby tried on dresses? And Shelby was also mad at herself. She should not have lowered her defenses around the girl. She should have known the little bitch had something up her sleeve.

And the little bitch had more.

Shelby and Vanessa raced to the house as soon as the Jaguar came to a stop. Each wanted to be the first to get to Leo, to tell her side of the story. Vanessa won, and her first words were, "Oh, Poppa, I've never been so embarrassed in my life!"

"I did not steal a scarf," Shelby said. She would not take any more of the shit Vanessa shoveled out, and unlike Vanessa, she would tell the truth. "Vanessa planted that scarf in my bag. She wanted to humiliate me."

"No, I didn't, Poppa." Vanessa threw herself into his arms.

"And what's more, she's been stealing things from me for months. I didn't want to tell you. I know how stressed out you've been about the movie, but it's your daughter who's the thief." Even then, Shelby knew she would not win in this situation as Leo looked back and forth at his daughter with love and his girlfriend with anger.

But Leo at least pretended to be fair. He disentangled Vanessa from his arms and held her at arm's length. "Did you steal from Shelby?" he said gently.

Vanessa shook her head, the tears falling rapidly and splashing on the tiled floor. Her timing was impeccable, and she waited, prettily sobbing until she could whisper: "Shelby's been sneaking into my room and sexually abusing me. Remember the other night? That wasn't the first time. Oh, Poppa!" And she threw herself in his arms again, knowing she had won.

Shelby shoved the *National Enquirer* with its ugly headline back into the metal box. She had always suspected Leo leaked the story about the alleged sexual assault to the press. He wanted to punish her for something she would never do, but he didn't need the scandal of a trial to ruin his sterling career. He said Vanessa was too fragile to put on the stand, but Shelby knew better. The fictitious story blew over quickly. Hollywood was fickle that way, but the damage had been done. With his many contacts, Leo made sure Shelby's career was over before it had really begun. But as it turned out, his career was virtually finished too. *Deceit* was an expensive, over-budget bomb the moment it was released, and Leo's career stalled, and then, like hers, disappeared into nothingness. Shelby had no idea what happened to the manipulative, conniving Vanessa, nor did she care.

Shelby panned her flashlight one final time around the projection room before landing, once again, on the projector. She took another step closer, just to prove to herself that she wasn't afraid of a silly machine. She had only imagined hearing the click and whirring of this machine the day before. Perhaps, too, stepping into such an old-fashioned movie theater brought back memories of her childhood when Barbara would take her to the movies in a place that looked very much like this one. When Shelby took a few more steps toward the machine, she could see a reel of film was loaded, ready to play. But she'd known that would be the case, hadn't she?

Shelby took a deep breath and flipped on the switch. Her heart beat painfully in her chest, but she would finish her search for clues in this place. She would get to the bottom of why a stranger in a small town would bequeath his business to her. The machine whirred to life, and through the window, Shelby could see the screen down below in the theater turn white. Numbers flashed, and then a picture came into focus. Shelby gasped. She'd been so sure this would be one of her films. But no.

Errol Gaylord sat behind his desk in the office of this theater, the office she had searched through before coming up here. He did look something like an elf with his bald head and pointed ears. But he happily smiled as he stared directly into the camera, and his voice sounded surprisingly deep when he began to speak. "So, Shelby, we meet at last. If you are watching this, you have accepted my gift, which makes me very happy. All of this," and he waved his arms to encompass her movie posters on the office walls, "is for you."

So far, so good, Shelby thought. The man had undoubtedly been an eccentric, but he seemed harmless enough right now.

Errol Gaylord continued. "You were probably not the prettiest or most talented actress of your generation."

"Thanks a lot," Shelby muttered, even though she knew it was true.

"But to me, you had a special quality that made you stand out from all the others. What is it they call it, the It quality?" he asked, then nodded. "Yes, I do believe that's correct." He pushed himself away from the desk and stood up. He was a very tiny man. The desk came up to his waist, but he walked around it to stand before the camera. "You had everything going for you, and then you threw it all away on that… that man!" he spat. His face darkened. "He was too old for you, my darling. He was not a good man, and you should have known better!"

Shelby wondered why she stood in the middle of a cobwebbed projection room, letting a dead man chastise her, yet she didn't move to turn off the machine.

Errol Gaylord began to pace, back and forth, in front of the camera. "And those allegations against you from his child! Of course, I did not believe a word of them, my darling. You would never do such a thing. But the girl got her comeuppance, didn't she? I made sure of that. Trust me."

Shelby gasped. "What do you mean?" she whispered. She had no idea what had become of Vanessa Spinelli. But had this deranged man done something to Vanessa in a misguided attempt to protect Shelby's honor? It did seem strange that the girl seemed to have disappeared. Shelby couldn't find her on Facebook and Instagram, and she had forced herself to look a time or two. But had this tiny man hurt Vanessa? Was he that crazy?

Errol Gaylord now wrung his hands as he paced. "And then you ran away. You should have stayed and fought, my love! You should have made more movies! But you ran away to Arizona. And all those men. Tsk tsk." Errol Gaylord stopped and put his face close to the camera. "You have been a very naughty girl, darling. You see, I have always known what you were up to, dear. People will do anything for enough money, but you already know that, don't you? Yes, people will do anything for the right price, including a cameraman named Hal Williams.

Shelby took a step back from that looming, now menacing face. Oh, God, this awful man had hired her father to stalk her for years. She hadn't seen her father since she was four and probably wouldn't recognize him now. He wouldn't have had to hide in bushes or behind trees. He could record her every move in broad daylight, and she was none the wiser. *Her life had never been her own.* Shelby braced herself against the glass of the window to keep her knees from buckling.

Errol Gaylord resumed his pacing. "I would have taken care of you like you deserved, my lovely Shelby. If only you would have found me sooner, we could have had such a wonderful life together."

"You are completely insane, you pervert!" Shelby pounded on the glass furiously, as if the image on the screen could feel the blows. What was she doing here, listening to the ravings of a madman? She reached for the switch to turn off the projector.

As if he knew what she was about to do, Errol Gaylord lifted his hand. "But wait! I have forgiven you for everything, my love, and now you are here. Now you will receive the ultimate gift of my devotion, which is priceless. Go to seat D-17, darling, and you will find a key to the storeroom behind the stage. Then you will know, once and for all, how very much I have loved you." Errol Gaylord blew her a kiss from his thin lips.

The screen dissolved to black.

Shelby wondered if she might be having a heart attack. The painful beating in her chest had not subsided during Errol Gaylord's insane rant, and now she felt a sharp pain in her left arm. And her jaw ached. Wasn't that another sign? Yet, for reasons she didn't understand, Shelby went down the steps to the lobby. Most of the candles burned low now, and Shelby had no idea how much time she had spent in the projection room. As if in a trance, she pulled open the heavy drapes and walked down the aisle toward Row D. Her flashlight revealed the torn fabric of the chairs, the tattered carpet that now lay in shreds. Cobwebs not only clustered in every corner but also covered most of the chairs. Except for D-17. The theater was old enough that the chairs still had ashtrays embedded in the armrests. And in the ashtray of D-17, Shelby found the key.

Now you will receive the ultimate gift of my devotion, which is priceless. Shelby, still trapped in the strange state of suspension that propelled her forward, found the stairs that led to the stage at the back of the screen. It was pitch-black in this space, and Shelby pointed the flashlight at the perimeter. She saw two doors. The first one did not budge when she inserted the key. *There's still hope,* she thought. Maybe the lock had rusted shut; she would never have to know what was behind it. But the key slid easily into the second lock. Shelby hesitated a moment before she pushed it all the way open and pointed her flashlight. The room was insulated with thick cinder blocks. It was as cold as a tomb . . .

She didn't scream; she didn't faint. Later, she would know she had gone into shock at the sight of the mummified body dressed in the bloody prom dress she wore in *Don't Close Your Eyes*. The rope around her neck was still wrapped around the beam above her, and the other items of clothing from Shelby's movies—the sexy lingerie, the red prostitute dress, and the orange jumpsuit—were displayed on headless dressmaker forms flanking her body. Shelby wanted to believe the poor woman had killed herself, but she knew better. *You will receive the ultimate gift of my devotion, which is priceless.* Errol Gaylord killed his wife to prove to Shelby how much he loved her. Shelby didn't know how long she stood there, staring, breathing in and out with shallow, ragged breaths.

She didn't lock the theater on her way out, nor did she gather up the remaining candles that still burned. It was a little past eight o'clock when she reached Marie Sherman's house, which no longer looked quaint and picture-perfect, but ominous and foreboding with its blood-stained carpet. A woman had been stabbed in this house; another woman had been murdered in the old movie theater. Shelby threw her belongings in her suitcases and hurried out to her car. She would leave this crazy, frightening town and never come back. She would raze the theater with all its contents and then sell the property. Yes, that was what she would do. She would demolish the building and the crime. She would act as if neither had been real.

Shelby had to inch her car down Elm Street because cars were parked bumper to bumper. She heard a roar coming from the Legion, and then the fire alarm blasted through town. *Maybe that horrible theater burned down,* Shelby thought. That's what she hoped. She hoped one candle left burning had sent the entire structure and the horrific secrets it held up in flames. The thought comforted her as she passed the city limit sign to Liberty and accelerated.

Shelby would never return to Liberty again, and she would never know that after fifty-three weeks of escalating frenzy, someone had finally won the Queen of Hearts Drawing. Someone, supposedly, had just gotten very lucky.

DEMOLITION DERBY

Officer Alan Morrison hoped that someone would finally win the damn drawing tonight. The Queen of Hearts game, sponsored by the American Legion, had been ongoing—the jackpot growing exponentially and then astronomically—for the past fifty-two weeks with no one choosing the envelope with the queen of hearts. Because the game included the jokers, bringing the total number of cards to fifty-four, only two cards remained tonight on the 53rd week of the drawing. If the person holding the drawn raffle ticket tonight didn't select the queen, the person whose raffle ticket was drawn next week would win automatically. Then the hysteria and frenzy, the drunken brawls and bad blood, and the crying and shrieking would end. And finally, the town would be at peace.

Yeah, right. Alan had only worked as a police officer in Liberty for two months, and there hadn't been a moment of peace. Perhaps the contagious mania of the drawing made people do crazy, unlawful acts. But it certainly seemed to Alan that in his short tenure here, many people in this town, either out of boredom or desperation, looked for trouble. According to a lot of the townsfolk, when the strip mines closed some years back, things started going to hell in a handbasket. With the loss of some of the highest-paying jobs in this rural, southern Illinois town, the town's population dwindled. But many, out of loyalty and a strong sense of community, decided to stay, despite the economic decline. Alan didn't really understand it. He'd been an Army brat, and his family followed his dad with every transfer. He'd always thought that picking up, moving, and starting over was what people *did*. But not the people in Liberty. They stayed, and lately, a lot of them had TROUBLE stamped on their foreheads.

Alan had responded to the usual calls in his weeks here, the domestic violence disputes, a few shoplifting incidents in Walmart, and way too many DUIs. The usual stuff for a police officer in any small town. However, Alan had also responded to a vandalism case when the town's "crazy person," as people here called the middle-aged schizophrenic who roamed Liberty's streets out of loneliness, threw a brick through the front window of the beauty shop. And then came the night when there was not one, not four, but ten robberies of local businesses in a single night. Alan knew a group of methheads who hung around by the Mississippi were responsible for the thefts, but he hadn't been able to put any of the three in jail because the ringleader, Tommy, was the nephew of the town mayor. "They've made some irresponsible choices," the town mayor told Alan, shrugging. "But they're harmless." Alan had to let it go.

However, the real humdinger of his cases up to that point came when a young hairstylist—rumored to be on meth but actually addicted to opioids—stole a houseboat from a man with cancer who was traveling up and down the Mississippi. Alan had interviewed Roxy when the vandalism occurred at the hair salon, so he was surprised when she took off in the houseboat right after another Queen of Hearts drawing. And she had taken her mother with her. Her mother wasn't in good health, and how Roxy hauled her into that boat Alan would never know, but when he had interviewed Roxy about the brick through the window, she had mentioned her mother at least three times. She was a devoted daughter, not a bad person who stole houseboats. So Alan made a phone call to the Coast Guard, asking for a favor. And sure enough, as he knew she would, Roxy brought the houseboat back, made a public apology, and drove off with the owner also aboard. As far as Alan was concerned, it was a happy ending for everybody. And that's how Alan liked things to be.

Unfortunately, the event that happened two weeks ago after the Queen of Hearts drawing did not end happily. He couldn't fix it because he got there too late. At least that's how Alan saw it, even though Pyle and Garcia, the other two officers on the force who also chaperoned the chaotic Thursday night drawing, kept telling him it wasn't his fault.

"A domestic that went too far," Pyle said.

"Probably booze and alcohol involved," Garcia said.

At twenty-nine, Alan didn't have the older officers' experience, but it seemed to him that both Pyle and Carcia were a little too complacent. People were a lot more complicated than those two gave them credit for, and many times, motives were not black and white. But this was the kicker. After being in law enforcement for five years—and the town before Liberty had also been small—Alan had never witnessed a shooting. He was surprised by how deeply it affected him—embarrassed about it, too, not that he would let the other two know. He also fervently hoped that his mind would not replay that brutal scene over and over again for the rest of his life. But it would. Every cop knew that you never forgot your first.

He'd been standing just inside the front door of the Legion, surveying the pandemonium. The Legion's two main rooms, the bar in front and the banquet room in back, had to be over capacity, but nothing could be done about it now. The crowd for the weekly drawing, along with the jackpot, had grown every week. It looked like the entire town had turned out for this night, along with plenty of people from small neighboring communities. Alan hoped whoever finally won this godforsaken drawing would be from Liberty. The citizens had grown very possessive about this enormous prize and would be very upset if someone from another town, someone not their own, walked away with the grand prize. Alan didn't know what kind of eruption would follow that occurrence, and he didn't want to find out. The residents did enough fighting among themselves after each drawing as it was.

Alan's trained ears thought he heard the unmistakable popping sound of a fired shot. Instinctively, his eyes searched the room. It was too crowded for him to see everyone's hands, but the ones he could see were all holding bottles of beer. Par for the course. He waited for another second. No screams of pain and no commotion, so it must have been the *pop* of a champagne cork, or perhaps a dropped glass or bottle. The Post's Commander was getting ready to draw the ticket for the grand drawing, the Queen of Hearts, from the large drum stuffed with $2 raffle tickets. He was a large, barrel-chested man, and he milked the moment for all it was worth. He explained the rules of the game, flexed his fingers, approached the drum, and then retreated as he thought of something else to say, something else to prolong his newfound fame as the master of ceremonies of the largest Queen of Hearts jackpot in Illinois history. The room sizzled with anticipation.

Alan decided to go outside to check things out, just to make sure. He'd started to sweat inside his long-sleeved, pressed blue shirt, and he didn't like it when he wasn't perfectly put together. His mother had taught him to iron at an early age, and Alan could iron a crease so exact that it looked as if it had been professionally done. He preferred not to think of his care with appearance as vanity. It was not vanity; it was a fact. He was a good-looking man, with his sandy blond hair and green-gold eyes with long lashes. His older sister, Amelia, had always called them his Barbie doll lashes, while his mother had always told him that he had a James Dean nose. Even if he hadn't been told such things from an early age, Alan would have figured it out. Girls started chasing him when he was in sixth grade and hadn't stopped. They didn't know it was a futile pursuit. Alan didn't want to be caught, and at the still young age of twenty-nine, he already thought of himself as a confirmed bachelor. Amelia's early troubled marriage and subsequent messy divorce had been blows that his family still reeled from. Alan refused to make that mistake.

It felt good to be outside. Even though it was a hot and humid night as summers in southern Illinois tended to produce, it felt cooler than the air inside the oven-like Legion that stank of sweat, beer, and a cocktail of different colognes and perfumes. And hairspray. Whatever new hairspray Trudy used now at Trudy's Beauty Boutique had a pungent, musty smell. He noticed the last time he went in for a haircut. Trudy had been so grateful for how he handled the rock through her front window incident that she offered him free haircuts.

"Come in anytime," she'd said, breathlessly. She seemed to catch herself just before she batted her eyes at Alan.

Oh, he knew that look well. "That's not necessary, ma'am."

"How many times do I have to tell you to call me Trudy?" She flirtatiously batted at his hand. "You can have all the free haircuts you want, indefinitely."

She was about ten years older than him and married. And this happened a lot to him. Still, Alan didn't want her to embarrass herself. "That's very nice of you. I'd be happy to have a couple of free haircuts, but it's not necessary."

"Oh, but it is! And I insist we leave the length of time open, okay? It's the least I can do since you fixed the window problem for me."

He'd taped a piece of cardboard over a hole and then driven poor Cliff Neeley to the psychiatric facility in Anna. However, Trudy did good work, and Alan was now very happy with the arrangement. He got a great haircut, and she got the chance to flirt. It worked out well for both of them.

Some of the other ladies in town had not been as subtle as Trudy. Maya, the curvaceous bartender at the Hideaway, had invited him over for a home-cooked meal during his second week in town. She seemed like a nice enough woman, and he happily accepted. Already, he'd grown tired of the fattening fare at Lolly's diner—a big fan of disgraced Paula Deen, Lolly added a stick of butter to every dish—and the unsatisfied hunger of a Lean Cuisine dinner. He arrived at Maya's on his day off in perfectly pressed khakis and a navy-blue polo shirt. Maya, who usually wore jeans and a Hideaway tank top the tavern sold for $12, had dressed in cut-offs so short that her butt cheeks hung out and a halter that barely covered the cantaloupe mounds of her breasts.

Alan always tried to be unfailingly polite, but the sight of Maya in the un-flattering get-up caught him off guard. With a start, he realized she was much older than he had initially thought and much too old to be wearing such an outfit. So instead of forcing out a compliment that would not come, he said, "Hello, Daisy Duke. Where are the other Dukes of Hazzard?"

But Maya was not offended. She laughed. "I just knew you had a sense of humor under that calm, cool exterior." She yanked him into her house.

She hadn't bothered to clean. Dirty clothes draped over the sofa and chairs, and scattered Legos—Maya hadn't mentioned she had a kid—made an obstacle course on the floor. The slovenliness of the place offended Alan a great deal more than Maya's appearance or possible kid. Being an extremely neat person himself, it appalled him when people couldn't take the time to hang up their clothes or pick up a fallen item. He then saw the pizza box on the coffee table, the napkins and paper plates beside it. "I thought you were going to cook dinner?"

Maya dismissively waved her hand. "Who has time to cook?"

"I was looking forward to it." Alan realized he was acting too stubborn for the situation, but the woman could have told him the truth. Alan always expected the truth, eventually.

Maya giggled, another thing she was too old to do with any grace. She rubbed her hand up his arm. "We don't have to eat the pizza—if you know what I mean."

Alan politely, yet firmly, told Maya that he wasn't interested in that kind of relationship with her, and Maya, like other women he'd been acquainted with, immediately asked, "Are you gay?" After Alan gently, yet firmly, assured her that he was not, Maya went with the other traditional assumption: "Some girl broke your heart, didn't she? Sure, that's it. Believe me, honey, I've been around that block a time or two."

That evening with Maya could have been scripted by other women he'd had similar evenings with. Alan did not know why women seemed to want an explanation when he explained that he didn't want a relationship, but they always did, and then they seemed relieved when they seized upon the notion that he had a broken heart. It seemed to bring them comfort, so Alan neither confirmed nor denied the allegation. And the funny thing was that the women seemed to like him more after that.

Alan heard a commotion coming from inside the Legion and wondered if someone had finally won. He checked the gun in his holster. He hadn't had the opportunity to use it yet in Liberty, and he hoped he wouldn't have to use it tonight. But he didn't have a clue as to how these people would react if someone finally won the drawing. This town had plenty of family feuds, feuds that went back for generations about some now-forgotten slight or argument. He knew the vast Ehlers clan, who fought among themselves often enough, held some grudge against the Pitts. Likewise, the Sulleys had some festering boil of a grievance against the Hepps. When alcohol was also added to the mix, as it was at every single get-together in this town, except for the church functions, someone or something could explode. Alan aimed to keep that explosion from happening tonight.

With his hand on his gun, Alan sensed a movement in his peripheral vision. He turned his head to the left and saw it: a flash of white against the dark-tinted window of a Mercedes. The Mercedes seemed odd enough. Alan couldn't think of a single person in this Ford and Chevy truck driving town who drove that type of vehicle. He saw it again, the flash of white. Something was not right with this situation; Alan could feel it in his bones. He walked quickly, purposely toward the strange car.

He could hear muffled screaming now, and Alan bent down to peer in the dark window of the driver's side, rapping with his knuckles on the glass. "Police! Open up!" And then his vision focused, and he could see a man on the passenger's side grab a young woman by her dark hair and start to pound, pound, pound her face against the steering wheel with swift, brutal intensity. His face, illuminated by the light pouring from the Legion, looked crazed.

"Stop! Open the door!" Alan wrenched at the handle, which didn't budge. He tried the back door, then ran around the car. All locked. He banged on the passenger's side window with the handle of his Glock, yelling and screaming. Another cacophony erupted from the Legion. No one could hear him, and it was too late to call for backup.

That's when he saw the glint through the passenger window, and that's when the woman somehow escaped from the man's grip on her hair and lunged at him. She clawed and slapped and kicked and fought while the blood poured from her face. He kept pointing the gun at her, and she kept scrabbling for it, and then they were writhing and twisting. The whole thing happened before his eyes so rapidly, and the thought that the couple could be in the throes of an intense passion, instead of a life-and-death struggle, lasted no more than a blink.

Alan raised his gun, pointing it at the window. "Police! Put down your weapon, or I'll shoot!" The struggle inside the car continued. The woman was on top, then the man, then the woman. More light shone into this side of the car, and Alan took aim. He called out one more time, "Police! Put down your weapon, or I'll shoot!"

The man's head appeared in the window, the crazed face, but he wasn't looking at Alan. He stared at the woman he had pinned beneath him, the gun pushed under her chin. Alan squeezed the trigger of his Glock and fired a shot through the window. The man collapsed on top of the girl, and everything went deathly quiet.

Alan had never been trained for this specific situation, but he knew what to do. The woman was pinned under the man; his weight could be crushing her. He bashed in what remained of the passenger window and reached in to unlock the door. With more strength than he knew he had, he heaved the man out of the car and reached for the woman. He didn't dare move her because she might have suffered more injuries, but she reached for his hand so he could pull her into a sitting position.

"Are you all right?" It was an absurd thing to ask. Her lip was split, her nose had obviously been broken, and her eyes had already started to swell shut. Yet she looked strangely serene.

"Is he dead?" she asked.

"Yes, ma'am. I'm calling you an ambulance right now." He reached for his phone. Alan knew she must be in shock, but she no longer seemed to be in distress. He wished he had a jacket to put over her shoulders. He wanted to offer comfort and support.

She turned her head slowly to look at him. "You saved me. Thank you."

She still had not let go of his hand, and he hadn't let go of hers. He waited until the ambulance arrived, and then he accompanied her to the hospital. No, he would never forget his first.

"We were gypped," Jared said, stirring his fifth or sixth Jack and Coke with a swizzle stick at the American Legion bar one hour after someone had just won the colossal 1.5 million dollar jackpot.

"The whole thing was rigged," Chelsea agreed, sipping her fifth or sixth Manhattan. She had started to drink that particular whiskey drink about a year before because of its fancy name. At home, however, she and Jared drank their whiskey neat. On the really bad nights, they didn't bother with the glasses at all.

Brian, the bartender, chucked the million empty beer bottles from all the people who had come up empty-handed into the trash. "You know the whole thing was fair and square, Chelsea," Brian said. "You were sitting in the front row when they took the vote."

"Well, now I think it was rigged," Chelsea said stubbornly, slurping her drink. Someone had inadvertently left out a bucket of sold raffle tickets from the drawing the week before, and the majority had decided to include that bucket of tickets in this week's Queen of Hearts event. But in two of the minor prize drawings leading up to the Queen of Hearts finale, two people held a ticket for the prize and then had to have another drawing with their two tickets. Sure, people had been good sports about it and all, but now Chelsea thought the whole thing smelled fishy. What stupid person would forget about an entire bucket of sold raffle tickets?

"I was really counting on that money." Jared was beginning to get that moony look on his face that happened before he either fell asleep or turned ornery.

Brian noticed Jared's look, too, as he should by now. "I'll let you have two more drinks before I'm cutting you off."

"Make them strong," Chelsea said. "We're nursing our wounds."

Brian still chucked beer bottles. "You're taking the whole thing too personally, Chelsea. It's a silly card game, a game of chance. Personally, I'm glad it's over. Maybe things can get back to normal in this town."

Chelsea had taken this drawing seriously. Every week for fifty-three weeks, she and Jared bought $20 worth of raffle tickets. They didn't miss a single Queen of Hearts for an entire year because a winner only got half the money if she wasn't present. For an entire year, Chelsea had focused her attention and centered her life around the hope of winning all that money. That hope, somewhere around week thirty, blossomed into a certainty. She would win, and her life would be transformed into something magical. Like in a fairy tale, she would live happily ever after. Now that hope was dashed, and Chelsea didn't know what to do with all the crushed pieces.

"At least the person who won is from Liberty." Jared didn't seem to remember that he still sat at the bar of the Legion. He pulled out his flask and poured a hefty amount of whiskey into his glass. Lucky for him that Brian's back was turned.

Brian heard, though. "Born and bred. She probably hasn't left Liberty for more than a few days at a time her entire life."

"And she's nice. Every time I go into the consignment shop, she asks how my little girl is doing. I think that's really, really nice." Jared's eyes teared up; he'd entered maudlin time.

Chelsea had no patience for this part of the process. "Cut that out, Jared. You haven't seen Remy in two years." Jared had fathered Remy with his girlfriend before Chelsea, who kicked him out shortly after the birth and moved to Carbondale, forty miles away. She'd called him a drunk, which was true. She'd also called him a bastard, which was not. Jared dutifully paid his child support, even though he didn't have any custodial rights. He sent gifts to the girl, too, when something caught his eye on the shelf at Walmart: a stuffed Elmo, My Little Pony, and pink, sparkly fou-fou dresses in size two. Remy was four now, and Jared just didn't get that she wasn't the same age as when he last saw her.

"But I love her." Jared let a single tear slip down his acne-scarred face. The maudlin phase demanded this.

"Give me a break," Chelsea said and told Brian she wanted another Manhattan.

Mandy Tanner might be a nice lady, but still. It wasn't fair. Chelsea had been so certain that she would win the jackpot tonight, so certain that she could taste it in her mouth like cotton candy. She arrived at the Legion early, as she always did, and downed a couple of drinks for good luck, as she always did, before taking her customary seat in the first row. She sat patiently through all the preliminary drawings for a free oil change at Manny's, a free haircut at Trudy's Beauty Boutique, a $25 gift certificate to Lolly's Diner, and two massaging seat covers from RV World. Her hands sweat so badly that she was afraid the tickets would turn to mush and be unreadable when her number was drawn. So she spread them out on her jean-clad broad thigh, her little soldiers waiting to be called to the front of the room to accept the prize of a lifetime.

Commander Atkins, at the front of the room, paced before the giant drum stuffed with thousands and thousands of tickets, rubbing his hands together gleefully. "And now for the main event, ladies and gentlemen. After fifty-three weeks of play, only two envelopes remain on the big board." He walked over to the board hung on the wall behind the drum and officials' table and pointed at the two lonely envelopes as if no one in the smelly, crowded room had noticed them before. "Only two envelopes remain. Tonight," his voice lowered, "someone in this room might become a millionaire."

He performed this schtick every single damn week, and tonight, of course, he dragged it out even more than in previous weeks. It drove Chelsea up the wall, and she wanted to shout, *Get on with it, you pompous asshole!* She could feel the sweat trickling down her ribcage. In three or four minutes, she would become a millionaire. She knew Jared watched the Commander just as intently as she did somewhere near the back of the room where he could be closer to the bar.

"This particular Queen of Hearts drawing has been most lucrative for our Post. Obviously." He laughed appreciatively. "With our share of the proceeds, we are going to . . ."

Blah, blah, blah. Chelsea always tuned out this part of his speech, the benefits to the town the Post would sponsor, such as the Head Start program and refurbishing the softball field's bleachers. Who cared about that stuff? She'd lived in Liberty all twenty-seven years of her life and didn't give a shit. She didn't have a kid—and if she got her way, she never would—and the bleachers at the softball field had been crummy and splintery for so long that no one noticed anymore. *Get on with it, you pompous asshole!*

"What would you do with 1.5 million dollars?" Commander Atkins started pointing at people in the crowd. "Would you pay off your house, buy a new car or boat? Would you travel around the world, or try to save the whales?"

Save the whales? That was a new one. Commander Atkins must have been reading one of his fishing magazines again. Or else he was trying to be funny— and failing, as usual. The man liked to drag out his fifteen minutes of fame every week, but this was getting ridiculous.

"Would you quit your job and live a life of leisure?" Commander Atkins had closed his eyes as if he could picture this dream.

It wasn't Chelsea's dream. She had spent so many hours daydreaming about what she would do with all the money that it would probably add up to about a month of her life. The first thing she would do is take a trip to Vegas and see what that was all about. And who knew? Maybe she'd get lucky on the roulette table and win even more money. She'd heard it was true that when you were on a lucky roll, everything you touched turned to gold. Jared wanted her to get a boob job, so she'd probably do that when she got back from Vegas. She'd buy a car, too, nothing too flashy, something like a Mustang convertible. And then she'd build the grandest house in town. That thought had come to her when the roof started leaking again in the dilapidated rental house she shared with Jared. She would build her dream house, and everything in it would be new. Every few years, she would replace things like the bathtubs and fixtures and flooring, and everything would be new again. Always new.

Chelsea didn't exactly know what Jared wanted to do with the money. He'd gone all over the map on that one. During one drunken rant, Jared said he wanted to buy a helicopter. In another, he wanted to open up a drone store, and in yet another, he wanted to move to Hawaii. Chelsea thought it was the Hawaii thing that made her realize Jared might not be the love of her life after all. It had never occurred to her to leave Liberty, and she didn't want to. Her parents and grandparents lived here, just as their parents and grandparents before them. The Uchtman name was solidly embedded in this town's roots, so why would she ever want to leave? If Jared fancied spending his half of the money moving to Hawaii, he would have to do it without her. That is, if she gave him half the money. Chelsea had been pondering the idea of persuading Jared to go 70/30. If he was drunk enough, she was pretty sure she could get him to sign some sort of agreement.

"I will give the wheel a final spin." The Commander grunted as he pushed the metal cylinder. "It's heavy tonight, folks." He made a big show of wiping his brow before giving it another big spin.

Chelsea had already been leaning forward in her chair. But now she perched on the very edge of her seat, her nose almost brushing her knee. This was it. This was when she shed her old life like a snake shedding its skin, and her magical new life began. No more boring nights, sitting on their lumpy couch, drinking whiskey, eating McDonald's, and playing video games. From now on, she would be sitting on a shiny leather couch with a view of the Mississippi, sipping Macallan 18. She could almost feel that smooth burn in her throat.

"Drum roll, please." About ten weeks ago, the Commander enlisted one of the high school drummers to come on Thursday nights to perform this one musical event: a single drumroll. Chelsea had to admit that it did add just the right touch of anticipation—as if she needed anymore.

With a flourish, the Commander reached into the drum and pulled out a single ticket, holding it up for all to see. "And the winning number is 185479!"

Chelsea's eyes darted to the tickets spread out on her legs. She scanned the numbers once before she heard: "Oh, my goodness, that's me!"

"I do believe the winner is present tonight in the form of Mandy Tanner. Come on up to the big board, Mandy!"

Chelsea couldn't believe it. She'd been so sure she'd win, but then again, she thought she would win every week. Chelsea watched as Mandy walked to the front, exclaiming the whole time. "I can't believe this. I've never attended the drawing before. I just can't believe it. This is my first time here." It was like rubbing salt into the wounds of the weekly faithful. And darting her eyes to the left and right, Chelsea was sure she wasn't the only person in the room who felt that way.

However, Chelsea still had hope. If the woman did not pick the correct envelope with the Queen of Hearts, one more drawing would be held next week, and that person would be an automatic winner. The noisy room grew as still as a morgue as Mandy, her cheeks flushed, pointed at the board. "Oh, I don't know." She shrugged. "I guess I'll take this one because it's closer to me." She shrugged helplessly again. "I don't know what I'm doing here. Honest, this is my first time."

The Commander took the envelope off the board, and with a deep breath— and after asking for an unprecedented second drum roll—removed the card from the envelope. He glanced at it, then held it close to his chest. "Ladies and gentlemen, Mandy has drawn," he flipped over the card and held it up high, "the queen of hearts! We have a winner!"

The noise erupted, a volcano of cheers and shrieks, and Chelsea was pretty sure some were wails of disappointment. That's what she wanted to do, wail. She skipped the check-awarding ceremony, as did many others, and fought her way to the bar where Jared had already saved her a seat. "That's that," he said and ordered drinks. They'd been sitting here ever since. The bar had mostly cleared, but Mandy could still hear plenty of people out in the parking lot.

"I guess we won't be quitting our day jobs." The more Jared drank, the more pronounced his southern, hillbilly-sounding drawl became. "We're going to be stuck in that damn Walmart for the rest of our goddamn lives." And just like that, it appeared, the righteous anger, the-world-is-against-me phase.

Unlike Jared, who stocked shelves at Walmart, Chelsea genuinely liked her job as a cashier. While unloading boxes and boxes of goods and placing them on shelves made Jared lament all that he did not possess in the world, Chelsea, while pushing a plethora of goods across the scanner, realized how much worthless crap most people bought. Still, they had come together over lunch in the break room a year and a half ago and bonded over their mutual dislike of Geraldine, the bitchy general manager. Geraldine sent out meaningless memos to remind people to wash their hands after using the restroom (duh), that there was a dress code forbidding ripped and torn jeans (fat chance), or that their pay would be docked every time they ate at the snack bar and didn't pay (she wouldn't dare).

And they bonded over their mutual love of whiskey. The subject came up immediately during that first lunch. Jared had a microwaved bean burrito in front of him (25 cents at Walmart), and after he had chewed down that first bite, which took a while because Jared's teeth were not the best, he said, "I like to party. I don't mean *party* party, like going to the taverns all the time, although I do that, too. I mean, I like to drink whiskey pretty much all the time."

She had noticed him around, of course, but it was the first time Chelsea really took a good look. Jared was older than her, thirty-four, and not particularly handsome. His face still bore his teenage acne scars, and his nose had a big bump in the middle from a childhood bike crash. He was tall and too skinny and slightly round-shouldered, but something about him appealed to her. His honesty, perhaps. Or maybe it was because he didn't give a damn what anyone else thought about him. That appealed to Chelsea, who felt the same.

"I love whiskey," she'd said, her cup of microwaved Ramen in front of her (also 25 cents at Walmart). "I've loved it ever since I was twelve and snuck into my dad's medicine cabinet and tasted it for the first time."

"Medicine cabinet?" Jared raised his eyebrows.

"A box in the storage shed where Dad hid his bottles of whiskey. He thought none of us knew what he was talking about when he said he needed to get something out of his medicine cabinet." He stared at her so intently that Chelsea felt like she should run a finger through her reddish-brown, curly hair, her best feature. But out of stubbornness, she did not. She let him recognize every freckle in her round face, let him check out her nonexistent chest. For a big-boned girl with wide hips and sturdy thighs, she had disproportionately small breasts.

Jared smiled, showing as few teeth as possible. "When we get a place together, we'll call wherever we store our whiskey our medicine cabinet."

"Deal," she said.

And that's how it began. The funny thing, though—and they commented on how funny it was all the time—was that Chelsea and Jared never got around to "storing" their whiskey anywhere. If a bottle appeared in the house, invariably, it was empty by the next morning. They'd wake up on the couch the morning after a straight-from-the bottle night, bleary-eyed, and when Jared would hold up the empty Jack bottle after fumbling around on the floor for it, he would then turn it over. Not a drop would fall to the ground. "It's magic," he would say, and Chelsea would laugh weakly. Then they'd throw on some clothes and stagger into work.

They were rarely late for work at the Walmart on the southern rim of Liberty. They both knew Geraldine was just looking for an excuse to fire them. Geraldine had not told either one of them that, nor had she given them any formal warnings. It didn't matter because they both just knew Geraldine was out to get them. So, the number one rule: Don't be late for work. The number two rule: Never buy the booze at Walmart. These two rules afforded the only code they lived by, and Chelsea and Jared abided by them.

But then the Queen of Hearts jackpot started to gather force and grow like a hurricane inside the town of Liberty, and Chelsea and Jared got sucked up into the eye of the storm. They drank every night, but Thursday nights became the apex of the week, the thrill that shattered the surrounding monotony. For the last fifty-two weeks, after no one won that night's drawing, Chelsea and Jared drank to their relief. They drank to dreams yet untarnished and hope not yet churned and spit out by the eye of the storm. Now that was all over. Chelsea wanted to cry in frustration, but she'd never been the crying sort.

"I bet Mandy uses some of that money for her daughter. She got beat up pretty bad in the parking lot here a couple of weeks ago. Some guy bashed her head into the steering wheel of his car a bunch of times. I heard she needs plastic surgery," Brian said now. He'd finally finished chucking out the empty beer bottles and moved on to washing the stack of highball glasses in the sink under the bar.

"Bastard," Jared spat. "What kind of man beats up on a girl? A chickenshit bastard, that's who!" Jared liberally spiked his eighth and last drink.

At that moment, Commander Atkins led the final entourage from the banquet room. He held Mandy's hand like a congenial father, and the woman still looked dazed and flushed. She carried an oversized cardboard Queen of Hearts check for the amount of 1.5 million dollars. It kept slapping against the young man's knees as he walked next to her; Chelsea recognized him as the reporter from the *Liberty Gazette*. He had also faithfully attended every drawing. Bringing up the rear was a silvery blond, stylish-looking woman whose stony face would have fit right in on Mount Rushmore.

Commander Atkins gave Mandy's hand a final pat. "We'll meet at the bank first thing tomorrow morning to get all the details finalized, Mandy. Congratulations again, my dear."

"Thank you," Mandy stammered. "I still can't believe it. I've never come to a drawing before, even though Trisha kept begging me to come. And then tonight I just needed to get out of the house. Things have been a mess lately—"

"Stop talking!" Trisha snapped. She grabbed Mandy's arm and yanked her toward the door. "You won. Everybody knows that, so shut up already."

"What are you so mad about?" Mandy asked as she was pulled through the door.

Grief rushed over Chelsea in one mammoth wave. It was really, truly over. And she had lost. "I'm going to take a smoke break," she said to Jared, who ranted about beating up the guy who had beat up the woman. In this phase, he was a blowhard, a self-righteous blowhard who knew all the answers to all the world's problems. In the morning, he wouldn't remember a damn thing about this one-sided conversation.

When Chelsea slid off the barstool, her feet had a hard time finding the floor. She gripped the edge of the counter, embarrassed. She was a young woman known for holding her drinks in this town. No, that wasn't quite right. She was *renowned* in this town for holding her liquor. She wasn't doing anything more than she did on a typical Thursday night. She had a couple of drinks before the drawing and six or seven here at the bar. Oh, wait. There'd been a couple of shots before they left the house. She and Jared had made some toasts to good luck. They had raised their mismatched glasses—somehow, and even though they both worked at Walmart, they had never gotten around to buying a proper set of dishes—and Chelsea had said, "When we win tonight, we're never coming back to this dump again."

"You know it, girl. Our real lives are about to start."

"Viva Las Vegas!" And they clinked glasses and drank. Chelsea had been so happy then, probably the happiest she'd ever been.

And look at her now, a mere three hours later, and all hope had been swallowed by a sinkhole. What's more, what were she and Jared going to look forward to now? The center of their social life had disappeared with the pick of a hidden card in a sealed envelope. What were they going to talk about? When Chelsea took the time to think about it, she and Jared had spent the majority of their time together fantasizing about winning the Queen of Hearts drawing. They'd made so many plans! True, some of them had been kind of stupid, like Jared wanting to own a drone store. And at one time, Chelsea had thought they could raise a bunch of goats and ponies and start a petting zoo at their new, beautiful home on the outskirts of town. Jared had laughed his head off about that idea, which made Chelsea even more stubbornly persistent. "It's a real thing," she'd said hotly.

And then Jared had dropped to the floor. "See? I'm rolling on the floor with laughter, Chelsea. A petting zoo!"

She'd acted all offended, grabbed the bottle of whiskey out of his hand, and gone out on the front porch to smoke and finish it off all by herself. She'd known it was a silly idea, really. The point was dreaming about the possibilities that the long-running drawing had provided in their lives. It had provided hours upon hours of entertainment. So now what were they going to do, sit around and drink every night without the wishful thinking/hoping/dreaming? It was a very dismal thought.

Chelsea knew she was weaving a little; her feet kept finding uneven ground. To cover that up, as she always did, she started jutting out her hips and doing a slow, exaggerated Marilyn Monroe type of sexy walk. It might not have wholly disguised her tipsiness, but it usually got a chuckle or a phony, high-pitched wolf whistle out of some of the bar regulars. Tonight, no one seemed to notice. It was like she had become invisible.

She pushed through the door and found a corner of the Legion to prop herself upon. It was so humid that beads of sweat immediately popped up along her scalp line like a string of oily pearls. Chelsea fumbled in the front pocket of her t-shirt for the crumpled pack of Camels. Chelsea always wore Hanes men's t-shirts with a front pocket over her left breast. Walmart carried them in a variety of colors, and Chelsea had them all. Tonight, she had on her red shirt. Looking down at it now, she could see it wasn't very clean. She couldn't remember the last time she'd done laundry, mostly because she hated going to the Laundromat. Which was right next door to Zelda's Consignment Shop, come to think of it. Which was owned by the woman who had just won the Queen of Hearts drawing and was now a millionaire.

Damn, damn, damn.

Chelsea flicked her Bic lighter against the tip of the Camel and inhaled deeply. She would get over this night eventually. She knew that. She would swallow her disappointment and digest it and then get on with life, working at Walmart, drinking nightly with Jared. She would see her parents, sister, and her three brats every Sunday for dinner after church. They had long since stopped trying to pull Chelsea back into the Pentecostal fold or whatever the church's newest preacher called it now.

When Chelsea renounced her Pentecostal upbringing at the age of sixteen by cutting her hair and exchanging her long dress for Levi jeans, her parents had been appalled, naturally. But they got over it. They always said they loved her, no matter what. And maybe they did. As cloistered a life as they lived, they most certainly would have heard of her drinking and smoking. Liberty was a small town, after all, but they never mentioned it. It was quite odd, but Chelsea's mother made the best fried chicken around, so Chelsea went to Sunday dinner. It was kind of nice. She had never once invited Jared to go with her. He was usually just getting up when she got home about two anyway, and it was time to start drinking again.

Chelsea lit her second cigarette from the dying butt of her first. It was still noisy out here in the parking lot and adjacent park, but it wasn't the widespread pandemonium people had been talking about for weeks. It looked like the weekly fight within the Ehlers clan was over. Sometimes it was cousin against cousin, other times, brother against brother. Whatever. It's how the large Ehlers family—it seemed like every third person in Liberty was named Ehlers—settled their disputes. On this night, Ronny and Donny, the thirty-year-old twins in the family, were wiping the blood off their mouths with the back of their hands and then clasping in a bear hug. It was kind of sweet, in a weird way. The family knew how to clear the air between members, and grudges did not last longer than a week.

A large group still gathered around the picnic tables clustered in the center of the park. Red and blue coolers holding beer were spaced evenly around the perimeter like guard dogs. Every so often, a burst of laughter would erupt from the group. At one point, a wiry old guy with a Duck Dynasty-looking beard jumped up on the picnic table and did an impression of something that looked like an ape. Whatever. The group cracked up. Chelsea thought it was odd. Like her, they were probably lubricating their disappointment, but unlike her, they were not wallowing. Tonight, she planned on wallowing and nursing her grief until she couldn't get her hands on any more alcohol.

"I hope you're not planning on driving tonight, Chelsea."

Chelsea dropped her lit cigarette. Officer Morrison had snuck up on her like a cat once again. Sometimes Chelsea wondered if he had it in for her. Every time she looked up during the Queen of Heart drawings the past few weeks, he seemed to be eyeing her. "No, sir. For the time being, I am not allowed to drive. As you very well know."

"Court day's coming right up." He stood there, hands on his hips, his right pinkie nestled against his Glock.

"I am aware." Chelsea tried hard to enunciate every vowel and consonant, but looking into those green-gold eyes of his, she knew she hadn't fooled him. Well, he was a cop and the one who had arrested her for a DUI two weeks ago. It had been so stupid. She and Jared had finished one bottle of Jim Beam, and Jared had decided he needed just a little more. "Don't you think we need a nightcap, Chelsea baby? I don't think I'll be able to sleep without a nightcap."

He'd had a lot more of the bottle than her, so stupidly, she thought she could still drive. Plus, he looked kind of pathetic, sprawled out on the couch like that, shirtless, his white, concave chest heaving with sweaty desperation. So she went. And Officer Morrison nabbed her just as she pulled into Partytime Liquors.

He was very nice about it and all. "I hate to see a young girl like you throw her life away by hurting herself or someone else in an alcohol-related accident."

He talked kind of funny, or at least it seemed funny at the time, clipped and polished, overly polite. Even in her not-quite drunken state, Chelsea knew better than to laugh. "Yes, sir." She did salute, though, which made him frown. Even frowning, he was a handsome man. Everyone in town had been talking about his movie star looks ever since he arrived, and even close up—when he gave her a breathalyzer test—she could see how smooth his skin was, how the pores were so tiny as to be almost invisible. However, he wasn't her type, mostly because he wouldn't look twice at a girl like her under normal circumstances. But she did like how she had his undivided attention right then.

Officer Morrison seemed genuinely sorry that he had to take her to jail to *follow procedure.* "But I won't handcuff you. And you can ride in the front of the car."

She appreciated not being treated like a criminal, even though he felt it was his duty to give her a lecture on the way to the county jail. He must have been about her age, but he acted like her teacher or something. "You should treat this arrest as a wake-up call, Chelsea Uchtman. No one was hurt this time. And just remember: It is never a good idea to drink and drive."

Unless you run out of alcohol, she wanted to say. But she kept agreeing with Officer Morrison, and he didn't lock her up or anything like that. He let her wait in the chair beside his desk for Tiffany, her only Walmart friend who had any money saved, to bail her out. And he even brought her a cup of thick, black coffee to sober her up, although she didn't feel the least bit drunk by then. She was touched by how nice he acted. And she was royally pissed off at Jared, who didn't answer his phone the ten times she called because he was passed out drunk on the couch. For the first time, Chelsea wondered if maybe she led a lifestyle that wasn't all fun and games. Sure, it seemed like a great idea, even exhilarating, those first few drinks of the night. But then it got sadder as the night wore on. Sometimes she and Jared ended up yelling and screaming at each other over the slightest infractions, like who ate the last Ding Dong or who forgot to buy toilet paper. And most mornings were sheer hell. "We should buy stock in Advil," they'd often joked, "and Gatorade." Maybe it wasn't funny.

"Take care," Officer Morrison said now. "And don't let that drunk boyfriend of yours drive either."

"I won't," she said, smiling as sweetly as she could, which wasn't sweet at all. She didn't have that kind of face. And Jared was going to drive them home tonight. Either that or they would have to walk almost a half-mile to their house, which neither of them was willing to do in this town that was so backward it didn't have a taxi or Uber service. But Jared drove really well when he was drunk; it was kind of amazing. When he was drunk, Jared could probably win the Indy 500.

Officer Morrison gave a final wave, and his right hand came to rest on his gun. It was true. Ever since Officer Morrison shot that guy who beat up the girl two weeks ago, he'd seemed to become very fond of his Glock. His hand would hover lovingly above it before his fingers would lightly touch the handle. People in this town thought he'd been a hero. Sure, there had been some kind of conduct investigation, but it was just cursory. The officer had shot a crazed man who would have murdered the girl if he hadn't interceded. The guy was a bonafide hero.

Chelsea lit a third cigarette, a secret smile toying at the corner of her lips now that Officer Morrison had gone inside the Legion. Little did he know, but he wasn't the only person who had a gun here tonight. Well, there were probably a lot of guns here tonight, with the Ehlers and Hepps and Pitts in attendance, but Chelsea would bet money she didn't have that she was the only girl here tonight in possession of a firearm. She didn't have a specific reason for buying the Ruger American Pistol. It wasn't like she wanted to hurt anyone, although she'd been awfully mad at Jared when he couldn't pull himself together enough to bail her out of jail. He'd been contrite when she got home the next morning, though. And then he cleaned the entire two-bedroom house and bought a real supper at Dave's Market, the Monday mostaccioli special, along with a bottle of Macallan 18, Chelsea's absolute favorite that she could rarely afford. They'd had a good night, no fights or anything. No sex either, but then they never did that anymore anyway.

And it certainly wasn't like Chelsea planned to harm herself. She'd never been one of those gloomy-assed people who liked to moan about how depressed they were all the time. She wanted to tell that type of person, *Get over yourself. Come on.* Who wasn't depressed from time to time? Who didn't have a few mornings a week when the idea of making it through another day seemed unbearable? It was a fact that life was hard and often sad, and occasionally, happy. Like the first drink of whiskey of the day. That was happiness. That was something to look forward to, wasn't it?

No, she'd bought the Ruger American Pistol because she wanted to. She'd walked past the gun counter at Walmart, and there it sat, front and center in the locked display case. It looked sleek and powerful, yet there was also something sexy about it. Chelsea had a hard time explaining even to herself why she just had to have that gun. Ray, the gun guy at Walmart, had taken it out and showed it to her and explained all its advantages in glowing terms. "She's a beauty," Ray had said, and Chelsea agreed. She bought it on Layaway and didn't even think to tell Jared. That Ruger was hers and hers alone, as of today at five o'clock, when she made the final payment at Walmart. It didn't occur to her that she had never shot a gun before and didn't know how to use it. "Cocked and locked," Ray said when he handed it over in its box. "17+1 in the chamber." That was good enough for Chelsea.

Chelsea stubbed out the Camel with the toe of her Converse. She was thirsty and wanted to go finish her drink. Then she and Jared would go home and polish off the bottle they'd opened earlier. Same old, same old. She looked up when she heard the scraping, thudding sound. She'd know that sound anywhere—she'd been in enough fender benders herself—and sure enough, down at the far end of the parking lot, a guy got out of his truck to see what he'd hit. "Goddamn it,

Sid. You didn't park in your goddamn lines and were too close to me. This is all your fault. You better have insurance, man."

Sid seemed to appear out of nowhere, stumbling to his truck. "Fuck you, Marty. You're the SOB who hit me. Your insurance better be willing to hand me a fistful of cash."

Marty stood, staring at the long scratch and cracking his knuckles. "Do you still have that ATV that needs a little work?"

Sid took off his Cardinals hat and wiped his sweaty forehead with his forearm. "Yeah. You still got that golf cart with the broken axle?"

"Sure do." They stared at the scratch in companionable silence. "Trade and call it even?"

"Deal." Sid reached into the bed of his truck and pulled out two Buds from a Styrofoam cooler. He handed one to Marty. "Fuck the insurance companies anyway. As soon as you report a claim, they jack up your premiums."

Marty tapped his beer can to Sid's. "That's right, buddy. Fuck the insurance companies."

Chelsea was gravely disappointed by this turn of events. Instead of being happy the two men had settled their dispute in a civil manner, she felt deflated. And a little bit angry. When Marty cracked his knuckles, she had been sure he would pop Sid in the mouth, and she would see some blood. She would see some violence, which would have seemed like a fitting ending to this topsy-turvy, disillusioning night.

Damn, damn, damn.

She turned to go back into the Legion. Chelsea was not a violent person by nature. She remembered in second grade when Carny Weston had pushed her into a mud puddle on purpose. "You're fat," she had taunted as she stood over Chelsea. It had been a deep, rutted puddle, and Chelsea struggled to sit up, face streaming with dirty water. Carny was about half her size, and Chelsea could have easily reached out and buckled her knees so that the girl would have landed in the puddle with her. But at church the day before, the preacher had gone on and on about how good Christians "turned the other cheek." So that's what Chelsea did. She turned her head, offering Carny a cheek. She'd fallen face-first into the puddle, so which cheek she should offer was a cloudy issue. But it didn't matter. Carny had already run off, laughing with her friends.

And there was that time during sophomore year in high school. Chelsea was still Pentecostal then, still wearing both her skirts and hair long. She was the only Pentecostal kid left in Liberty High because the other students of the faith had left the public school and started at the new charter school, Pentecostal Christian Academy. When Chelsea went to her locker between Algebra and Geology, someone had written FREAK all over it in black spray paint. It wasn't the first time that had happened, and she would do as she had before, go and tell the principal. Chelsea hadn't named any names in the vandalism, although she had her suspicions. However, this time when she opened her locker, she saw a curly reddish-brown lock of hair hanging from the central hook. It looked a lot like her hair, but it couldn't be. She had never cut her hair; it was against the faith. Chelsea could feel eyes upon her as it took a moment, then two, for the realization to set in. She reached for the back of her head, feeling the hole at the nape where the hair had been. She knew it had to be Terrence, the rude boy who sat behind her in Algebra, the boy who repeatedly stabbed her in the back with his pencil and kicked her chair, muttering insults. But she didn't tell a single soul.

Shortly after that incident, Chelsea renounced her Pentecostal faith, or faith of any kind, for that matter. She started to wear jeans, Converse tennis shoes, and what would become her signature t-shirt with the front pocket over her left breast, over her heart. She cut her hair very, very short in an attempt to look the exact opposite of how she had before. She wanted so much to fit in that when she was taunted about her radical new look, she would only smile and say something like, "I'm the new and improved Chelsea Uchtman." She'd say it jokingly, airily, but it didn't matter. Her classmates still didn't seem to like her any better, and Chelsea just didn't understand why. She was a nice person, a good person. She stopped going to church, which made her mother cry all the time, and she altered her appearance for them. What was she doing wrong?

The taunting grew worse. It became so bad that it ran like a mantra in Chelsea's head day and night: "Hey, Lesbo, are you a girl or a guy, a cunt or a prick?" A specific group of football players could be held responsible for most of the vile, vicious remarks, which Chelsea told herself was funny when she tried to make herself feel better. Everyone knew Liberty High always had the worst football team in the county, yet these guys walked through the halls like they were some kind of jock superstars. And that one semester, they decided to focus their vulgarity on Chelsea. But she didn't tell.

She hid in the bathroom a lot during those three months. If she saw the group of four, wearing letterman jackets and walking four abreast down the hallway, she would duck into the bathroom and lock herself in a stall. She acted like a coward, she knew that, but it was better to be a coward than to take their pornographic abuse. And perhaps the worst part about it was that no one offered to take her side. Not one single person stood up for her. A couple of girls had been nice to her in Home Ec, a class that Chelsea despised, a class that she absolutely sucked at, but even they were nowhere around when the football jocks attacked Chelsea.

So it was par for the course when the inevitable happened. No one was around. She had stayed after school to help Mr. Smith, the social studies teacher, take down the Spring Fling decorations, a dance she had not attended because no one had asked her, and she didn't want to go alone. She was at her locker, gathering up her books to go home when she heard the heavy, thumping footsteps. She knew it was the four. The four inept football players had decided to go out for track this year, discus and javelin, and practice had just ended.

Chelsea slowly closed her locker. She could smell their grassy sweat when they were still ten feet away.

"Hey, Lesbo," Bo, the leader said. "Are you a girl or a guy, a cunt or a prick?" The others, who all looked remarkably similar to Bo with their broad chests and squashed in-looking faces, snickered. Together, they looked like a litter of bulldog puppies.

The school's front door was behind them, as was the bathroom, her place of refuge. Chelsea had no choice but to walk straight ahead, toward them. And then stop before their wall of solid flesh. "Excuse me," she said, staring at the floor. "I need to get home." Amazingly, at a sign from Bo, they parted ranks.

Chelsea was granted one swift second of relief, but that was all she would get. The four followed her down the hall with their disgusting chant, "Hey, Lesbo, are you a girl or a guy, a cunt or a prick?"

"Leave me alone," she murmured, too terrified to raise her voice. Something bad was going to happen. She could feel it in her bones, as her grandma used to say. Where had Mr. Smith gone? Where was the janitor, Fred?

Bo had heard. "It speaks!" he boomed. "The creature has a voice!"

Chelsea was almost to the bathroom door. She would be safe in there, she thought. She knew the graffiti scrawled on every stall in that place of refuge. Later, when she let her mind go back to that afternoon, she would see how stupid she had been, how naive. But at the time, she only wanted to get into the safety of that Lysol-smelling room, get into a stall, and lock the door. She should have run down that hall for all she was worth. Perhaps then someone would have seen that she needed help, that she was being pursued by evil, malicious forces. But she ducked into the bathroom.

They followed. "Anybody want to bet? Girl or guy?" Bo asked. The other three seemed jumpy, from nerves or excitement Chelsea couldn't say. "I say it's time to find out. Grab it!"

She tried to scream, but a big, sweaty palm engulfed her face as they wrestled her to the cold tiles of the floor. Chelsea tried to kick and struggle, but they quickly subdued her, pinning her arms and legs to the floor, immobilizing her. She felt her body turn to stone, and she turned her head to the side as Bo yanked down her jeans, tangling them around her ankles. Chelsea tried to concentrate on anything but what was happening to her. She could see her distorted reflection in the stainless steel of the skinny pipe under the sink. In the corner stood a bucket with a mop, as if Fred had left in a hurry. Had Fred known what these four awful people were going to do to her? Had Mr. Smith? Why had they all disappeared?

"Ta-da!" Bo said as he ripped off her underwear and held up the cotton panties. "Tighty-whities," he said. The other three laughed on cue. Then Bo pried her legs open—Chelsea hadn't realized that she had clamped them together—and peered closely. Chelsea could feel his hot breath on her inner thighs. "We have a girl, gentlemen. The mystery has been solved. See for yourself." Chelsea supposed the other three looked, but she'd closed her eyes.

"Let's get out of here," one of them said nervously.

"Yeah, we've had our fun. We should let her go." A different voice.

"Don't even think about it, Bo." The third voice sounded urgent.

Chelsea's eyes were still closed, but she heard the thump of his tennis shoes go around her head. She heard the clank of the silver metal bucket as he extracted the mop. "One more thing," Bo said, his voice heavy, raspy. "I'm going to teach this bitch a lesson."

What lesson do I need to learn? Fluttered across her mind before she felt the sharp jab of the broom handle, before she felt it tearing her flesh, before she felt the blood trickling down her inner thighs. *What did I do wrong?* Again, the sharp thrust of the broom handle, deeper this time, sent bolts of pain through her body. Chelsea saw black dots spin across her closed eyelids.

"That's enough, Bo." The third voice sounded very far away. "You've made your point. Let's go, man."

Chelsea didn't think she stayed unconscious for very long. She was a tough person, and she'd taken the abuse of her classmates for years. This was just one more thing, and she would swallow it, digest it, and get on with her life. She was sore, yes, but she told herself it wasn't too bad. Stoically, she pulled a long line of paper towels from the dispenser and wet them in the sink, and stoically, she washed the blood from between her legs. She had been a virgin before this, and now she didn't know what she was. It didn't really matter.

From that point on, she wouldn't care what other people thought of her, and she wouldn't let it bother her either. If she didn't mention this incident to anyone, if she didn't verbalize it, it would just disappear. So she never uttered a word to a single person, and wonder of wonders, those four jocks left her alone after that. When they passed her in the hallway, they averted their eyes from her defiant stare. Once, Chelsea thought she saw a blush of shame spread across Bo's cheeks, but she couldn't be sure. A few years later, when someone told her Bo had been killed in Iraq, it took Chelsea a minute or so to remember who he was. And then a slow smile spread across her round face.

The second she walked back into the Legion, it hit her again like a baseball bat. It was all over. Someone—not her—had drawn the queen of hearts, and her beautiful house filled with everything new would never happen. She could see through the door of the bar into the deserted banquet hall where tickets littered the floor like brown, funereal confetti, and still more losing tickets lay dying in the drum. Soon, someone would sweep the floor and empty the drum, and all the thousands upon thousands of possibilities would be trash.

Jared still sat at the bar, ranting about the guy who beat up a girl. Chelsea could tell just by looking at his fiery red face and his wild, darting eyes that

Jared had fully entered into the ornery phase of his drinking, and she felt glad. Witnessing that fender bender outside the Legion had given her a plan. She now knew what she needed to do to make herself feel better about losing so much. She now had the perfect solution for how to end this night with the bang that it deserved. She downed the rest of her Manhattan and reached into Jared's back jeans pocket for his flask. There wasn't a lot in there, but it was enough to renew her buzz and jack up her adrenaline. It was time to act, to take matters into her own hands.

Chelsea had to prop up Jared on the walk to the car by slinging his arm around her shoulder. It was a good thing they always got to the drawing early and snagged a parking spot close to the door. Boy, he was drunk tonight. Rip-roaring, perfectly drunk. She shoved him in behind the wheel of their old Honda and took out the Ruger box from the trunk before she settled herself into the passenger seat. Neither one of them bothered with seatbelts; they never did. They'd long ago agreed that a car crash wouldn't be a bad way to go.

"You know how, when we go to the Demolition Derby in Du Quoin every year, you say you want to enter it next year?"

"Hell, yeah, I want to smash up some cars for fun one of these days." Jared beat his fists on the steering wheel in excitement. It was a good thing.

"How about we do it tonight?" There were still quite a few cars in the parking lot, maybe twenty or so unoccupied vehicles. It would be perfect.

"Huh?" Jared swiveled his head toward her, momentarily confused.

"Gentleman, start your engine! We are in a demolition derby now. These cars around you need to be taken out. Smash 'em! Crash 'em! Demolish these suckers! Go! Go! Go!"

Jared didn't need any more incentive than that. He backed out, squealing tires, and rammed into the car directly behind them. The jolt had them both bouncing all over the seats, but Jared did it again. Then he rammed his front fender into the side of a Buick parked sideways, collapsing the door. "Fucking A, man!" Jared yelled through the open window. "You lose, sucker!"

Oh, it was glorious! It was the most exciting thing she had ever done in her entire life! Screw the Queen of Hearts drawing! This was a hundred times better than winning a stupid game. This felt like living. "Keep going!" She yelled over the smashing, collapsing metal. The cars started to look like tin cans, and Jared made quick work of them. He really was quite a good driver when he was drunk. It was amazing.

It only lasted a couple of minutes—but it seemed like they'd been smashing into cars for hours—when people started running. "Jared! Jared!" she yelled. "We have to get out of here. I want to drive through town, fast." Jared obeyed, squealing more tires and laying rubber as he peeled out of the Legion parking lot. "Faster!" she kept saying as he headed toward Main Street. "Faster!"

Jared, too far gone at that point, didn't even care what she did next. He didn't blink an eye when she took the Ruger from the box and lifted herself to sit atop the door in the open window. It was a tight squeeze, secure. It was all good when she fired that first shot into the clock tower on the square. It was all good as she fired randomly at the storefronts and into the air. She didn't know how many bullets were in the gun. She just kept shooting. Even though she heard the siren of the approaching police car, she kept shooting.

"Look at us, Jared!" she screamed at one point. "We're like Bonnie and Clyde!"

She didn't remember if she told Jared to drive to Mandy's house, or if he just did it out of instinct. He could be kind of savvy that way sometimes. As they drove toward Mandy's house, Jared kept accelerating. Chelsea's hair whipped around her face and flew into her mouth. The sharp, wet air brought tears to her eyes. She didn't think she wanted to shoot Mandy. She just wanted to scare her. She just wanted her to know it wasn't fair that she won. That's all.

Jared took the final corner on two wheels. Mandy closed her eyes in bliss, in happiness, opening them just in time to see Mandy's house—and the large Weeping Willow tree flying toward her. The scream died in her throat.

His siren blaring, Officer Alan Morrison called over the loudspeaker. "Pull over!" The drunken fool bounced off trash cans and curbs and stop signs as he circled the town square for the third time. "Pull over, Jared!"

Alan's adrenaline was already pumping when he saw Chelsea position herself in the car's open window and start shooting. He now had a very critical situation on his hands, and his heart started galloping. Someone could get seriously hurt here. She shot randomly, hitting the clock tower and then a few store windows. One bullet might have ricocheted off the grandstand. Alan just didn't understand it. She was a nice girl who repeatedly made bad choices, as so many young women in this town did, and now she was about to throw her life away. Hadn't he warned her about that? Hadn't he told her that she needed to get herself together when he arrested her for a DUI? Of course, he had. But she hadn't listened. None of them ever listened. They just kept pulling the same shit over and over again.

"Put your weapon down, Chelsea!" He called over the speaker. Alan doubted she even heard him in her drunken delirium. He held his breath when she leaned so far back in the window that her hair dragged along the ground, and when she struggled back up just before her head bashed into a fire hydrant, he breathed a sigh of relief. If the young woman was as fortunate as a cat to have nine lives, she would use them all up tonight.

He had to blame himself at least a little for the inevitable disaster unfolding right in front of his eyes. Since saving Stephanie Nelson from her crazed lover two weeks before, he might have gotten a little cocky. He'd even come to believe he had a kind of sixth sense when it came to ferreting out brewing trouble. Ha! The last laugh was on him. Of all the possible scenarios running through his mind tonight, the night when so many dreams would end and so many people would be angry and discouraged, he had not prepared himself for this one. People would be drinking a lot, that was a given, and Alan had considered the fights that would break out—and they had, as always—possible shootings and stabbings, but he hadn't counted on a joyride through town with shots fired randomly at innocent people.

Nor had he counted on a suicide spree, and that must be what they were doing. They demolished all the remaining cars in the Legion parking lot, and now it would appear that they were intent on destroying themselves. Jared finally tired of the square and took off down one of the side streets jutting out of Main Street like spokes on a wheel. He sideswiped the Liberty Savings and Loan on the final turn, and Chelsea's hair again scraped the street.

But she struggled up again, and she was weaving and laughing and waving the gun and yelling to Jared, "Faster! Faster!"

"Pull over, Jared and Chelsea!" It was a futile plea, and Alan knew it. He was as close to their car as he could safely get, and he had no way to head them off. The only glimmer of hope he had was that they ran out of gas, but he wasn't going to count on it. Jared made another turn onto Meadow Lane, and Alan suddenly knew where they were heading. He immediately called Pyle and Garcia for backup.

They were going to Mandy's house and the person who had won the Queen of Hearts drawing. Stephanie also stayed there now. He ought to know. Alan had taken this route countless times in the last two weeks. He told himself it was all part of his patrolling duties, but he knew better. He wanted to see Stephanie again, but he didn't know if it was appropriate or not. It was a first for him. Brought up to be polite and use good manners, he had somehow failed to learn what a man did when he became genuinely interested in a woman. He had inspired many futile pursuits, but when it came to how he should act when he was the pursuer, Alan didn't have a clue.

Jared followed Chelsea's command and drove even faster now, zigzagging even more erratically. Alan glanced down at his speedometer: 70 mph. This would not end well; he knew that. Yet there was nothing he could do about it. It was like watching a house disappear suddenly and totally into a sinkhole. It was like watching a building implode or a dam collapse. It was like watching a snake swallow a mouse. Once the wheels had been set in motion, there was nothing you could do about it.

It was like when his mother was diagnosed with Stage 4 breast cancer and refused to get any kind of treatment. "I'm not letting them cut off my breast," she had said to Alan.

"This isn't a time to be vain, Mom." He'd said it gently. He and his mother had always been close, united in solidarity when the Sergeant Major forgot he was in his own home and began to bark orders at them. He understood, too, that she had always depended upon her beauty and her good figure to define her.

"It's not vanity, Alan." She already looked pale and thin. And nestled in the wingback chair by the front window, she looked as fragile as a porcelain figurine. "I just don't see the point in prolonging things."

"Please." There, he'd said it. If she wanted him to beg her to go for treatment, then he would do it. "Please have the surgery. Please have the chemo and radiation, Mom."

Then he'd gotten on his knees next to her chair, taken her hand, and cried like a baby. When the Sergeant Major came in, Alan thought for sure he'd be rebuked, just like when he was a child and then a teenager, but Dad said nothing. Instead, his father knelt on the other side of his wife and added his tears and pleas. But that beautiful, stubborn woman would not change her mind. She would not budge an inch; she died four months later.

It was time. As Alan watched in horror, Jared sped the final few yards down Meadow Lane. Mandy's house stood near the end of the street, but right before Jared got there, he jerked the wheel to the left, jumped the curb, mowed down the neighbor's rose bushes, and plowed deep into the branches of the Weeping Willow. The air vibrated with the sound of the crash.

Alan heard a guttural cry as he screeched to a halt, the siren still blaring, and bolted from the car. Only later did he realize that he was the one who made that grief-stricken sound. Because of the long, hanging branches, Alan couldn't see how bad it was, but the old Honda had not burst into flames. That was one good thing.

As Alan tentatively crept toward the Weeping Willow, he heard neighbors coming out onto their porches. He heard Garcia and Pyle's siren approaching, and he heard someone calling for an ambulance. He parted the snapped branches with his flashlight. Steam escaped from the crumpled hood, but other than that, it was silent. He ran the flashlight over the car, seeing everything he had feared: Jared, head thrown back, impaled by the steering column, and Chelsea, still wedged into the window and hanging out of it, eyes staring lifelessly into the dark branches of the tree. Alan knelt and took her head gently in his hands. A single trickle of blood ran from the corner of her mouth, but her face didn't have another scratch. *She must have broken her neck,* Alan thought. He hoped that she had died instantly, that she hadn't felt any pain.

"You okay, Morrison?" Pyle put a hand on his shoulder. "This is the tough kind—when they're young."

"This is so needless. I don't understand."

"Booze and domestic violence," Pyle said. "All variations on the same theme."

"No, no." Alan sorrowfully shook his head. "I think this had to do with the Queen of Hearts drawing. I think they died of disappointment."

"That damn drawing. I'm glad it's over."

The ambulance arrived, and Alan backed out of the overhanging branches. When he reached up to wipe the dripping sweat from his face, he realized he'd been crying. He was a police officer. He wasn't supposed to cry, at least not on duty. When alone, he still teared up over his beautiful mother.

He looked up to see Stephanie staring at him from the Tanners' yard next door, her face still heavily bandaged. She told him she would have to have plastic surgery in the hospital after it happened, and he'd said something hokey like, "You'll still be beautiful." The bastard who banged her head against the steering wheel had knocked out a few of her teeth, but it still seemed like a lovely smile to Alan when she smiled back. And her aquamarine eyes. He could not stop thinking about them.

Stephanie reached out her arms to him, and Alan suddenly knew precisely the right thing to do. He crossed over to her, buried his face in her neck, and let her hold him.

BESTIES

Trisha attacked the stain with the scrub brush she found under Marie Sherman's kitchen sink. It was too late. It was too late for many things, yet Trisha attacked the dried bloodstain with ferocity. The stain had already been set, rooted deeply into the fibers of the carpet when Sophie found Marie's body. Marie had lain in her own coagulating blood for two days before her friend Sophie became concerned and ventured over. Sophie, in her late 70s like Marie, didn't have the sense God gave a goose egg, so instead of the rational thing to do—calling the paramedics and the police—she called Trisha. "There's blood everywhere," Sophie yelled into the phone. Because she was hard of hearing, Sophie assumed that everyone else was equally disadvantaged. "It's everywhere!"

Understandably, Sophie was upset, but that didn't mean Trisha would cut her any slack. Trisha had no patience with incompetent people. "Does she have a pulse?"

"I… I… don't know," Sophie hiccupped into the phone. "I don't want to touch her. There's blood everywhere!"

Sophie, even in her advanced age, was so irritating. And so was Marie, and so was her other friend Nadine. Trisha called them The Church Ladies because they wore their Presbyterian religion like a badge of honor that elevated them far, far above mere flawed mortals, when the fact of the matter was that they were as flawed, if not more so, than everybody else. Trisha had never seen anyone who had mastered the look of disdain like her aunt Marie.

"Fine. I'll be right there. And for heaven's sake, Sophie, don't touch anything. Do you hear me?"

"I really need a glass of water." Sophie's thin, trembling voice suggested that this was true.

"Absolutely not, Sophie! The police are going to be dusting for fingerprints, and I don't want you to mess up the crime scene."

"Oh, my," Sophie said.

Trisha called the police and ambulance on her way over. She was dressed in her lululemon workout clothes and had wanted to get in a good workout on her elliptical trainer before lunch. It was another thing that irritated her. Trisha hated having her workout routine disrupted. At forty-five, she was rail-thin and in the best shape of her life. She worked hard at it, exercising six days a week and following an Atkins-inspired diet. Now, this morning would be shot to hell—all because of Marie.

Marie was Trisha's uncle Leland's second wife. His first wife, Maggie, had been such a sweet, warm person. Trisha had loved her aunt Maggie, who sewed clothes for her dolls and made snickerdoodle cookies that made her house smell of cinnamon. But after that lovely woman died from septicemia caused by a ruptured appendix, Leland must have decided to take up with someone who was the complete opposite. Which turned out to be Marie, a stranger who blew into town one day. Her truck broke down on the side of the road, and it was Leland who offered her a ride into Liberty. And that was all it took for Marie to worm her way into Leland's heart and move into Maggie's house.

The whole thing had always smelled fishy to Trisha. People didn't just show up in Liberty, a small, rural town in southern Illinois, for no reason. True, it was a rather pretty little town located on the Mississippi, and thirty-some years ago, jobs were plentiful because the coal mines still operated. But Marie must have been on her way somewhere else when Fate changed her mind. She had been a middle-aged woman traveling alone—with only one suitcase, mind you—when she cast her spell on Leland, an unsuspecting, grief-stricken man. Trisha always theorized that Marie was running away from someplace or someone. Not that Marie would tell you if you asked. Trisha had tried many, many times, to no avail. No, Marie would get that holier-than-thou look on her face and say, "My life began the second I met Leland." Trisha would roll her eyes.

So Trisha and her aunt were not close, but that morning when she arrived at Marie's house before the paramedics, Trisha couldn't help but feel sorry for the woman. And appalled. And outraged. Marie still lay on the floor just as Sophie had found her. (It appeared that Sophie had not dared to move an inch since talking to Trisha. Even her Jitterbug phone was still pressed to her ear.) Marie's underwear was tangled at her ankles, and what looked to be an ordinary steak knife protruded from her abdomen. Trisha quickly looked away, surprised at the tears that came to her eyes. Trisha had not cried in fourteen years and prided herself on that accomplishment.

When she stooped down to check Marie's pulse, the sight of Marie's naked, white, vulnerable neck made Trisha feel even worse for the stuck-up old lady.

The attacker had stolen Marie's pearls, a gift from Leland, and Marie's pride and joy. Trisha felt a surprisingly strong pulse in Marie's wrist, and in a rare gesture of empathy, she took Marie's hand. "I'm here now, Marie. The ambulance is on its way."

Marie's eyelids fluttered, and then it looked like she struggled to open them. When she finally managed that, and Trisha thought it must have taken a Herculean effort, she tried to wet her dry lips. "Sophie, go get a glass of water for Marie," Trisha said.

"You said not to move." Sophie still hadn't budged.

"Go get the damn water," Trisha snapped. And after a second or two, Sophie trotted off.

Marie's voice was so faint that Trisha had to put her ear directly over Marie's lips. "Don't, don't—" Marie whispered. "Please."

Trisha immediately knew what Marie meant. A proud woman, she didn't want the paramedics to see her in this condition. It was a no-brainer for Trisha. She quickly pulled up the woman's underpants, figuring they would find out about the sexual assault soon enough in the emergency room. If poor Marie ever got to the ER. Sometimes Liberty's only ambulance was called to one of the neighboring small towns. It was too bad that a sick or injured person in this town couldn't call ahead and make a reservation.

Sophie returned with the glass of water, and surprisingly enough, noticed right away what Trisha had done in the name of her aunt's modesty. "Oh, my," she said.

"Don't you dare say a word when the police and paramedics arrive," Trisha warned.

"I won't." She vehemently shook her head. "And that's the way Marie would want it. You're a good niece to her, Trisha."

No, she wasn't, but Trisha didn't feel like getting into an argument with the likes of Sophie on that day. When the EMTs finally arrived a minute or two later, they loaded Marie into the ambulance, where she suffered a series of small strokes. So Liberty Memorial Hospital helicoptered the woman to Missouri Baptist in St. Louis, then transferred her to a rehab center in Des Peres. It was the kind of story that Trisha would have usually spread all over town by now, but she didn't that time, in part because it felt too rawly personal, even though the tragic events had not actually happened to her. Secondly, she had not been to visit Marie. As far as Trisha knew, she was Marie's only living relative. Trisha's no-good sister in Pasadena didn't count, so it was up to Trisha to take responsibility for the old woman. And Trisha did not want that responsibility. She and Marie had never liked each other, never gotten along until that one brief connection right before the EMTs arrived.

To compensate, Trisha tried to rent out Marie's house to make a little extra money for her. Leland was a veteran, so Marie's benefits had to be decent, but she might need some more cash sooner or later. Trisha thought it was an excellent plan to assuage her guilt. She was relatively new to the real estate business, and to say business wasn't booming was an understatement. Business was lousy. Most of the Liberty homes had been built in the 1940s and 50s, and most needed extensive repairs. Business was so bad that Trisha had only sold one home in the six months she'd been selling real estate. That only happened because she sold one friend's house to another friend. Now the friends weren't speaking to each other or to her. Lesson learned, but she'd get the hang of it. Then came the email from Shelby Williams in Scottsdale, Arizona. She'd seen Marie's house advertised online and wanted to rent it for a month. An entire month! Trisha thought her luck had changed.

Fat chance. The woman had been pleasant enough, Trisha supposed, but the whole thing seemed odd. She claimed Errol Gaylord had left her his old, falling-down, probably haunted movie theater in his will because he had been a big fan of hers when she was an actress some years back. But they weren't even related! In fact, Shelby said she had never met the man who had bequeathed her such an extravagant gift. Now Trisha knew Errol Gaylord had been just bat-crazy enough to do something like that, but still. The elfin-looking old guy could have left that movie theater to plenty of people in this town. Like her, for example. She would have razed the old building and constructed a business that the town really needed, maybe a decent gym like LA Fitness or something. God knew the people in this town needed something like that. Liberty had plenty of overweight people waddling around.

But a commission was a commission, and Trisha decided she would play nice with Shelby Williams. Naturally, the first thing Trisha did after she met Shelby was google her, and wonder of wonders, Shelby Williams had been in four movies that Trisha had never heard of. Even though the actress's pictures in the old films looked nothing like the Shelby Williams who had rented Aunt Marie's house, Trisha was impressed. And she was not an easily impressed woman. Yet a movie star was a movie star, and after the disappointing disaster of last night, Trisha had marched herself over here this morning to have a cup of coffee with the woman and ask for her autograph. Maybe she could be friends with this former actress. At least then she would have something that Mandy didn't have. At the thought of Mandy, her best friend for years and years, Trisha attacked the bloodstain on the carpet more ferociously.

However, when Trisha arrived this morning with a bag of blueberry muffins from Dave's Market and two cups of steaming, strong coffee from Lolly's Diner, she found the house deserted. The front door was wide open like it had been flung and stuck there, dirty dishes were stacked haphazardly in the sink, and all the drawers in the bedroom bureau had been pulled out and dumped on the floor. The first thing that Trisha did was check and see if Shelby Williams had stolen anything. She hadn't. Her aunt's various vases and trinkets and silver-framed pictures were still in their precise places. Trisha allowed herself a few moments of relief, and then she got good and mad. The nerve of the woman to up and leave town and not tell her! Trisha had been nothing but friendly to her. Yet the alleged actress (Trisha was starting to think this woman had stolen the actress's name to draw attention to herself) hadn't even had the decency to leave a note with the keys that had been thrown onto the dining room table. That's what Trisha got for being nice. She'd only asked for half the rent up-front, and she knew hell would freeze over before she ever saw the other half.

Trisha's phone, on the floor next to the bucket of sudsy water, pinged once again. Trisha knew who it was. Damn it, she did. The winner of the 1.5 million dollar Queen of Hearts drawing at the Legion last night wanted to gloat, and Trisha couldn't bear the thought of it. Even when she pulled up to Aunt Marie's house this morning and looked across the street at the marquee above the Legion's front door, she felt a tidal wave of disappointment so intense that her knees buckled. She came dangerously close to screaming at the top of her lungs: "It's not fair!" She'd been going to the weekly Thursday night drawing for months now, always hoping that her number would be pulled out of the massive drum, and she would be the one to walk to the big board at the front of the banquet room and select the envelope containing the queen of hearts. She'd been faithful in her attendance and even more diligent than usual about her appearance, in case she got her picture in the paper. And for what? Her best friend, who Trisha had persuaded to come, had never attended a drawing in her life, yet her number was drawn, and she was the lucky one who chose the queen of hearts.

It wasn't fair!

Trisha's phone rang now, and after checking to see that it was indeed Mandy, Trisha leaned back on her haunches and threw the scrub brush into the bucket. It was too late to get out the dried bloodstain, and the only reason she'd tried yet again to do so was that she had so much pent-up anger and frustration. Reluctantly, Trisha reached for her phone. She might as well get this over with. "Hello, Mandy." She forced a cheerful tone into her voice. "How's the million-aire doing today?"

"I still can't believe it."

"So you've said." And said, and said. Last night, when the *Liberty Gazette* reporter interviewed her, that's all Mandy could repeat. It would be one boring article. Trisha took some satisfaction in that.

"My phone hasn't stopped ringing."

"Offering congratulations or wanting a handout?" Liberty had a lot of people out of work, and it wouldn't surprise Trisha a bit if people immediately started sniffing around the newly minted millionaire's door. Knowing Mandy, she would probably be compelled to give a person money to pay some medical bills or fix a car. Trisha, on the other hand, would not be so inclined. Not that it mattered now.

"A little of both, but mostly congratulations. When I met Commander Atkins at the bank this morning to move the money into my account, that new guy they hired told me he wanted to be my personal financial planner. Can you believe it? I don't even know what a financial planner does."

Trisha didn't know what a financial planner did either, but she said, "That might be a good idea."

"I told him I'd think about it. I've never had a lot of money at one time before." Mandy took a drink of something on her end. "It's a little scary."

"I can think of worse positions to be in." Trisha didn't try very hard to keep the sarcasm at bay. What was Mandy whining about? Granted, she hadn't had an easy life, but now she was a millionaire. Problems would be more palatable when drenched with money. At least that's how it seemed to Trisha.

Mandy, as usual, ignored Trisha's sarcasm. "I'm afraid people are going to start treating me differently now."

"I know people are going to start treating you differently now."

"Does that include you?" Mandy asked pointedly. "I know what's going through your head, Trisha. You're very disappointed that you didn't win, and you've gone to every single drawing. I hadn't been to any, and then I waltz in and win the grand prize. And I only went because of your insistence. You were trying to get my mind off Stephanie's medical bills and the fact that my sixteen-year-old is either very pregnant or about to take over as the Goodyear Blimp."

That pretty much summed it up. "I'm happy for you," Trisha said through clenched teeth. "Or I will be, soon enough."

"If that's all you can give me right now, I'll take it." Then came the sound of a refrigerator opening and closing on Mandy's end. "Anyway, the drawing is not the reason I called you." Then came the unmistakable glug of pouring.

"Are you drinking a glass of wine?" Trisha asked.

"Yep. Would you like to come over and join me?"

Trisha smiled for the first time in days. "It's ten o'clock in the morning, Mandy."

"So what?"

"I guess you do have a right to celebrate."

"I'm not celebrating. It's more like I'm numbing my problems."

Trisha's entire body tensed. They had been so careful for so long now, and Mandy hadn't suspected a thing. It was no different now; everything should be fine. "Oh? Problems?"

"You know how I've suspected for months that Neal was having an affair?"

"And I've repeatedly told you that I know everything that goes on in this town. If Neal was having an affair, I would have heard about it," Trisha said uneasily. "You should be celebrating today, Mandy, not torturing yourself."

Mandy paused to take a drink. "I'm not torturing myself, and in a way, I'm relieved. I'm not crazy, and I'm not making things up like Neal constantly accuses me of doing. I now have definite proof."

Trisha couldn't move from her position on the floor. Every muscle had gone rigid. "What kind of proof?"

"I found a silk scarf in Neal's truck." Mandy paused to take another drink. "It looks like one of yours."

"I'm sure a lot of women in this town wear silk scarves," Trisha said slowly, faintly. How could this be? They had been so careful.

"True, true." It sounded as if Mandy took another deep pull on her wine. "But how many people in this town wear Poison by Christian Dior?" When Trisha failed to respond, Mandy answered her own question. "I can only think of one. You."

Since freshman year in high school, Trisha and Mandy had been there for each other through all the joys and upheavals that thirty years of friendship could bestow, so Trisha found herself at a loss to explain her jealousy of her best friend. But there it was, a pure green dragon of a thing that had festered and grown throughout those years. It didn't make any sense at all. Mandy's life had been as far from a Lifetime movie as a person could get—an abusive childhood, failed marriages, a wayward daughter—while Trisha's life, on the surface, seemed relatively sedate and orderly. Trisha had sometimes wondered if she lived vicariously through Mandy's trials and tribulations to compensate for the lack of excitement in her own life. Trisha also wondered if the crux of the matter was that she often felt bored and unhappy in her quiet life, while Mandy, despite all the turd balls life had thrown at her, more often than not seemed to be content. That, too, didn't make any sense, but there it was. She was insanely jealous of her best friend.

However, Trisha would swear up and down that jealousy was not why she took up with her best friend's husband. It was not. But Trisha didn't want to dwell on that now as she drove over to Mandy's house. She did not want to go. Dear God, Trisha didn't want to go. But she did owe Mandy some kind of explanation. Now that the truth no longer lurked around in the shadows, she should at least try to articulate why she and Neal had been seeing each other for nearly two years. The only problem, though, was that she couldn't come up with a single good reason. Not one. It wasn't like she and Neal had fallen madly in love with one another. Maybe they had been passionate in the first few months, but now their weekly trysts had become as much of a habit as her morning coffee. Yet she continued to betray her best friend for no good reason at all.

A car honked at her as she blew through a red light at the only traffic light in town. Shaken, Trisha pulled over. She was on the town square and had no recollection of driving here. It wasn't even on the way to Mandy's house, yet she was parked in front of Funtown Billiards, one of the businesses that her husband, Bill, owned. He also owned the Tastee Freeze and Mr. Lucky's Tavern, so in the eyes of the citizens of Liberty, she and Bill were well off. Years ago, she worked at the makeup counter at JCPenney in the Carbondale mall, but she quit the moment she found out she was pregnant. Dear Lord, it had been the happiest day of her life when she took the home pregnancy test and finally saw a positive result. She immediately called JCPenney and quit, and then she called her best friend. Not Bill but Mandy, who wept tears of joy. "I'm so happy for you," she'd said.

Married to Bill at the age of twenty, Trisha had tried for ten long years to get pregnant. There was no reason they couldn't get pregnant, they had been told by numerous doctors, even though Bill's sperm count was on the low side, and Trisha had a cyst on her ovary. "You're both young and healthy," another had said. Yet every month brought fresh disappointment. Trisha watched in dismay as her former classmates and friends had baby after baby like it was the easiest thing in the world. One friend, Carol Ehlers, already had eight children, and another, Earlene Pitt, had six. And she couldn't even have one.

"Who wants that many kids anyway?" Mandy said when Trisha pointed out the sheer volume of the Ehlers and Pitt clans. "If you want a kid so bad, I'll give you mine."

She'd laughed, but Trisha knew Mandy didn't think it was very funny. Her daughter Stephanie, twelve years old, was already a handful, running around with a group of boys all destined for Juvie. "I think I better start from scratch. I wouldn't know what to do with a twelve-year-old," she'd added, just to be polite.

"I don't know what to do with a twelve-year-old either." Again, Mandy gave a rueful laugh. "Just keep trying, Trisha. I know it's going to happen for you. And the fun is in the trying, right?" This time, Mandy's laughter sounded genuine.

Trisha cleared her throat. "Mm, sure, I guess." As close as she was to Mandy, she wasn't about to discuss what went on behind her and Bill's bedroom door, how unfulfilling she found her sex life to be. Mandy, on the other hand, hadn't been married to Neal for very long, and they were still clearly in the honeymoon stage of their relationship. And naturally, Trisha was jealous of that, too. She and Bill had never been genuinely passionate about each other but had married more out of convenience than love. They'd known each other since they were kids, and their families had been friends for years, so it was just assumed Trisha and Bill would eventually marry. And so they did, in a lavish ceremony—by Liberty's standards—at St. Joe's, followed by a prime rib dinner and dance at the Legion. They'd even had a seven-piece band come down from St. Louis to play. It had been the social event of the season. It was just too bad it had been all downhill from there.

But when she finally got pregnant, Trisha thought it would change everything. A baby would bring them closer together and solve all their problems. Trisha was sure of that. What's more, once she had a baby, she would no longer be lonely. Sure, she had Mandy, but Mandy didn't have a lot of free time these days, what with her new husband, wild child, and new business. She had recently purchased Zelda's Consignment Shop and had thrown herself full throttle into running it. Trisha was happy, sort of, that Mandy had finally found her calling, but she found herself with a lot of empty time on her hands. Since her parents' boating accident on Lake Kincaid, Trisha felt at a loss. She'd never been close to her older sister, who had moved to California as soon as she graduated. She might as well have fallen off the face of the earth, as far as Trisha was concerned. Patti was the proverbial buxom, ditzy blonde who'd had the good fortune to marry a man who owned half a dozen citrus groves. It always made Trisha mad when she thought of how lucky her undeserving sister had been.

But now she would have her own family, and Trisha felt special for the first time in her life. She was creating a human being in her body, the most miraculous of miracles, but before she even had time to revel in her newfound happiness, Mandy, naturally, had to go and spoil it.

"Guess what?" Mandy said when she burst through Trisha's front door a week later. "I'm pregnant, too! This is going to be so much fun. Our due dates are only four days apart, so we'll be going through everything at the same time! Can you believe it?"

"No," Trisha said sullenly. This was supposed to be her special time. Mandy had already had her turn, and now here she stood, pregnant and glowing. There was no other word for it. While Trisha had spent the better part of the morning crouched over the toilet bowl, her best friend had the nerve to *glow* with good pregnant health.

Mandy hugged her, hard. "Wouldn't it be something if our kids are best friends, too?"

"It sure would." Trisha tried to catch Mandy's contagious happiness, to no avail. She didn't want her child to play second fiddle to Mandy's, as she had to her best friend. She'd never voiced the second-fiddle sentiment to Mandy, although it should have been obvious enough. Mandy had been homecoming queen, while Trisha hadn't even made the court. Mandy had been a cheerleader, while Trisha had only been the mascot, disguised in a hot, itchy falcon costume. Mandy had dated the most popular boy in the senior class, and Trisha had… Bill. And that was just high school. It didn't really matter what Mandy did or did not accomplish. People just automatically liked her. Trisha's reputation was less stellar. She knew people called her *prickly* behind her back. And it stung because it was true.

True to form, Mandy sailed through her pregnancy, while Trisha struggled with morning sickness and lethargy. Mandy only gained twenty-five pounds, while Trisha gained a staggering fifty. Mandy's feet and ankles didn't swell; Trisha's did. Mandy didn't get stuck in the cushions of her couch and embarrassingly ask her husband to hoist her up, which took an incredible amount of grunting on his part. Nor did Mandy split a seam in the crack of her maternity jeans when she knelt to take communion. And Mandy didn't have a twenty-two-hour labor, but rather, plopped out a baby girl in two hours flat.

But oh, it was worth it! After that never-ending labor, when Trisha held her baby boy in her arms for the first time and saw his perfect little face, she knew it had all been worth it. He was beautiful, her little Ryan, just perfect. For the first and only time in her life, Trisha felt utterly content. Finally, she had a purpose, and she vowed to be the best mother she could be.

And she was. Everyone told her so. She dressed Ryan in the cutest coordinating outfits and didn't go out of the house without applying sunscreen on his delicate skin. She read stacks of books on parenting and pureed her own baby food, freezing the sweet potatoes and green beans and butternut squash in ice cube trays. She was punctual with Ryan's immunizations and diligently kept a detailed baby book. She saved a lock of his hair from his first haircut at eighteen months. And she did not compare her son to Mandy's Clara, even when Clara reached all the milestones ahead of Ryan: the first tooth, rolling over, sitting up, and walking. Trisha didn't care about that. All she cared about was her healthy and happy baby.

"Don't you let Ryan get dirty every once in a while?" Mandy had dropped by that June afternoon, Clara in tow, Clara, who now splashed through a mud puddle while Mandy and Trisha sat and watched their children from the back patio, glasses of lemonade in front of them.

"Ryan doesn't like to get dirty." Trisha watched Ryan play quietly with a dump truck on the grass.

"All kids like to get dirty," Mandy said with authority.

"Not Ryan."

Mandy pulled her sunglasses down her nose and looked over the rims. "Oh, come on, Trisha. Hasn't Ryan ever thrown food or played with his own poop?"

"That's disgusting."

"That's called having a kid."

"Speak for yourself." Ryan's blonde curls shone in the sunlight. *He could be a child model,* Trisha thought. *He's that beautiful.* At twenty-two months, he was the prettiest baby she had ever seen. And that definitely included dark-haired Clara, who now had streaks of mud all over her legs. She lifted her pink dress over her head, exposing her soggy, saggy diaper.

Mandy changed the subject. "I'll bring my world-famous potato salad tomorrow. Anything else?"

Trisha and Neal would be hosting their annual June barbecue the next day, and Trisha looked forward to it. It would be the first party she'd thrown since Ryan's birth, and she'd been planning it for weeks. Trisha couldn't wait to show off her perfect little boy. Now that he was walking and beginning to talk, he was a real charmer. She smiled and waved at him before turning back to Mandy. "A bag of ice would be good."

"Will do." Trisha drained her lemonade. "I've got to run now. Neal will be home soon, and I haven't even thought about supper." She walked over to Clara and scooped her out of the puddle. Holding her with one arm like a football tucked to her side, Mandy said, "Come on, kiddo." She patted Ryan on the head on her way to her car. "He is one clean little boy, Trisha. See you tomorrow."

"I am perfectly capable of watching my son for an hour while you get ready for the party," Bill said.

"He's fine right here with me," Trisha said, shifting Ryan from one hip to another. Since before dawn, she'd been up preparing the seven-layer salad, the corn dip, and forming the ground beef into thick patties. When Ryan awoke at six o'clock, Trisha fed him and put him in the Pack 'n Play. He tired quickly of that, so she moved him to the swing. That, too, was not to his liking, so she put him back in the highchair and gave him Cheerios. When he grew tired of that after a whopping three minutes, she resorted to holding him as she chopped vegetables and readied the paper plates and napkins. Even Trisha, who rarely admitted defeat, found it slow going with only one hand to work with.

"I'll give Ryan his bath and dress him for the day while you finish up." When she made no move to hand over the baby, his voice turned to wheedling, pleading. "Come on, Trisha, he's my son, too."

It was an argument they'd had many times before. When he was in a really petulant mood, Bill would accuse Trisha of being overly protective of Ryan. It was a hard argument for Trisha to win—because it was true. She didn't like to let Ryan out of her sight. In the twenty-two months of his life, she had never hired a babysitter and rarely let anyone else hold him. And that included her husband. Trisha did not think Bill gave Ryan one hundred percent of his attention, a point proven one winter Saturday morning when she left the living room for mere seconds to go to the bathroom. When she returned, Bill was engrossed in a golf game on TV, and Ryan had crawled dangerously close to a space heater that Bill wasn't supposed to turn on in the first place.

Boy, she'd let him have it that time. "See?" she'd said. "If you are not completely focused on the baby *all the time*, dangerous things can happen."

"I turned my attention away for one second, Trisha. That's it." Bill was foolishly indignant.

"But you can't do that!"

"Phil Mickelson just made an eagle on that hole!"

"I think our baby is more important than a stupid golf game." She picked up Ryan and held him close to her heart while she glared at her husband.

"Oh, for crying out loud, Trisha, nothing bad happened. The baby's fine."

"But it *could* have, Bill. That's the point."

"What are you going to do when the kid goes to school, Trisha, sit in the back of the room and watch him like a hawk? Or knowing you, you'll probably fold yourself into one of those tiny chairs and sit right next to him. And God forbid the teacher gives the kid a pair of safety scissors to cut his ABCs out of construction paper or a pencil with a pointed end. What will you do? Have her fired?" Bill was on a roll now. "You'll probably open his carton of milk for him, too," Bill added and then had the nerve to chuckle.

Trisha couldn't bear the thought of Ryan going to school. In the back of her mind, she'd stored the idea of homeschooling him, but she wasn't going to bring it up now. "We'll cross that bridge when we come to it," she snapped. Bill could make fun of her all he liked, but Trisha was convinced that Ryan would only be safe if he was under her supervision.

"You're running out of time," Bill reminded her now, his arms outstretched toward Ryan.

Trisha glanced at the sunflower clock on the kitchen wall. That was true, unfortunately. She still had to finish the salsa and somehow get herself ready for the party. Where had all the time gone? She'd planned and planned, yet she still ran short on time. For once, she needed help. Reluctantly, she handed the baby to him. "Be sure the bathwater isn't too hot. His outfit is on the layette, the blue t-shirt with the sailboat, and the matching shorts with the anchor."

"Aye, aye, sir!" Bill gave her a mocking salute. To the baby, he said, "Come on, buddy, we're going to have some male bonding time. Maybe we'll have time to turn on the Cardinals game."

"That's not funny!" she called to his retreating back.

"Or maybe we can find some porn on one of those pay-per-view channels," Bill shouted.

"Still not funny," she muttered as she picked up a knife and went to work on the poblano chiles for the salsa. She worked quickly and efficiently, but without the baby nearby, she felt lost, untethered. She worked faster still. However, when she went upstairs to change into her blue sundress for the party (the one that matched Ryan's outfit), she peeked into the bathroom. Ryan gleefully splashed water, and Bill was right there with a hand on his back. So Trisha let herself relax for just a moment. Maybe she should let Bill start caring for Ryan for an hour here and there, as long as she stayed within listening distance. It was something to think about.

The guests started to arrive shortly after noon. They'd sent invitations to forty people this year, and everyone had accepted. Trisha took that as a good sign. She hadn't been out and about much since the baby's birth, and she'd heard (from Mandy, mainly) that some people were ticked off at her. She'd given up her seat on the Beautification Committee and hadn't overseen the Christmas tree lighting ceremony in the town square for two years now. She'd also stopped going to town meetings where she had once been a vocal participant. She was the one who got the town to hire a dog catcher, and she was the one responsible for installing the one traffic light at the busiest intersection in town. But all that fell by the wayside once Ryan was born. He had been worth the wait, and he was everything to her.

"What a great turnout." As usual, Mandy arrived at the party last with her new husband Neal and baby Clara, who she again carried like a football. Mandy swore up and down that she didn't arrive late to events on purpose, that she didn't consciously try to make a late, grand entrance. Trisha didn't believe her. She was dressed to the nines in a hot pink dress with straps that crisscrossed in the back, exposing her slender, tanned shoulders and back. She still wore her blonde hair long, as she had in high school, and all eyes turned to look at her when she walked in the door. Especially the men's eyes, and Trisha didn't miss seeing her husband's face when he got a load of Mandy. Trisha would let him have it for that later. ("Your tongue practically hung out of your mouth, Bill," she would say to him. "You looked like a dog in heat.")

"Even the weather is cooperating today. It's not too hot or humid. Here." Mandy held out a bag from Dave's Market. "I didn't have time to make my world-famous potato salad, which is not all that great to begin with." Mandy laughed, her bright cornflower blue eyes crinkling with good humor. "Dave's is better anyway."

"Mandy," Trisha said evenly, "you know I always like to serve my guests homemade dishes at my parties." Trisha abided by that strict rule. It just figured Mandy would go and mess it up.

"Just put it in a pretty bowl, Trisha, and no one will know the difference."

"And here's a bag of ice." Neal carried the twenty-pound bag over his shoulder. He was a tall, big-boned man with a body that would probably turn to fat in a few years. Trisha had invited the new couple over for dinner a couple of times in the last year. Neal was on the quiet side but seemed nice enough. He even let Mandy win at Pictionary, which wasn't easy to do. Mandy was terrible at the game.

Trisha directed Neal to the cooler of beer and soft drinks outside and then said to Mandy, "Help yourself to a glass of wine." She nodded toward the steel bucket filled with ice and bottles of chardonnay and sauvignon blanc.

"You don't have to twist my arm." She put down Clara and poured a hefty amount of chardonnay into a red Solo cup. "And before you ask, Stephanie's not coming. She's grounded again. Mrs. Schneider's watching her. It sure is handy having her next door."

Trisha decided not to announce how happy she felt about the unpredictable Stephanie not coming to the party. She was sneaky, and someone would have to keep an eye on her all the time, or she'd be sneaking beers out of the cooler.

"Something's missing in this picture," Mandy said, staring at Trisha. "Oh, yes, the baby. Where's Ryan? I don't think I've seen you without him since he's been born."

"He's with Bill." Trisha glanced out the window above the kitchen sink. Yes, they were still there. Bill held the baby, who smiled and waved at everybody.

Trisha would get him soon and take over, introducing him and showing off their matching outfits. It had been an hour and a half since she'd allowed Bill to take Ryan, and it was too long. But guests started arriving as soon as she finished her makeup, and she'd been busy greeting people, pouring drinks, and passing around the chips and salsa. However, her radar still focused on her baby. It was almost as if she could *feel* where he was at all times.

Mandy joined her at the window. "It looks like they're having a good time. It's nice to see a father with his kid, you know?"

Coming from anyone else, Trisha would have thought that remark carried a hint of reproach, but not with Mandy. It was a genuine observation. "I guess I should let Bill spend more time with Ryan."

Mandy patted her arm. "Whatever you feel comfortable with, honey. You waited a long time for this baby."

Trisha covered Mandy's hand with her own. Mandy really was a dear friend, a good person. "Yes. Shall we go outside and join the party?"

It was, without a doubt, the most successful party she had ever hosted. The temperature stayed put at a reasonable 79 degrees, and people had dressed for the occasion, as they always did for her parties. The ladies wore colorful dresses, and even the men had ditched their usual slogan t-shirts for collared shirts tucked neatly into their pants. Trisha had rented a big tent and two long tables where the food would be served, and a bouncing house for the ten or so kids in attendance. Trisha could already see that little Clara had made it into the bouncing house and seemed unperturbed as the other jumping, older kids jostled her around.

But Trisha wasn't about to let Ryan into that filthy rubber nest of germs. She couldn't risk him catching anything from the other kids, and he wasn't used to so much noise and mayhem. Not her son. Her son liked to play quietly with his trucks and stuffed animals. Lately, she had let him pound on the bottoms of her pots with a wooden spoon when she prepared dinner. He didn't bang willy-nilly, though. Not her son. Trisha was convinced he tapped out a definite rhythm, slowly and deliberately. She had pointed out her son's musical acumen to Bill. "Look at how talented Ryan is. I think he's going to be a musician." Bill had not been as impressed. "The kid sometimes misses the pot altogether, Trisha. He looks a little uncoordinated to me." Bill just didn't get how extraordinary their son was. It was beyond annoying.

Trisha walked over to Bill and held out her hands. "My turn," and as soon as he was safe in the cocoon of her arms, Ryan nestled his sweet blond head into her neck. It was her idea of heaven, and she could relax now. It was her turn to show off as she went around to the ladies, most of whom she'd known all her life, and introduced her son. Of course, most of them had seen him before when he was first born, and some of them had dropped by gifts, but now Ryan was a little person. He had a personality—albeit a quiet one; he didn't talk much—and a full head of hair and dimples. However, her little jaunt around the yard wasn't as satisfying as she would have hoped. She heard the usual "cute kid" and "my, he's grown," but being in the presence of her son didn't seem to excite the women as much as Trisha would have liked. Earlene Pitt actually said to her, "You and your son are wearing matching outfits. Cute. Haha." But then again, Earlene had six kids and was jaded. What did she know? And Trisha had never cared much for her anyway.

Trisha realized she had to give Ryan back to Bill when she served the food. Mandy offered to take him, but she let her own kid run wild and would probably put Ryan down somewhere and lose him. So Trisha was forced to hand him to Bill, who had somehow gotten involved in an animated conversation about the merits of various lawn fertilizers. Neal manned the grill, and Neal placed the burgers and the hot dogs neatly on her best platter and handed it to her. "Is there anything else I can do to help?" he asked.

"You're a guest here, Neal. You've already done more than enough to help me." Trisha looked pointedly at Bill, who didn't bother to glance her way. He had a beer in his hand, and his face was already flushed. Bill, unlike many other men in this town, wasn't a big drinker. He didn't even go and drink at his own bar, Mr. Lucky's, but judging from the two rosy splotches of color on his cheek, Trisha would guess that he was on his second or third beer.

Still, she had no other choice but to give him their son. "Go easy on the beer, okay, Bill?" she said as she handed over the baby.

"This is my second beer, Trisha."

Trisha could tell she'd embarrassed him in front of his friends, but she didn't care. Ryan's welfare should be their top priority, and Bill should take a lesson from her. She'd been nursing one glass of wine since the guests arrived. "Just go easy, okay?"

"I guess we know who calls the shots in this house." Ray Pitt's laughter was too loud. He'd probably had a six-pack before he even arrived at the party. Everyone in town knew Ray liked his Budweiser.

Bill's face turned a deeper shade of red, and she knew she'd bear some consequences for upstaging her husband in front of his friends. It wasn't the first time. Bill, being Bill, would probably give her the silent treatment for a couple of days. Trisha didn't know why Bill thought the silent bit made a big impression on her, but it didn't phase her at all. She rather liked it when he didn't talk about his damn sports teams and how business was going. But Trisha had to admit she did feel a little bad now. And more than anything, she didn't want to spoil the upbeat mood of the party. "I only meant that it's time to eat. We can't have people drinking too many beers on an empty stomach, can we? This party is just getting started, and both Bill and I want everyone to have a good time."

Ray Pitt raised his beer can. "Here, here. You and Bill always know how to throw a great party."

"Thank you." Trisha smiled sweetly to show there were no hard feelings. Minor crisis averted, Trisha went back into the house to bring out all the food, noticing as she passed all her guests that everyone seemed to be enjoying themselves. She really did know how to throw a fabulous party.

"Someone should tell these people they eat too much." Mandy, helping Trisha in the kitchen, threw away a handful of paper plates. Then she started to hand her the empty serving bowls. "Seriously, what is it about people and free food?"

"If you put food in front of people at a party, they will eat it." Trisha finally felt like she could relax some. Everyone had been fed, and as always, she'd had plenty of food. She'd also had a second glass of wine, which had definitely helped in the relaxation department.

Mandy laughed. "I guess I have to include myself in that group. I had seconds on everything. My compliments to the chef."

"Thanks, Mandy, but why are we wasting our time in here? I can take care of all of this later. Let's go join the party."

"You've never let a dirty dish sit longer than five minutes, Trisha. I know the real reason you want to join the party, but I'm in perfect agreement. Let's go."

"Is it that obvious?"

"If you crane your neck any farther looking out that window, you're going to need to go to a chiropractor. Come on, girlfriend." Mandy threw her dishtowel on the counter.

Trisha laughed as she followed her friend out the back door. It was true. She had left Ryan in the care of Earlene Pitt, at Earlene's insistence, when she brought in the serving bowls. She couldn't flat-out tell Earlene, "No, I don't trust you," in the presence of the other women, all of whom were experienced mothers. Besides, Ryan was behaving beautifully. It was way past his nap time, but he bravely bobbed around like a drunken little soldier, allowing people to pick him up from time to time. She should really take him up for a nap, but she knew she would worry about him more out of her sight. Even if she had the baby monitor at her side, she was afraid she wouldn't be able to hear him above all the laughter.

And there was a lot of laughter. The fourteen women in the backyard played a rousing round of The Dollar Game. Trisha loved that game. Every woman started with three one-dollar bills, then rolled the dice to determine if the bills went to the person on her left, right, or into the communal pot. It was a game that could go on forever without too much at stake. She took a chair at the table and pulled Ryan into her lap, relieved that he was safe in her arms once again. The women started a new round when she and Mandy arrived, and Trisha got immediately immersed in the game. When Ryan squirmed in her lap, she put him down, but she kept an eye on him. He didn't roam far, and he didn't follow Clara and the other kids back into the bouncing nest of germs. Her son was such a good boy, such an angel.

The men had moved to the front yard where Bill had set up the wickets that morning for croquet games. From the sound of it, Trisha could tell they had decided to play for money, too. She could hear the thwack of the balls, the occasional cheer, the occasional curse. From time to time, one of the men would return to the cooler in the backyard and fish out beers to take back to the front.

Trisha wondered why one of the dimwits didn't have the good sense to pick up the cooler and move it to the front lawn. But no. She could hear them arguing about whose turn it was to make the next beer run. It seemed to have become a part of the game, so Trisha kept her mouth shut and let them make the whole drink retrieval process harder than it needed to be.

The women, too, drank wine as they nibbled on peach cobbler and fudge brownies. Trisha didn't know who had brought the steel bucket with the wine bottles outside, but she wouldn't mention it. Likewise, when a woman went into her kitchen to get another bottle of wine out of the refrigerator, she didn't give a second thought about them nosing around in her house. She hadn't thought she'd missed being in the company of other women after Ryan was born. But now, sitting in her large, comfortable backyard, drinking wine and talking about everything and nothing, she felt happier than she had in a long time. Every time Mandy caught her eye, Trisha smiled, and Mandy nodded approvingly. She'd been telling Trisha for months that she needed to get out of the house more often.

They all heard the deep, resonant *thwack* of the croquet ball hitting metal followed by the anguished, "Shit!"

"What was that?" Mandy asked, her eyes wide.

"I don't know what it was, but I know that voice. It's Bill." Ryan, startled by the unexpected noise, or finally exhausted, began to cry. Trisha immediately went to him and picked him up. "Shh, Ryan. It's okay, baby. Nothing's going to hurt you."

Bill came tearing around the corner of the house. "Where are my car keys, Trisha?" Sweat coursed down the sides of his face. "I've got to move the car because that damn Ray Pitt thinks he's swinging a golf club. He just put a big dent in the driver's side door, and if I don't move my Caddy, he's probably going to bust out a window next."

"Oh, no." However, Trisha didn't feel especially bad about the damage done to Bill's beloved white Cadillac. She'd joked more than once that he loved that car more than he did her. Unfortunately, it probably wasn't a joke.

"Where are my keys? You drove the Caddy last, Trisha!" Bill shouted to be heard over Ryan, who had started to howl as if he were in pain.

"I only drove your precious car because mine was in the shop. Otherwise, I wouldn't dream—"

Bill grabbed her by the shoulders. "Where are my damn keys?"

He didn't shake her, but Trisha felt the accusation from the heat of his hands. And she could feel the open stares of the women upon them. With her irate husband and squalling child, they didn't make the perfect tableau Trisha had tried so hard to create. "They're in my damn purse," she hissed. She'd meant to put them in the bowl on the table by the front door like she always did, but she hadn't for some reason.

He let go of her shoulders with an unmistakable thrust. "You should have put the keys back where they belonged," he said, just as everyone in the backyard heard another dull *thwack!* "Goddammit!"

Bill was ruining their perfect party, their idyllic afternoon, and now he was making the baby claw at her face and neck. "Here! Take Ryan inside for his nap while you get the keys."

"I don't have time."

"It's only a stupid car, Bill. You have insurance, and now, after the way you've behaved in front of my friends, you owe me." She wished her words were daggers as she whispered them into his ear. She would never forgive him for this. Never.

She had never seen him so angry as he took Ryan roughly from her arms, and she automatically recoiled. He looked as if he hated her at that instant, and she hadn't really done anything wrong. Ryan continued to wail as Bill stomped into the house, but seconds later, all was quiet.

Her legs shook as she made her way back to the table and took her seat. She took a sip from her wine glass. Her hand, too, looked palsied. "Let's get back to the game, ladies. Whose turn is it?"

"Mine." Mandy scooped up the dice. "Men and their cars." She shook her head. "I've never understood it. Do you remember my no-good second husband? He had that souped-up Camaro with the fart can on it that you could hear all over town. When that car got stolen, he cried like a baby. I, on the other hand, jumped for joy. When the insurance money came in—and that car was the only thing the louse ever insured—I deposited it in my account and left him. So, on second thought, I guess the souped-up Camaro was good for something." When some of the other ladies laughed nervously, Mandy looked at Trisha and winked.

God bless her, Trisha thought. She was trying to break the tension. That's what good friends did. "It's only a car. Bill will get over this."

A few minutes later, the women sitting in the backyard listened to the Cadillac roar angrily to life and the screech of tires before they heard another sickening thudding sound, before they heard the screech of brakes, before they heard another scream.

The scream, again, came from Bill.

Trisha would never have made it through the next hours, days, weeks, months, and years if it hadn't been for Mandy. She was right by Trisha's side as the condolences flooded in, then dribbled away, then stopped altogether. It was a tragedy that people didn't like to talk about, suffering too awful to contemplate. Losing a child was unthinkable, heartbreaking, horrific, but when that child was lost needlessly, through an accidental chain of events, well… People thought it was best to put it all behind them and get on with their lives.

But Trisha and Bill would never put the death of their twenty-two-month son behind them. All they could do was limp along after the initial shock numbed to a dull ache, after all the painful accusations had been hurled so many times that they became meaningless, after the awful fact of events.

"You should have put the baby in his crib!" Trisha would scream tearfully.

"You should have put the baby down for a nap an hour before!" Bill would return.

"Why didn't you make sure the door closed when you went back outside to move your damn car?" Trisha, by that point, would be beating Bill's chest with her fists.

"Why didn't you put the keys in the bowl by the front door? I wouldn't have had to go into the backyard, and you would not have given me the baby!" Bill would cover his face with his hands and sink to the floor, not to escape her futile blows but by the enormity of his grief. He had backed over their baby in his own driveway. He had killed their son.

The details would never be quite clear to Trisha. Bill claimed he had put Ryan in the Pack 'n Play in the kitchen while he ran outside to move the Cadillac. Trisha suspected this was not so. Ryan hadn't yet mastered the art of climbing out of it, so Trisha thought it was more likely that Bill had set the baby down and dashed out the front door, not taking the care to latch it properly behind him. When Bill returned outside, an argument erupted over something that no one at the party could now remember, and no one noticed the baby boy who had toddled out of the house and made his way to the end of the driveway. Bill, furious over his car, had jumped in and started it, not bothering to check behind him, rammed it into reverse, and stomped on the accelerator. And then it was too late.

How did people ever recover from such a disaster? They didn't. They went back, eventually, to their everyday lives, with gaping holes in their hearts and precious memories locked into vaults in their souls. They took pills to sleep at night and anti-anxiety meds to stumble through each day. Over time, they stopped ranting about all the things that could have been and cohabited rotely and dully within the confines of their now empty house. Trisha and Bill never contemplated divorce; it wasn't an option. Like it or not, they were now bound together by the worst tragedy of all, and there was nothing they could do about it.

But through it all, Trisha had Mandy, who brought over food and movies and books, who sometimes did nothing more than hold Trisha's hand as she cried out a lifetime's supply of tears. But one day, Trisha woke up and found she had no more tears left to cry. At Mandy's gentle urging, she rejoined Liberty's Beautification Committee and threw herself into all the other civic duties she had performed before Ryan. Trisha rejoined with an almost frantic gusto, and with this renewed social interaction, Trisha became obsessively interested in the affairs of the people in Liberty. She collected and dispensed the town gossip, thriving on the misfortunes of others. If she ever stopped to analyze this obsessive need of hers, Trisha would have concluded that she did so because she wanted to know she was not the only person who had suffered grave loss and disappointment. She was not the only person who bore her sorrow like a crown of thorns. But Trisha kept herself too desperately busy to consider such a thing.

After driving around town for more than an hour, retracing the streets that were as familiar to her as her own reflection, Trisha had still not come up with a line of defense. Mandy expected her, Trisha knew that, and she probably wanted some explanation. But Trisha didn't have one. She could tell Mandy that she and Neal had come together out of mutual loneliness, which was partly true, at least on her part. She could tell Mandy that the whole thing had happened by accident. About two years ago, Trisha had run into Neal at Partytime Liquors, where they were both buying lottery tickets.

Surprised, she had asked, "Does Mandy know you buy lottery tickets?" Trisha knew that money was tight in the Tanner household because Mandy told her often enough. She also knew Mandy would think Neal was throwing away good money on such an extravagant impossibility.

Neal had looked sheepish. "I can't say that she does. Does Bill know you play the lottery?"

"Of course not. But I figure it's not really any of his business." The truth of the matter was that Bill probably wouldn't give a damn one way or the other. Other than their big house, about the only thing they still shared was a joint checking account. Yet Bill never mentioned the withdrawals she took out at the off-track betting bar she frequented in Carbondale, nor did she mention his checks made out to a massage parlor in Marion. If Bill still cared a shred about her, it seemed to Trisha that he would have the courtesy to use a credit card. But he didn't.

"You're not going to tell Mandy, are you?"

"Absolutely not. We all have our little secrets, don't we?" She realized her laugh sounded flirtatious only after the fact.

"Then, we'll call this *our* little secret, okay?"

Trisha remembered the Lotto jackpot was 38 million dollars for that week, but she didn't remember who actually asked the other to go to the Hideaway for a drink. They were very chaste that first time, sitting as they were at a local bar. It wasn't until the next week that they started to cross the bridge over into Missouri and get a motel room in Perryville.

After another twenty minutes, Trisha could not prolong the inevitable any longer. She pulled into Mandy's driveway, relieved to see that Neal's truck wasn't there. For a fleeting moment, she thought she should call Neal and get their story straight. Maybe they could still come up with a credible excuse for her scarf being in his truck. She'd had car trouble, and he'd given her a lift, or she'd left the scarf at Mandy's, and Neal had hoped to return it. But then Trisha looked up and saw Mandy's heart-shaped face peering out the front window, staring directly at her.

And for the first time, at the sight of that dear, trusting face, Trisha felt what she should have felt all along: fear, remorse, shame. She'd had an ulterior motive for sleeping with her best friend's husband all along. It was jealousy, pure and simple. She'd always been jealous of Mandy's imperfect, sloppy life, but it was more than that. Her jealousy sprouted from Mandy's ability to bounce back from all the disappointment and heartbreak and still remain a good, kind person. Mandy didn't have it in her to be cruel or vindictive.

But then again, Mandy had never been betrayed by her oldest, dearest friend. What if Mandy had decided to cut Trisha completely out of her life? Trisha couldn't bear the thought. All along, she'd thought Mandy had more to lose than she did in this scenario. She would lose her husband and maybe some self-respect. Everyone in town would talk about "poor Mandy," who had been blind to her husband's affair with her best friend.

But Trisha had been wrong. She was the one who would lose the most. She would lose the most important person in her life, the person she had most depended upon, the person whose good cheer and kindness she had most certainly taken advantage of. She would lose the only person who had brought her back to life after her son's tragic death. During the history of their friendship, they had been through so much together, and she was the one who had ruined it, possibly beyond repair.

Trisha wanted to cover her face with her hands to block the look in Mandy's eyes. She wanted to drive away like the coward that she was, but then Mandy was on the front porch, beckoning. "Are you going to sit in your car all day, Trisha? Come on in."

It seemed to take Trisha forever to move her heavy legs, get out of the car, and up the front steps. She followed Mandy inside to the kitchen where they had spent so many hours talking over coffee or wine, over salad lunches, and at times, chocolate cake from Dave's Market when they celebrated something. Trisha had always refused the cake. She wished she hadn't now. She wished she'd let herself enjoy a slice of that rich, moist cake as much as Mandy had.

She sat down at her usual place and watched as Mandy got a bottle of wine from the refrigerator, another glass from the cabinet, filled the new glass and her own, and brought them to the table. Mandy sat in her usual spot. She didn't look as if she had been crying, nor did she look especially angry. She took a sip of her wine, twirled her glass by the stem, took another sip.

"Please say something," Trisha begged when long minutes had ticked by.

Mandy reached for something on the seat of the chair next to her and pulled up Trisha's Hermès silk scarf. "I believe this is yours." She pushed it across the table to Trisha.

Trisha couldn't move as the scarf laid there like the accusation it was. "Please say something. Yell at me. Throw something. Call me a bitch. *Something.* I deserve it."

Mandy looked at her now, her fading blue eyes focused and alert. "Would that make you feel better, Trisha? If I call you a bitch?"

"Yes." Trisha wanted Mandy to rake her over the coals, to scream and yell. This calm, controlled Mandy was not normal. It wasn't the lively, animated Mandy that she knew and loved. Trisha wondered how many glasses of wine Mandy had drunk.

"It's always about you, isn't it?"

Trisha could not respond to the stinging truth of that.

Mandy took another sip of wine. Her newly refilled glass was almost empty. "Okay, I have a question for you: *Why?* Why did you have an affair with my husband?"

It was the question that Trisha knew would come. It was a logical question. It was also the one question she didn't want to answer, but she knew that their friendship, the most important thing in her life, was at stake. "I was jealous of you. I've always been jealous of you, Mandy."

Mandy started to laugh. "That's the most ridiculous thing I've ever heard!" She laughed harder, grabbing at her midriff, gasping. Then she started to choke and sputter, a flush spreading across her face.

Trisha immediately sprang from her chair and filled a glass with water. Pounding on Mandy's back, she said, "Drink this." She stood there until Mandy got her breathing under control, then pushed her chair next to Mandy and took her hands. "I'm so sorry. Please forgive me, Mandy. Please. I don't know what I'd do without you. *Please.*"

"You're crying. You're the woman who never cries, Trisha, but you're crying now."

Surprised, Trisha reached up and felt her wet cheeks. She didn't try to blink back the tears that still streamed from her eyes. "Will you ever forgive me?"

Mandy reached again for her wine glass. "Do you love him?"

Trisha shook her head miserably.

"Me neither." Mandy raised her glass.

"Will you ever forgive me?" Trisha asked again, desperate for an answer. She moved her chair an inch or two closer to Mandy's and felt relieved when Mandy didn't pull away.

Just then, Trisha heard the front door open and slam shut, and girlish voices filled the house, moving closer. Stephanie, her face still bandaged, the skin around her eyes a bluish-yellow, walked in. Her former boyfriend had beat her up two weeks earlier, and after leaving town years before, she'd moved home indefinitely to recover. Mandy would probably have to pay for her plastic surgery. Too late, Trisha realized she should have brought over a casserole or ham. She should have taken Mandy out to lunch to offer her condolences, but she hadn't. Trisha hadn't even stopped by the consignment shop to see how Mandy was doing. She had not been a good friend in that regard either.

Clara followed, and Trisha had to trap the gasp in her throat when she saw how bloated and enormous the girl looked. It was hard to believe this was the same little girl who had bravely wandered into the bouncing house at that fateful June barbecue. Clara denied that she was pregnant, but she must be, Trisha thought, as she saw Clara's swollen feet leaking out of the loose slippers she wore, the lumbering way she walked. Ryan would have been her age now, Trisha thought. *What would her blonde angel have looked like now?* She stifled a sob, but no one seemed to notice.

"You're the talk of the town, Mom." It was hard to decipher the words coming from

Stephanie's mouth. Her lip had been split during the beating, her teeth knocked out.

"Yeah, we're the daughters of a millionaire," Clara huffed, eyeing Trisha suspiciously as she drank directly out of a carton of milk.

Mandy turned her gaze away from her daughters and back to Trisha, looking straight into her eyes.

Will you please forgive me? Trisha silently begged.

Without unlocking her gaze from Trisha, Mandy drained the last bead of wine from her glass. "It's hard to believe, isn't it, girls? But I guess it's true. I picked the queen of hearts. I hit the jackpot this time."

THE TROLL PARADE

Neal Tanner knew the parade was a bad idea from the start. When his wife, Mandy, won the Queen of Hearts jackpot at the American Legion the week before and became an instant millionaire, everyone in the small town of Liberty seemed to be very happy for her. She was a local gal, born and bred in this town—as was he—and everyone said it couldn't have happened to a nicer person.

"That woman has worked hard her entire life," Daisy, who worked behind the counter at Dave's Market, said to him two days after his wife became a millionaire. "She deserves to be on Easy Street."

"If I couldn't win, I'm glad it was her," said Ray Pitt when Neal ran into him at the Circle K that same day. It was saying a lot for Ray, who had attended every single Queen of Hearts drawing for nearly a year before Mandy—who had never attended a single drawing—walked in and had her ticket drawn from the big drum. And then picked the sealed envelope with the queen of hearts and won the 1.5 million dollar jackpot. It was saying a lot for Ray because everyone knew he was a sore loser and a bad sport.

"Mandy's always been nice to me." Darlene Sutton had stopped Neal on the street outside of the post office. "Once when I was flat broke, she advanced me some money on my kids' outgrown jeans and t-shirts before she even sold them. Say, do you think she's going to keep that consignment shop of hers now that she's a millionaire? I sure hope she does. She's sold a lot of stuff for me."

"I don't know," Neal said. Zelda's Consignment Shop, his wife's business on Main Street, had always run on fumes. Mandy worked there before she bought it from the original owner, Zelda, fifteen years ago. Neal knew Mandy loved that business because it was hers and hers alone.

"Well, anyway, tell her I said congratulations. It couldn't have happened to a nicer person." Darlene, her mail in hand, looked like she was ready to chat a while about his wife's good fortune. "Say, do you think—"

"Sure thing, Darlene," he said quickly, getting into his truck. "Take care."

Neal didn't know if his wife planned on keeping her consignment shop or not; they weren't exactly on speaking terms. The day before, she had found his lover's scarf in his truck. His lover of two years, Trisha, happened to be Mandy's best friend, and now he was up shit's creek without a paddle. The affair had been a mistake from the start. Both he and Trisha knew that, yet they had dragged out the damn thing as if it had been an unwanted obligation rather than a pleasure.

"I know," Mandy said when he got home from his job at Damon's RV World late yesterday afternoon. When she saw Neal's eyes dart to the two wine glasses on the table, she added, "Trisha was here."

Neal knew he had no defense, and he didn't deserve one. He'd cheated on his wife with her best friend, which was a major *faux pas* in anyone's book. He still loved Mandy, of that he was sure, but he hadn't slept with her in quite a while. When he started up with Trisha, he'd become confused about the whole thing. He was already cheating on Mandy with her best friend, but if he slept with Mandy while he was sleeping with Trisha, would he be cheating on Trisha as well? He couldn't figure it out.

He still stood in the center of the kitchen. "Now what?"

"I don't know." Mandy had a cup of coffee in front of her, along with a half-eaten chocolate cake, a sure sign that she was upset.

"Do you want me to move out?"

"Where would you go?" Mandy took a large bite of cake, then pushed the plate away.

"I could go to Max's Motel." The old motel on the south end of town, next to the Walmart, was as dilapidated as a barely-functioning business could get. But if he was going to be in the doghouse, he might as well be in one that punished him properly.

"Don't be silly," Mandy said. "You already sleep in the den. Besides, do you know how much it would cost to spend weeks in a motel, even one that crappy?"

He hadn't had time to think of that yet, but then things were different now. The reality of Mandy's newfound wealth hadn't had a chance to settle in his brain. That staggering amount of money seemed unreal to him. "Well," he said hesitantly. "You did just win the big jackpot at the American Legion."

"Oh, right." Mandy nodded. "There is *that*." She picked up the half-eaten cake, walked past him, and dumped it in the garbage can. "I would say your sense of timing is very unfortunate, Neal."

He deserved that too, rightfully so. He'd been drinking a beer at the Hideaway Tavern when he heard the news that someone had finally won the

Queen of Hearts drawing. The bar had become more and more deserted on Thursday nights as the jackpot grew, which was why Neal liked it there. He enjoyed the peace and quiet of the place. He lived in a house dominated by women. Even before Stephanie, Mandy's daughter from a previous marriage, returned home, wreaking more havoc, Mandy and his own daughter Clara had incessantly bickered. So Neal especially liked to escape to the Hideaway on Thursday nights.

But at nine o'clock, the door to the Hideaway banged open and clamoring, shouting people rushed in, jostling him at his seat at the bar. "There's finally been a winner!" a guy Neal didn't know yelled. Many people from neighboring towns had started to come to the drawing as it grew outlandishly large.

"Yeah? Who?" Maya, the buxom bartender, expertly uncapped a row of beer bottles.

"What was her name?" The guy turned to his friend.

"Mandy something," he said. "Who cares? It wasn't us."

"Isn't that your wife's name?" Maya asked Neal.

"Yes, but she doesn't go to those drawings."

But a few seconds later, Tucker Aldean, Liberty's mayor, entered the Hideaway. He rushed over when he spied Neal. "Congratulations, buddy!" He clapped Neal on the back. "It looks like you've just come into some money."

"What are you talking about?" Neal reached into his pocket for stray dollar bills to pay his tab. The noise was too much for him. Most of these people were dead-drunk already and had no business drinking anymore. Maya shouldn't be serving them, but there she stood, handing out bottle after bottle. Too many accidents were waiting to happen in this place.

"Mandy won the jackpot." Tucker drank thirstily from the bottle.

"Mandy doesn't go to the drawings." Neal signaled for Maya.

"She went to this one, and she won, buddy. You guys have it made now. Do you think you'll quit your job?"

"Of course not." Neal could barely hear Tucker over the escalating noise. None of it made any sense. "Besides, if Mandy won, it would be her money."

"You're married, buddy. What's hers is yours, what's yours is hers—at least that's what my wife tells me. Haha." He clapped Neal on the back again. "Let me buy you a beer."

"No, I've got to get going." Neal knew Illinois wasn't a community property state. He didn't know why he had that piece of information stored in his brain, but it reared its head now. It didn't matter, though, because Mandy couldn't have possibly won, no matter what Tucker Aldean said. Everyone knew he exaggerated when he drank.

But it was true. Mandy, who had always claimed that she was the unluckiest person on earth, had won. Mandy, who had never bought a raffle ticket or scratch-off lottery ticket in her life, was now a millionaire. It was all that the people of Liberty could talk about. Before, it had been the frenzy of the escalating pot and the chance of winning. Now, all that attention focused on his wife. Neal knew this because he didn't move out. He and Mandy only spoke when necessary, but it seemed as if they had formed some kind of truce, at least for the time being.

It was heady stuff in the first few days. Mandy's phone didn't stop ringing with people offering congratulations and tentatively asking if she might spare a hundred or two. Mandy, as always, remained cordial and nice to these requests. "I'll have to talk to my accountant first," she told caller after caller. "And then I'll see what I can do." Then a steady line of people began knocking on their front door. Some brought gifts: a basket of tomatoes or corn from their gardens, bouquets of wildflowers, mason jars of homemade peaches and preserves. Many wanted to tell her their stories of woe or hardship; a few requested donations to so-called charitable causes that Neal had never heard of and suspected didn't exist. But Mandy, to her credit, gave the same response to that parade of people, "I'll have to talk to my accountant first. And then I'll see what I can do."

"I don't like all this attention," Mandy said on Tuesday, the fifth day after the drawing. "And these people are making me too sad."

"We're going to have to move." Neal, gratified that Mandy shared this with him, was only half-joking.

"Don't be silly, Neal. I'm not going anywhere. This is my home."

Neal noticed she said *my* home, not *our* home, but he had not yet earned the right to mention such a thing. "Some of these people are getting really pushy, honey."

"Don't call me *honey*," Mandy said absently. She wandered back to the kitchen, her place of refuge. "Were you there when the man told me about his son with leukemia or the woman who told me that she would die if she didn't get a kidney transplant? Or what about the woman who brought her tiny little boy who has that elephant man disease? I don't remember what it's called."

"Proteus syndrome. Yes, I was there, Mandy." Perhaps she was too distracted to notice he hadn't left her side and not gone to work since the stream of moochers, as he had begun to call them, started arriving in droves. Stephanie called them the parasites, and Clara, also unkindly, called them the spongers. Mandy didn't call them anything at all but listened to each and every sob story. Sometimes she was too kind for her own good, and Neal knew he would have to protect her, whether she liked it or not.

On Wednesday, day six after the drawing, the first of the nasty letters arrived. Neal had walked to the end of the driveway and retrieved the mail that day. He was starting to feel that it wasn't safe for Mandy or the girls to go out. People had begun to camp out on their lawn, and he would give it one more day, hoping the novelty would wear off before he called Officer Alan Morrison, the man Stephanie happened to be dating now. It was getting ridiculous. He hurried back inside, walking around the side of the house and in the back door before he opened the letter with Mandy's name scrawled in black on the front of the envelope. There was no return address, and the letter hadn't been posted. Mandy wasn't around, so he opened it quickly, knowing it would be bad news.

It was. "Dear bitch," the note began. It looked as if it had been written in crayon, waxy and smudgy and childish. "I know what you did all those years ago. If you don't put $100,000 cash in a black garbage bag and put it under the north bleachers of the softball field in 48 hours, I will tell them EVERYTHING."

The note was preposterous, yet sinister at the same time. Neal knew Mandy had never so much as stolen a pack of gum or picked up a stray quarter that did not belong to her, so the person who sent this note must be off his rocker. But Neal had a sick, unsettling feeling deep in his gut. He knew this would only be the first of many disagreeable notes. This person, in his fiendishly clever imagination, had chosen to try to blackmail Mandy. Neal heard Mandy coming and quickly pushed the letter to the bottom of the trashcan. It was absolutely ridiculous, and he wasn't even going to bother telling Mandy about it. However, and even more disturbing, Neal knew the tide of goodwill toward his wife had changed. People were becoming angry, desperate.

Mandy was on the phone when she walked into the kitchen. "Well, okay… when you put it that way." Neal could hear the reluctance in her voice. "If you think it will be good for the town… You know how much I love this town… Yes, I'll do it. I'll be in the parade."

A parade? Neal knew it was a bad idea.

Clara did not want to go to the parade, yet Mom dragged her to Trudy's Beauty Boutique to get her hair done. It was sheer agony. All the old ladies in the shop fawned over her mom like she was some kind of movie star or something. Even Trudy, generally a pretty cool lady, acted like Mom was something special.

"I guess I'm really going to have to make you look like a million bucks now, aren't I Mandy?" Trudy mixed hair dye in a plastic bowl. "I'm thinking highlights. What about you?"

"Just do my hair like you always do, Trudy." To her credit, Mom looked a little embarrassed by all the attention.

Trudy, clearly disappointed by that answer, said, "Oh, come on. Like it or not, you're a celebrity now. You've got to look the part."

Mom sighed but in a nice way. "Sure. Okay. Whatever you want to do, Trudy. You're the expert here."

Gina and Joanne, two of the town's nosiest busybodies, stood right next to Mom's chair, breathing on her. "You're going to go on a cruise, aren't you, Mandy? That's what I would do, go on an around-the-world cruise." Gina rifled through the large purse hanging on her arm. "I have some pamphlets right here."

"I'd buy a Mercedes," Joanne said eagerly. "Aren't you going to buy a new car, Mandy? That old Buick you drive has got to be at least ten years old. A new car is definitely the way to go. I guess it doesn't have to be a Mercedes. A BMW would be just as good."

Mom shifted in her chair as if she were trying to get away from the two hovering ladies. "I haven't decided anything yet. This whole millionaire thing hasn't really sunk in."

More women entered the shop and went directly to Mom, crowding around her as Trudy worked, asking her questions and chattering excitedly about the stupid parade and how Mom was the guest of honor. She would be riding on the biggest float, not in a car or the back of the fire engine. Clara had seen the float; it was truly hideous. The float, built on a large flatbed truck, wasn't covered with carnations like most floats, but with fake money glued all over it. It even had a throne in the middle that looked like the queen of hearts playing card. Clara asked Darryl Hubert, the town's maintenance man who built the float, "Are you going to make her wear a stupid crown, too?" She'd been kidding, but Darryl had said, "You bet."

"Are you sure you only want a trim?" Sue asked. Sue was the hairstylist who had replaced Roxy Morton, which made Clara kind of sad. Everyone knew Roxy was a doper, but she'd been nice. When she ran off with a guy traveling down the Mississippi on a houseboat, people said all kinds of mean things about her. It was one of the many things that Clara hated about Liberty. A lot of people were just downright nasty.

"Your hair would look a lot fuller if I took off a few inches." Sue looked hopeful, scissors poised.

"I guess it would match my face then, wouldn't it?"

Sue cleared her throat. "Um . . ."

"Just a trim."

Sue went to work without another word, and Clara closed her eyes. When she was younger, she used to think she became invisible when she closed her eyes. Boy, did she wish that were true now, but it sure wasn't. No one could miss her from a mile away. She'd gotten so large and bloated during the past few months that she sometimes didn't recognize herself when she accidentally caught a sideways glimpse of the huge young woman reflected and framed in the hallway mirror. She'd cried about it, in the beginning, when the weight started to pile on, and there was nothing she could do about it. She didn't cry now, not even in secret. She just wanted it all to be over.

She would be sixteen next month on August 12, and the only daydream Clara had about her mom winning all that money was that she could now buy Clara a car. Then Clara would just drive away, vanish. Of course, because of her condition, she hadn't even gotten her permit yet, but that didn't even figure in because a daydream could be anything you wanted it to be. But it would probably kill Mom if she did something like that. She'd cried for weeks when Stephanie left town at eighteen "to pursue her dreams." Ha! Stephanie ended up as a stripper in Champaign. What kind of dream was that?

Linda Aldean, the mayor's wife, rushed into the shop just then. As usual, she looked all out of breath. She was always like that, acting like she was in a big hurry, but it seemed to Stephanie that she really had nowhere to go. "There you are, Mandy! I've been looking all over town for you. I have something I want to ask you."

Here we go again, Clara thought. All week long, ever since her mom won the Queen of Hearts jackpot, people had been calling and coming to their door, asking for money. They were a bunch of spongers, every single one of them. It seemed to Clara that people should have more dignity than that, but not in this town. No, every single one of them wanted to take advantage of Mom's good nature, and the sad thing about it was that she'd probably end up giving it to them. Her mom was a softie, gullible, too nice, but it had sure worked to Clara's advantage over the last few months.

"You're pregnant," Mom said for the millionth time.

"No, I'm not."

"You're depressed, then."

"Hello, Mom! I'm fifteen. It goes with the territory."

Dad seemed oblivious to everything that went on in the house—or maybe he was just too busy fucking his girlfriend—but then Mom brought in Stephanie to get to the heart of the matter. Because her half-sister was twelve years older than her, Clara and she had never been close. That wasn't the case now. After Stephanie got her face bashed in by her boyfriend, she changed. She was no longer beautiful, and even after extensive plastic surgery might not ever be again, but it didn't seem to bother her too much. Stephanie confided in Clara that she finally felt at peace now that she was no longer with Jere. "We were abusive to each other," she told Clara. "I'm glad he's dead." The handsome police officer, Alan Morrison, shot Jere just as he was about to murder Stephanie. And now *he* was Stephanie's new boyfriend.

"Oh, what a tangled web we weave," Clara said to Stephanie.

"Shut up. When are you going to tell Mom the truth? Do you really think she doesn't know?"

It had been something to do, and they'd made a pact. They trusted each other. Clara and her two best friends, Kristen and Katie, had been sitting around her living room on a Saturday night once again. They were all three on the softball team, and Clara had often wondered if it was because of the softball team that the three of them didn't get dates. Didn't most guys think female softball players were gay? Well, they weren't. They might not have been as pretty as some of the other girls in school, but they weren't butt-ugly or anything like that. Clara knew she was a "big girl," but it wasn't like she was fat, and neither were Kristen and Katie.

"I know some FFA boys are having a party at Jesse Norman's house tonight. Let's crash it, do something exciting for once." Kristen twirled a piece of her short, blond hair around her finger. She would have been a lot prettier if she ditched her black-framed glasses.

"I don't know." But Clara was intrigued. She'd had a crush on Jesse Norman all year.

"Let's make it interesting. Let's make a pact. We're all going to lose our virginity tonight." Katie was, in fact, rather stocky, but she had enormous boobs that she was secretly proud of.

"Where did that come from?" Clara stared at her.

"I know most of the girls in our class aren't virgins," Katie said with authority.

"How do you know that?" Clara had never really thought about it before.

"Let's just say that I *know*."

Kristen giggled nervously. "Virginity, who needs it?"

It was only that, merely a whim, something to do, that led the three girls over to Jesse Norman's house, shivering in the cold early November night. Jesse lived on a farm about a half-mile from town, so it was a good thing they all had tennis shoes on. They had all three changed into some skimpy tops, though, that they found in the back of Stephanie's old closet. *The boys won't let us come in,* Clara thought. *There's nothing to worry about.* She pretended she wasn't scared as she joined in the chatter with her friends.

But they were invited in. "The more, the merrier," Jesse said when he opened the door. He was tall, with light brown hair brushing the collar of his plaid shirt. Clara thought he looked something like Justin Bieber, but her friends scoffed at that observation.

Clara had heard about these high school parties, the parties held in houses when the parents weren't home, or at Boss' Lake, an old strip-mining pit just outside of town. They happened almost every weekend, she'd heard, but entering into that social realm was an entirely new experience for her. It wasn't all guys, as she'd secretly feared. In fact, it seemed to be most of the kids from the junior and senior classes. They were the only sophomores there, and it made her feel special. Looking at the shining faces of her friends, Clara could tell they felt the same.

Beer, tequila, vodka, pot. All seemed to be in abundant supply. At first, Clara hesitated when someone handed her a red Solo cup filled with a clear liquid. She didn't know what kind of booze it was, but it tasted good, once she got the hang of it. "Let's dance," Katie yelled over the din. "We can't stand in this corner forever."

Clara could have stood in the corner forever, watching in fascination as couples gyrated against each other in time to the loud music, kissed, disappeared for a while—presumably to an unseen bedroom—and returned, flushed and giggling, self-satisfied smirks on their faces. But she did dance, sloshing some of her drink on the floor. Clara was a pretty good dancer, if she did say so herself, having practiced many hours in the privacy of her bedroom. She drank some more.

"Remember the pact," Katie said sometime later. "Jesse's standing right over there, Clara. He's been staring at you all night, and he hasn't been with anyone else. Go for it!"

Clara had stolen small glasses of wine from the bottle in the refrigerator at home before, but she had never had a lot of alcohol at one time. She'd never been drunk. Clara didn't feel drunk right then either, just an incredible feeling of liberation and excitement. She, too, had noticed Jesse staring at her. Could it be that he felt the same way she did? She sauntered over to him, trying to be sexy, trying to play it cool.

"Hi, Clara," he said, smiling. "You're looking good tonight. Let me refill your drink." He turned his back just for a moment and then handed her an almost overflowing drink.

She could have fainted with happiness. Jesse had noticed her! It was hard to have a conversation over the loud music, so they mostly smiled. The drink was gone before she knew it. She wondered if she should ask him to dance, or would that be too bold of her? She didn't know the protocol, but she knew she felt happy, so happy.

And a little dizzy. The room's edges started to blur together, but Clara noticed Kristen and Katie were both talking to boys. "Whoa," she said, grabbing onto the dining room table that had transformed into a bar for this party. "That was a strong drink."

"Liquid courage." Jesse took her cup and again turned his back as he refilled it.

She laughed. She wasn't quite sure what Jesse meant, but he didn't seem like he would leave her side. Clara couldn't believe it. Maybe it was a kind of date, although people didn't really date anymore. She drank some more. When she looked around the room sometime later, she didn't see Kristen or Katie. *The pact. Oh, no.* She wasn't sure she wanted to do that tonight… but the next thing she knew, she had stumbled into Jesse's arms.

"Hey, now," he said. "Maybe you need some fresh air."

He was so kind. Good-looking and kind. Clara nodded, gulped. "That would be great."

Jesse led her out to the back screened-in porch, but the brisk air didn't revive her. If anything, it made her feel drunker, woozier. "I better sit down." She made her way to the couch under the back row of windows and landed in a sprawl.

And then Jesse landed on top of her, kissing her, pawing at her low-cut tank top. "Wait," she mumbled into his chest. "No, wait." He didn't seem to hear her as he moved his hands down her body. Then he was struggling with the zipper of her jeans. *These are my good jeans,* she thought distantly. *I hope he doesn't rip them.*

Jesse panted loudly now, his breath hot and boozy on her face. "Do you have protection?"

That was the last thing she remembered before she came to. She hadn't been out long. She could hear the party still in full swing, and it was still pitch-dark outside. She struggled to pull up her pants, not daring to look at the couch. Maybe nothing had happened. She still had on her panties. Maybe Jesse had been a gentleman when she passed out. Maybe she was still a virgin. Clara got slowly to her feet, and when she felt the bile, she reached for a trash can and vomited. She wiped her hand across her mouth. She felt better now.

She passed Jesse on her way to the front door. "It was like fucking a corpse," he told a group of friends, and they laughed.

But Clara knew he wasn't talking about her. Jesse was a gentleman.

"We've been looking all over for you." Katie grabbed her arm. "We've got to get home. It's late."

Walking was good. The cold air slapped at Clara's face, turned her body numb. *Nothing happened,* she told herself. Wouldn't she remember if something had happened? Tomorrow, her life would go back to normal. She didn't have to worry about a thing. Jesse Norman was a nice guy, not a creep who took advantage of passed out girls. She knew that about him at least, didn't she?

Katie, teeth chattering, said, "You know I didn't mean it about a pact to lose our virginity, right, guys? I was joking. I'm still a virgin, of course."

"Me, too. I want to be in love when I have sex for the first time. I'm not saying I'm going to wait until I'm married, but you know." Kristen had lost her glasses at the party and walked between them, letting Clara and Katie stumble her along. "I think the guys spiked the girls' drinks."

Clara said nothing at all when she dropped to her knees and vomited again, violently. She would never tell them that Jesse Norman might have drugged her drink. He might have raped her. And she might have deserved it.

"So, how do you like it?" Sue handed Clara a mirror and tried, unsuccessfully, to twirl the chair around so Clara could see the back.

It was hideous. Without asking, Sue had taken a curling iron and made "beach waves" to "frame her face." But she looked so hopeful that Clara didn't have the heart to tell her what she really thought. "Um… nice?" She needed to get out of the chair, out of the salon, right now. She was having another one of her hot flashes, and in the mirror, Clara could see beads of sweat starting to trickle down the sides of her face, into the "beach waves."

"Mom will take care of this." Clara lumbered ungracefully out of the tight chair. "She's got the big bucks now, you know, so you'll probably get a big, fat tip."

"Do you think so?" Sue's eyes went wide with excitement.

It was sickening. People were so weird about money. "I've got to go." Clara, struggling with the plastic cape, finally broke herself free. Mom still sat in Trudy's chair, surrounded by clamoring women, and no one noticed Clara leaving the shop.

It was the story of her life these days. She was as big as a house, yet people didn't seem to *see* her. It was like looking at her embarrassed them or something, which seemed weird because she should have been the embarrassed one. And she was embarrassed, but even more than that, she was mad as hell. At herself, mostly. She'd made one stupid mistake that ruined her life. And she didn't know what to do about it.

"Everyone in this family is a professional when it comes to denial," Stephanie said to her one evening when they were alone, watching TV.

"I don't know what you're talking about." Stephanie didn't move her eyes from the screen. She didn't trust herself to meet Stephanie's frank stare.

"Eventually, you will have a baby, Clara. There's no escaping that fact."

"Says who?"

Clara rarely left her house these days, so the humid blanket of heat hitting her as she left the salon surprised her. In the hour or so she had been inside Trudy's, the temperature must have risen twenty degrees. It was torturous. What kind of stupid town would have a parade on this hot day in late July? The dimwits of Liberty would. It just figured. Well, Clara would have none of that. It was inhumane to stand in the hot sun on a day in the upper 90s. It was a good reason not to go. Never mind that she didn't want people to see her anymore. She'd cut off all contact with her so-called friends, and if they got a load of her now, they would *know*. Clara couldn't bear the thought.

"There you are." Mandy emerged from the salon. "We might as well walk the few blocks to where they're setting up the parade. We'll leave the car here. I don't think we can get a parking space any closer."

Clara hadn't noticed before, but now she saw that the street was lined with parked cars. She could also hear the high school band warming up in the distance, along with the sounds of a gathering crowd. "This is insane."

"I know, but Tucker Aldean said the parade will be good for the town. A reason to celebrate always brings a town together."

"Who cares?" Around her mom, Clara always resorted to her most sullen self. She wasn't sure why she took out her unhappiness on Mom; she just did. It was like she couldn't help herself.

"I do. I've always loved this town. The people, for the most part, are good and decent."

"Ha!" Stephanie had a point about Mom and denial, for sure.

"Oh, honey, don't be that way. Not today. I'm nervous enough as it is."

That was news to Clara. "What are you nervous about?"

"Oh, I don't know." Mom tried to hurry Clara along, but with her enormous bulk, it was slow going. "People might throw tomatoes or something." Mom laughed. She looked good, with her newly highlighted blond hair. She'd also worn her best white linen slacks and a red, white, and blue striped shirt. Clara thought her blatant display of patriotism was overkill, for sure, but she kept her mouth shut for once.

It was sheer agony when they got to the staging area. Everyone in town, despite the oppressive heat, seemed to have shown up. Clara knew most people liked her mom. Who wouldn't? She was compulsively nice to everyone, even the nasty people who talked about her behind her back. Dad was already there, standing beside the hideous Queen of Hearts float. To Clara's horror, she saw that Darryl Hubert had now added colored, twinkling lights that draped the sides of the truck and snaked up around the throne Mom was supposed to sit on. "Oh, God," she muttered.

"Shh," Mom said. "The man tried his best."

Clara closed her eyes. It wasn't easy to hide in plain sight, but she would do her best. If she ran into any of her so-called friends, or worse, Jesse Norman, she would just *die*. She would, right on the spot, just up and *die*. She hadn't seen anyone from school now for over two months. Getting through the last months of school had been hard enough when she took to wearing her dad's old surplus Army jacket to cover up her expanding waistline. She told everyone she had a thyroid condition that made her gain weight. After school ended, she told Kristen and Katie that she had a highly contagious case of mono. When they continued to call and text, Clara stopped responding. Finally, she got a joint text from both of them: "If you don't want to be our friend anymore, FINE. We don't NEED you." Clara had cried over that, but it had to be done. She was now on her own.

"Easy there." Dad had his hand on Mom's arm, helping her onto the garish, rickety float.

Mom pushed it away. "I can do this on my own, Neal."

It served him right. Stephanie had been right all along about Dad having an affair with Trisha Yardley. Clara had sworn up and down that it couldn't be true. Dad and Trisha couldn't stand each other. And when Clara and Stephanie followed Dad to Carbondale one day, tailing him like a couple of inept spies, he hadn't done anything wrong. He'd gone to look at a horse, of all things, and Clara hadn't heard him mention anything about buying a horse since then. (It was too bad. She would have liked having a horse.) But Clara had been dead wrong about her dad. She wasn't sure what to think of him now, but she knew she wouldn't adore him like she used to. It would serve him right.

Clara had been spot-on. Mom looked pretty stupid sitting on that fake throne, and when she dutifully put on the phony tiara, Clara cringed. She hoped people weren't going to laugh at her or throw tomatoes or rotten eggs. And where was Stephanie in all this? Stephanie, at least, would tell Mom to take off the stupid tiara. Stephanie might have even torn off the twinkling lights and thrown them at Darryl Hubert, telling him they were ridiculous. Stephanie was capable of doing such things. But she'd begged off the parade this morning. All she had to do was point at her bashed-in, bandaged face. It was her get-out-of-jail-free card.

The float finally lumbered off, following the mayor's car, the fire engine, the antique cars, and the marching band. The Queen of Hearts float was the finale, and even though Darryl Hubert drove slowly, Mom still rocked from side to side. At her feet sat two large metal buckets of candy. In Liberty, every vehicle had to toss out candy along the parade route to the little kids, although Clara had seen grown men and women scramble for the Tootsie Rolls and Smarties and Dubble Bubbles many times. It was shameful. Were they starving or something? Whatever. In Liberty, the candy tossing at parades was mandatory.

With the float now inching down the road, Clara's hiding place was gone, and she was exposed. Mom probably expected her to follow along or something, meeting her later at the American Legion for the potluck. That would be a madhouse. Clara didn't know how this many people could fit into the Legion's two rooms. Strangely, she did feel like maybe she should follow the parade route to protect her mom. Which was utterly stupid. What could she possibly do to help if someone called Mom names or jeered, or if people started to throw things at her? She couldn't even bend over anymore to put on her shoes. She was helpless to defend anyone.

And she, not Mom, would be the laughingstock of this parade. Everyone would finally get a load of her and *know*. Jesse Norman would surely be along the parade route somewhere, along with Kristen and Katie. It was unfathomable to Clara that neither Mom nor Dad recognized that fact, but she did have to admit that denial came in pretty handy every once in a while. Thankfully, no one looked at her now. The crowd that had been in the staging area had followed the parade, much like the throngs who followed Tiger Woods or Rickie Fowler from hole to hole on PGA tournaments on TV. For sure, it was a herd mentality, and Clara supposed she should be grateful for this one small thing.

She headed home. The heat made her even more sluggish than usual, the sun beating down on and melting her "beach waves." All she wanted to do was go home to her air-conditioned house and put her heavy feet and legs up on the coffee table. She couldn't see her feet, but she knew her pink fuzzy slippers—the only shoes that fit—were filthy. She hadn't had lunch, and she was ravenous, like always. Maybe Mom had picked up a bag of glazed donuts from Dave's Market. Maybe Stephanie was around and would watch an episode of *Fixer Upper* with her. It was unbelievable, but true. Stephanie, of all people, had become her only friend.

She walked slowly, miserably toward home. It was sheer agony. Her feet hurt, her back ached, and the old Old Style t-shirt of Dad's she wore stuck to her body like cellophane. She huffed and puffed, trying to get air into her lungs. She wouldn't make it. She passed by one of the splintery picnic tables in the grove next to the Mississippi. She would have to rest a bit before she could continue on her journey, and she made her way to the table and sat down. It felt a little cooler here under the trees by the river, but not much. She was so tired. Maybe if she rested her head on her arms for only a moment, she would feel up to the task of getting home.

The smell of pot, not the voices, awakened her. Disoriented, it took her a moment to remember where she was. She raised her head, pushing the matted hair from her cheeks. The voices came from behind a row of bushes, male voices, and then the crushing of a beer can.

"Maybe we can kidnap the bitch. We can send a note to the husband, telling him that if he wants to see his bitch-wife alive again, he better hand over the cash," came the voice floating over the hedges.

"I don't know. It's her money, right? Maybe he can't get it out of the bank or something. I know that if I won that kind of money, I wouldn't let my old lady touch a damn penny of it," a second voice said.

"Shit. You might have a point." Coughing. "Don't hog the joint." Coughing. "Doesn't the bitch have a daughter?"

"There's two. The one that got beat up and the tub of lard. Shit, she could be in the circus she's so fat."

"It doesn't mean the bitch doesn't love her and wouldn't pay good money to get her back."

"Fuck, man, what if we had to feed her for a week or two? It might not be worth it." Voice two laughed meanly. "I mean, what the fuck?"

Clara, heart pounding, had heard enough. What if they looked over the bushes and saw her? Would they kidnap her right now? She was a huge sitting duck.

Clara hadn't moved so quickly in months. Her need to get out of there was so strong that she walked/jogged toward the street, her stomach banging heavily on her thighs. She lost a slipper somewhere along the way, but she didn't go back to retrieve it. She had to get home. She had to tell Stephanie that Mom was in danger, that they were all in danger.

When Clara finally burst in the back door, Stephanie sat at the kitchen table, her computer before her. She looked up. "Holy shit, Clara. You look like you've seen a ghost."

"I heard… at the grove… some guys talking about… kidnapping Mom or me or you," she gasped. "We're in danger!"

"Calm down." Stephanie led her to a kitchen chair that wobbled under her weight and brought her a glass of water. She waited until Clara drank the whole thing, and her breathing returned to normal. "Take a look at this." She turned the computer screen toward Clara.

Clara's heart started to pound all over again. People were saying the nastiest things about Mom. Some posts said she didn't deserve to win 1.5 million dollars. Others said she ought to give the money to someone more deserving. One said she better watch her back, and one said she should go to jail for killing her family. "What do you make of this?" Clara pointed at the last post.

Stephanie shrugged. "I don't know. Some nutcase. But Mom's all over social media, and it isn't good. Jealousy does strange things to people."

"Money does strange things to people."

"True." Stephanie shut down the computer. "Enough of this. Maybe I shouldn't have shown you in your condition."

"Shut up."

"I would have been very disappointed if you didn't say that." Stephanie flinched when she smiled. Her split lip wasn't completely healed yet.

Clara thought of Mom, now at the Legion, surrounded by all those crazy people. Clara didn't care what Mom said about the kindness of people in Liberty. To her, right now, they all seemed dangerous and crazy. "What are we going to do? Should we tell Dad?"

"He's worthless," Stephanie scoffed.

Clara didn't take offense. She, too, wasn't a big fan of Dad's right now. "Then what?"

Stephanie picked up her phone. "I'm calling Alan."

"What do you think of Goat Yoga?" Mandy had her back to him, busily rewashing her hands at the kitchen sink. She'd been doing that a lot since the parade two days before, obsessively scrubbing her hands with Dial antibacterial soap.

They were the first words she had spoken to Neal since the parade and potluck, and he gratefully grabbed at the crumb of conversation. "I've never heard of it. Is it a real thing?"

"Of course, it's a real thing. People practice yoga with goats. It's supposed to be very soothing."

"I don't get it," he admitted, wondering where Mandy was going with this. Since the parade, Mandy had seemed preoccupied, distracted, and at times, confused. Yet when people knocked on their front door—and the moochers still came with sad stories and outstretched hands—Mandy smiled kindly and said, "I'll have to talk to my accountant first. And then I'll see what I can do." Neal knew that Mandy had not yet talked to an accountant. He also knew she wasn't sleeping at night. From the fold-out bed in the den, he could hear her roaming the upstairs hallway, descending the stairs, and then the sound of voices from the TV. Knowing Mandy, Neal would bet that it was some old black and white movie on the TCM channel. She always watched those when she wanted to escape.

"I think the goats climb on you while you're stretching and stuff."

Mandy had grown up on a farm, but with her alcoholic father and four no-good brothers running the place, Neal doubted they'd had goats, or chickens or cows or sheep, for that matter. Before they perished in a house fire, the men in Mandy's family stayed busy drinking and fighting. Neal's mind went immediately to the first blackmail note, but he pushed it away. Mandy had now received quite a few more like it, but he never let her see any of them. His wife was too fragile, and in many ways, too innocent to be exposed to such things.

Unfortunately, Mandy did know about the unkind things being said about her on social media. She might never have known about it if Stephanie and Clara hadn't pounced on her the second they came home from the parade. "Would you look at all this trash talk about you?" Stephanie had shoved the computer in her mom's face.

"I think someone's going to try to kidnap you, Mom, or maybe they'll kidnap Stephanie or me." Clara's fear was genuine, her face streaked, her newly coiffed hairdo now smashed back to its original lankiness. Neal reached out to her, his baby girl who had grown so sullen and large, so unhappy, but Clara sidestepped his arms. She'd barely spoken to him since she found out about his affair. And Neal knew he deserved that, too.

"I already called Alan, and he's going to patrol our neighborhood regularly." Even with all the bandages on her face, Neal could see how Stephanie's eyes lit up when she mentioned the officer's name. He couldn't remember when Mandy had stopped looking at him like that. He couldn't remember when he started to take her for granted.

"Oh, dear. Is that really necessary?" The crease between Mandy's eyes deepened. "All this hullabaloo will die down quickly enough. You know how people are in this town."

"Mom!" Stephanie threw her hands up in the air. "You need to take this seriously!"

"The kidnappers said I belonged in a circus." Clara's pale face flushed crimson. "They said I was a tub of lard!"

"No one is getting kidnapped," Mandy said. "I'm bushed. I think I'll go upstairs and take a nap. You're on your own for dinner, girls. I couldn't eat another bite. Trisha brought that tortellini pasta salad to the potluck, which has always been my favorite . . ." The three remaining in the kitchen heard her voice trail off tiredly as she walked out of the room.

Clara and Stephanie stood there, staring at each other. Not at him, though. It was like he didn't exist for them anymore at the mention of Trisha's name. "What the hell?" Stephanie sputtered.

Clara shrugged. "You know Mom."

"That's the problem. I do." Stephanie got in a long, mean glare at Neal before she scooped up her computer and left.

"It's just you and me, kid," Neal said to Clara, reaching for her again.

"Not anymore." Clara's glare looked like a perfect replica of her sister's before she lumbered off. And Neal was left alone.

The parade hadn't been too bad. Mandy had smiled bravely, waving at all the spectators lined up along Main Street, waving like the former beauty queen that she was. Neal had been put in his place by Darryl when he announced that he wanted to ride on the float, standing behind his wife. He wanted to do it for her own protection, but it did no good trying to explain that to Darryl.

"No can do, buddy. You're riding in the cab with me. Mandy's the star of the show, not you, pal."

"But what if people spit at her or something?" It was Neal's greatest fear, and he couldn't stand the thought of Mandy suffering that ignoble gesture of contempt.

Darryl looked at him incredulously. "Why would they do that? Everyone in Liberty loves Mandy. They're *happy* she won the Queen of Hearts jackpot, man. It couldn't have happened to a nicer person."

Neal's worst fear about the parade had not come true, but he sat in the cab of the truck, vigilant and wary, scanning the crowd suspiciously. He had a feeling that if he saw the face of the person who had sent the blackmail note to Mandy, he would just *know*. But then what would he do? Jump out of the truck and punch the guy? Neal had never hit another person in his life, but he would do it for Mandy now. If physical violence got him back in her good graces, he would do it. He would become her knight in shining armor.

"What are you muttering about, man?" Darryl asked as they approached the Legion.

"Nothing." He would now never be Mandy's knight in shining armor. He had never been, but she'd loved him anyway. And he had ruined it. She would never trust him again, and now that she had all this money, she didn't need him at all.

They let too many people into the Legion for the potluck. People were supposed to buy tickets to come to the dinner, with the proceeds going to the town's Beautification Committee and volunteer fire department. But many of the people who crowded into the bar and banquet rooms hadn't purchased a ticket. No one was checking at the door anyway, so it was inevitable that people wanted to come in and gawk at Mandy like she was some freak of nature. "She's the only millionaire in town," Neal heard someone say. "I got good and drunk the night Mandy won the jackpot," someone else said. "Nobody should have that kind of money," a drunk guy at the bar thundered. "She should share the wealth."

And then that damn Darryl brought in the throne from the float, and even though Mandy demurred, insisting that she didn't want to do it, the post commander, a blustery guy named Atkins, practically pushed her into the seat. Mandy, being Mandy, was a good sport about it as people clustered around her. Neal wouldn't have been surprised if people started bending down and kissing her hand like she was the Pope or something. Neal tried to get as close to her as possible, but a wave of people kept pushing him away, so anxious were they to get close to his wife, to have a little bit of her newfound glory shine upon them. They congratulated her; they gushed over her; they asked for money. And through it all, Mandy's smile never wavered.

"It's shameful, isn't it?"

Of all people, it had to be Trisha who had swum to his side. "She's handling it well." Neal didn't take his eyes off Mandy.

"Is she really, or is she burying what she's feeling with chocolate cake and old TCM movies?"

That hit the nail on the head exactly. It pained Neal that Trisha had been in Mandy's life so much longer than he had—and probably knew her better, too. "She's handling it well," he said stubbornly.

Trisha's perfume, Poison, the perfume he had once found so enticing, now repelled him. It was hard to imagine now, but just weeks ago, he and Trisha had boozily come up with a plan to leave their spouses and buy a horse farm in Tennessee. By God, he'd even gone to Carbondale to look at a stud horse. How ludicrous. He didn't know anything about horses. Neal glanced at her quickly; Trisha did not look well. Always too thin, she now looked haggard. She hadn't bothered to cover the circles under her eyes with makeup, which was so unlike her.

"I miss Mandy." It was loud in the room, but Neal could hear her perfectly. He could hear the pain in her voice. "I only hope she can forgive me one day."

Me, too. But Neal didn't say it out loud. He didn't take his eyes off his wife.

"Bill's leaving me. We lost a son together, but we stuck it out."

Neal had been at the barbecue on that day fourteen years ago. He'd always been thankful that he'd been in the bathroom in the house when Bill accidentally drove over their twenty-two-month-old son. Neal hadn't been in the front yard when it happened, but when he ran outside, the sight sickened him. To this day, it was the most horrific thing Neal had ever seen. He didn't know how anyone could live through such a tragedy.

"But now he's going to leave me. He packed his bags this morning." Trisha's voice sounded like it was full of tears, but Neal didn't look at her. "He was just looking for an excuse, and the funny thing is that I don't blame him. I guess I got what I deserved."

Me, too. But Neal didn't say that out loud either. He didn't take his eyes off his wife.

"Doesn't everyone like baby goats?" Mandy's voice brought Neal back to the kitchen as she dried her hands, then squirted Dial into her palm and began scrubbing again.

"I've never thought about it one way or the other."

Stephanie, who was now always around and had no plans to leave, walked into the kitchen. Even though she and Neal had never been close, he couldn't blame her for this. Where would Stephanie go? She had always been damaged, but now she bore the proof of that on her battered face and body. And it was no surprise that she was the only person bold enough in this family to voice what they'd all been thinking: "What are you trying to do, Mom? Wash the taint of money off your hands?"

"Clean hands, pure heart," Mandy said, scrubbing away.

"Give me a break, Mom. You're freaking out, and you know it."

"Don't talk to your mom that way, Stephanie," Neal said rotely. It was an old habit.

"Go to hell, Neal." Stephanie abandoned whatever she had planned to do in the kitchen and went out the back door, slamming it behind her.

Mandy, at the sink, didn't flinch. "I could buy a little farm a mile or two outside of town and buy a group of goats. What is it called, a herd?"

"I think it's called a trip or a tribe." Neal had no idea where that piece of trivial information had come from. It was just like when he told Tucker Aldean that Illinois wasn't a community property state on the night Mandy won the Queen of Hearts jackpot. He kept watching as Mandy scrubbed her hands raw before he asked, "Would you buy back your father's farm? I heard it was for sale again." That unfortunate piece of property had changed hands many times since the fire.

"Goodness, no!" Mandy shuddered. "That place is cursed."

"What do you mean?" Neal, again, thought of the blackmail note. And the indecent post on Facebook that said Mandy had killed her family. Why did people come up with such hurtful untruths and hurl them at innocent people? It made no sense at all to Neal.

Mandy went on as if she hadn't heard the question. "People keep asking me what I'm going to do with all the money. I'm going to pay for Stephanie's plastic surgery, of course, and then Clara has been hinting she wants a car. Other than that, I don't know."

"Plastic surgery might be very expensive," Neal ventured. "I don't know what kind of insurance Stephanie has, or if she has any at all from the place she worked at in Champaign." Mandy had mandated that none of them were going to say *strip club* in this house. She wouldn't allow it. "It could be that the surgery takes up most of the money."

Mandy spun around from the sink, her hands dripping. "Do you really think so, Neal?" she asked excitedly. "Do you really think Stephanie's surgeries will use up all the money? Wouldn't that be fantastic? Then I wouldn't have to worry about all these sad, poor people who need money to feed their families or pay for an operation to cure their dying children. I wouldn't have to bear their burdens." Mandy clawed at her cheeks with her still-dripping hands. "It's like *Sophie's Choice* on steroids!"

"You don't have to bear their burdens, Mandy." The anguish on his wife's face distressed him. He should make her an appointment with their family doctor. Maybe old Doc Jenkins could give her something to calm her nerves. "Their problems are not your problems."

"Oh, but they are, Neal! I'm the one who won all this money. It shouldn't have happened. I shouldn't have even been there that night, but then Trisha—" Mandy stopped, the look on her face now stricken.

"Honey." Neal rose from his chair.

"Don't call me *honey*." Mandy buried her face in her hands. "I can't stand it!"

Neal knew Mandy wasn't only talking about the money. She was talking about him, too, and the breakdown of their marriage because of what he had done. She also referred to the betrayal and possible loss of her best friend. A woman as good as Mandy didn't deserve any of this. Winning so much money would make most people happy, but not Mandy, not her.

"Mandy." He approached her quietly, slowly. He wanted to put his arms around her to comfort her. If she would allow him only that, maybe they could start again, rebuild their marriage, and put the past behind them. Maybe she could find it in her kind heart to forgive him.

She felt him coming. "Stop right there, Neal." She lifted her wet face from her hands. "Don't come any closer. I've had enough of people glomming all over me lately."

"That's not fair," Neal said, hurt. He'd only wanted to comfort her. And then another thought came to him. To him, it seemed obvious, but maybe he should make it perfectly clear to her. "You know I don't want any of your money, Mandy."

She opened her eyes wide. "You mean you wouldn't be thrilled if I bought Damon's RV World for you? You'd finally be the boss of your own business. How does that sound?"

He'd worked so many years for that insufferable Bart, who had, over the years, probably stiffed him out of thousands of dollars. It was just a fleeting thought, quick as a gnat, but it must have put a spark of longing in his eyes. "You'd do that, Mandy?"

The look she gave him was inscrutable. "Just as I thought." His wife turned back to the sink, turned on the faucet, squirted the antibacterial soap in both palms, and began to scrub harder.

Her mom was going crazy, no question about it. Between answering her phone and the knocks on their door (the spongers still intruded; they had no sense of pride), if Mom wasn't washing her hands like a possessed person, she was scribbling notes on old receipts from Dave's Market. Not on actual notebook paper or on a computer, but on these tiny scraps of wrinkled paper. Clara didn't know why she'd saved them in the first place, but they were everywhere around the house now. Stephanie finally went around the house with a trash can, collecting all the crumpled balls, but Mom told her to *cut it out!* Since Mom hardly ever yelled, even Stephenie seemed surprised. "Fine," she'd said. "Have it your way." She upended the trash can on the spot and started kicking the scraps of paper every which way. "Are you happy now?"

"Yes, Stephanie, I'm happy now." Mom clearly was not. "I'm going through a process here. I need to keep all these notes until I decide what I'm going to do with the money."

"You could be a little more organized about it," Stephanie muttered.

"Fine." Mom stopped chewing on the end of her Bic pen. "I'm calling a family meeting."

"A what?" Stephanie said.

"Just sit your butt in the chair, Stephanie. All of you, sit down."

It was so weird. They were all in the kitchen anyway—even Dad, who hung around the house like a kicked puppy all day long—so Mom could have started talking right there and then, but instead, she sat there waiting until they all trooped over to the table to join her. "Here's what I've been thinking."

She was definitely off her rocker. Everyone sat there while she went on and on about who needed the money the most. The families with sick and dying children topped the list, but she was in a quandary about how much money each one should get. "How much would an operation like that cost?" she asked at one point. Then she went off on a tangent about how the money would be better spent by donating it to national organizations like St. Jude's or the American Red Cross. "But maybe I should be thinking globally. UNICEF is a worthy charity. Or maybe Doctors Without Borders?" Then, after about an hour of that, she started to wring her hands. "Seriously, I'm thinking about burying the money and forgetting this whole nightmare ever happened."

"Most people would think this is a blessing." Dad sat, arms crossed, his long legs perpendicular to the kitchen table because they didn't fit underneath it. "You can take care of your family, Mandy. Set up a trust or put a chunk of money into a CD. They're safe. Or you could pay off the mortgage on the house."

Clara noticed that Dad said, *your* family, not *our* family. She was starving, as usual, but she didn't dare move. "Or you could spend it. New cars all around would be nice." She wasn't sure if all her hints about a new car had sunk in. Mom had trouble focusing these days.

Stephanie, surprisingly quiet during Mom's erratic monologue, finally said, "I don't want you to feel obligated to pay for my plastic surgery. I got myself into this mess."

"Stop it!" Mom said sharply. "That's the one thing I am sure about spending this impossible money on." She looked at Clara. "And a new car for Clara. My children deserve something out of all this chaos."

"Mandy, you don't have to decide what to do with the rest of the money yet. It hasn't even been two weeks. Give it time."

Both Clara and Stephanie, who had been ignoring Dad most of the time, nodded in approval. It was good advice.

But Mom saw it differently. "But it's such a burden! There are so many sad people in this town, people in need. I can't stand it one second longer!"

Dad pulled his phone out of his shirt pocket. "Enough is enough. I'm calling Doc Jenkins. You need anti-anxiety meds or something."

Stephanie perked up. "And ask the old guy for a refill on my pain meds. I'm running low."

"Oh!" Mom pushed her chair back from the table and ran from the room, sobbing.

"She is so losing it," Stephanie said, shaking her head.

"Don't talk about your mother like that," Dad said automatically, his phone to his ear. "Hello, Doc? I need to ask you a favor."

"I'm going to the consignment shop today," Mom announced a couple of days later. "I don't care what Officer Morrison says." She seemed a little better, calmer, although she refused to take the Valium Doc Jenkins had prescribed.

Stephanie, on the other hand, had no problem popping an Oxy whenever the mood struck. "You can call him, Alan, Mom, now that I'm dating him."

Wonder of wonders, that coaxed a smile from Mom. But then again, who wouldn't like Alan? He was handsome in a clean-cut way—like one of the Jonas brothers—and polite without being too smarmy. Clara had felt much safer with him patrolling the neighborhood frequently, and even safer on the nights when he came in to drink a cup of coffee and make goo-goo eyes at Stephanie. Clara couldn't figure it out. Stephanie looked like she'd been in a war, yet Alan couldn't take his eyes off her. She hated to think she was jealous of Stephanie's happiness, but she was just a little bit. Jesse Norman had not looked at her like that in her brief moment of utter joy at the party—before it happened. Now he would never look at her like that. Clara knew this to be true.

Alan had told them all to stay in the house as much as possible, "until this whole Queen of Hearts frenzy blows over." Except for brief excursions to Dave's Market for food, they'd all obeyed him and were glad for it. On the night someone started throwing gravel at their windows, Alan was there. On the night the door handle jiggled ominously on the front door, Alan was there. And on the night a carload of guys TPd their front lawn and threw eggs onto the porch, Alan was there to go outside and chase them off. All he had to do was stand on the front porch and look handsome and official, and the guys piled into the car and took off, tires screeching. Alan told them he thought it was a bunch of teenagers. Clara wondered if Jesse Norman had been one of them.

"It won't last forever," Alan had assured them. And he seemed to be right. Most of the danger seemed to have passed. Oh, spongers still came to the door and called, and people still posted nasty things, but the inherent threat seemed to have lessened. And they were all a little stir-crazy, even Clara, who had been cooped up in the house for months before Mom won the jackpot.

"I'll go with you, Mom. I could sweep the floor or something." Clara had to turn away at the look of happiness in her mom's eyes. She'd been a shit for so long that Mom had probably forgotten that she was, deep down, a nice person.

"What the hell? I'll go, too. Just give me a minute to fix my face. Haha." Stephanie tugged on her cowboy boots, the really nice ones that she said she'd give to Clara when it was all over, the boots Clara shamelessly coveted, even though she knew they would never fit her.

"I'm not comfortable with the three of you going alone." Dad stood uncertainly, and Clara found, to her surprise, that she had started to feel a little sorry for him over the last few days. They'd all been pretty mean to him, ignoring him and such.

Mom only hesitated a second or two. "All right. We'll all go."

They were all in the best mood they'd been in for days when they pulled up in front of Zelda's Consignment Shop. "When are you going to change the name to Mandy's Consignment Shop, Mom?" Clara asked for the millionth time.

"Oh, I don't know." Mom waved her hand in front of her face like she always did. "Zelda was always so good to me. I like to think she's still part of the place."

Clara noticed the front shade of the shop covering the big picture window was pulled down. Her mom never pulled it down because she thought it was good advertising to leave it up. Clara had always thought that was wishful thinking on her part. Many people in this town would prefer to go to Walmart and buy clothes and dishes and towels and knickknacks, rather than the used stuff in this store. Her mom took everything people brought her, even the most threadbare of clothes, to resell. And Clara knew for a fact that Mom, eventually, when items had been sitting on shelves or hanging on hooks in the store for years, would take them to the Goodwill in Carbondale. She thought it was a big secret or something, but Clara knew.

Mom, too, seemed to sense that something was off. "I would have sworn I left that shade open."

"I've been saying for years that you need a security camera, Mandy," Dad said.

"Maybe we should call Alan." Stephanie stood staring at the store, her hands on her slim hips. "It's Sunday, his day off, and I know he'll be in church. But I also know he'll come if I call him."

Alan went to St. Joe's, the Catholic Church in town, and so far, he hadn't persuaded Stephanie to go with him. It being Sunday, Clara knew most people in town would be at church, which would explain why Main Street felt so deserted. Her family went to the Lutheran Church on Easter and Christmas, but other than that, forget about it. Clara had never questioned that oddity until now. She liked Pastor Welles, and she'd enjoyed sitting in the church with its tall stained-glass windows and hard wooden pews. Clara felt a movement in her stomach, that familiar tapping she tried so hard to ignore. Maybe Pastor Welles, who probably didn't remember her anyway, would be someone she could talk to, a religious stranger who wasn't supposed to pass judgment but listen and offer advice. At least that's what Clara thought pastors were supposed to do. It was something to think about.

"I'll go in first." Dad started for the front door.

"No, Neal, stop." Dad stopped immediately. "It's my store, and I'll go in first." Mom already had the key in her hand when she walked to the door. But even Clara, a few feet away, could now see that the lock had been broken.

"I'm calling Alan."

But Mom ignored Stephanie and pushed open the door. It swung wide, and the stench of gasoline came pouring out.

"Mandy, please! It might be dangerous." Dad grabbed Mom's arm, but she shook him off.

And the first thing Mom did was open the shade. Clara pushed by Dad and went into the store. The strong smell hit her, and she thought she might be sick, but this one time, Clara would be there for her mom, who looked strangely calm as she surveyed her store.

Clara couldn't believe it. She'd expected to see it empty, the shelves and hangers bare, but that wasn't the case. Or she expected to see dishes broken and scattered, ripped clothing, but that wasn't the case either. "What happened here? Did someone get scared off before they could set the place on fire? I don't understand."

"Maybe someone had a change of heart," Mom said.

"Oh, please, Mom, stop it. This is still vandalism." Stephanie had come into the store. Her gaze landed on the front counter, where the cash register sat. "Your ugly little dolls are gone, though, Mom."

Clara's eyes went to the place on the counter where Mom's collection of forty-some trolls with different colored hair and colorful outfits used to be. For some reason, Mom had always had a soft spot for those little dolls, and she wouldn't let Clara play with them when she was a kid. Clara had always resented that, even though she'd never been a doll kind of girl.

"My trolls."

"They were hideous. And creepy." Stephanie rubbed her shoulders as if she were cold, but it was stifling in the place. The air conditioning hadn't been turned on for days.

"For your information, Stephanie, those little people are known as good luck trolls, or gonk trolls, in the United Kingdom."

"So you've told me. Still creepy, Mom."

Mom went on as if she hadn't heard Stephanie. "My grandmother gave me my first troll when I was seven, and I've collected them ever since. If I hadn't had her after my mom died, I don't know what I would have done. She was a good person." Mom went to sit on the stool behind the counter, where Stephanie knew she spent a good deal of time staring out the window when she was out of work to do. "It's not like I thought they actually brought me good luck. I'm not a superstitious person."

Clara noticed out of the corner of her eye that Alan had arrived. He stood just inside the door, not saying a word. He, too, stared at Mom.

"In fact, I never thought I was a lucky person at all."

"Honey." Dad looked like he didn't know what to do, but then he moved. He went behind the counter and tentatively put a hand on her shoulder. He seemed relieved when she didn't brush it off. "We can fix this."

"Without a doubt, we can fix this. With a little work, a little scrubbing, everything can be fixed."

Stephanie moved over to Alan and whispered something in his ear. "You can file a report," he said.

"No, no." Mom waved her hand in front of her face again. "I don't need to replace the trolls." She reached under the counter and brought up a box. "Here, Clara, these are for you, for the baby. Every time something nice came in, I saved it in this box for you."

Stephanie appeared at Clara's side magically, holding her up when the relief made her knees buckle. "This gasoline," she said. "It's making me feel faint."

"You can give it up now," Stephanie whispered in her ear.

"Shut up," Clara whispered back as she squeezed her sister's hand.

Mom found her old green shopkeeper's apron under the counter and pulled it over her head. Then she reached for her dust rag and started to wipe the counter where the troll dolls had stood for so many years. "After everything that's happened, I've realized I am a lucky person. And I'm not talking about the Queen of Hearts jackpot. I have a few ideas about that money, but I'm narrowing it down. No more scribbled notes."

Dad took Mom's cue and went to the back and got a mop and bucket.

Mom polished the empty counter that used to display her trolls until it gleamed. "I do know one thing, though. I'm going to knock this town's socks off!" She started laughing, but she didn't sound at all crazy. She sounded happy.

EROSION

Tucker Aldean, the youngest man ever to be elected mayor of Liberty—a statistic he was exorbitantly and not secretly proud of—usually took his morning coffee at Lolly's Diner. The people of his town thought that was because he was a man of the people, a man who listened with an open ear to their petty griping and unrealistic suggestions. Tucker let them believe that. After all, he did want to be reelected again. It wasn't because of the money, which was nonexistent, but because Tucker liked the prestige of being the mayor, even in a town as small as Liberty. However, Tucker mainly went to Lolly's for coffee and stale donuts because he wanted to escape his house, with its four clamoring children, and his wife.

Tucker didn't have that excuse to escape to Lolly's on this particular morning in early August. His wife, Linda, had shipped all four kids to church camp, and the house was blissfully quiet. Even Linda, who repeatedly reprimanded the children to keep them in line, or if that wasn't necessary, turned her scolding to her husband—the gutters needed to be cleaned; the faucet at the kitchen sink leaked again; the front screen door was so loose it flapped in the wind—had immersed herself in the *Liberty Gazette.*

So the house, with only the exceptions of their clinking coffee cups and the grandfather clock in the hall (Linda's sole, useless inheritance from her grandmother), was silent. Tucker, to his surprise, found it strangely unsettling. The children, two boys and two girls, ages 12, 11, 9, and 7, weren't kicking each other under the table, laughing, crying, or dawdling over their oatmeal. All of them hated oatmeal, but Linda insisted it was the most nutritious breakfast, and

264

they would eat it *or else.* "Would it be so bad to give them Frosted Flakes every once in a while?" he had been naive enough to ask once. "Not in this house," Linda said with such authority that he never brought up the subject again.

It was also strange to see Linda in such repose. She was usually a person of constant movement, both in the house and about town. Anyone watching her buzz from one room to the next, or from one errand or meeting to the next, knew she was a woman on a mission. Tucker never understood the purpose of her charging hither and thither, and he had never asked. Linda didn't like to be questioned. They'd married young, at eighteen, and that had been understood from the start. Now, sixteen years later, it was a fundamental statute of their marriage.

"Oh, this is sad." Linda looked at him over the top of the paper to make sure he paid attention to her. "Mitchell McHenry died."

"The drunken poet finally kicked the bucket, huh? Don't tell me. It was his liver."

"This is nothing to joke about, Tucker. He was always such a sad old man, drinking his life away in bars every night. I don't think I ever got a chance to talk to him, but I always felt sorry for him."

"He didn't say much to anyone." Tucker was surprised when Linda reached up to touch a single tear at the corner of her eye. They were both thirty-four, but she still looked good, with her close-cropped light brown hair and slender figure. He, on the other hand, hadn't fared so well. He'd noticed this morning that his brown hair had receded a little more, exposing more of his high forehead. His head would soon look like a balloon. He was also developing a paunch from too many beers at the local taverns. It wasn't his fault. Because he was the mayor, people often bought him drinks he didn't want. But he drank them anyway. He couldn't offend his constituents.

"How old was the guy?" Tucker genuinely wanted to know.

"It doesn't say."

"Where was he born? Was he a teacher like everyone thought? Was he ever married?"

Linda scanned the paper. "It doesn't say any of those things, Tucker. This is not exactly an obituary. I mean, it's more of an article written by that young guy at the paper, Brad Taylor. Weren't they friends?"

"Can I see that?" Tucker held out his hand, half expecting Linda to say, "I'm not finished yet," but she reluctantly handed it over.

Tucker scanned the short article, which was nothing more than three short paragraphs. It simply stated that Mitchell McHenry had been a fixture at the local taverns for years. After a couple of beers, and if someone bought him a shot of Jack Daniels, he could be coaxed up onto a barstool where he would recite poems of Walt Whitman: "When Lilacs Last in the Dooryard Bloom'd" or "O Captain! My Captain!" or "Out of the Cradle Endlessly Rocking." The article said his voice was deep and resonant, and he was an avid devotee of the

Transcendentalists. It also mentioned that Mitchell was a quiet man who lived on Pine Street, with no known living relatives. There would not be a memorial service.

"This doesn't say anything about the man that I didn't already know," Tucker said, disappointed. He knew he wasn't alone in his lack of information. For years, there had been speculation and gossip in the town about the mysterious man who just showed up one day and started drinking in the local taverns and reciting poems. With his shaggy grey hair, beard, and tweed jacket, the man looked like a relic from the past; in fact, he looked a lot like Walt Whitman himself. Tucker knew this because he'd googled it when he got home from Mr. Lucky's one night after Mitchell had given an hour-long recitation, and uncharacteristically, charged with his electrifying performance, had jumped down from the barstool himself. His head held high, Mitchell marched out of the tavern, leaving an unfinished beer on the bar.

"Didn't he have a limp? I always thought it was an old war injury, something like that." Linda had refilled their coffee cups while Tucker read. She'd started buying Starbucks French Roast, an unnecessary extravagance in Tucker's opinion, but he didn't mention it.

"Could be. The guy might have been fifty or eighty, and no one knew his age or anything else about him. The shaggy old man didn't have the gift of gab. He sure as hell didn't kiss the Blarney Stone." Tucker felt himself starting on a roll.

"Unlike someone we know," Linda said quickly, to shut him up. "I still think it's sad."

"The guy could have talked if he wanted to. People in this town are easy to talk to."

Linda acted like she didn't hear him. "I wonder how he died," she mused. She picked up her phone. "I know. I'll call Trisha Yardley. She knows everything that goes on in this town."

Tucker listened patiently to the one-sided conversation. He liked gossip as much as anyone in this town—and needed it to get his job done—but some women in this town treated gossiping like a holy vocation. And Tucker was powerless to change that much conviction. "Well?" he said when Linda got off the phone.

Linda reached to the corner of her hazel eye to blockade another tear from escaping. "This is quite sad, Tucker. According to Trisha, no one had seen the drunken poet in a few days. At first, no one thought much about it because the guy liked to frequent different taverns on different nights."

Tucker nodded. He'd seen the guy at all the taverns in town over the years (what did that say about him? he wondered), and in each bar, Mitchell had a specific barstool he liked to sit on. He didn't like it when someone sat next to him, so no one did. To Tucker, that was an admirable sign of respect from the people in this town, his constituents. Sometimes they knew when to give a guy his space.

"Lenny, the bartender at Mr. Lucky's, finally got worried on Thursday when Mitchell didn't show, so on Friday morning at around eleven—Lenny doesn't get up early because he works late, you know—he went over to Mitchell's apartment on Pine Street. He knocked and knocked, but no one came to the door. Then he got really worried." Linda held up her hand when she saw that Tucker wanted to speak. "And I know what you're thinking, Tucker, but no, no gross smell came from the apartment."

"I was not going to ask that."

"Yes, you were. Anyway, Lenny punched in the glass on the door, just like they do in the movies, and reached in and unlocked it." She took a deep breath, sniffled. "He found the poor man in his bed, fully clothed, with an empty bottle of whiskey in one hand, vodka in the other. Vials of pills were on the nightstand, but Trisha didn't know if they were prescription or not."

"Suicide?" Tucker had a hard time spitting out the word. For once in his life, he was as near speechless as he could get. The thought of that poor man finally drinking himself to death in earnest was one of the saddest things he'd ever heard.

"It gets worse."

Tucker recovered quickly. "How can it get worse? The man is dead." Sometimes his wife bewildered him.

Linda took another deep breath. "Lenny said he saw thousands of unopened letters scattered all over the apartment, letters he'd written to a woman named Kay Ballant that he never sent."

"So?" Tucker stared at her blankly.

"You are such a man, Tucker! Don't you see? The poor man had probably been drinking himself to death all these years over unrequited love or a long-lost woman. Something like that. Doesn't that just break your heart?" Linda sniffled for real now and reached for her paper napkin to blow her nose.

"Isn't the new chemistry teacher at Liberty High named Ellie Ballant?"

"I wouldn't know, Tucker. Our children are not in high school yet. But trust me. When they do get to high school, I will know every teacher's name. And anyway, you're missing my point. This is a very sad story about a man who drank himself to death over love."

Tucker's mind spun, not over a man who would kill himself over love, but how this singular event could somehow benefit the town. When Mandy Tanner won the 1.5 million dollar Queen of Hearts drawing three weeks ago, he'd organized a parade. To his way of thinking, nothing like a celebration, complete with a parade, could bring a town together and boost morale. The people in this town certainly needed something to celebrate, with unemployment at an all-time high and small businesses closing. He'd been about the age of his oldest son when Liberty was in its heyday, but once the coal mines shut down, the town and the people in it had witnessed a slow yet steady decline. Tucker was always trying to come up with new ideas to cheer up the people and help small businesses. As mayor, he wanted this goal to be his signature on the town, and after a succession of re-elections, his legacy.

Unfortunately, the parade and the following potluck at the American Legion hadn't had the desired effect. It had not brought the people in this town closer together. Desperate and jealous people stalked Mandy anyway, in person, by mail, and on social media. Even her business, Zelda's Consignment Shop, had been vandalized. The perpetrators threw gasoline over everything in the store, and Tucker knew they would have burned it down if one of them had thought to bring a lighter or matches. He knew this because the ringleader was his nephew Tommy, who ran around with the other meth heads in town. Tucker's older sister Tina made Tommy confess to Tucker, just as she had when Tommy and his gang robbed ten businesses in Liberty in a single night. Officer Alan Morrison knew who was responsible for the crimes, but Tucker had asked him to keep it under wraps. It was one of the perks of being a mayor in a small town. Family connections trumped misdemeanor charges.

"The drunken poet was a fixture in this town. He probably didn't know it, but he meant a lot to the people of Liberty." He waited for Linda's approving nod. She knew as well as he did that he was stretching things a bit here. He did have a tendency to do that, especially when he'd been drinking. Everyone knew it.

"He will be missed, and he should be honored." Tucker waited again for Linda's approving nod. "We, as a town, will hold a public memorial for the man."

"Whoever gives the eulogy should mention that he died for love." Linda's hazel eyes glowed with conviction.

"He drank himself to death, Linda." Tucker's sense of truth often came at the most inopportune moments, and at Linda's glare, he amended his statement. "The drunken poet was a great man who died for love. It might not be true, but it has a good ring to it, doesn't it?"

Linda was already on it and on her phone. "Hello, Trisha? Could you spread the word about—"

"I wouldn't mind coming in for a nightcap." The guy, who said his name was Kansas, leaned across the seat of his old pickup and put his hand on her thigh.

"You've been very kind," Roxy said as she scooted away and opened the door. "But like I told you, I've been gone for weeks, and there's not a thing in my refrigerator."

"Your refrigerator is not what I'm interested in."

Roxy didn't want to be rude to the guy, but after hitchhiking all the way from New Roads, Louisiana, she was sick and tired of this kind of behavior from the men who offered her a ride. "I have a boyfriend," she said. "And he's the jealous type." It wasn't true, and Roxy didn't like to lie, but desperate times called for desperate measures. She'd read that someplace.

"I've driven miles out of my way," Kansas whined. "I deserve something for my time."

Roxy supposed he had a point, but she wouldn't give him what he wanted. And other than that, she had nothing to offer. On the houseboat, she'd left behind the garbage bag with what was left of the money Tommy stole—along with her mother, Rosemary. "I'll tell you what. Drop by Trudy's Beauty Boutique tomorrow, and I'll give you a free haircut." Roxy hoped she still had a job as a hairstylist at Trudy's, but she had kind of run off without notice. She hoped Trudy would forgive her and let her come back to work. She was dead-broke.

Roxy could hear him calling her all the expected vile names as she walked up the rickety steps to trailer #9 and let herself inside. She locked the door behind her, not that it would do any good. Any decent-sized man could ram the flimsy door and barge inside. But Roxy had faith he wouldn't do that. He wasn't as bad as the man who had pushed her out of his semi when she wouldn't give him a blowjob. They'd been at a truck stop just outside of Nashville, and she'd landed *splat!* on the asphalt. Her tailbone still ached from that experience, but at least the guy had thrown her backpack out after her. That was something to be grateful for.

Roxy flipped the switch next to the door, and wonder of wonders, the lights came on. She'd expected the electricity would have been turned off for nonpayment, but it hadn't. It was something else to be grateful for. It wasn't much, but it was something, and Roxy would take any crumb of happiness she could get. She had always been a happy person, but it was hard going after the events that happened on the boat.

She should never have stolen Calvin's houseboat, *Shameless*. It had seemed like a good idea at the time, though, because she just knew Tommy would pin those ten robberies that night on her. He'd told her so. Plus, she realized that her addiction to Oxy and Percocet had gotten out of control. It had started to affect her good looks, and like Rosemary always said, "Once your looks go, kid, you've lost everything." Rosemary was a perfect example of that. All her years of hard drinking and smoking caught up to her, but good. She was only forty-four, but she looked like she was twenty years older. She needed oxygen for her COPD, but she was still Rosemary, feisty and strong-willed. Roxy loved her so much. That's why she couldn't leave her behind in the trailer. That's why she'd dragged her onto the houseboat in a rubber tire, hoping against hope that Calvin wouldn't catch on and leave the Queen of Hearts drawing early.

In retrospect, perhaps her biggest mistake had been coming back to get Calvin the next morning. She'd had no intention of doing that. She was really getting the hang of driving the houseboat, and she and Rosemary were having a fine time, eating peanut butter and jelly sandwiches and drinking Mountain Dew and talking about all the new places they would see. The two of them, who hardly ever set foot outside of Liberty, would see something of the world and meet all new people. River people, Calvin had called them. He said he'd been met with nothing but kindness on his travels up and down the Mississippi.

But then the Coast Guard pulled her over just before they got to St. Louis. She'd been scared to death, sure that she'd end up in jail now, but the guy had told her to go back home. "The police officer in Liberty said you won't be in any trouble if you return the boat." Rosemary knew he was talking about the handsome new officer in town, Alan Morrison. She'd met him when Cliff Neeley threw a brick through the front window of Trudy's. He'd been nice to Cliff then, too. So she'd told the Coast Guard, "Okay, I'll return the boat."

She'd turned the boat around, and when she was sure that the Coast Guard wasn't following, she'd said to Rosemary, "I don't want to go back home. Maybe we can drive right by Liberty and make it to Louisiana. We can see New Orleans."

Rosemary had found a pack of Calvin's Marlboros and was smoking, something she wasn't supposed to do. "I don't want to go back either. Heck, we've barely gotten started." She inhaled, coughed.

"Put out the cigarette, Mom."

"I think better when I smoke." Rosemary inhaled, coughed. "Say, why don't we bring Calvin onboard with us? He would know how to fix the boat if it breaks, and the guy does have cancer."

Rosemary, too, had read the article about Calvin in the *Liberty Gazette*. Two years before, he'd been diagnosed with cancer. The cancerous cells came from his bone marrow and attached to his sinuses. He was in the hospital for a long time on a ventilator, and when he came to in hospice, he wasn't expected to live. But he did live, so he then decided to fulfill a lifelong dream of traveling the Mississippi on a houseboat.

"But he's in love with me, Mom. He's over fifty, and I'm only twenty-two. He's a nice guy, but don't you think that's kind of creepy?" Roxy felt bad talking about Calvin that way—he was a nice guy—so she added, "I think he's more your type."

"I suppose I could take one for the team," Rosemary said. "It's been a long time since I've been with a man, but I'm pretty sure I've still got it."

Roxy would never point out to her mom that, actually, she didn't have it anymore. Sitting there wreathed in smoke, Rosemary looked more like a wizened elf than a forty-four-year-old woman. "Would you really do that for me?"

"Sure thing, baby. I'll make a play for the old man."

Roxy wasn't surprised to see that a sizable crowd had gathered at the small dock in Liberty. She knew she had some degree of notoriety in town, mostly because of her fondness for hillbilly heroin. The group of tweakers Roxy hung around with didn't help her reputation either. She could see Tommy in the crowd looking at her with his zombie eyes. Roxy almost expected him to jump into the water and make his way to the boat, demanding that she give back the garbage bag of loot he had stolen from Partytime Liquors and other businesses in town.

But Calvin upstaged everyone when he dropped to his knees and proclaimed his love for her. "Roxy, will you marry me?"

Rosemary had made her arduous way to the deck of the houseboat and was true to her word. "Now, Calvin, my Roxy here is young enough to be your daughter. I'm closer to your age, honey. Why don't you come on board, and we can talk about this?"

That was all the invitation Calvin needed, and then there were three of them on the boat as they headed south. "I am going to make you fall in love with me," Calvin told Roxy, breathlessly.

"We'll see about that," she said. With Rosemary there to keep an eye on her, Roxy felt safe. She and Rosemary shared the small narrow bed, while Calvin, being a gentleman, slept in the one shabby recliner. Once or twice, when Roxy awoke in the middle of the night, she saw Calvin staring at her with such intense, unabashed longing that she wanted to crawl out of her skin. It was that creepy. But it was okay during the day, in the beginning. Rosemary played her part and flirted shamelessly with Calvin, but Calvin, it would seem, only had eyes for Roxy.

But then she got sick, and even that did not deter Calvin's devotion. He hovered over her incessantly. "You poor girl. You must be seasick. We'll stop in the next town, and I'll buy you some Pepto-Bismol and ginger ale."

Roxy, curled into a fetal position on the bed, could only moan.

While Calvin went into Hannibal to get his remedy, Rosemary asked bluntly, "Are you pregnant, Roxy? Mind you, I'm not one to judge. I was twenty-two when I had you, and sure, it threw me for a loop, but everything worked out okay in the end."

"I'm not pregnant, Mom." At least Roxy didn't think so. She hadn't slept with Tommy in six or seven weeks, but it wasn't pregnancy that concerned her during those sick, aching days. She and Rosemary had brought a lot of stuff with them on this trip, including the falling-apart quilt that Grandma had made, a shadow box of pictures from Roxy's short stint as a majorette, and all the tools of Roxy's trade: scissors and brushes and boxes of hair dye. But Roxy had neglected to bring the most important thing of all, the one thing that made her the happiest. She had forgotten to bring her stash of Oxycontin. She couldn't say this to her own mother, though. It was the one thing Roxy had ever kept hidden from her, the extent of her opioid addiction. "Like Calvin said, I have seasickness or motion sickness or something like that."

After a week or so, Roxy felt better physically but still felt overcome by a numbing lethargy. It was the strangest thing. She had always loved the Mississippi River and had spent countless hours on the banks of the river getting high or simply enjoying the peacefulness that the muddy, flowing water brought to her. But now she could see that dreaming of all the places the river could take her was much more exciting than being on an old boat, making slow progress to the next town, where Calvin would get off to tell his stories and rely upon the kindness of strangers. It wasn't glamorous at all, no matter what Calvin had said when he was interviewed for the article in the *Liberty Gazette*, it was downright boring. In essence, Calvin was no more than a freeloader who told the same stories over and over again, portraying himself as a hero who had survived cancer, a man now brave enough to follow his own dream.

Roxy liked to think of herself as a kind person, but enough was enough. "Calvin," she finally said, exasperated. "I have some money. You don't need to beg for a loaf of bread or a basket of peaches."

Calvin seemed genuinely surprised by this assessment of his intentions. "Roxy, sweetheart, people like to give me those things. It makes them feel better about themselves."

"I don't know about that, Calvin. I think they just feel sorry for you."

Before Calvin could open his mouth, Rosemary piped up. "Well, if that's the case, Calvin, would you ask the next person to give you a couple of juicy steaks? I've got a hankering for a T-bone." She, too, seemed to have grown listless and bored as one day ran into the next without distinction. For the most part, she camped out in the shabby recliner and smoked Calvin's Marlboros, hacking and wheezing. Her oxygen tank sat unused and empty in a corner, next to a rusty propeller that had no use but to take up precious space. The cabin overflowed with such useless scraps of junk. And it was starting to smell in the cabin too, a combination of unwashed bodies and old food and gasoline fumes.

"Mom, I'm going to refill your oxygen tank in the next town."

"Why bother? I always hated that thing. It made me feel like a dog tied to a fence."

"You have COPD. You need that oxygen."

"No, I don't. This sea air is clearing my lungs."

"We're on a *river*."

"Whatever." Rosemary's coughing fit became so violent that it almost knocked her out of her chair. "All better now," she said when she could catch her breath.

"Will you marry me, Roxy?"

Roxy had forgotten Calvin was even in the cabin. He repeatedly and incessantly asked her the question as if that would win her over—or wear her down. "Calvin, I am never going to marry you." When they finally reached New Orleans, Roxy would pack up Rosemary, and they would leave.

Roxy never thought she'd miss Liberty so much, but she did. She'd started to daydream about winning the Queen of Hearts drawing again. She went to that drawing every week, hoping her ticket would be pulled out of the big drum. She could see herself walking to the front of the room and selecting the envelope with the queen of hearts as if it were happening in front of her eyes. She'd begun to get the feeling that winning the jackpot might be her true destiny, not this houseboat, not Calvin's puppy dog eyes following her every move, not even New Orleans. Roxy wanted to go home; she wanted her old life. She craved her Oxy. Until then, she would try to make the best of it, but it was hard going.

"Why are we traveling so slowly?" Roxy asked Calvin one day. She thought it was a day in mid-July, but it might have been more toward the end of the month. After her illness and after the opioids were finally out of her system, the days seemed to flow seamlessly together like the river itself. On some days, the really bad ones, Calvin decided they would circle back to the town they'd just left because he wanted to say hello and "shoot the breeze" with someone he thought was a new friend. So all Roxy knew for sure on that day was that it was unbearably hot, and they weren't even going fast enough to generate any kind of breeze. It was hard to breathe in the still, thick air.

"Ah," Calvin said, "there is a very important reason for that, my dear Roxy." When she didn't act the least bit interested, Calvin said, "Shall I tell you why, my lovely girl?"

"Could I stop you?" The man loved to talk, to tell stories, any story, and as the days passed, Roxy learned to block out the sound of his voice. The guy never shut up, and it seemed to Roxy that Calvin's constant harping should have made the trip more interesting. But it hadn't. Calvin's musings on everything from the price of gas to the meaning of life rambled with no discernible direction, and this trip was still as boring as the days were long. She felt bad thinking that about Calvin. He was a decent guy—he hadn't tried to kiss her or feel her up or pounce on her once—but since they were on his boat, they were at his mercy. And at the rate they were going, it would take them at least another month to get to New Orleans.

Calvin, at the helm, smiled happily. "The Minnesota Department of Natural Resources near Red Wing conducted a study on the river from 1989 through 1992. That research showed that high-energy wakes from motorboats can greatly accelerate natural erosion. The wakes can cause the banks to erode by as much as two feet per year on the inside of a riverbend and up to fourteen feet on the outside of the riverbend over three years!"

"Amazing," Roxy said dully.

"No, my dear, it's a tragedy!" he corrected her. "I am not going to contribute to the erosion of the mighty Mississippi. That's why we travel slowly. That, and to take in all the sights along this mightiest of rivers. Did you see that bald eagle yesterday? It's a majestic bird, the bald eagle."

Roxy hadn't paid much attention to the birds during her stint on the houseboat, and it wasn't the bald eagle she thought about now as she walked toward Trudy's Beauty Boutique to beg for her old job back. It was the erosion she thought about as she walked past lawns that had been green and lush when she left but were now brown and dry. The spring flowers had withered and now hung limply. She'd always thought of Liberty as a pretty little town, but now it looked weatherbeaten and a little sad. The town might have been eroding all around her for quite a while, but she'd never noticed because she was almost always high. When people used to complain to her about the dog days of summer, Roxy honestly hadn't known what they meant. But now she got it. Summer eroded all around her, and it wasn't pretty.

Last night, she scoured the trailer for her stash of Oxy. She knew she shouldn't take any drugs. She'd been clean for a while now, but she wanted to have those pills in her possession *just in case*. After all, she had just survived a traumatic period in her life. Didn't she deserve a little security, maybe a tiny bit of happiness? And maybe that tiny spark of happiness would set her back on the right track. Rosemary had always called Roxy her "ray of sunshine." And Roxy desperately wanted to be that person again, even if she didn't know if it was still possible, not after what happened. But she frantically searched the messy trailer—they'd left in such a hurry—sure that she had a half-full vial of pills somewhere. But it wasn't in the medicine cabinet, under her mattress, or in the back of the silverware drawer, all her usual hiding spots.

Her precious pills were nowhere to be found. It was only after Roxy checked underneath every couch cushion, in every drawer, in the dirty laundry hamper, and in the sink crammed with crusty dishes, that she realized the screen on Rosemary's bedroom window was missing. Someone must have come into the trailer and stolen her pills. And she knew the culprit: Tommy. It had to be Tommy. He probably thought it would be payback because she had left town with his stolen money. But she didn't dare confront Tommy about the theft. He was probably so far gone by now that there was no telling what he would do. A meth head zombie could be so unpredictable.

Despite her exhaustion and despite finding a lone Budweiser in the refrigerator, Roxy spent a restless night on the airbed in the closet she called a bedroom. She couldn't bear the thought of climbing into the tangled sheets of Rosemary's more comfortable bed. She didn't want to smell the cheap perfume Rosemary bought at Family Dollar. Nor did Roxy want to see the pictures of her and her mother that Rosemary had crammed on her nightstand and taped on all the walls. Roxy knew it would be her undoing, so she closed the door to Rosemary's room. Maybe in a day or two, she could stand to go back in there. Maybe not.

Darlene Sutton, her neighbor, seemed happy to see her when Roxy went over early in the morning to use her phone. It was another thing Roxy no longer had, her phone. Calvin said it was probably on the boat somewhere, but Roxy knew that wasn't true. She suspected that Calvin, one night when she finally fell asleep, had taken the phone out of her backpack and thrown it overboard. "You're always looking at that thing," he'd told her more than once. "Look around you. There's so much to see. Smell the roses, dear Roxy." All Roxy saw around her was muddy water and weedy, eroding river banks. No roses.

"You must have had such an exciting adventure. I have to say, you were the talk of the town for a while there," Darlene said as she handed over her phone. "I want to hear all about it."

Darlene liked to talk, which might be a problem. "I'm kind of in a hurry right now, Darlene. Maybe later?" Darlene was kind, but Roxy had no intention of returning later.

"How's Rosemary?"

"She's sleeping." It was a kind of truth.

"The poor thing must be tuckered out."

"You could say that." Roxy stood uneasily. She didn't want Darlene to hear her call old Doc Jenkins and beg for a prescription for Oxy for Rosemary. Since Rosemary hurt her back in a work-related accident at the Cake Mix Factory years ago, Roxy had been refilling the prescription for herself.

"Go on. Make your call." Darlene crossed her arms.

"I think I left something on the stove. I'll be right back." The call didn't take long. The receptionist, a mean girl who Roxy had gone to school with, said Doc Jenkins was on vacation, and no, no one else in the office could write a prescription at this time.

Roxy felt panicked enough at this turn of events—what was she going to do now?—but when she returned the phone to Darlene, her one remaining hope, a long shot of daunting odds, splintered. "Did you hear that Mandy Tanner won the 1.5 million Queen of Hearts jackpot? It couldn't have happened to a nicer person, but some people have all the luck, you know?"

"I hadn't heard." Roxy's voice was faint. On the houseboat, she'd begun to believe winning that jackpot was her true destiny; it was the daydream that kept her going. Perseverance had to count for something, didn't it? She had gone to that drawing every single week. And then she stole *Shameless*, and every opportunity for happiness dropped away, one by one.

"Why, Roxy, you look like the sky has fallen! Come on, where's that pretty smile of yours?"

Roxy tried a wobbly smile. "Better?"

"You bet. Aren't you glad to be home?"

"There's no place like Liberty."

Roxy didn't even have money to buy gas for her ancient VW Beetle, and now her stomach rumbled as she opened the door to Trudy's Beauty Boutique. It was still very early, and mercifully, Trudy was the only person in the salon. Roxy knew she liked to get there first to do inventory and prepare for the day.

"I see you got your window fixed." Roxy decided to be factual before she begged. It seemed like a lifetime ago that Cliff Neeley threw a brick through the front window. Roxy wondered if Cliff was back from the mental institution in Anna. She wondered if he had drugs. Surely, a schizophrenic took drugs of some kind.

"When did you get back?" Trudy's voice didn't sound overly friendly.

"Last night." Roxy's eyes immediately went to her old station and saw it was stocked with scissors, combs, mousse, gel, a curling iron, and a blow dryer. A picture of a little blonde girl taped to the mirror also proclaimed transferred ownership. A new person had marked Roxy's old territory.

Trudy noticed. "I had to hire someone else, Roxy. You left without notice, and I didn't know if you were coming back."

"I understand." Not only did Roxy's smile wobble precariously, but her voice did, too.

"Listen, Roxy, you became unreliable, and I can't afford to have a stylist who's using." Trudy's voice softened.

"I'm not using. I've been clean for a while now."

"How was I supposed to know that, honey? You took off on that boat, and no one thought you'd come back… Oh, now, Roxy, don't cry."

"I'm not crying," Roxy said as a tear dripped off the end of her nose. Another hope dashed, and Roxy couldn't say she was too surprised by this. Since she had the unfortunate idea to steal that houseboat, it was the way things were going.

"Is everything okay?" Trudy came closer, assessing. "You don't look like your normal self."

"I'm not high." Dear Lord, Roxy wished she were. She'd take anything, maybe even meth, which she'd sworn to Rosemary that she would never take, to make the sadness disappear, to make the world look bright and shiny again.

"That's not what I mean." Trudy took Roxy's chin in her hand and turned her face toward the light. "Is that a bruise on your cheek?"

Roxy thought she'd done a decent job with her makeup this morning, but in the light of the shop, she could see how unevenly she'd applied it, the un-blended edge of too-dark foundation on her jawline. It was embarrassing. She was supposed to be a professional when it came to hair and makeup.

"When was the last time you ate?"

Roxy shrugged. She wanted to crawl into Trudy's arms, but she didn't dare. She might not ever leave.

"I think I have a twenty in my purse."

"No, thank you, Trudy." Roxy had never begged, never asked for a handout, not even on the boat with Calvin, who thought that's what people were supposed to do. And she didn't want to take Trudy's money now. It was kind of funny if Roxy stopped to think about it. She'd always thought people hit rock bottom when they were on drugs, not when they quit.

Trudy gave Roxy that assessing look again. "Now, you listen to me, Roxy. I know a girl in trouble when I see one." When Roxy started to protest, Trudy shook her head firmly. "Believe me. I've been there. Did I ever tell you about the time I spent in Chicago when I was trying to make a go of it as a singer?"

"You did what?" Roxy had always thought of Trudy as the most dependable yet unexciting person she had ever met. She didn't mean it in a bad way, of course, but Trudy had never seemed like an adventurous sort to her. It just proved that you couldn't judge a book by its cover. Roxy had read that somewhere, and now it almost made sense.

"Come on, Roxy. I have some donuts in the back I picked up from Dave's Market this morning. I'll tell you all about my adventure, and then you can tell me about yours." She took Roxy by the elbow, steering her toward the back room of the salon where Roxy could smell the delicious aroma of coffee brewing. "Then I think we can come up with a plan. I have an idea."

Tucker was beside himself with excitement over his newest scheme to bring the town of Liberty together. If a parade for a well-liked townswoman who had just become a millionaire wouldn't do the trick—and he was still scratching his head over that one—a memorial for a prominent citizen would certainly give the people of his town something to commemorate. After all, it was a known fact that two singular events in life brought families and friends together the most: weddings and funerals. Since no one of any note was getting married that August in Liberty, a funeral it would have to be. And Tucker planned to make it grand. After he held the service—and no church in town would be big enough for that—maybe he could organize a funeral procession as they did in New Orleans, complete with a jazz band and spectators joining in and forming a second line. Oh, Tucker had big plans, all right. Big plans.

He didn't waste any time. On the morning that he and Linda came up with this wonderful idea, he called his old buddy Don, the principal of Liberty High, and reserved the high school gym for the event, which would be held the next Saturday. Then he'd gotten on his computer and designed a flyer, which was pretty good if he did say so himself. Tucker didn't have an actual picture of the drunken poet, so he used one he found of Walt Whitman on the internet, figuring that no one in town would know the difference. Besides, the picture of Whitman was of a much spiffier man than McHenry, who had always looked, despite his bravado when he recited his verses, a little on the downtrodden, shaggy side. Satisfied, Tucker went to his cubbyhole of an office in the town hall and made copies. Now he needed to distribute them all over town.

But before he did that, Tucker decided he would put an announcement in the *Liberty Gazette,* just to cover all the bases. If the good people of Liberty, his loyal constituents, did not happen to patronize a local business during the next week—and that would be a shame, in Tucker's opinion—they would surely read about it in the paper. Rather than make a phone call, Tucker decided to go in person to the newspaper office located just off Main Street. And that was Tucker's first inkling that he might have jumped the gun.

"Why are you doing this?" Brad Taylor, the young man who had written the drunken poet's obituary that was not quite an obituary said. "Mitchell would not have wanted this kind of attention. He was a quiet man who liked to read his books on Transcendentalism—when he wasn't drinking, I mean." Brad was still young enough to blush.

"Nonsense. Everyone wants to go out with a bang. Everyone wants to have a large crowd at his funeral." At least Tucker did. That's why he worked so hard at his non-paying job as mayor. Before being elected, he had only been the owner of a lowly lawn mower repair business. Now he was somebody in this town. He hoped to have the grandest funeral that Liberty had ever seen when his time came.

"Not Mitchell," Brad said firmly. "He was a quiet guy who only wanted to be left alone. We should respect that, Tucker."

"If you knew him so well, you should be the one to give the eulogy." Tucker would not show his irritation to a loyal constituent, but he was getting a little miffed. Some people just didn't get it.

"No, thank you, Tucker. I didn't know him well enough."

"I thought you guys were friends or something."

"Not really."

"Okay, then," Tucker tried to remember Linda's exact words from that morning. "How about all those letters to his unrequited love? Maybe that woman could give the eulogy if you're so dead set against it."

"I don't think that would be appropriate either."

"Why the hell not?" Tucker wanted to pick up the scrawny little guy by the scruff of his neck and give him a good shake. But as mayor, he could not do that.

"I refuse to divulge my sources, Tucker."

"What kind of bullshit is that?"

"It's called reporter's privilege."

"I don't care what it's called, Brad. I just want to know why the unrequited love lady won't give the drunk guy's eulogy."

"Maybe that's your answer right there, Tucker." Brad snatched the typed memorial announcement from Tucker's hand. "But I'll run this for you anyway. It'll be in Thursday's edition."

"Thanks a lot, buddy." But then Tucker shook Brad's hand to show there were no hard feelings. "I'm sure I can find someone else in town who would be *honored* to give the drunken poet's eulogy."

"Good luck with that." And Brad turned and went back into his office, which was even smaller than Tucker's.

It bothered Tucker that the little twerp got the last word, but he would not let that exchange get him down. This public memorial service was a good idea; he could feel it in his bones. And everyone in town knew Brad Taylor had a stick up his butt. He took his job so seriously that you would have thought he wrote for the *New York Times* instead of a small-town newspaper that only published once a week.

Tucker's next stop was at the only florist in town, The Garden Spot, owned by Carrie Young. A couple of years older than Tucker, she had been a looker in high school, but you would never know it now. When they reached their twenties and thirties, some people seemed to grow outward in an ever-expanding circle. Carrie was one of them. But Tucker liked Carrie, and they had a minor flirtation thing going on the rare occasions he came into her shop. "Hey, sexy," he said to her when he walked in.

"Hey, handsome."

"What's a gorgeous woman like you doing in a place like this?" Tucker leaned over the counter.

"For starters, I own the place, as you well know." Evidently, Carrie wasn't in a flirting mood today. "What's the occasion—birthday, anniversary, apology?"

Tucker lifted his frame from the counter. He'd hoped to pave the way to his request, but Carrie wasn't in the mood. "None of the above. Here." He handed her a flyer. "Would you put this in your window?"

Carrie glanced down at the picture but didn't stop putting ferns into a multicolored arrangement in a vase on the counter. "Who's Mitchell McHenry?"

Tucker hadn't considered this. All the bar patrons in the seven taverns in Liberty knew the guy, but the people who didn't frequent those establishments might not. "The drunken poet. He's the one who recites poems in the bars when he's had a few."

Carrie sniffed. "I guess that's why I didn't recognize him."

Tucker remembered, too late, that Carrie was born-again a few years back, but he plunged ahead anyway. "Let me tell you about Mitchell McHenry. He might have been a drunk, but that doesn't necessarily mean he wasn't a good person. Who are we to judge, right, Carrie?" Tucker could see he had her attention now, and he shifted into high gear. "I mean, the poor man was probably sad and lonely, a lost soul. As far as anyone knows, he had no living relatives. The poor, poor man. Can you imagine? And then he dies, destitute and alone."

Carrie glanced at the flyer again. "It says here that he was a prominent fixture in this town. Doesn't that mean people knew him?"

She wasn't making his pitch easy. "A prominent *fixture*, as in, he was *around*."

Carrie rolled her eyes. "That describes a lot of people in this town." She inserted the last fern into the arrangement. "So okay, I'll post the flyer."

"That's really pretty." Tucker nodded toward the arrangement. "I'll take forty of those." At Carrie's wide-eyed stare, he hurried on. "I'm sure you, being a good Christian and all, would love to donate those to the memorial service, a service that will bring this town together to honor one of its own."

"No."

Tucker cupped his hand around his ear. "What was that?"

"I said, *no*. I'm not donating forty expensive arrangements of out-of-season flowers to a drunk man's funeral. However, I would be happy to take cash or a credit card for the purchase."

"All right. How about if you donate ten?" Tucker considered himself to be a reasonable man. If ten was all he could get, he'd take it.

"Absolutely not, over my dead body, you must be crazy. I'm not donating anything."

Tucker was out of ammunition. "Fine. I'll pay for them."

"Now we're talking." Carrie reached for a pen and a pad of paper. "You want ten arrangements, just like this."

Tucker headed toward the door. "No, I want forty. Bill them to the town," he called over his shoulder. He would worry about what he had just done to the town's meager resources later.

The cost of the flowers would be exorbitant. And added to that would be the cost of the runner Tucker wanted to put down in the center of the gym, the banners along the wall (after he took down all the Liberty Falcon ones), and the jazz band he had already hired from St. Louis to march down the street New Orleans-style. And then there was something else he hadn't considered. Of course, the drunken poet didn't have a burial spot in the Liberty Cemetery on the south side of town. But now that he had a band already hired with nonexistent town money, that band needed a final destination. Tucker made another stop at Carruthers Funeral home, where Mitchell McHenry's ashes still resided, unclaimed, and took care of that. And then old man Carruthers talked him into buying an ornate brass urn, (further reinforcing Tucker's belief that funeral homes preyed on the grief-stricken). So now the drunken poet would be buried in a fancy urn in a plot the size of a shoebox in his adopted hometown.

But Tucker had an ace up his sleeve. He would go to the source—i.e., the patrons of the bars the drunken poet had frequented, which was all of them. Surely, his fellow drinkers, his comrades in arms, would shell out a few bucks for the man who had entertained them with the poetry of Walt Whitman for all those years. Surely, those fellow imbibers would be happy to contribute to the old man's memorial and final resting spot. Mitchell McHenry was one of their own. All Tucker had to do was make sure they were drunk enough.

He waited until the good people, his constituents, at Mr. Lucky's felt no pain at ten o'clock on Tuesday evening. Tucker was also feeling pretty darn good by that point himself. He loved to gab and joke around with all the guys at the bar, and as usual, he'd been the recipient of four or five free beers. He felt so good, in fact, that he had almost forgotten his purpose. No one in the place had mentioned the drunken poet once. Rather than sitting empty out of respect, his usual barstool now contained the overflowing butt of Stoney Hiney, who all the guys called Hiney, naturally.

But Tucker eventually remembered his mission and slid from his own barstool and made his way over to Hiney. He tapped him on the shoulder. "Hey, buddy, could you get up for a second? I need to make an announcement."

"I ain't leaving this stool. I'm going to sit here until I'm good and drunk. I got fired from American Aluminum today. I deserve to get drunk."

Tucker hadn't heard the news that American Aluminum was laying off employees. It was one more blow to Liberty and further reason why the town needed an opportunity to support one another. He felt bad for the guy, he truly did, but this town needed a beacon of light more than Hiney needed another beer. "Come on, Hiney, I need to make an announcement, and it has to be from this stool. It's the drunken poet's stool."

"Not anymore. That old drunk is dead."

"Dead but not forgotten."

"Yeah, right." Hiney pressed the beer bottle to his lips. He looked like a blowfish. "Dead is dead."

Since the drunken poet's barstool wasn't an option, Tucker decided he had only one course of action left. He would jump up on the bar itself to plead his case. The bar was crowded on this Tuesday night because the Cardinals were playing the Cubs. It was a rivalry so fierce that it had inspired numerous fights in this town, and all eyes were riveted to the TV hanging above the bar. However, jumping onto the bar was not an easy task. Tucker wasn't as agile as he used to be, and the beers he drank were not helping his cause. He ended up crawling onto the bar and ungracefully wobbling to an upright position. "Gentlemen, may I have your attention?"

"What in the hell are you doing, Tucker? Am I going to have to cut you off?"

Lenny, the bartender, was a burly guy, but he looked so much smaller from Tucker's lofty vantage point. Tucker briefly wondered if he should ask Lenny to give the drunken poet's eulogy. He was the one who had found him, after all. It was an excellent idea.

"Get off the bar, Tucker. You're blocking the TV," Ray Pitt said.

"I have an announcement to make. Well, it's actually more of a request."

"Get off the damn bar, or I'll knock you off."

"In a minute, Ray." Tucker thought how easy it would be to kick Ray in the face, but that wouldn't be very mayoral of him. And he always had to take into consideration the next election. He needed every vote he could get, even one from the obnoxious Ray Pitt.

Everyone in the bar started to clamor now—"get off, get down, the Cardinals are up to bat"—and Tucker knew he didn't have much time. "Gentlemen, as you know, our dear friend Mitchell McHenry has departed this earth. It is only fitting that we, the people of Liberty, honor him in the fashion he deserves. To that end, I am asking you for donations to—"

The next thing he knew, Tucker was facedown on the bar. He'd landed with a jarring thud, and beer bottles rolled all around him. It took him a second, perhaps two, to realize what had just happened. That obnoxious Ray Pitt had pulled his leg right out from under him. But that wasn't the worst part. The worst part was that people were *laughing* at him, laughing loud and hard. He could not find a shred of dignity in his present circumstances. He was the mayor of this town, a position that should be respected, but now he was facedown on a sticky bar, and people were poking at him, *poking*. Word about this travesty would soon be all over town, and he would be the butt of jokes for weeks, maybe months to come. He could not bear it.

The tavern door banged open, and Tucker could hear a voice. It sounded like one of the Ehlers clan, saying, "Did you hear? There was a fire at the trailer park."

"Good. Somebody finally burned the white trash in this town," Ray Pitt said meanly.

Tucker had managed to get in a sitting position. "Shut up, Ray."

"You've got a beer nut smashed on your forehead," Ray said, taking a swig of beer.

"No, no," the Ehlers boy said. "It's just one trailer, the one that belongs to Roxy Morton. She's back in town, but she wasn't home. They say she lost everything."

"That poor girl," someone said.

"And the best part is," the Ehlers boy waited a beat for his *coup de grâce*, "they arrested Tommy Newton. I mean, he was standing right there with a can of gasoline in his hands, probably strung out on meth, as usual."

"That lowlife finally got what he deserves." Ray took a swig of beer, and then in a loud voice, said, "Say, Tucker, isn't that little creep your nephew? I don't think you're going to get him out of this one."

"It's just a summer cold."

It was not a summer cold. Roxy had helplessly watched as Rosemary grew grayer by the day, as she continued, despite Roxy's objections and admonishments, to smoke and drink in the shabby recliner. Roxy could no longer say that she would refill the oxygen tank at the next town because the tank had disappeared. Roxy suspected that Rosemary, with the help of Calvin, had thrown it overboard. They'd become as thick as thieves, those two, whiling away the hours smoking and drinking, and in Rosemary's case, staring into the distance with glassy eyes, and in Calvin's, talking about the woman in Louisiana who baked him pies.

On this day, Rosemary looked even worse than usual. Her eyes were yellow and jaundiced, her breathing shallow and labored. Roxy couldn't stand it one second longer. "Mom, do you have a death wish or something?"

"Doesn't everyone?" Rosemary's fingers, too, were yellow, stained from the thousands of cigarettes she'd smoked on this boat ride to hell.

Roxy and Rosemary should never have gotten on this houseboat. It had changed them both for the worse, and the longer they stayed on the boat, the more the power of the river eroded their vitality and motivation. Both of them had become shells of who they used to be, and Roxy didn't understand how that could have happened. Yet she seemed incapable of staving off the inevitable.

"We're getting off the boat," she said. "Come on, Mom. I'm taking you to the hospital."

They were docked at New Roads, Louisiana, but neither had ventured off this cursed boat. It was as if they had both become victims of Stockholm syndrome, and Roxy wasn't sure who their captor was—Calvin or the Mississippi. Roxy took Rosemary's hands and tried to pull her up, but Rosemary, nothing but skin and bones now, turned to dead weight. "Fine. I'll carry you."

"Now hold on a second, my dear Roxy. There is nothing wrong with Rosemary. Like she said, it's just a summer cold."

"No, it isn't." Roxy put her arms around Rosemary. "Put your arm over my shoulders, Mom, and I'll pick you up." Then she whispered, urgently, "Please, Mom. We have to get off this boat." When Rosemary didn't respond, Roxy did it for her. Holding Rosemary firmly, Roxy lifted.

"You have always been a good girl, Roxy. I love you."

"I love you, too." Rosemary was more unwieldy in her arms than heavy, but Roxy was not a very big girl either, and it still wouldn't be easy to carry her into town and find a hospital. She needed help. "Calvin, can you give me a hand here?"

"This is not a good idea, my dear Roxy." Calvin wrung his hands. He, too, with his bloodshot eyes and sallow skin, looked the worse for wear since they began this ill-fated trip. "I want people I meet to think this boat is a bearer of good tidings."

"Give me a break, Calvin." It wasn't the first time Roxy thought Calvin had lost touch with reality. She dripped with sweat now, and so did Rosemary, which made her slippery. And they hadn't even made it out of the cabin yet.

"Besides, it's starting to rain." A not-too-distant crack of lightning followed by the loud boom of thunder accentuated his point.

In her determination to get Rosemary off the boat, Roxy hadn't even noticed that the steady drops of rain had grown more determined, incessant. It was the kind of sudden, torrential storm that used to terrify her as a child. Rosemary would always make a fort out of blankets and pop some corn, and she would sit with Roxy in the makeshift fort and tell her stories, making her feel safe and secure until the storm passed.

"Please, Calvin." Roxy hated to ask anyone for anything, but she would make an exception for her mother. She needed help.

"Only if you marry me."

"Calvin, I am never going to marry you."

"Not even for the sake of your mother?"

Roxy couldn't believe it. "Are you blackmailing me?"

"I will help you if you marry me."

Calvin was barely taller than Roxy, but right then, he looked crazed and a little sinister. During the trip, he'd gotten rid of her and Rosemary's cell phones, and most of the time, he dissuaded them from leaving the boat in the towns where they docked unless he accompanied them. "There's nothing in this town worth seeing," he would say, or "It's too hot for you two ladies to be out and about." He also claimed that the radio on the boat was broken. "We don't need anyone's help," he would say. "I know how to take care of *Shameless*." Roxy realized what he'd done now; he'd isolated them to make them totally dependent upon him. Roxy didn't know whether it had been intentional on Calvin's part, but it didn't matter now. For some reason, she and Rosemary had allowed it to happen. She and Rosemary had passively played Calvin's game. No more.

Without another word to Calvin, Roxy slowly made her way to the narrow side deck. She shifted Rosemary in her arms, but her mother didn't make a sound. Her eyes were closed, but she was still breathing. Roxy could feel the shallow rise and fall of her chest against her own. Instinctively, Roxy knew she didn't have much time. She must hurry.

As soon as Roxy stepped out of the cabin and onto the deck, she and her mother were drenched. The pelting rain seemed to be coming from every direction, and the wind, too, was relentless in its attack. Roxy had never been in a hurricane, but she thought she might be in one now. The old deck's wooden boards were as slick as ice, and the entire boat heaved on the churning water of the river. She wanted to grab onto the railing to steady herself, but that was impossible. She held Rosemary in her arms.

And then she didn't. It happened so fast that Roxy would never be sure if the angry river rocked the boat violently and pushed her against the railing, or if she stumbled on her own. Or if Calvin had pushed her. He stood there beside her now, and she was hanging over the railing, her arms empty, her mother dropped into the Mississippi and quickly swallowed.

"She can't swim!" she screamed above the roar. She grabbed Calvin by his t-shirt and yelled into this face. "We have to do something!"

"Roxy, she's gone!" He yelled back, looking stricken and old, his thin hair plastered to his skull. "Honey—"

But Roxy didn't waste another second. She pushed him away, climbed onto the railing, and jumped into the water. This could not be how it would all end for Rosemary, who was terrified of water. Yet she had come onto this horrible boat because of Roxy. Roxy had told her that they would see the world, that this would be their big adventure. So because of Roxy, her mother had agreed.

"We're taking a vacation on a houseboat," Roxy had said firmly on the night she planned to steal Calvin Phillips' houseboat.

Rosemary nodded. "Damn right, we are."

And now Rosemary was somewhere in the Mississippi, and it was all Roxy's fault.

Roxy found her, caught in the anchor chain, and after repeated attempts, diving and surfacing, diving and surfacing, untangled her by feel rather than sight. When she bobbed to the surface for the final time with her arm around Rosemary, Roxy dragged her to the ladder on the side of the boat. Calvin still stood on the deck, wringing his hands. But he did help get Rosemary onto the boat and then onto the narrow bed in the cabin.

Roxy stood panting as she looked at Rosemary's lifeless form on the bed. She'd tried to give her mother CPR for over an hour before she would admit to herself that Rosemary was truly gone. And now, the first time in her life, she felt utterly alone and terrified. Her mother had always been there for her, in her own peculiar way. For the most part, she had sheltered Roxy from the drunk and violent men she used to bring home. On the nights when she was too drunk to protect her daughter, she did feel bad about it. She would take Roxy to a movie and let her buy popcorn and a soda and even a candy bar. According to so-called normal standards, Rosemary might not have been the best mother in the world, but to Roxy, she had been perfect.

"Marry me, Roxy. I'll take care of you now."

"Calvin, I am never going to marry you," Roxy said listlessly, suddenly exhausted and numb. She could say so many nasty things to Calvin, but she had never been that kind of person, and out of grief, she didn't want to start now. And really, this wasn't his fault. She was the one who had stolen his houseboat. She was the one responsible for this terrible turn of events. She would suffer for the rest of her life because of this. And she deserved it.

She gave Rosemary a sponge bath and combed her hair. She applied her mom's makeup like she used to do before Rosemary went to St. Joe's to play bingo on Saturday nights. Her mother used to feel so good about herself on those nights. Then she gave Rosemary a final kiss on her cold cheek. "You look like a million bucks, Mom."

Then Roxy grabbed her backpack, got off the boat without looking back, and started walking towards Liberty.

"Tucker, I know you've put a lot of work into this memorial service for the drunken poet, but I think you need to cancel it." Linda still sat at the kitchen table in her gardening clothes, drinking iced tea, and hadn't made a move to change into her black dress. The memorial service started in an hour.

"I won't do it." And the fact of the matter was that he couldn't. Banners proclaiming the drunken poet's importance to Liberty already hung on the gym walls, and the expensive flower arrangements—Tucker had almost had a heart attack when he saw what Carrie Young charged for those—lined the embroidered white runner. And the ornamental urn sat on a tall table next to a picture of Mitchell McHenry, aka Walt Whitman. Except for the urn and Walt Whitman's picture, the place looked like many weddings he had attended at the American Legion. Oh, and he couldn't forget about the jazz band from St. Louis. He'd heard they arrived and had set up in the bandstand in the town square. There was no going back now.

He was already dressed in his one good black suit, a red carnation in his lapel. "If I remember correctly, Linda, you thought this was a good idea just the other day."

"I know, I know. But who would have thought that Trudy would organize a Poker Run to benefit poor Roxy Morton? I mean, it is a sadder story than the drunken poet's. The girl is truly down on her luck. She lost her mother on that houseboat, and then your nephew burned down her trailer, and she lost everything." Linda still made no move to change her clothes.

That blasted Trudy. Why did she have to organize a Poker Run on the very day he had planned the drunken poet's funeral? Tucker was still reeling from that blow. People in this town seemed to have forgotten that Roxy Morton was an opioid addict who hung around with the meth heads down by the river, including his damn, no-account nephew. His sister Tina was furious with Tucker because he refused to bail out the loser one more time. He couldn't if he wanted to save any remnant of his reputation in Liberty. During the last week, his prospects of being re-elected mayor had eroded daily, what with his nephew's scandal and the humiliating incident in the bar and the lack of support for the drunken poet's memorial service. Who would have thought that the people of Liberty would consider it a waste of money to honor one of their own? Where was their civic pride?

"Honey," Linda said gently, and Linda never said anything gently, "maybe it's time to admit defeat."

"Never! A prominent figure in this town needs to be recognized!"

"A prominent *fixture.*"

"Whatever. People in this town have no respect for the dead."

"Of course they do. But perhaps people in this town feel it's more worthwhile to spend time and money on a young girl who desperately needs help."

"I'm not giving up." Tucker adjusted his tie and collar. He'd forgotten how unbearably hot his wool suit was in the summer. "People could go to both events."

"They both start at the same time," Linda pointed out.

"It would be nice to have your support." Right now, Tucker would be grateful to have support from *anybody,* but that wasn't the way things were going. "Please get dressed, Linda."

"You go on ahead, and I'll meet you there." Linda still made no move toward the bedroom. She reached for the pitcher of iced tea and poured herself another glass.

"It's going to look really bad if my wife doesn't show up."

"No one's going to show up, Tucker," Linda said quietly.

"Sure they will," Tucker insisted stubbornly. But he began to doubt himself. It was a new sensation, and he didn't like it one bit.

"The word around town is that you've been using the town's money to pay for the memorial service. People aren't happy about it, Tucker."

Tucker gaped at her. Where had she heard that? And then he knew. Genevieve Bradley, the town treasurer, was a blabbermouth if there ever was one. She'd looked at him funny yesterday when he went into his cubbyhole of an office. "I'm going to pay it back."

"I think it's called embezzlement."

"It's called *borrowing*! And I'm going to pay it back!" Tucker was sweating profusely now. If the good people of Liberty, his constituents, now thought he was a thief… Well, he was up shit's creek without a paddle. He would never regain the people's trust or his reputation. All he'd wanted was to do something nice for a lonely man, and this was how the town repaid him? He felt like a man condemned before he'd had a fair trial.

"Cancel the service, Tucker."

Tucker didn't bother to answer her. He went out the back door, slamming it shut behind him, but even that gave him no satisfaction. People in Liberty did not understand that he had planned this memorial service for the good of the *entire town*. The drunken poet's funeral was supposed to display the people's goodwill and respect for one another, and he would still give the drunken poet the send-off he deserved, even if he was the only person there. He'd gone this far, and he couldn't go back.

Tucker was not the only person at the service. He'd had to walk to the gym in the oppressive heat because he discovered he had a flat tire when he went out to his car. Four of them. On closer inspection, Tucker saw that the tires had been slashed. This, he knew, was only a portent of things to come. Sure, it might have been a teenage prank, but Tucker couldn't convince himself that this was the case. Only a week ago, he'd been well-liked by the town, popular, and now people slashed his tires and threatened him. Tucker had always considered himself to be an upbeat type of guy, but the thought that people now disliked him depressed him greatly. After this funeral was over, he would have to think of some way to get back into the town's good graces. If Tucker had to sell his lawn mower repair business, he would do it. Of course, then he would be just another one of the unemployed. He walked faster, sweating. He'd think of all that later.

Groups of motorcyclists roared past him, with groups of bicyclists trailing behind. They were all participating in the blasted Poker Run for the opioid-addicted, hapless Roxy Morton, traveling from bar to bar, collecting cards to make a poker hand. Under normal circumstances, Tucker would have thought it was a commendable idea, especially if he'd thought of it himself. But not now. It was Roxy's Poker Run that had ruined his memorial for the drunken poet. The citizens' attention had been easily diverted by a silly game. He supposed he shouldn't have been surprised. Look how crazy everyone had gotten when the Queen of Hearts jackpot rose above a million dollars. They were fickle, all of them.

Tucker had worked himself into a righteous rage, mostly directed at Roxy Morton, by the time he arrived at the gym. He'd taken off his suit jacket, and now his white shirt clung to his wet body like a second skin. He was late. He'd prepared himself for an empty gym, thanks to his pessimistic wife, so he was surprised and insanely gratified when he saw a small figure sitting in the front row. As he grew closer, he could see it was Roxy Morton, dressed in shorts and a t-shirt, head bowed as if in prayer.

He took the seat beside her. "What are you doing here? Aren't you supposed to be at your Poker Run?" Tucker had never been this close to the girl before and was surprised to see how young she looked, how pretty, with her blonde hair gathered into a bun at the nape of her neck. When she raised her clear green eyes to look at him, he had to admit that she didn't look like an addict, at least not now. What she looked like was an incredibly sad young woman.

"I'd rather be here."

"Did you know Mitchell McHenry?"

"No. I mean, I saw him around town sometimes." Roxy trained her eyes on the urn. "I once wondered if he was my father."

"Seriously? I didn't think the drunken poet had any relatives in town."

Roxy gave a small smile. "He probably wasn't, though. You see, my mom never told me who my father was. Not that it matters now. She died recently. Drowned." A sob escaped from Roxy's small frame. "And it's all my fault."

Before Tucker realized what she was doing, Roxy had buried her face in his wet shirt and was sobbing in earnest. Unused to such a blatant display of emotion, Tucker didn't know what to do. "There, there." He gingerly patted her on the back. "I'm sure it wasn't your fault."

"It was!" Tucker could feel her lips moving on his shoulder. "I was trying to get her off the boat, and I slipped or something and dropped her into the water."

"I'm sure you didn't mean to do that." Tucker didn't know if what she said was true or not, but he did know that what Roxy felt was real. The poor girl was distraught. She had suffered some kind of tragedy, and her grief was so palpable that it seemed like another presence in the large, empty gym. He reached into his suit jacket for a soggy handkerchief and let her cry.

When at last she composed herself and straightened up, wiping at her tears, she said, "Is it all right if I pretend that this service is for Rosemary, too?"

"We don't have to pretend. We'll make this a memorial for both of them." And Tucker knew with certainty that this was a good idea. He had planned a memorial service for the drunken poet, a forgotten, lonely man, but perhaps Roxy's mother, too, had been a forgotten, lonely soul. And perhaps he had misjudged Roxy harshly and unfairly, just as the people in this town were now doing to him. Tucker hated to admit defeat, ever, but maybe, just maybe, he had been wrong about a few things here and there.

He patted Roxy's hand, truly grateful that at least she, out of all the town's citizens, seemed to understand his need to commemorate a man who hadn't amounted to much by ordinary standards but still *mattered,* nonetheless. So he gave his grandiose eulogy for Mitchell McHenry, which paled in comparison to Roxy's short, eloquent tribute to her mother: "She might not have been perfect, but she tried her best. I will always love her."

When the joint service ended, Tucker, almost shyly, told Roxy that he had hired a New Orleans-style jazz band to lead a procession to the cemetery. "We're probably going to be the only two people marching, though."

"Rosemary and I always wanted to go to New Orleans. That's where we were headed on the boat." Roxy's eyes shone. "I think it's perfect."

So the two of them followed the jazz band to the cemetery and laid the drunken poet to rest. Roxy tentatively took Tucker's hand, and he let her. "I'm always going to think of Rosemary as being here, too. Now neither one of them will be alone."

Just beyond the cemetery, the Mississippi flowed past, and Roxy gazed longingly at it. Tucker, misunderstanding her gaze, asked quickly, "You're not thinking of doing anything foolish, are you?" If what Roxy had told him was true, he was afraid of what she might be thinking. Unlike the trivial, stupid mistakes he had made out of pride more than anything else, Roxy had to learn to live with genuine tragedy.

"No." She turned to him. "Are you?"

Tucker knew what she meant and shook his head. "No, not anymore."

Roxy turned her gaze back to the river to where a small boat sped by. "Did you know that research showed that high energy wakes from motorboats can greatly accelerate natural erosion along the Mississippi?"

"That makes perfect sense," Tucker said, nodding. It explained so much.

LABOR OF LOVE

"This is all the progress you've made?" Jillian asked as she walked through the small, cluttered rooms of the not-so-grand Colonial on Waverly Way. "I mean, you've been here for something like five weeks, and there's still crap everywhere."

"I've been here for seven weeks, Jillian, and believe me, we've made a lot of *progress*. You wouldn't believe the amount of stuff she accumulated after Pop died, and trying to get her to part with anything is like trying to take away the needle from a heroin addict."

"Nice one, Robert. Our mother is off to church, and you compare her to a heroin addict."

At forty-eight and three years older than Robert, Jillian was still just as irritating as she'd been when they were kids. Over these last long weeks in his small hometown of Liberty, he had repeatedly asked her—begged her, even—to come down from her home in West Des Moines and help him with the monumental task of cleaning out their eighty-year-old mother's house. Jillian hadn't even bothered to invent a good excuse for not coming. She'd simply said, "I don't want to, Robert."

"All I'm saying is that it's incredibly painful to get her to part with anything. She demands to see everything I want to put in a garbage bag. And if that's not bad enough, she even goes out to the dumpster in the alley in the middle of the night and fishes out stuff I've already thrown away." Robert kicked at a box full of old calendars that the First National Bank of Liberty gave out every Christmas to its loyal customers. Their mother had saved every single one for decades.

"Oh, come on, Robert. It can't be that bad." In the kitchen, Jillian picked up a cracked thermos that Robert vaguely remembered had been in his lunchbox in second grade. "See this? It's trash."

"Trust me. It's not that easy. You might think it's trash, and I might think it's trash, but our mother does not."

Jillian, who had done nothing to help so far, sighed wearily. Her tall, angular figure sagged against the counter. Jillian dyed her short hair red, which did nothing to decrease the sharpness of her features. "Angela was always such a bitch."

"She's not being a bitch, Jillian," Robert said, feeling the very new need to defend his mother. To him, the most surprising thing that had happened in his weeks back in Liberty was the discovery that their mother wasn't who he had always thought she was. All their lives, from childhood into adulthood, their mother had seemed cold, distant, and overly judgmental. Neither Robert nor Jillian had been especially close to her, always preferring to go to Pop for advice and support. Pop had been dead for almost twenty-five years, yet neither he nor Jillian had made an effort to really get to know Angela in the ensuing years when she'd been alone. And lonely. Robert understood that now.

To Robert's great surprise during this arduous task, he had seen his mother smile and laugh on occasion. He had also seen her cry over old pictures and a homemade birthday card Jillian had made for her in third grade. After an especially bad day of sorting through Pop's old clothes, he'd heard her crying in her bedroom in the middle of the night. He wasn't sure what to do about it but knew he should at least check on her. He'd cracked open the door and saw her sitting in the middle of the bed, holding Pop's old powder blue leisure suit from the 1970s, the rest of his clothes scattered about her, as if she were taking turns holding each shirt or pair of pants or tie. Robert had carefully closed the door before she noticed him. The next morning, she had returned the items of clothing to the boxes marked "Charity," acting like nothing out of the ordinary had happened, as if she had not spent the night holding them and crying. "What do you want for breakfast, Robert?" she had asked him.

"What do you mean she's not a bitch? Has she ever visited you in Chicago? Did she at least call and support you after your two disastrous marriages ended in divorce?" Jillian glared at him as if he had betrayed her. They'd always been allies before when it came to distrusting their mother.

Why had he wanted her to come? Robert wondered, glaring back. It would seem that Jillian's porcupine quills, the ones she'd sprouted during her rebellious teenage years, were still as prickly as ever. He took a deep breath. It wouldn't do any good to rise to her bait, and he did need her help, unfortunately. "You'll see, Jillian," he said evenly. "It's like every little thing she gives up diminishes her somehow." Before Jillian could open her mouth to say something else mean—and Robert knew she had plenty of ammunition—he hurried on. "Maybe that's not the best way to put it, but you'll see. She's changed. She seems to be moving so much slower these days, and sometimes she doesn't get out of bed until eight o'clock." Mother, in the old days, had considered sleeping past six a.m. something of a sin.

"She's eighty, Robert!" Jillian sputtered. "Of course she's moving slower these days, and last winter, she tripped over a chair leg and bruised her hip. That's why we're doing this. We have to get her out of this junk-filled house and into some kind of assisted living facility."

"She's called me Jacob a few times." Pop's name had been Jacob.

"Oh," Jillian said, taken aback. "Are you saying she's got dementia or Alzheimer's? Is she losing touch with reality or something?"

"I think it's more wishful thinking." Robert could understand Jillian's surprise. After Pop died in a fire, their mother had been so angry that she never uttered his name in their presence. Robert knew now that he and Jillian had been told a story to protect them, to leave untarnished their memory of Pop. They'd been told that Pop, a member of the volunteer fire department, had died heroically trying to save a woman named Tina and her two young children. But Robert knew now that Pop had already been in the house when the fire started; he'd been having an affair with Tina for years. Mother had told him the truth shortly after he arrived. She hadn't told Jillian, and Robert realized right then that he wasn't going to tell her either.

"I didn't think she even liked Pop, let alone loved him." They were in the family room then, and Jillian picked up a silver-framed family picture that had been taken of the four of them after church one Sunday. "Look at the body language here. They're as far apart as possible." Jillian had taken one lousy psych course in college and still considered herself to be an expert on the subject.

"I'm pretty sure that she loved him very much."

"She sure had a weird way of showing it." Jillian put the picture back on its crowded little table. "I'm beginning to think that being in this claustrophobic small town again has made you crazy. Or maybe the old woman has you brainwashed."

"Maybe we should get to work," Robert said, changing the subject. He couldn't even begin to explain to Jillian what he had yet to understand himself. After spending so much time with Mother, Robert did now see her in a different, kinder light. It's not as if he thought he and Jillian had been wrong for so many years. Angela Walker could still be as petty as the next person, and he had been privy to many outbursts that bordered on temper tantrums. Right now, she wasn't speaking to Sophie, one of her best friends, over an argument that had something to do with the church music on one particular Sunday. He did realize, however, that she wasn't perfect; none of them were. And it was okay.

"Fine. Let's get to work." They were back in the kitchen, and Jillian grabbed a construction-size garbage bag and began stuffing it with odds and ends from the counters: old envelopes with writing on the back, recipe cards, pens and pencils, a small cork bulletin board with phone numbers and memos still attached. "The sooner we get done here, the sooner I can go home."

Robert sighed. Jillian just didn't get it. When Mother returned from playing the piano at the Presbyterian Church, she would immediately take everything out of the bag and put it back exactly where it once was. Only after she examined each and every item, thought about it for a while, put something back into the bag, then reconsidered and retrieved it—the process could go on for hours—only then would she end up putting a fraction of what she considered to be priceless memorabilia into the bag for good. After weeks, Robert had finally accepted the fact that she needed to do this; she had to do this for her own peace of mind.

"Have you made arrangements at The Cedars yet?" Jillian stuffed away. "Angela needs to pick out what furniture she wants to take with her."

The Cedars was Liberty's biggest nursing home, and Angela refused to talk about the imminent move. Years before, she had said she refused to burden her children by moving in with them in Chicago or West Des Moines when her time came. Lately, though, she'd been dropping hints that Robert had not yet deciphered, such as: "Maybe I won't have to move anywhere," or "Maybe there's another alternative." He had poured himself another cup of coffee while he watched Jillian's futile efforts. Robert had to admit he had slowed down during his time in Liberty. He also had to admit it wasn't necessarily a bad thing. "I haven't called the nursing home yet. I haven't had time," he lied. All he'd had in Liberty was time. At first, he'd thought of it as a punishment, but now he didn't.

"God, Robert! Am I going to have to do everything?"

Mother came in the back door just then and stood in the kitchen. She dropped her armful of hymnals, but not to greet her long-lost daughter. "Jillian! Dear Lord, what are you doing?"

Robert calmly sipped his coffee and managed, somehow, to keep the smug smile off his face as their frail little mother wrestled the garbage bag from Jillian's hands and began to replace everything to its rightful position back on the counter. "Everything has its place, Jillian," she said in a familiar, scolding voice. "Did I not teach you to respect that?"

Robert kept mostly to himself during the seven weeks in Liberty. And somewhere along the line, this trip had gathered an air of finality. Naturally, that feeling stemmed from the nature of the trip. He was, after all, helping his mother clean out his childhood home, one scrap of paper and a pair of pantyhose at a time. Once all the relics of his long-ago life disappeared, this house and the lives it had sheltered would be gone. The new family who bought this house would effectively erase all the memories that had gone before.

This wasn't as sad to Robert as perhaps it should have been. He'd been happy growing up in the Colonial on Waverly, a popular, cocky kid, the star of his high school basketball team, the know-it-all smart-ass who thought he would leave this podunk town and set the world on fire. That was not what happened. He was a twice-divorced, middling graphic design artist who was thinking of buying a parrot, for fuck's sake. Yet this trip had given him time to reflect not only on his failures but also on his future. For the first time in years, Robert could see a glimmer of hope. After this chapter was finally closed, perhaps he could get out of the rut he'd dug himself and move on. Towards what, he wasn't sure. However, he did know that this would be his last trip to Liberty, Illinois, and that knowledge brought freedom.

Robert hadn't tried to contact old friends who were no longer friends, nor had he frequented the town's taverns to feed on local gossip during his time in Liberty. However, as much as Robert had tried to keep his head down and mind his own business, he did feel like there was one thing he needed to do before he left the town for good. His former high school girlfriend, Mandy, had won the Queen of Hearts jackpot at the American Legion a couple of weeks before, and he wanted to congratulate her. That jackpot, eventually reaching 1.5 million dollars, had been the talk of the town for weeks. Robert, despite himself, had gotten somewhat interested in the whole spectacle. And he, like everyone else in this town, had followed the paper trail in the weekly *Liberty Gazette*, the articles announcing that there was no winner yet, which implied that there was still hope for all. And then Mandy, a person whom he used to love, had finally won the biggest prize of all.

"Can you believe it? Someone finally won that cursed jackpot." Angela said she didn't condone such a blatant display of gambling, yet she followed the Queen of Hearts drawing just like everyone else in town. She held the proof in her hands, the latest copy of the *Liberty Gazette*. "Mandy Tanner. Did you know her in high school?"

"It was a small high school, Mother. Everyone knew everyone." Robert wasn't surprised that Angela didn't recall that Mandy had been his girlfriend, the homecoming queen to his king. He'd never brought her over to meet his folks, mostly because he knew his mother would get that condescending look on her face just to make Mandy uncomfortable. Pop would have been decent; he would have known Mandy from when he taught her middle-school social studies. But his mother had been a different story. He hadn't wanted to subject Mandy to that. At the time, he thought he was protecting her.

And maybe he'd been right. "That family of hers was such a disgrace!" Angela said, carefully refolding the paper with shaking hands. "All those drunken Malone men running around and getting in fights." She shook her head woefully. "And then their house burned down and killed the whole sorry lot of them, probably because they were too drunk to know what was happening. Good riddance."

"Jesus, Mother." Even after weeks in this house, and even after their tentative, budding new relationship, his mother could still say things that appalled him.

"Do not take the Lord's name in vain in my house, Robert. I will not allow it."

"Sorry," Robert said rotely. Then, out of a misguided, too-late desire to defend Mandy, he said, "She was a nice girl." He'd thought she was more than nice.

He'd told her he loved her, but then Robert had started to behave badly, telling her how much he couldn't wait to leave this godforsaken place, even though he knew it hurt her because she had no plans or any money to leave Liberty. And then when she told him she was pregnant, he'd behaved even worse. He'd offered to get the money to pay for an abortion. When she told him she lost the baby a little while later, he behaved atrociously. He'd been relieved, and after dumping her on her family's rundown front porch after the senior prom, he'd never called her again.

He'd seen Mandy twice in the weeks he'd been in Liberty. The first time, on the Fourth of July, he'd walked into her store, Zelda's Consignment Shop, to get Angela out of the heat. If he'd known Mandy was now the proprietor of Zelda's, he'd forgotten all about it, so he wasn't prepared to see her when she popped up like a Jack-in-the-Box from behind the front counter. He recognized her instantly. She was older, of course, a little heavier, a little more war-torn, as was he, but she had the same engaging smile and blue eyes. It had been an awkward encounter; it was impossible to say anything meaningful in five minutes after twenty-seven years of being virtual strangers. To make matters worse, Angela fixated on a scarf and would have stolen it, too, if Mandy had not diffused the situation.

The second time he saw Mandy had been as bizarre and awkward as the first. She appeared on Angela's front porch late one night to show him a picture of a little girl. Mandy was drunk—Robert could smell it on her breath—and thrust the photo under his nose. "Here," she said. Robert had no idea why Mandy would show him this picture. "Don't you see?" she had said. Robert thought he'd said the little girl was cute, which hadn't seemed like enough for Mandy. She left as quickly as she'd arrived. Robert doubted that Mandy would even remember the incident in the morning. Perhaps she had confused him with someone else? Perhaps she had gone to the wrong door? He quickly forgot about the whole thing; it meant nothing.

But now, on this day, the second one since Jillian's arrival, Robert saw his opportunity to escape and walk uptown to Mandy's shop to congratulate her. He would let Jillian shoulder the burden of trying to get their mother to part with a few more pieces of her past. They were sorting through the old roll-top desk, its drawers and cubbyholes, and as usual, it was slow going.

Jillian, her voice scalding with impatience, said, "You don't need to keep a ball of rubber bands or empty bottles of Bayer."

"They might come in handy someday," Mother insisted.

Jillian threw up her hands in disgust. "No, they won't, Mother! At this rate, we're never going to finish."

"I don't have anywhere else I need to be," Mother said sweetly.

Jillian mumbled an unintelligible string of swear words, then marched into the kitchen and poured herself a tumbler of chardonnay. She'd brought a case of wine with her from Des Moines, and the bottles diminished at an impressive rate. Mother, who abhorred having any kind of alcohol in the house—and Jillian knew that very well—kept sweetly smiling, pretending not to notice. Robert would give that round to Angela.

Jillian just didn't get it yet, and Robert couldn't blame her. It had taken him days and weeks of frustration and numerous worthless arguments to realize that Angela, in her way, was being stubborn because she wanted to spend more time with her children. It was incredibly sad that she thought this was the only way to keep them close, and once Robert figured it out, he started to cut her some slack. On some days, rather than go round and round in circles, he would say, "Why don't we call it a day and watch *Scarface*? You pop the corn, and I'll put the movie in the VCR." Angela always willingly, gratefully agreed. Robert didn't even want to think about the fight that would ensure when it came time to sort through Angela's beloved gangster movies and ancient VCR. It would not be pretty.

With Jillian and his mother at a stalemate, Robert made his escape and walked uptown in the oppressive heat. It had been a summer without much rain, and even though the forecast called for thunderstorms later in the day, Robert didn't see any signs of dark clouds as he walked past dry, lifeless lawns and drooping hydrangea bushes. But he did see three little girls running through a sprinkler in one yard, and two boys rode by on their bicycles, baseball mitts dangling from the handlebars. It was surprisingly comforting to see kids being kids. Being childless himself—his two ex-wives had not wanted children, which had been fine with him at the time—he'd only heard stories about how unpredictable kids could be, how difficult. However, when it came to what kids did in the summertime, they all seemed to enjoy pretty much the same things, the same activities he'd done as a kid in this town. He'd loved the freedom that summer and the release from school brought. It was only when a man got older that he realized that freedom was an illusion.

Mandy sat in her usual place on a stool behind the front counter when Robert pushed open the door. If she was surprised to see him this time, she didn't let on. "It's two in the afternoon, and you're my first customer of the day. Do you smell gasoline?"

Confused, Robert said, "Gasoline? Or do you mean gas? Do you have a gas leak?"

Mandy smiled. She looked tired. "I mean gasoline. Vandals broke in here a couple of days ago and doused everything. We've been cleaning like crazy."

"Why would they do that?"

Mandy waved her hand in front of her face, a gesture she'd made since high school. "Oh, it's the whole Queen of Hearts thing." And then she filled him in on the people who had camped out in her front yard asking for money, the people who called and asked for money, and the people who had thrown eggs and rocks at her house. "Mind you, I'm not complaining," she finished.

"People don't always try to put their best foot forward. They're not bad people. They just got a little carried away."

"It sounds like a bunch of sore losers to me." It was no wonder she looked tired, and the feeling that suddenly came over him felt so foreign, so unexpected, that he didn't recognize it at first. Then he remembered. He hadn't felt it in a long time, perhaps it had been years, but he wanted to take Mandy in his arms and hold her. She was heavier than she used to be, but a physical memory resurfaced, unbidden. The first time he'd kissed her at a party at Boss' Lake after the homecoming dance. They didn't join the party. Instead, they sat in his restored Mustang, and he took her in his arms…

"Robert? Are you okay? You look like you've seen a ghost, or maybe it's the heat. Dear Lord, it's hot out today." She fetched him a glass of lemonade from a jar on the counter. "I usually reserve this for paying customers," she laughed, "but seeing as you're under the weather and all." She handed him the glass.

He drank thirstily, his eyes on the jar of lemonade on the counter and not on her. He had no idea where that feeling—or was it a vision?—had come from. To cover his embarrassment, he finally said, "Something is different here." He pointed at the counter. "The last time I was here, I think you had more stuff on that corner. Is something missing?"

"Oh, yes. My troll doll collection. My grandmother gave me my first troll when I was seven, and I've collected them ever since. They were the only thing in the store not for sale, yet they were the only thing the vandals took. Don't you think that's odd?" Mandy laughed.

Robert thought the whole conversation was odd. Mandy seemed a bit manic. It seemed like she tried too hard to pretend that everything was normal when clearly her life was never going to be the same again. Or perhaps she was just feeling uncomfortable around him, which he could understand. He felt the same. Being in her presence brought back too many long-forgotten, buried memories. People said you never forgot your first love, which Robert had always thought was total bullshit. But maybe it wasn't. Being in Mandy's presence was starting to make him remember certain feelings, too, about how it felt to be young and hopeful. He shook his head; he was reading too much into the situation. The time in Liberty had clouded his hard-earned, jaded outlook on life. But perhaps he had been wrong about that as well?

Mandy glanced at the shop's front door, and Robert realized it wasn't the first time she had given the door a worried look since he entered. "Are you expecting someone? I don't want to keep you if you have an appointment or something." He remembered his mission then. "I only stopped by to congratulate you on winning the jackpot. Do you have any big plans for the money?" He refilled his glass with lemonade to avoid looking at her. "Are you going to keep the store?"

"There's no question that I'm going to keep the store!" Mandy's voice sounded too loud in the empty room. "I don't know what I'd do without this place."

"I thought that you might take a long trip, or maybe move? I don't know. A lot of people who came into that kind of money would . . ." he faltered. He didn't know where he was going with that train of thought.

"I'm not moving away from Liberty, Robert. Are we going to have the same conversation we had twenty-seven years ago?"

He had offended her, and he immediately knew why. It had been their last conversation.

"God, Mandy, don't you want to get out of this small town? There aren't that many job opportunities here, and besides, don't you want to meet new people, go to different places? Come on, this town is downright claustrophobic sometimes."

"I like this town," she said in a small voice.

"This podunk town is fine for some people." He was waving both hands in the air, trying to prove his point. "But some people want more out of life, you know?"

"What about me? Don't you love me?"

Robert finally met her eye to eye. "I'm sorry," he said, hoping she knew everything he meant in that simple apology.

"I'm sorry, too," she whispered.

Robert could see that her eyes shone with tears, but he didn't understand. What did she have to be sorry about? He was about to ask her, his mouth open, the words ready to spill forth, when the front door opened, and a young woman with a bruised and discolored face burst in. She looked vaguely familiar to him, and then he remembered. He had seen her picture in the *Liberty Gazette*. The "before" picture at the top of the article described how she had been attacked by a boyfriend in the parking lot of the American Legion at a Thursday night Queen of Hearts drawing. The attack occurred a couple of weeks before Mandy won.

"I know, I know. I'm late, but I have a perfectly good reason, Mom. Clara's acting even weirder today than usual, and I said to her, 'Are you finally going to have that baby, little sister?' And she, of course, said, 'What are you talking about? I'm not pregnant.' Sheesh! We all know how this story's going to play out, don't we?"

Mandy stood stock-still, staring at first Robert then Stephanie, her eyes wide.

"Oh, and I saw Trisha going into Lolly's Diner. She said she'd order you a piece of chocolate cake. What, like it's some kind of bribe? I can't believe you've agreed to talk to her after what she did to you. The bitch slept with your husband, and you're probably going to forgive her. Shit, Mom, if my best friend did that to me, I'd probably scratch her eyes out, but not you. I just don't get it."

"Stephanie." Mandy choked out.

The girl seemed to notice Robert for the first time and stuck out her hand. "Hi, I'm Stephanie."

Stephanie. The night that Mandy had appeared out of nowhere on his front porch, she had a picture of a little girl, her daughter Stephanie. *"Don't you see?"* she had asked him. The article in the paper had said that the attacked young woman was in her late twenties, hadn't it? Had it also stated that Mandy was her mother, and he missed that critical piece of information? Robert, his heart pounding, slowly held out his hand. "I'm Robert." He couldn't stop staring rudely at her face.

"I know, I know. I used to look much better than this before my face got bashed into a steering wheel. Haha. I'm going to have to rely on the miracles of plastic surgery, thanks to my millionaire Mom."

"You look fine to me," Robert stuttered. He could think of nothing else to say. The girl looked like a train wreck, but he could see by her jet-black hair and aquamarine eyes that she used to be very pretty. His eyes used to be that color before they faded to a nondescript blue. *Oh, God.* He turned to Mandy.

She refused to look at him. "Stephanie, why don't you go in the storeroom and start sorting through that box of clothes Darlene Sutton sent over."

"I thought I was supposed to *man* the store while you patched things up with that bitch best friend of yours," Stephanie said, petulant. Robert recognized that note of protest in her voice, too. And he realized that until recently, it was the exact tone of voice he used to address his own mother.

Mandy's hands fluttered like birds around her face. "Please, Stephanie, could you for once just do as I ask?"

"Jesus, Mom, make up your mind. And why are you so jumpy?" But Stephanie, after a moment's hesitation, marched into the back anyway.

"Mandy, I don't know what to say… I didn't know." Robert tried desperately to grab onto one of the many thoughts that spun in his head. Had he had a daughter all these years? Robert wanted to hope he would have been a big enough person to own up to the responsibility all those years ago, but sadly, he knew the answer to that. But if he had, he wondered how it would have changed things, altered his untethered, self-centered life. He might have been a better man if he'd known. But it was too late for all of that. All he could hope for was that he would do the right thing now.

"Don't say anything." Mandy had composed herself once Stephanie left the room, and her voice sounded calm.

"I'm sorry." His voice broke.

Mandy shook her head firmly. "There's nothing to be sorry about, Robert. Everything worked out the way it should."

"Please let me try to make it up to you, to her." Robert didn't know what that would entail. He didn't know how to establish a relationship with a grown daughter, a stranger, but he would try—if Mandy would let him.

"No, Robert, it's too late."

Mandy's voice was not unkind, but it was clear that she would not change her mind. And Robert didn't blame her. She'd had years to come to her decision, and he had to respect that, even though his heart felt the heaviest it had ever felt. For a brief second, he had a daughter; he had found that glimmer of hope. Then it was gone as suddenly as it appeared.

Mandy picked up her purse, signaling it was time for Robert to leave. "Go home and help your mother. She needs you." She walked to the front door and held it open to usher him out. "By the way, I think you coming home to help your mother is very noble, Robert."

He stumbled out the door, tripping on the raised wood of the old door sweep. He was having trouble putting one foot in front of the other. "I am not noble."

Mandy, even after all these years, was still unfailingly polite. "Oh, Robert, don't be so hard on yourself." She shut the door securely behind them and adjusted the purse strap on her shoulder. She faced him for the last time, and her last words to him were: "A lot has happened to me recently, and I've come to the conclusion that most people aren't noble. However, actions are a different thing altogether. I do believe that actions can be noble."

And then she turned and walked towards Lolly's Diner to meet her friend, and he turned in the opposite direction, towards home to help his mother.

Clara was not going to have this baby. *She would not.* Purposefully, she hadn't read any books on childbirth and what to expect during labor, as if that could stave off the inevitable. Purposely, she had not let herself think that the end result of all these endless months, which seemed like an eternity to Clara, would be an actual living, breathing baby. She still didn't want to think about that when the pain in her lower back grew more relentless. All she'd wanted for nine months was for this *thing* to be over. And then she could get on with her life, pretending like none of it had ever existed, the party at Jesse's where she'd been too drunk to remember what happened (had he drugged and raped her?), or the slow disconnect from her family and friends that had been her own doing.

Today was August 10, and Clara would be sixteen in two days. It wasn't like she expected a Sweet Sixteen or anything like that, especially since she no longer had any friends left to invite. She'd made sure of that. However, Clara had expected her mom and dad and sister Stephanie to at least acknowledge that she had a birthday coming up. But no. Everyone in her family was too wrapped up in the 1.5 million jackpot Mom had won at the Queen of Hearts drawing. It had been hard on Mom, all those spongers with their hands out and sob stories tugging at her heartstrings and making her crazy. It was a fact: Mom was too nice for her own good. However, she had been true to her word and gotten Clara a new car. Well, it was a used Subaru (the safest car around, her mom said), but it was good enough for Clara. Mom hadn't said it was for Clara's birthday, though. She'd just dropped the keys on the kitchen table and said, "Here you go, sweetheart."

No one in her family seemed to remember that Clara didn't have a driver's license or even a permit for that matter, which was a definite plus in Clara's book. Since school let out in May, she'd been hunkering down in their house watching TV and eating anything she could get her hands on, too self-conscious to venture out in public and show herself. She had become enormous, so big, in fact, that the couch cushion she sat on for hours on end had flattened like a pancake. And lately, even her dad's XX-large old flannel shirts didn't fit. Then Stephanie, the only member of her family who seemed to get what was truly happening, found Clara sitting on the couch wrapped in a sheet. (She'd been going for a toga look, but she hadn't quite pulled it off.) Stephanie took pity on her and bought a couple of tent-like muumuus from Walmart.

"These are the largest items of clothing I could find." She threw them on Clara's sheet-wrapped body sprawled on the flat-as-a-pancake sofa cushion. "Lucky for you that a lot of fat people shop at Walmart." But then her voice softened, which was saying a lot for her acid-tongued older sister. "Are you finally going to admit you're pregnant?"

"I think I have a thyroid condition." That was the lie Stephanie told all her friends, back when she still had friends. The muumuus were all splashed with flowers, hideous, but Clara knew she had no choice. Either she wore the muumuus, or she started walking around butt-naked. It would not be a pretty sight.

Stephanie threw up her hands. "Unbelievable! What's the matter with you, Clara? Do you think you're the Virgin Mary or something?" Stephanie seemed ready to pounce, but then she changed her mind. "Well, I guess it's not just you, is it? This family gives denial a whole new meaning."

"Shut up," Clara said.

"You're such an idiot that it's getting harder and harder to be around you. But you know I love you, right?" Stephanie didn't wait for an answer before she stomped off.

Clara was glad Stephanie left before she could see her cry. And it wasn't because she'd been reduced to wearing muumuus. Clara couldn't remember Stephanie ever telling her that she loved her, but it sure made her feel a little bit better. As gigantic as she had become, Clara felt like just a shell of her former self around people; she'd felt that way for months. But Stephanie saw her for what she really was. And Stephanie loved her anyway.

Later that same day, Mom dropped the car keys on the table, and Clara felt better than she had in a long time. Maybe it was because she knew, without admitting it to anyone, that this whole ordeal would soon be over. However, Clara preferred to think it was because she now had her very own car. A car meant she now had more freedom than she'd ever had, and Clara planned on taking full advantage of that—as soon as she learned to drive a stick shift. But that was a minor drawback. Clara found a tutorial on YouTube, and after a few false starts and stalls, and once she figured out how to push the seat back as far as it would go so that she could wedge herself behind the wheel, she took her first road trip two days later.

Well, it wasn't so much a road trip as a cruise around town. But it was a start, and that was the important thing. Clara felt powerful and all-knowing behind the Subaru wheel—even if it was hard to breathe—which lasted until she got to the only stoplight in town on Main Street and stalled the car. The lone truck behind her was mean enough to honk when she couldn't find the right gear, and Clara was flushed and agitated when the guy finally gave up and drove around her. "Hey, that's illegal!" she yelled at him, just to make some kind of a point. But hell, she didn't know if it was illegal or not since she'd never read the stupid book that sat on her dresser, *Rules of the Road,* or something like that. Whatever. She would follow her own rules from now on. Well, she would as soon as this whole ordeal was over.

She drove, fitfully, through town. It looked so much smaller from Clara's new vantage point behind the wheel, the houses closer together and the streets narrower than when she used to walk everywhere. People she passed waved at her—Liberty was a waving kind of town—and Clara wondered if they recognized her. In a way, she wanted them to, so they would think to themselves, "Look at Clara Tanner, all grown up!" And in another way, she didn't want them to recognize her because they would probably say something like, "That can't be Clara Tanner, can it? Lordy, Lordy, what in the world *happened* to her?" Clara waved back anyway, smiling happily. It seemed like the right thing to do.

Without quite meaning to, or maybe she had planned it all along, Clara found herself on the road leading to Jesse's house. He lived on a farm about a half-mile from Liberty, and as she drove now, Clara remembered walking this same route on that cold day last November. She and Kristen and Katie, her best friends, had decided to crash the Saturday night party of the upperclassmen of Liberty High. They thought they were so daring, so adventurous as they walked along this road. It was Katie who'd had the bright idea of making a pact: They would all lose their virginity on that very night. That, too, was heady, titillating stuff. But as Clara approached the house now, she wished she'd said *no* right then and there. She wished she could rewind all the events that led to her passing out on a couch on the porch and all that came afterward. Clara would play it all differently now. She wouldn't drink so much, she wouldn't let Jesse "fix" her drinks (had he drugged her?), and she wouldn't be stupid enough to think that a boy like Jesse Norman would be interested in a girl like her.

The house looked deserted, so Clara parked next to the ditch in front and stared at the white clapboard house, the setting of her greatest triumph and most humiliating defeat. The farmhouse looked too innocently ordinary to have housed the scene of that raucous party, with teenagers, hormones out of control, drinking and smoking and hooking up. It looked like a Norman Rockwell painting, not the place where Jesse Norman had raped her when she passed out. Clara thought she had run out of rage during the past nine months, but she found it returning now, full-throttle. She shouldn't let Jesse get away with what he'd done to her. She thought he was a gentleman, but he wasn't. Oh, no, he was not a gentleman. And he, too, should have to bear the consequences. He, too, should suffer as she suffered.

Clara pounded on the steering wheel. *It wasn't fair.*

Just then, the front door of the farmhouse opened, and Jesse appeared as if Clara's rage had conjured him out of thin air. He noticed the Subaru and lifted his hand in the Liberty-friendly wave, and then he purposely walked towards her. He could not have recognized the car because Mom said she bought it on Craigslist from a guy in Carbondale. So why was Jesse walking closer, waving, smiling? Did he recognize her? She'd done the best she could do to disguise herself over the last months. She'd eaten herself to the size of a house in an attempt to become invisible. Clara thought she'd been ready to see him, to confront him, but she was not. She wished she could vanish before his eyes, disappear in a puff of smoke, but that was impossible. She wished she'd worn a hat. Panicked, Clara turned the key in the ignition.

The car sputtered, died. She tried again. Nothing. He was almost to the car, and if she hurried, she could still get out of here before he got close enough to recognize her, *to see.* She tried the Subaru a third time, pumped on the gas, shifted gears. *Nada.* With nothing else to do, she tried to scrunch down in the seat, but it was hopeless. She was like a bug pinned to a spreading board, a specimen waiting to be examined. And then Jesse would *know.*

"Did you run out of gas?" Jesse stood at the driver's side window, peering in.

He was so close that Clara could smell his spicy cologne, the same one he'd worn the night of the party. The scent made her dizzy, and then she felt the bile rise in the back of her throat. She was afraid she might be sick. "What?" she asked faintly. He was too close. If only she'd figured out how the air conditioning worked, she wouldn't have the windows rolled down. He wouldn't be so threateningly, heartbreakingly close to her.

He reached in and tapped a gauge on the dashboard. "Just as I thought. You're out of gas." He straightened up. "I've got a gas can in the garage. I can have you fixed up in no time." He walked away, whistling.

He hadn't recognized her. Somehow, that seemed worse than anything he could have done to her. *Anything else,* she reminded herself. He had already profoundly damaged her, and while she'd wallowed in misery, he'd been nonchalantly going on his way, whistling. *It wasn't fair.* She would let him have it when he returned—if he recognized her. The night he took her virginity had meant everything to her, but to Jesse, it had been unremarkable, not worth remembering. *How dare he!*

Jesse returned with the gas can. "Don't worry about a thing. I'll do this for you." He went to the side of the car with the gas cap.

He might have glanced into the car, but Clara couldn't be sure. She pushed her lank, dark hair off her damp face. She was perspiring heavily and could feel the hideous floral muumuu cling to every fold of her body. Now was her opportunity, her one chance to get even, her last chance to tell him the truth. She opened her mouth, but nothing came out.

"You're lucky I was home. Usually, I'd be out in the fields at this time of day, but I'm home packing. I joined the Marines. Leave for basic training tomorrow." He screwed on the lid of the gas cap.

Did Jesse think he was making conversation with a stranger, someone who happened to be passing through Liberty and ran out of gas right in front of his house? Maybe he did recognize her and was trying to play it cool. She didn't know anything about boys, despite her present condition. Not one damn thing.

Jesse tapped the car's fender. "You're all set. That ought to get you to the gas station."

What came out of Clara's mouth wasn't anything she expected. "Are you scared?" she asked. He was standing at the rear of the car, and she was looking at him through the rearview mirror. He was every bit as handsome as she remembered—she still thought he looked like Justin Bieber—but he looked different, older maybe.

"A little," he said. He rocked on his heels. "Are you?"

"Terrified." Her voice shook.

"Yeah." He nodded and turned his face toward the house. "I better get back to packing. You take care." He gave the hood of the car a final pat.

It was not nearly enough, but Clara knew that's all she would ever get from Jesse Norman.

Clara wanted to stay on the couch and never leave again when she got back from her road trip to Jesse's house. She didn't feel at all well. Her stomach churned queasily, and her insides felt heavy and hot. It was a weird feeling. But Mom wouldn't take *no* for an answer. "Get your behind into the kitchen, Clara Jean Tanner. We're having a family dinner. Participation is mandatory."

It was sheer agony, these family dinners that Mom had grown so fond of ever since she found out about Dad and Trisha. It was like she tried too hard to pretend they were still a normal family when they clearly were not. Her mom was a millionaire now, for one thing. And then there was Stephanie, who invariably started an argument and wouldn't eat anything unless Mom pureed her food in a blender. (It was so gross, seeing her suck up meatloaf or roast beef through a straw.) And then there was Dad, who still moped around like a kicked puppy, even though it became more apparent with every passing day that Mom wasn't going to throw him out any time soon. Yet they came together and faked "family" time to make Mom happy.

Mom passed around a big bowl of beef stroganoff. She'd bought it at Dave's Market, naturally, but she thought that if she put it in a nice bowl, it was the same as if she'd made it herself. "I have an announcement to make," she said, scooping out the stroganoff.

They all looked at her expectantly, waiting, until Stephanie said, "What are you waiting for, Mom, a drum roll?"

"That would be nice."

Sighing, Stephanie drummed her fingers on the table. "Spill it, Mom."

"I've decided what I'm going to do with the money, or as I like to call it, my ill-gotten gains." Then she laughed.

"There's no need to hurry," Dad said. "We need to straighten out the tax situation before you come to any major decision." Dad had been preaching caution about the jackpot for going on three weeks now. He said he was protecting Mom's best interests, but Clara sometimes wondered if he hoped she would share the loot with him. Clara knew there was fat chance of that happening.

"Yes, Neal, we'll pay the taxes first." She gave him a look that said, *You're raining on my parade,* but it wasn't mean or anything. She often acted impatient towards him, but Clara knew for a fact that Dad had been sleeping in their bedroom for the last couple of nights.

"Don't do anything stupid, Mom." Stephanie slurped through her straw. She'd worked in the consignment shop that day and had been very cranky since she got home. She'd told Clara a strange man had been in the shop that day, and he'd given her the creeps. "It was like something went through me, you know?" she'd said to Clara when she got home. Clara did know what she meant by that. She'd felt the same way when she looked at Jesse through her rearview mirror.

"Would someone please pass the stroganoff?" Clara asked. The bowl had stalled by Stephanie. Despite her queasiness, Clara was starving. When everyone had taken what they wanted, she would finish off what was left.

"After taxes," Mom continued as if there hadn't been any interruptions, "I'll put aside money for Stephanie's surgery and Clara's college education."

Clara looked up from her plate. This was news to her. She hadn't even begun to think about college yet, or if she even wanted to go. This *thing* she was going through had put everything else on hold indefinitely. But Mom looked so proud of herself that Clara nodded. "Thanks, Mom."

Satisfied, Mom played her trump card. "Then I'm going to set up the Liberty Relief Fund. Isn't that a wonderful idea?" She beamed. Mom's smile made her look almost pretty.

"What's a relief fund?" Clara, whose lower back had been aching steadily all day—had she wedged herself behind the wheel of the Subaru too tightly?—desperately wanted some relief. She'd taken some baby aspirin, but it hadn't done a damn thing.

"I'm going to put the rest of the jackpot money into an account the town will control. When a person in Liberty finds himself in a desperate situation, say he lost his job, or can't make his mortgage payment, he can apply for funds." Mom, looking at the quizzical faces around the dinner table, plowed on desperately. "The government sets up disaster relief funds all the time, and this is no different."

Clara fully expected Stephanie to say something nasty, like "that's the stupidest idea I ever heard of," but she didn't. "So, the relief fund will benefit the town, but you don't have to make the decision who deserves the money and who doesn't."

"Exactly!" Mom went back to beaming.

Clara didn't get it at all. A lot of people in Liberty had been downright mean to Mom after she won the jackpot. For Pete's sake, a group of meth heads had vandalized the consignment shop. But that was Mom for you, a Good Samaritan to the end. A sharp pain traveled across Clara's abdomen, and she let out a small gasp. "Oh!"

Mom, immediately concerned but for the wrong reason, said, "You don't think it's a good idea, Clara?"

"I think it's a good idea, Mom," she said in a whispery voice, not daring to move a muscle for fear it would incite more pain. "Maybe the people in town will leave you alone now."

"Exactly!"

Dad finally spoke up. "The town could set up a board to be in charge of making the donations to the most worthy causes."

"Kind of like a parole board," Stephanie said, smirking as best she could with her battered face.

"No, Stephanie," Dad sighed. "Maybe a couple of pastors or someone else the people in this town wouldn't argue with."

"I was thinking of Tucker Aldean, the mayor," Mom said firmly.

Another sharp pain shot across Clara's abdomen, and she quickly clapped her hand over her mouth to stifle a moan. But as usual, no one paid the least bit of attention to her.

Dad leaned forward in his chair. Because his legs were so long, he couldn't sit facing the table. "Now, Mandy," he said carefully, knowing he wasn't out of the doghouse yet. "After that fiasco with the drunken poet's funeral, no one in town particularly likes the man anymore. Do I need to remind you that he used the town's money, *wasted* the town's money for that harebrained idea?"

Mom picked up her fork again, signaling that the matter was settled. "I thought the memorial service was a noble gesture on his part, and I would have gone if I wasn't so busy cleaning up the shop. Besides, I always liked the man, and I think he deserves a second chance." She took a sip of her wine and looked pointedly at Dad. "Don't you agree that people deserve a second chance, Neal?"

Angela Walker felt exceptionally tired that evening, and it had nothing to do with the fact that it was almost her bedtime. It was bone-weary exhaustion that seemed to have settled in her very marrow. She and her children, Robert and Jillian, had spent most of the afternoon and the better part of the evening boxing up her collectibles. And she had many collections now: silver spoons, thimbles, Precious Moments figurines, sheet music, Barbie dolls, antique lamps, and old hymnals and Bibles. And that was just the tip of the iceberg. Neither Jillian nor

Robert knew she had other boxes of collectibles: porcelain dolls, silk scarves, decks of cards, and Christmas ornaments in every shape, color, and size. Angela stored it all in Tremont's Storage Garage on the north side of the railroad tracks running through the center of town. She paid the man forty-five dollars a month for that privilege. It seemed like an outlandish amount of money to Angela, but she considered it to be a necessary expense.

Yes, Robert and Jillian would blow a gasket when they found out about that little secret, discovering she had even more "unnecessary junk," as they so unceremoniously called it. But all those collectibles were not junk, nor were they unnecessary, at least not to Angela. She had spent years combing through mounds of items at yard sales and flea markets and craft fairs to lovingly assemble her collections, and each item selected gave Angela a feeling of accomplishment. Each item also gave her something tangible to hold onto in a world that was so fleeting and fast-paced, a world where it was so hard to find anything or anyone a person could hold onto and keep.

"Mother of God!" Jillian bellowed, holding up a pair of Raggedy Ann and Andy dolls conjoined, their rag hands tied together. "Who in their right mind would want a pair of Siamese Raggedy Ann and Andy dolls? They're so creepy!"

"Put them in the charity box," Robert said calmly. "Maybe a poor kid in Africa would want them."

"Right. A starving kid in Sudan would want something like this. Give me a break. They're trash." Jillian threw the dolls into a giant garbage bag and took a swig of wine. Jillian had been steadily drinking all day, and the more she drank, the more sarcastic she became. She'd always been that way, quick to anger, quick to judge, quick to discard.

They're collectibles, Angela said, or thought she said. Neither of her children seemed to hear her. It had been going on like this all afternoon. Angela would think she had said something, but either the words didn't come out, getting tangled somewhere between her brain and her mouth, or her children were ignoring her. It didn't really matter now, though. Come hell or high water, her children were determined to throw away her life one piece at a time, effectively destroying her, effectively erasing her. Angela had expected this, of course. She was old now, useless in their eyes.

Perhaps she had always been useless to them. Angela would be the first to admit she had not been the best mother. It wasn't as if she hadn't tried. She had tried very hard in her way, but motherhood and the selflessness it involved had not come easily to her. She could blame her own mother, who had always been indifferent to Angela, her only child, but that was all water under the bridge now, and it wasn't the real reason anyway. The real reason was that Angela had been so in love with her husband that she didn't feel like she had anything left over to give to her children. Loving Jacob had been an all-consuming curse that almost destroyed her.

She'd had no illusions from the start. She knew when she married Jacob that she loved him more than he loved her. She wasn't even his only girlfriend at the time, but desperate to hold onto him, she'd told him that she was pregnant when she was not. Jacob might not have been trustworthy when it came to fidelity, but he was honorable when it came to doing the right thing. Two months after they married, when she finally admitted to him that she had lied, Jacob looked at her with such sorrow. She knew she had wounded him with her betrayal, but he didn't yell, which wasn't his style, or call her a liar, which she was. Instead, he had sadly shaken his head and said, "We'll have to make the best of it, then."

So *making the best of it* became the foundation of their marriage. And being a hopelessly in-love fool, Angela had grabbed onto that morsel. She also ridiculously thought she could make Jacob love her over time. She cooked his favorite meals, kept a clean house, took great care with her appearance, and eventually gave him a daughter and son. She hadn't wanted children, even though it was expected at the time, but she wanted to make Jacob happy. In a sense, it backfired on her. Jacob was indeed crazy over those kids. He doted on them, and she became even more lost in the background of his life when she became the bad cop to his good cop in the parenting department. He would have let them do or have anything they wanted, while she was the one who had to be the disciplinarian, the voice of reason. Somewhere along the line, without her totally grasping the situation, she seemed to lose the respect of all of them.

Still, she tried, in her way. It wasn't easy to love people who did not love her back. But Angela thought that through sheer perseverance, by adhering to a strict code of conduct, she could change the situation. She turned a blind eye to Jacob's various dalliances in those early years. Oh, once the kids were in bed, she would get in her car and drive around town until she spotted Jacob's red convertible parked in front of one woman's house or another. (She'd even conceded to that frivolous purchase, one they couldn't afford on his teacher's salary.) She never knocked on the woman's door and made a scene, although she had every right to do so. No, every single time, she'd thought to herself: *This will pass. This will be the last time.* She'd go home and pretend to be asleep when he finally, without apology, crept into their bed. In the morning, she would fix his breakfast of bacon and eggs, pack the kids' school lunches, and tell herself that soon, very soon, Jacob would come to his senses and see that she was the only woman who truly loved him.

And then Jacob got involved with a young woman named Tina. Despite Angela's hours of prayer, regular church attendance, and the thousands of hymns she played, Jacob ultimately betrayed her. He fell in love with another woman. Tina wasn't like his other flings, and Angela could sense that from the start. Jacob grew blatant about his attachment to her, sometimes not even coming home at night. He made no apologies. When Jacob fathered her two sons, he did not express any regret or remorse. He didn't say anything at all, but Angela knew. Oh, yes, she knew, but she kept putting one foot in front of the other, praying and hoping that Jacob would see the truth of what they meant to each other, that he would take her in his arms and say, "You're the one I love, Angela."

But when Jacob started to move some of his possessions over to Tina's house—a pair of pants, boots, a razor, a toothbrush—Angela finally understood that Jacob's commitment was not to her, that it might never have been to her. Desperate, she found his Colt .45 in the garage and confronted him. She shook so hard that she almost dropped the weapon when she pointed it at his face and said, "You have to choose, Jacob. It's that woman or me." Angela had never held a gun before, but she was determined to use it either on him or herself on that night.

"I can't help who I love, Angela," Jacob had said, with something that looked like pity on his face. "You need to let me go." Then he turned and left the house.

He wasn't going to come back this time; Angela knew that. She crawled into bed, cradling the gun. For years, she had devoted herself to that man. She had prayed, waited. Her children were out of the house by then, and she had no one, no one at all. She would kill herself. She would end it all. She put the gun to her temple time and again, but she couldn't make herself pull the trigger. She cried, and then finally fell asleep, only to be awakened by the fire chief, who told her that Jacob was dead. Perhaps she should have felt relieved that it was all over, but she was not. She was so angry with him, so lost without him, and she couldn't help but feel that she was the one who had driven him away, into the arms of another woman, and then back into a raging fire to rescue the woman he truly loved. Angela was the one to blame, not Jacob. She had not been enough for him.

"I've had enough of this shit. Let's go to Mr. Lucky's and get a drink." Jillian kicked a garbage bag. She was too old to act like such a child, but that was Jillian's way.

"I'd say you've had enough, all right."

Robert had dark circles under his eyes, and Angela wondered why she hadn't noticed them before. He'd seemed like a different man these past few weeks, sadder, kinder. Angela didn't know what had happened to change him from the cocky young man he used to be. Life, she supposed. Life changed everyone. Looking at him now, she could finally admit it. She had always favored Robert over Jillian, who had been so difficult from the start. Mothers and daughters were supposed to be close, but that hadn't been the case with Angela and her daughter. For the first time, Angela wondered if it was because they had both been vying for Jacob's love. It was sad that this realization had come so late in the game.

"When did you become a middle-aged prude?" Jillian had already picked up her heavy purse.

She looked tired, too, and every bit of her forty-eight years. She'd been brave enough to give birth to three children, and surprisingly, she seemed to love all three very much. Angela wondered how she'd managed it, to spread love lavishly and equally. It must be a gift of some sort. Maybe Angela would have understood if she'd been around her grandchildren more, but it was too late for that now.

"Fine." Robert didn't look unhappy to leave the house. He turned to Angela. "We'll only be gone for an hour or so. Do you want me to pick up some ice cream from the Tastee Freeze on the way back? They're open until midnight."

This had become something of a ritual for them during these last weeks, but now that, too, was over. "No, Robert, not tonight."

"We'll pick some up anyway," Jillian decided as they went out the door. "In case you change your mind, Mother."

I love you, Angela said, or thought she said. Neither of her children seemed to hear her, so maybe it had not come out right. A low, long-distance humming, something akin to music, had started in her head, but it wasn't at all unpleasant. In fact, it was almost comforting. Angela had always found that music, especially her beloved church hymns, brought her a sense of peace. Maybe the sound would lull her to sleep, and sleep would be a good thing right now. She was so tired, more tired than she had ever been before. Bed. She must make her way to bed.

Angela had played the piano at the Liberty Presbyterian Church for almost forty years, and now, as she sat in a chair in the front room, she stared lovingly at the old piano. Jacob had bought her that piano for their tenth wedding anniversary, a gift that had touched her to her very core. She'd thought then, all those years ago, that there was still hope for them, that the piano meant Jacob had finally conceded to her love. That hope vanished quickly enough, but the piano still reminded her of happier times. She had spent a lot of hours on that piano bench, her hands on the keys, feeling as close to contentment as she ever could. She arose from the chair slowly, bones aching and creaking, and made her slow way to the bench. She sat.

She would play one song before retiring, only one. One last song would be enough. Angela poised her hands on the keys and began to play "Amazing Grace," Jacob's favorite hymn. She would play it through, verse by verse, each stroke of the key like a heartbeat until the last note lingered and faded away. And then the silence would bring peace.

It was sheer agony. Clara had used the expression many times in her life when she found herself in awkward or uncomfortable situations, like when Mom dragged her to Trudy's Beauty Boutique to get her hair done. It was on the day of the stupid parade the town threw for Mom after she won the 1.5 million Queen of Hearts jackpot. Or when Clara had to sit through long, drawn-out family dinners at the kitchen table and couldn't escape to the family room to watch some mindless reality show on TV. But now Clara knew she'd had no idea what *sheer agony* meant. This *thing* she was going through gave a new definition to those words. Clara felt as if her body was trying to turn itself inside out, and she could do nothing to stop it.

She was in labor, and all the denials in the world would not prevent the inevitable from happening. Something desperately tried to claw itself out of her body, and from the feel of things, this unknown being would make Clara pay for all her months of evading the irrefutable truth. Oh, yes, this was payback, big time. Clara had somehow managed to make it through the family dinner, even as the pains in her lower back and across her abdomen grew sharper, stronger, steadier. When she was finally allowed to excuse herself from the table, she made her way to her room. Clara had no memory of actually climbing the steps, but she was suddenly in her room, leaning against the closed door, moaning as quietly as she could. If she could just make it to her bed, she would be safe. She would close her eyes, and maybe when this was all over, she would wake up and find out that it had only been a dream.

That was so not happening. Clara stifled another moan as the next pain almost brought her to her knees.

"Clara?" Stephanie knocked at the door. "Are you okay? You got a funny look on your face about halfway through dinner."

Clara didn't think anyone had been paying any attention to her, but leave it to Stephanie to ferret out a "funny look." Maybe she should tell Stephanie the truth and ask her for help, but she wouldn't be able to bear Stephanie's *I told you so* look when she saw that she'd obviously been right all along. Stephanie used to lie and say she was a nurse, but Clara doubted if Stephanie even knew how to put on a band-aid. She wouldn't be any help at all. Plus, Clara didn't want Stephanie to see her like this. She didn't exactly know what would happen, but she was pretty sure that it would be messy.

The pain stopped, and Clara managed to say in an almost natural voice, "It's just heartburn. I'm fine, Stephanie."

"You have got to be the most stubborn person I have ever met." Stephanie kicked the door. "And if you think you can have a baby alone, you have also got to be the stupidest person I ever met." Stephanie kicked the door again before stomping down the stairs, loudly swearing the whole way.

Stephanie was wrong. Clara would have this baby alone. She'd suffered through the last nine months alone anyway, so what was the big deal? It was true that Mom had wanted to take her to see a doctor, and it was true that both Mom and Stephanie had tried to get her to at least admit she was pregnant, but other than that, she alone was the one who had to bear the burden of her own cross. She'd made such a stupid mistake. She'd fallen into the same trap so many teenage girls fell into, and she should have known better. She only had herself to blame, so it was only fitting that she see this thing through to the bitter end. Alone.

But wait. Clara couldn't have the baby here on her childhood bed with its pink sheets and homemade quilt. One of her aunts had made the quilt for her when she was small, and tiny multicolored unicorns danced across the surface. Mom would probably kill her if she ruined a family heirloom with all the muck and whatever would come out of her. As if on cue, something inside her burst, and Stephanie felt warm liquid rush down her legs and puddle on the floor. Oh, God, she was already making a mess. Mom was going to kill her, for sure.

Where could she go? If she could just get in her car and drive somewhere far away, everything would be all right. But she couldn't do that because she had come straight home after leaving Jesse's house that afternoon—it seemed like a lifetime ago—and she hadn't stopped at the gas station to get gas. Her car was parked on the driveway, empty and useless. She couldn't risk running out of gas before she got to the Circle K, and besides, she didn't have any money. She wouldn't get her allowance until Saturday.

It came back to her then. Just a couple of days ago, when Stephanie had been especially disgusted with her yet again, she'd said: *What's the matter with you, Clara? Do you think you're the Virgin Mary or something?* Of course she didn't think she was the Virgin Mary. She'd had sex once, sort of, and gotten pregnant. But Mary gave birth in a barn, so couldn't she? Jesse lived on a farm, which naturally had a barn, and if she could manage to walk there, it would be the perfect place. It seemed like poetic justice, or something like that, to have the thing born on the same farm where it was mistakenly conceived. And if a barn was good enough for the Virgin Mary, it was good enough for Clara.

What did she need to take with her? Every TV show that Clara watched had someone fetch plenty of towels when a person went into labor. That would be a cinch. All she had to do was go into the bathroom and gather an armload of towels, walk downstairs, past the family room where everyone probably watched TV, and through the kitchen to the laundry room in the back of the house. The laundry room was right off the kitchen by the backdoor, so it would be easy. The hard part would be getting past her family. Another wave of pain gathered force in the middle of Clara's body. She knew she had to hurry.

It proved to be even easier than she thought it would be. Clara walked past the arched doorway of the family room, clutching the towels to her abdomen for dear life. In a weird way, they comforted her, and holding onto the soft cotton seemed to make the pain lessen. But it would return. Clara knew that and walked as quickly as she could. Stephanie wasn't in front of the TV. She'd probably gone out with her new boyfriend, the cop who'd saved her life on the night she was attacked. And Mom and Dad were sitting on the couch, Mom nestled under Dad's shoulder. It was kind of sickening but also kind of sweet. It looked like Mom was going to let Dad off the hook for cheating on her. That would be Mom for you.

Clara walked out the back door and kept going. She knew her feet were moving, but it was like they had turned into concrete slabs. Each step required a great deal of effort, and clutching the towels wasn't holding the pain at bay anymore. At this snail's pace, she would never make it to Jesse's farm. She could no longer hold in the gasps because the agony in her abdomen was constant now, searing. When she made it to the small grove with the splintery picnic tables on the edge of the Mississippi, Clara knew she could go no farther. It was the same grove where she'd stopped to rest after the parade and overheard the tweakers talking about kidnapping her and Stephanie. One of them had called her a tub of lard, but Clara was beyond caring about that now, or if the tweakers were even nearby. She haphazardly spread the towels under the trees farthest from the picnic tables and fell to her hands and knees.

The thing was tearing her apart, her body ripping in two. Sweat poured off her face and soaked the ground. She stifled the screams by putting one of the towels in her mouth, and she tasted blood. In her more lucid moments, she tried telling herself that this would be over soon, but the next second, she knew it would never be over. Clara didn't know what time it was or how long she'd been in this hell; it seemed to go on and on. Then she gave a mighty push and felt something wet and slimy slither out of her body. She fell onto her back, panting. Was the agony finally over?

She could feel the thing between her thighs, but she wouldn't touch it. No, she would not. Except for the crickets chirping and the sound of the Mississippi lapping insistently against the riverbank, all was quiet. Was the thing dead? Had she done something wrong? Then the thing started to cry, softly at first, like a whimpering puppy, but then its cries grew louder. What did it want from her? And then Clara heard another sound, a rustling, and something broke through the bushes, shining a light on her.

"Oh, my goodness!"

At first, Clara thought it was an angel with blonde hair illuminated around her face like a halo. But angels didn't carry phones they used for flashlights, did they? Then the angel bent down, and Clara recognized Roxy, the girl who used to work at Trudy's Beauty Boutique before she ran away on that houseboat. Clara had always liked Roxy.

"Lucky for you, I have some scissors. I always carry the tools of my trade, you know?" Her voice was soft, soothing, as she bent down and cut something, talking all the while. "I've been walking along the river every night at about this time. It calms me, you know?" She pulled her shirt over her head and did something with the thing. "I sure never expected to see anything like this, though." Her laugh sounded like bells. "She's a beauty, all ten fingers and toes. You did a good job, Clara." She finished what she was doing and handed the wrapped package to Clara. "Here's your beautiful little girl."

"It's okay. I don't need to see it." Just as she had been doing for nine months, Clara had given no thought to what would happen when this thing was over. Roxy seemed to like it, though. Roxy had made it stop crying. Maybe she should ask Roxy to take it? Wait a minute. What had Roxy said? *Here's your beautiful little girl.* She had a baby girl.

"Go on." Roxy nudged the package closer. "Take a look."

Reluctantly, Clara did so, but only because Roxy was being so nice. She peered into the makeshift blanket, and while Roxy held the flashlight, Clara could see a small face, the tiny nose and rosebud lips, the blue eyes wide and staring straight at her. She didn't mean to do it, but she reached for the baby, who seemed to fit into the crook of her arm as if she belonged. Clara thought it was sweat dripping down onto the baby's cheek, but it was not.

"What are you going to name her?" Roxy knelt next to Clara and her baby.

"I don't know." Clara gently stroked the little cheek and felt as if something hard inside her—the ball of shame and anger and grief—melted just a little.

"I saw Officer Morrison and your sister Stephanie drive by a few minutes ago. Should I give them a call? You should probably go to the hospital or something," Roxy said in that same soothing voice.

"In a minute." Clara placed her hand on the baby's small chest without unlocking her gaze from the baby's blue eyes that looked so much like hers. She could feel her heartbeat, and it was surprisingly strong for such a tiny, living being. Even more surprising was that the baby's heartbeat seemed in perfect sync with her own. Clara reached for her baby's small hand, knowing that once she held it, she would never let go.

TO MY READERS:

Thank you for reading *Queen of Hearts*. I have completed twelve additional novels, each a distinct and interesting story with great characters. If you liked *Queen of Hearts*, I believe you would like my other novels as well, and of course, I would love for you to read them.

Please visit the Library page at *LaurieLisa.com* for more details on my other novels:

- *The Wine Club*
- *Across the Street*
- *The Light Tower*
- *Hollister McClane*
- *"star-cross'd lovers"*
- *David's Women*
- *Family Mythology*
- *Hospitality House*
- *Donny's Well*
- *Salon Confidential*
- *Sunday Brunch*
- *The Wine Cellar*

Along with *Queen of Hearts, The Wine Club, Across the Street, The Light Tower* and *Hollister McClane* are all available now on Amazon and other retailers in print, eBook and audiobook formats. You can also join my Readers List at *LaurieLisa.com* to receive news and updates on the release dates for my other novels, make personal requests to me directly, and ask questions about my books.

I look forward to hearing from you!

Laurie.

www.ingramcontent.com/pod-product-compliance
Lightning Source LLC
Chambersburg PA
CBHW061556190726
48288CB00007B/2051